NATASHA MADDEN

FAE COURT SERIES

II

Rise of the Druid Queen

Book Cover by Geka

First Edition edition published by Natasha Madden

Content Warning

This book is an adult romance, and is intended for 18+ audiences. It contains themes that may be confronting to some readers.

- Sex Scenes
- Blood/ Gore
- Violence
- Psychological torture
- Anxiety/ Panic attacks
- Kidnapping/ Holding against will

Dedication

To those who long to be swept away into worlds woven with magic and mystery.
To the dreamers who turn pages in search of escape, of wonder, of something more.
To anyone who has ever wished they could become someone else, live a different life, or stand at the edge of an impossible adventure—
This story is for you.
May you find yourself lost in its pages...

Glossary

Villages and Cities

Skora - The capital of the Unseelie Court.

Starlight City - The capital of the Seelie Court.

Pinehelm - A village near the Evergreens castle, surrounded by towering pines.

Mistbourne – A village located on the edge of the river that flows in from the Dead Sea. It is surrounded by a mystical mist that blankets the town, hiding it from unwanted travelers.

Ethereal Peaks – A treacherous mountain top surrounded by swirling mists.

Elysium Bluffs – Elysium Bluffs is perched atop breath-taking cliffs overlooking the ocean.

Stonewillow – A village full of whimsical treehouses intricately woven within ancient willow trees, blending stone and nature harmoniously.

Skywarden – This is home to winged shifters and fishermen. Situated on towering cliffs, it overlooks the Sea of Storms.

Escalle – A small village between the ancient expand of forest and the veil to the Outlands.

Outlands – This is where the evil and condemned are sent to live out life sentences for their crimes. The veil surrounding the Outlands acts as a prison, keeping them inside.

Deadlands and Valley of the Dead – These are two sections of the Outlands.

Creatures and Beasts

Deadling – A twisted, humanoid creature that dwells in the darkness. Their skin is hollow and grey, stretched tightly over malformed frames, and their bulging, milky eyes lack pupils. Once thought to be human, they are now consumed by shadow.

Outcasts – Fae who have either been exiled from the Seelie or Unseelie Courts or have chosen to live outside their laws. Mistrusted by both factions, they are known for their unpredictability and fierce independence.

Vurien – A gentle, bat-like creature known for their harmless nature. Often seen fluttering through the night skies, they are drawn to moonlight and tend to avoid conflict.

Frostflare – A rare forest guardian that resembles slender blue foxes with distinctive white sigils marked on their foreheads. They are solitary beings, rarely seen, and are said to appear only in times of great need.

Bellowig – A large, carnivorous squirrel. Agile and aggressive, they are known for attacking in packs and leaving little behind.

Willowroot – A delicate species of fairy, no more than 2.5 inches tall. They only communicate through sign language.

Luxaryn – A majestic white beast resembling a winged lion with two horns jutting from its thick, snowy mane. Rare and awe-inspiring, the luxaryn are said to appear only to those with pure intent.

Evergreens
Spring Court
StoneWillow
Valley of the Dead
Deadlands
Pinehelm
Outlands
Ethereal Peaks
Escalle
Dead Sea
Magic Veil
N
W
E
S
Mistbourne
Sea of Starlight
Autumn Court
Skora
Summer Court
Fuar Mt
City of Starlight
Mermaid Bay
Moonlight Bay
Winter Court
Elysium Bluffs
Skywarden
Frostfall
Sea of Storms

Chapter One

Everly

The wind howls as it whips violently around me, threatening to tear me from my perch high in the tree. My hair, once neatly braided, is now a wild, tangled mess, ripped free by the relentless icy gusts. I narrow my eyes, struggling to see through the blinding expanse of white snow that surrounds me. I almost want to laugh at the state I find myself in. Snowflakes cling to my eyelashes, and the crisp, biting air causes my breath to form clouds in front of me. My fingertips throb with pain, raw from desperately clutching onto the rough bark of the tree as I climb as high as I can. In my haste, I didn't think to grab gloves before leaving the cabin this morning. My mind was on other things like Maxon and my friends.

"What the hell do you think you're doing?"

I jerk against the tree trunk, my fingers digging deeper into the hard, unforgiving frozen bark.

The cold bites at my skin, but it's nothing compared to the fury simmering beneath the surface. A menacing growl slips past my lips as I glare down at the forest floor, frustration and anger boiling within me.

Below, Alivar stands with his hands on his hips looking up at me with that infuriatingly calm expression, like he has all the time in the world.

"Trying to figure out which way to go," I mutter through clenched teeth, fighting back the snarky comments threatening to spill out.

"Maxon will have my neck if anything happens to you." Alivar's voice is maddeningly level. "That includes catching a cold."

The mention of Maxon's name sends a sharp pain through my chest. I grit my teeth, my chest aching with the weight of everything I've lost.

"Well, if you'd just taken me back to Skora I wouldn't be out here!" I snap, the words filled with bitterness.

Without warning, Alivar appears next to me, portaling onto the branch like it's the most natural thing in the world. I yelp in surprise, my stomach lurching as my heart gives a hard thump against my ribs. Instinctively, I tighten my grip on the tree, my knuckles turning white from the effort.

"Don't do that!" I shriek, wishing I could let go of the tree long enough to slap that infuriating smirk off his face.

Alivar merely shrugs, his white-blonde hair whipping around his face as he studies me with those piercing eyes of his. Unlike me, he has no need to cling to the tree for dear life. He crouches down on the branch, perfectly balanced, as if standing on solid ground.

"You're here with good reason. Plus, it's only been a day," he says, his voice annoyingly reasonable.

"A day too long," I growl back, my frustration boiling over.

Alivar shakes his head, extending a hand toward me. "Come on, let's go."

For a brief, heart-stopping moment, hope surges within me. My mouth opens, ready to demand he take me back to Skora, but before I can speak, Alivar shakes his head again, cutting off my words.

"Not back to Skora. Not yet."

The hope that flared up just moments ago fizzles out, replaced by a burning disappointment that gnaws at my insides. I clench my jaw, the cold seeping deeper into my bones, making the tree bark feel like ice against my skin.

"Then no," I retort, my voice cold and defiant.

Alivar's expression shifts, his eyes narrowing as if I've just sprouted a second head. "Everly," he growls, the sound low and dangerous. "Your lips are turning blue. Don't be so stubborn."

His violet eyes flash, the intensity of his gaze sending a shiver down my spine. They remind me so much of Maxon's eyes, except for the blue ring around Alivar's irises instead of the silver ring that would flare to life in Maxon's. The similarity is almost too much to bear.

But even as I sit here, freezing and frustrated, I can't bring myself to trust him completely—not when I'm so far from where I want to be, and especially not when those eyes, so much like Maxon's, seem to see right through me.

I look back out over the frozen Winter Court, the snow-covered landscape stretching out before me. Behind me, the majestic mountains tower high, their snow-capped peaks reaching toward the sky, disappearing into the clouds.

The vast expanse of icy plains is a sharp contrast to the warmth I crave. Above everything else, I desire the comfort and security of Maxon's arms around me. The thought of his tender touch fills me with an ache that only he can soothe. I desperately need to know he's okay.

Where did that demon take him?

My thoughts begin to spiral, racing through worst-case scenarios, making my breathing become shallow and rapid. The sound of my own heartbeat fills my ears, a constant reminder of the anxiety racing through me. I shiver involuntarily as the icy air bites at my exposed skin. An exasperated sigh comes from Alivar.

I shoot him glare, my teeth knocking together.

"Why are you being stubborn?" he grouses. "Look, I promise in a few days you will be back in Skora."

"They need me now!"

"Once, I'm sure, it's safe to return."

"It's my home!"

Alivar narrows his eyes. "Well aware, Princess. Anyway, you can't leave without saying goodbye to Felix. He would be devastated."

With a sigh, I roll my eyes. The damn house cat. Who would have ever guessed that the Seelie Prince, of all people, had a secret cabin hidden away in the midst of the frozen Winter Court? And that it's occupied by a friendly pet cat, no less? The idea of such a regal figure caring for something as ordinary as a house cat is almost laughable, yet here I am, caught up in this strange reality.

Alivar watches me closely, his expression a mixture of patience and mild amusement as he holds out his hand to me again. It's clear he's waiting for me to make a decision, and despite my irritation, I know I don't really have a choice. With a resigned breath, I slowly reach out and slip my hand into his, feeling the familiar hum of magic ghosting over my skin. It's a sensation that sends a shiver down my spine, both comforting and unsettling at the same time.

Just as his hand tightens around mine the air shifts, and suddenly, a portal appears beneath us. It's as if the ground drops out from under me, and before I can fully comprehend what's happening, the world tilts on its axis. A rush of adrenaline surges through me, my heart pounding in my chest as the reality of the situation hits me like a ton of bricks.

We're falling.

The sensation of freefall grips me, the cold wind whipping past my face as we plunge into the unknown. My stomach lurches, and I can't stop the scream that rips from my throat, carried away by the howling wind. The world around me blurs into a dizzying swirl of colors and shapes, the icy air stinging my skin as we plummet through the portal.

Time seems to stretch and compress all at once, the fall both endless and instantaneous. My hand tightens around Alivar's, the only solid thing in a world turned upside down. His grip is steady, reassuring even, but it does little to calm the wild thrum of fear coursing through me.

Finally, with a jarring thud, we land on solid ground, the sudden stop knocking the breath from my lungs. I stumble, my legs wobbling beneath me as I try to regain my balance. The world spins for a moment longer before finally coming to a halt, leaving me breathless and disoriented.

As I catch my breath, I glance around, taking in the cabin.

Sitting calmly by the fire is Alivar, Felix the cat perched on the arm of the chair by his side. Its black fur gleams strangely in the light, and it regards me with a look of quiet amusement, as if it knows more than it lets on.

Chapter Two

Maxon

I release a groan as I shift uncomfortably on the cold, merciless stone floor. The length of chain between my ankles and wrists is only about a foot, leaving me with barely enough room to move. The one around my neck, anchoring me to the wall, is even shorter, pulling tight with every slight movement. Each time I try to adjust my position, the shackles constrict further, biting into my skin and forcing me into painful submission. The only relief comes when I manage to stay completely still, my back pressed against the rough wall—a near-impossible task given the so-called accommodations.

I look down at the shackles encasing my wrists and see dried blood crusted on my skin. These aren't ordinary shackles like the iron ones most would use for the fae. They're made from wyvern bones, ancient and powerful, rendering all of my magic utterly useless.

I can feel the cold, dead weight of them around my wrists, ankles, and neck, sapping the strength I would normally draw from within.

It's as if they've cut me off from a vital part of myself, leaving me hollow and helpless.

Leave it to the fucking Shadoweaver to have the perfect cell waiting for me. I shouldn't be surprised really—this is exactly the kind of meticulous cruelty he's known for. But I can't help the bitter thoughts that flood my mind as I tug futilely at the chains. Where in the world did he even find wyvern bones? The creatures have been extinct for centuries, their remains scattered and nearly impossible to come by. Yet here I am, bound by the very essence of one, trapped in a cell that feels more like a grave.

My body throbs with pain, every muscle and joint screaming from the strain of being unable to move for so long. The stone beneath me offers no comfort, and the relentless thirst gnaws at the edges of my sanity, intensifying the disorientation that has been creeping in since the moment I was chained here. It's only been two days but it feels like a lifetime. The blood loss and the wyvern bones draining my magic have left me in a state of desperate need, my body teetering on the brink of collapse.

I've faced countless dangers before, but this . . . this is different. The physical agony is one thing, but the knowledge that I'm slowly being drained, not just of blood but of my very essence, is a terror all in itself. My thoughts keep drifting, struggling to stay coherent, but one pressing concern cuts through the haze; I have yet to discuss a crucial matter with Everly.

The bond between us is new, fragile yet powerful. Once mated, I will need to feed from her during every new moon—a necessity for my kind, one that's as much about maintaining my strength as it is about deepening our connection. But, I'm uncertain if druids share the same characteristics as the high fae in this regard. Will she, too, begin to feel the effects of our separation? Will the bond pull at her, making her feel the same gnawing emptiness that's growing within me?

Movement in my periphery has me tensing. A thick mass of shadows forms in the open archway, two crimson eyes staring at me from in its depths. I tip my head back against the stone and close my eyes.

"You look like shit," the mass hisses, its voice slithering over the stone walls like a cold, unfeeling wind.

I force my eyes open to thin slits, my throat dry as sandpaper. "Back for more?" The rasped words grate against the rawness in my throat.

The shadowy form slowly solidifies, transforming into the demon I've come to loathe. In the flickering torchlight, her black hair gleams like polished onyx, a stark contrast to the dim, filthy surroundings. Surprisingly, her white silk kimono, adorned with delicate red flowers, remains immaculate—untouched by the blood that should stain it. That's new. Her eyes, a striking crimson red, gleam with a sinister light, betraying the twisted satisfaction she gets in this game she likes to play.

"You're just so delicious," she purrs, stepping closer with a predatory grace.

Disgust twists my features into a snarl. My lip curls, and I let out a low growl, which reverberates in the confined space.

The demon tips her head back and laughs, the sound scraping against my nerves like nails on a chalkboard.

"Fucking demon," I spit, venom lacing each word.

Her head snaps down, and before I can react, she's straddling me, her weight pressing down on my already aching body. Her hand fists my hair, tipping my head back, the pain scattering across my scalp.

"I told you. My name is Yumekui," she whispers, her breath hot against my skin.

My lips peel back over my fangs, a silent snarl of defiance. "Your name is of no concern to me," I snarl, refusing to give her the satisfaction of acknowledgment.

Her lips tilt into a sinister smile, and with a flick of her wrist, a dagger materializes in her hand. The blade gleams wickedly in the dim light, promising pain. "For royalty, you really have no manners." She tsks, feigning disappointment as she lightly trails the blade against my skin, drawing out the tension in the air.

The sensation sends a shiver across my body, a mix of fear and rage simmering beneath the surface. But I refuse to give her the pleasure of seeing me break. Not now. Not ever.

Placing the tip of her finger on the dagger, she twirls it, a bead of red blood forming. Slowly, she puts her finger in her mouth, sucking the blood from it while those crimson eyes never leave mine.

With a swift motion she drags her dagger across my chest, leaving a searing pain in its wake. Air hisses between my teeth as a fiery pain burns a path over my body.

Humming in approval, she leans forward and drags her tongue across the wound, lapping at the blood. With each passing second, the burn intensifies, creeping through my veins like acid. She is fucking infecting me with her foul poison.

I try to move, but my restraints tighten, keeping me in place.

"You could end this pain and help us," the shadows whisper.

"Never!" I roar.

I would endure an eternity of this pain if it meant Everly would be safe. I hate that she's out there alone.

No, not alone. Alivar got her out of the city, but has he taken her back? Is she under Raiden's protection? Fuck, I hope so. If he has her . . .

Anger and jealousy burn in the pit of my stomach, momentarily blocking the pain.

I want nothing more than to open our bond to see how she's doing, but I can't risk it.

Chapter Three

Everly

Alivar smartly vanished earlier, leaving me in this secluded cabin with strict instructions not to step outside again. The cabin's suspiciously well-stocked, almost as if someone anticipated my every need. Clothes in my size, enough food to last weeks, even little comforts like a warm blanket draped over the worn leather couch. It's too convenient, too perfect, and the unease gnaws at me.

But despite the cozy setup, the pull of the world outside still tugs at me. I can't just sit here idle, while my thoughts run rampant. Which is why I decide to collect more firewood. Though, in truth, I have no idea what I'm doing. There isn't much to find, just a few damp, half-rotted branches scattered around the clearing. But it's given me something to do, a way to keep my hands busy and my mind off the mounting anxiety.

The cabin's solitude is starting to wear on me. Alone with nothing but my thoughts, my imagination conjures up all sorts of horrors. What is happening in Skora? What is Maxon going through?

The images in my mind grow darker with every passing minute.

"Stop, Everly. You'll drive yourself mad," I mutter, shaking my head as if the motion can somehow dislodge the spiraling thoughts. But the fear is like a living thing, slithering through my mind, whispering doubts and dread that refuse to be silenced.

As I trudge through the snow, a sudden breeze tosses my hair across my face, causing me to momentarily lose sight of my path. The air, crisp and biting, carries with it a subtle fragrance of pine, adding a touch of freshness to the wintry landscape. I gather a small amount of firewood and make my way back to the cabin, feeling the cold nip at my cheeks.

Approaching the cabin door, I pause, my gaze drawn to the darkening forest beyond. The towering trees stand tall and silent, their branches swaying gently in the breeze, as if whispering hidden secrets only they hold.

Felix, with his sleek midnight black fur and piercing green eyes, waits by the front door of the cabin, his distinct features contrasting against the white background.

"I'm back."

Felix meows loudly, seemingly protesting my departure from the cabin once again. Rolling my eyes, I push open the door and let out a sigh. My attempt to explore the area has proven to be unhelpful. Even my magic seems dormant here, as if it's too cold to function.

Swinging open the wooden door, I step inside and bang my boots on the mat to remove any excess snow. Felix follows closely behind, winding his tail around my leg as he enters. The cabin is small and cozy, with a single spacious room and a bathroom tucked away. If not for the circumstances, I might actually enjoy the cabin with its frost-kissed windows which exude an icy elegance that perfectly frames the breathtaking view of the snow-capped mountains.

I pick up a log and make my way over to the fireplace by the far wall. Squatting down, I carefully place the wood on the fire, making sure it's secure and won't roll out. The last thing I need is to catch the cabin on fire. I stare into the flames, becoming lost in the captivating dance as it flickers. My mind naturally wanders to Maxon and the rest of the group. I've had no way to know their fate after the Shadoweaver's pet unleashed her army of creatures at the city's gates. I have tirelessly tried to connect with Maxon through our bond but he's deliberately blocked any connection. The fact I can still feel his heartbeat next to mine provides the only sense of solace I have in this moment.

In a robotic motion, I remove my gloves, dropping them to the floor. My soul is heavy with so much pain, it's a feeling I'm unfamiliar with. Fighting back tears, I hold my hands out in front of the fire, relishing the warmth as I flex my fingers. Slowly, I lower myself the rest of the way to the floor, settling in front of the fire, becoming lost in the flames.

My skin relentlessly itches, a desperate sensation that consumes me. The overwhelming need to find my way back fills my every thought. If Alivar stubbornly refuses, I am left with no option but to forge my own way. I refuse to remain hidden out here while others suffer.

Zaria's soft feline eyes, shimmering like pools of amber, vividly appear in my mind, instantly shattering my heart into countless pieces. A surge of tears wells up, and I fight to hold them back. I need to be there for my friend to provide solace during her unfathomable loss. Rayna was always so bright and bubbly, and I know how close the sisters were. The thought of the immense pain Zaria must be enduring breaks me. The haunting image of the light vanishing from Rayna's eyes as she desperately sprinted toward me etches itself forever into the depths of my memory. She sacrificed her own life in a valiant attempt to reach me, and the weight of that moment presses down on my soul like an anchor, pulling me deeper into the abyss of grief and guilt.

The weight of it hits hard—so many lives stolen, and all because of that demon. *Yumekui.* In the past twenty-four hours my fear has morphed into a smoldering anger, seeping into the depths of my being. The burning desire to grow stronger, to learn my magic, consumes me like a relentless flame flickering in my chest.

I crave to unlock the depths of my magic, to train and hone my skills, so I can bury those who threaten the people I love. My fury will know no bounds, and I vow to do whatever it takes to stop the Shadoweaver.

I need to know every intricate detail of the Shadoweaver's plan to use me as his escape route from prison and what his intentions are. But first I need to get home, regroup, and find out who has been working with Alivar behind Maxon's back. I don't know why it bothers me so much that someone we trusted was working with Alivar to feed him information. I think I'm still sore about him showing up when I was bathing, to be honest.

With a sense of restlessness, I absentmindedly pick at a loose thread on my pants, the repetitive motion providing a small sense of satisfaction.

To my surprise, Alivar has a selection of the dresses I designed, accompanied by matching pants and boots, already here in the cabin. It's kind of unsettling how prepared he was for me. Maxon's claim that the Seelie Prince has a personal interest in me seemed dubious at first. However, being in this place has made me question my initial doubts.

Unable to sit by the fire any longer, I wander through the cabin, curiosity propelling me to open every cupboard and drawer. The creaking sound of the old wooden furniture echoes through the silent room adding to the rustic charm of the place. As I sift through the various items, I stumble upon a stack of blank paper neatly tucked away in one of the drawers. The untouched sheets, pristine and white, stand in stark contrast to the weathered surroundings. Next to the paper, I find a tin filled with an assortment of pencils, their tips perfectly sharpened.

Maybe if I did some drawings, it would help quieten the racing thoughts in my mind. So, I sit down at the small wooden table near the window and pick up a pencil. My hand hovers over the paper, and my mind goes blank.

I drop my head to the table and bang it softly against the wood several times.

The prickling sensation of magic rises in the air, sending my senses into overdrive. I look over my shoulder to see Alivar standing in the middle of the room. Pushing the hood from his head, he grins at me. My teeth clamp together and my eyes narrow, sending him a glare before going back to my drawing. Every line I sketch is more aggressive than the last, a silent rebellion against his presence.

"I brought dinner," he says, his tone calm but edged with irritation.

"I don't want to eat." My voice is flat, final.

The conversation should end there.

"Don't be stupid. You need to eat."

I turn in my seat and face him, my eyes falling on the lifeless rabbit he lifts into the air. Disgust curls my lip as I take in the sight.

"I don't eat meat."

His expression shifts from frustration to bewilderment. "You don't . . . You don't eat meat? Are you serious?"

"Deadly." My eyes flare with defiance, and I raise my chin, daring him to challenge me.

"How did Maxon ever put up with you?" he mutters, more to himself than to me, but the words hit their mark.

Pain slices through my chest, sharp and unforgiving. I blow out an aggravated breath trying to expel the hurt, but it lingers, heavy and suffocating.

"You're an asshole," I snap, the insult escaping before I can stop it.

His eyes widen at my outburst.

"I saved you," he counters.

"You've held me here for–"

"Twenty-four hours, Everly. Not an eternity!" His patience is wearing thin, and it shows in the clipped tone of his words.

I stand abruptly, my chair scraping loudly against the wooden floor. "It feels like an eternity, Alivar!" The words burst from me, raw and unfiltered.

The room falls into a tense silence, the air thick with unspoken accusations and simmering anger.

"Once I'm sure the threat is gone, that the city and Castle Vesner are safe, I will take you back. Yumekui could still be lurking in the forest, waiting to snatch you. If I allowed that to happen, then all those lives would have been lost. And for what? When I get the all clear, I will return you."

My heart sinks like a heavy stone down into the pit of my stomach, making it twist and churn with guilt. The realization hits me like a punch to the gut—I don't want to endanger anyone else. I've been selfish, thinking only of my own fear and desperation. So many people have already died, their lives snuffed out like candles in a storm, all because of the cursed blood that runs through my veins. My blood, the key to setting the Shadoweaver free from his ancient prison.

The thought makes my chest tighten, a cold sweat breaking out on my skin. I can't shake the images of those who have fallen. Their faces flash through my mind, one after another. Each loss is a fresh wound, a new scar on my soul. And yet, here I am; still alive, still breathing, still a threat to everyone around me.

With a deep, shaky breath, I settle back into my chair, my movements slow and deliberate as I try to steady myself. I brush my long blonde hair away from my face, the strands falling back stubbornly, as if they, too, were burdened by the weight of my guilt.

"Alivar?" I say softly, my voice trembling despite my efforts to keep it steady.

"Yeah?" he grunts as he heads toward the kitchen and casually tosses the lifeless rabbit onto the counter. The sound is enough to make me cringe, and my stomach churns with nausea.

"What do you know about the Shadoweaver?"

Alivar turns and leans back on the counter. He folds his arms over his chest and stares at me. Silence stretches on, and I shift uncomfortably. The force of his piercing gaze intensifies, making me want to take the words back. Just as frustration builds up, he finally speaks.

"If he gets his hands on you, I know he will leave nothing but destruction in his wake."

His words stir something fierce within me. A sharp mix of dread and determination.

"How do we stop him?" I ask, my emotions rising, tightening my throat, making the words emerge strained and barely audible.

Fear, anger, desperation. But the one taking up the most space? Guilt.

With a heavy sigh, Alivar moves that piercing gaze to stare out the window. "The Shadoweaver has been imprisoned for centuries, deep in the mountains of the Deadlands."

"Why not just kill him?"

"He can't be killed. Our ancestors did what they could in trapping him. No one knows where exactly. He commands the dark, the shadows, and those who dwell in it."

The image of countless deadlings swarming the city flashes vividly in my mind.

"Why does he need me?" I whisper, my fingernails digging into my legs as I scrunch up the fabric of my dress. "I mean, I get it's my blood that unlocks the prison he is in, but why? Why me?"

"You are the strongest of your kind. It was the druids along with the Guardians, who imprisoned him in his cavern deep in the mountains. So, it is your blood that will unlock the spell, only your blood holds the magic required to do so. The fact that you were able to open the gate from the human world to here and without even realizing it, is just a testament to that power."

My mind goes blank and my lips part on an exhale.

"Once you master your abilities, you will wield more magic than those who came before you. The blood that flows in your veins holds the power to command armies, a legacy of ancient strength. Why do you think my mother was so pissed when your parents denied us a marriage treaty? Why she is so pissed that I didn't find you first?"

"I don't feel as powerful as you say," I mutter, looking out the window at the snowy landscape.

Despite being an all-powerful druid, I couldn't save Maxon, Rayna, Lavina, or protect the city. I sure don't feel like I'm someone great.

"From the moment you were born, it was clear you were destined for greatness. It was whispered on the wind."

"The prophecy?"

Alivar nods, and the words run through my mind.

It was from the whispers of ancient trees and the murmurs of the sacred groves.
A druid princess, born under a crescent moon's gentle glow, shall wield power unmeasured in realms both high and low.
With magic deep within, she'll rise, her destiny unknown,
To shake the faerie realm, where mystic secrets are sown.
Her heart a beacon of the woods, her spirit strong and free,
She'll dance with stars and call the winds.

Beneath the moon's enchanting light, she'll rise to claim her throne,
Uniting realms of faerie, her power fully grown.
With wisdom, love, and courage, she'll mend what once was torn,
For in her hands, the faerie world shall be reborn.

"How do we stop him?" I whisper, repeating my earlier question.

"I don't know."

Chapter Four

Maxon

My head lolls to the side, the wyvern bones tightening around my neck with a cruel, unyielding grip. It jolts me back to reality, the harsh reminder that there's no respite here. Every inch of my body aches, a relentless symphony of pain that seems to pulse with every beat of my heart. Hunger is a constant, gnawing presence, a feral craving that claws at my insides, demanding the one thing I'm desperate to avoid—blood.

If it weren't for my injuries and these bones stopping me from healing, I wouldn't be craving blood at all. I know they're waiting, lurking in the shadows, calculating. They're biding their time, waiting until the hunger becomes unbearable, until I'm so desperate that I'm driven to feed from the fucking demon. But I can't do that. If I give in, everything will fall apart. It's a line I can't cross without losing Everly forever. There would be no coming back from that, no redemption, no second chances.

Just an irreversible plunge into chaos that would consume everything I'm fighting to protect.

I close my eyes, feeling the coolness of the wall against the back of my head. The silence that wraps around me is like another layer of stone—heavier than the walls, heavier than the cold. My throat, parched and scratchy, longs for a sip of water. I can go several weeks without food and water, but given my condition, I'm not sure I'd last that long. Without my mates blood, my body was as useful as a mere fucking mortals. My injuries will stop healing altogether, and infection would spread. Turning me into something neither dead or alive.

A harsh scraping sound echoes through the dimly lit tunnel, causing my attention to fixate on its entrance. A putrid stench wafts through the air, assaulting my nostrils, and I struggle to suppress the urge to retch. The overwhelming odor can only be attributed to one creature in my knowledge—a deadling.

The air thickens with an eerie stillness, as I strain to make out any other sounds. There is a faint stir in the tunnel, a delicate shift in the atmosphere that catches my attention.

A predator.

My primal instincts are finely tuned to detect any threats. Something that my father and Nolan ingrained in me since I was young.

The faint scent of decay and earth fills my nostrils, intensifying the growing sense of dread within me. The sound of its claws scraping against the stone reverberates through my small area. I can almost taste the adrenaline in the air as I tighten my fists, my knuckles turning white with tension.

The grotesque hand, with its elongated fingers and sharp, curved nails, inches closer, as if taunting me.

I only have a small amount of wyvern chains to work with, but I can dispatch the creature easily enough. Its sunken, gaunt features make my lips curl in disgust. The deadling's milky white orbs blink as its head tilts at an unnatural angle, slinking into the room just feet from me. Its presence fills the space with an oppressive, foul aura.

My grip tightens on the chains as I grit my teeth, waiting for it to make its move. The air feels thick, the deadling's hunger palpable in its gaze. Its intentions flash in its eyes a moment before it lunges, mouth open wide, emitting a guttural hiss. I don't give it a chance to touch me. In a swift motion, I twist the creature around, wrapping the chain across its neck. Pulling it against my body, the wyvern chain glows faintly, reacting to the dark magic that animates the deadling. It thrashes violently, but I hold firm, using every ounce of my strength to keep the chain tight. The deadling's claws swipe at the air, narrowly missing my face. Its screeching grows louder, the sound reverberating through the room. Its unnatural strength pushes against me, crushing me against the stone wall.

Growling, I pull tighter, feeling the chain dig into its decaying flesh. The deadling's movements become more frantic, its death throes an eerie dance of desperation. Using my legs, I pin it down, and with one final, violent shudder, it goes limp, collapsing against me. I shove it off me onto the floor and wipe my face with the back of my hand as I sit panting, my heart pounding in my chest. The tension slowly ebbs away, replaced by a sense of grim satisfaction.

I glance around the room, my body thrumming with adrenaline. There could be more lurking in the shadows waiting for their chance to strike. I can't let my guard down, not even for a moment.

Chapter Five

Everly

It has been three days since Alivar brought me here, but each moment feels like an eternity. The days drag on, making time itself feel sluggish and oppressive. I let out a muted growl, frustration bubbling up inside me. This is ridiculous.

I need to focus on something else, so I close my eyes, and focus on my magic, desperately seeking the power that once flowed so freely.

Feeling a faint flicker in my chest, I reach for it, coaxing it. A tingling sensation spreads over my skin, making the hairs on my body rise, but that's it. I can't summon a wall of water or command vines to rip from the earth.

I cross my legs, adjusting my clothing around me. The white breeches, made from the softest material, offer some comfort, as does the white, off-the-shoulder, ruffled tunic.

The gold and blue overdress that laces up over the basic clothes is gorgeous with its high splits for easier movement, and the gold ties adding a touch of elegance.

I also love how there is a loop at the end of the long sleeves that goes over my pointer finger.

However, today, the beauty of my attire feels meaningless, a hollow adornment that does nothing to ease my turmoil. Desperation claws at me, a relentless force I can't shake, no matter how hard I try.

I close my eyes and focus, trying again to summon the magic that once flowed so effortlessly through me. I picture the rush of water, its power and grace; the strength of the vines, twisting and unfurling with life; the delicate beauty of the roses that bloom in the castle's gardens, their petals soft and vibrant. But all I can manage is a flicker, a faint spark of energy that sputters and dies before it can fully ignite. My magic is now reduced to a mere trickle, trapped, suppressed by some unseen force that I can't identify. The entire situation is maddening.

My shoulders slump, and I glance back toward the kitchen. "Maybe I need to eat."

But the thought of food does little to stir my appetite. I'm too preoccupied with thoughts of escape, of regaining my magic and breaking Maxon free from the Shadoweaver. Felix meows loudly, brushing up against me. I drop my hand and glide it over his back, eliciting a gentle purr from him as he leans into my touch.

Drawing a deep breath, I close my eyes and focus once more on the flicker of magic within me. This time, I channel all my frustration, anger, and desperation into it, willing it to grow, to ignite into the powerful force it once was.

As I concentrate, I feel a slight shift, a spark of hope. It's faint, but it's there. I latch onto it, nurturing it, coaxing it to grow. The tingling sensation intensifies, spreading through my body, and I feel a surge of energy. It's not much, but it's a start. And it's enough to remind me that I am not powerless.

Out of nowhere, a chilling howl slices through the wind, sharp and eerie, freezing me in place. Was that . . . My heart skips a beat as I strain to listen, the sound echoing in my mind.

Quickly, I scramble to my feet, cursing under my breath.

"Damn it," I mutter, nearly tripping over the flowing fabric of my dress as I stumble toward the window. My fingers clutch the edge of the windowsill as I lean close to the cold glass.

I heard it. I know I did.

My eyes scan the clearing and the tall pines that encircle the cabin like silent sentinels. My shoulders slump in disappointment. I must be imagining things. It couldn't possibly be— Another chorus of howls shatters the silence, louder and closer this time. I inhale sharply, my pulse quickening as the realization hits me like a lightning bolt.

It is *them!*

Panic and exhilaration surge through me in equal measure as I sprint toward the front door. I grab the handle and wrench the door open with a force that sends it crashing against the wall, the sound of splintering wood ringing in the cold air. I don't care. The only thing that matters is getting outside, finding them.

Stepping out onto the porch, I'm immediately greeted by a dazzling white landscape, the snow stretching endlessly in every direction, covering everything in a thick, pristine blanket. I take a few hesitant steps forward, spinning around slowly, my breath coming out in visible puffs of steam. A gust of icy wind whips across my cheeks, sending a shiver down my spine but I barely notice it. My eyes are locked on the towering trees in the distance, scanning for any sign of movement.

Then, amidst the sea of white, a flash of vibrant blue catches my eye. My breath hitches. I watch, mesmerized, as a frostflare bursts from the snow-covered ground, its powerful legs propelling it effortlessly over a fallen tree. Its fur, a brilliant blue that glistens like sapphires, stands out starkly against the snowy backdrop, each strand shimmering as if touched by magic. The creature's eyes glow like radiant white orbs, and the peculiar markings on its forehead emit a soft, ethereal light, adding to its otherworldly appearance.

My mouth falls open in awe, but before I can fully process the sight, two enormous white wolves leap over the same fallen tree, their movements graceful and powerful, their fur blending seamlessly with the snow. Eyes, sharp and intelligent, lock onto me, and in that moment, I know.

"Nymeria! Anika!" My voice cracks with the tidal wave of emotions that fill me. A mix of joy, relief, and overwhelming love burst from me. I start running to meet them; the snow crunching under my feet. My heart soars as they bound toward me, their forms growing larger, more defined with each passing second.

Both wolves tip their heads back, howling in unison as they come sprinting down the hill. This time I'm unable to stop my tears, a sob breaking free.

The frostflare dashes toward me with incredible speed, its paws barely touching the ground, and not a single impression left in the snow. Bracing for impact, I watch as it explodes into a cloud of blue, shimmering dust just inches away. *What the hell?*

I don't have time to process what just happened, because I'm knocked off my feet. The moment I hit the ground, a cold rush of snow engulfs my back.

Anika and Nymeria playfully nudge me, their soft fur brushing gently against my skin as they nestle into my embrace. Their presence is a balm to my wounded heart, a reminder that I'm not as alone as I've been feeling.

"I can't believe you're both here. How did you find me?" My voice trembles with disbelief and gratitude. I reach out to stroke their fur, feeling the familiar texture beneath my fingers, and it grounds me in this surreal moment.

They both move away slightly, creating just enough space for me to sit up properly. The chill of the snow seeps into me, but I barely notice, too focused on the two magnificent creatures before me.

'The fox brought us here,' Anika's voice echoes in my mind, calm and sure, as if it's the most natural thing in the world.

"Wait, but if you're here." My thoughts race as I trail off, connecting the dots. They're supposed to be with Maxon. "What happened?"

Anika and Nymeria exchange a look, their eyes full of sorrow that sends a fresh wave of fear through me.

'The demon took our king before we could reach him,' Anika's voice comes again.

'We are sorry,' Nymeria adds, her tone laced with sadness.

The significance of their words crashes down on me, and I pull them close, wrapping my arms tightly around each of their necks. The softness of their fur against my face is a small comfort, but it does little to ease the ache in my chest. Tears flow freely down my cheeks, hot and unrelenting, mingling with the cold air. My sobs fill the silence, a raw, guttural sound born from the deep sorrow of knowing that Maxon is now alone in the enemy's den.

"It's not your fault." I say, barely audible. Though my heart is breaking, I try to soothe them. "Thank you for finding me."

'The fox led us here and said you needed us,' Nymeria explains, her words offering a faint glimmer of hope in the darkness that has settled around us.

I take a shaky breath, struggling to regain my composure. I can feel the snow seeping into my clothes, the cold biting at my skin, but it's nothing compared to the numbness I feel inside.

I stand, brushing the snow from my clothes with trembling hands. "I do need you," I admit, looking down at them. "I always do."

Chapter Six

Everly

Relentlessly, I pace the length of the cabin, my annoyance simmering dangerously close to boiling over with every passing minute. Nymeria and Anika's steady gazes follow my every step from their spot by the fireplace, their presence a silent reminder that I'm not alone—but their quiet observation does little to soothe the storm raging inside me. The gentle crackling of the fire, once a source of comfort, now only heightens my agitation, each pop and hiss like a match striking against my already frayed nerves.

If things were different, I might love it here. The snow-covered landscape outside the window is breathtaking, a winter wonderland that would normally fill me with awe. But today, none of it matters. The beauty, the tranquility—it's all lost on me, swallowed up by the desperation eating away inside.

If I stopped pacing and actually sorted through my feelings, I'd see I'm desperate to get back because I don't want people to think I've abandoned them or that I've switched sides.

My eyes dart to the window, the outside world taunting me with its freedom. Felix's sharp eyes track my every move from his perch on the windowsill, his furry face tilting slightly as if he's trying to figure out what's going on in my head. He probably thinks I've lost my mind. Maybe I have.

"He can't keep me here. I'm not his prisoner," I snap, my voice cracking.

The words echo in the small cabin, bouncing off the walls and coming back to me, a harsh reminder of the reality I'm trying so hard to deny. I have absolutely no control of anything right now.

I stomp my foot against the wooden floorboards, the sound loud and jarring in the otherwise quiet room. My fingers flex and curl, itching with the need to fight, to break something, anything, just to release the tension coiled tight within me.

Suddenly, the unmistakable sensation of magic prickles along my skin, and I whirl around to see a portal materializing before my eyes. Pulse hammering in my throat, I storm over to Alivar without even giving him a chance to speak.

"We are leaving."

Alivar's eyebrow lifts in surprise, his arms crossing over his chest. "I don't–"

"Now." Irritation pulses through me like a live wire.

"–take orders from you," he finishes, the portal blinking out behind him.

Nymeria and Anika flank me, their low growls rumbling through the cabin, rattling the icy windows.

A ghost of a smile crosses Alivar's lips as he observes the three of us. "Fine."

My head jerks back in surprise. "Really?"

Alivar is silent for a long moment, his gaze unwavering. "Yes."

"Okay, then let's go!" I say with disbelief and urgency.

"Where would you like to go, Princess?" he says, teasingly.

"Don't mess with me, Alivar."

"Wouldn't dare, Princess."

Felix gracefully leaps from the windowsill and approaches me. His emerald feline eyes flash, catching the light in a way that feels unnatural. I squint, tilting my head slightly as if adjusting my angle might reveal some hidden truth. Is that magic?

Before I can dwell on it, a sudden, swirling pulse of energy erupts from him, shimmering like a veil being pulled away. My breath catches as I take an instinctive step back, only to collide with Anika. The impact jolts me, and my arms flail out to steady myself, the air suddenly thick with magic. It's not just a trick of the light—Felix stands at the center of it all, the magic wrapping around him like a second skin.

"What the hell?" I whisper, my hand landing on my chest as if to keep my heart from free.

"Princess," the fae standing before me purrs, his green eyes the only familiar feature in his transformed visage. Short black fur covers his entire humanoid body, giving him a sleek, shadowy appearance. A tail sways behind him, mirroring the restless energy in his stance. Around his face, a tuft of fur forms a wild mane, accentuating the pointed ears protruding from the top of his head. Long black hair cascades down his back, blending seamlessly with the dark fur. His hands and feet end in sharp, formidable claws, completing the image of a creature both fierce and otherworldly.

I've never in my life seen a being quite like him, but that's not saying much, I did grow up in the human world.

"Felix?" I whisper, completely off kilter.

"Yes."

I blink several times, trying to process what I'm seeing. The cat—no, Felix—just transformed into the humanoid figure now standing in front of me, his form shifting with an almost fluid grace. My mind struggles to catch up with the impossible reality unfolding before me.

My voice is unsteady as I grapple with the bizarre sight. "What's going on?"

Felix's gaze meets mine, and there's a slight hiss in his tone as he responds, "I was concealing you while you were here."

"Huh?" My confusion deepens, the meaning of his words slipping through my fingers like sand.

Alivar steps in, his voice calm but tinged with something that makes my skin prickle. "Felix here is a unique type of fae. He can nullify magic, and is excellent at cloaking," he explains, as if it's the most normal thing in the world.

The realization crashes into me, sharp and bitter like a blade twisting in my gut. "You had me watched and my magic concealed?" I snap, spinning on Alivar with a fury that sets my blood on fire. My hands clench into fists at my sides, and I can barely contain the urge to lash out.

Alivar just shrugs, as if my anger is nothing more than a mild inconvenience. He runs a hand through his hair, his expression indifferent. "I couldn't have you drawing attention to yourself. To be honest, I'm surprised they found you," he says, casting a frown in the direction of Nymeria and Anika.

The wolves bristle at his scrutiny, but before I can retort, Felix interjects, his tone relaxed, almost bored, "The frostflare lead them here."

"What?" Alivar's brows furrow, his confusion mirroring mine, but for entirely different reasons.

Felix's tail flicks back and forth in an almost lazy manner, though there's a sharpness in his eerie green eyes as he turns his gaze back to Alivar. "Doesn't matter."

Alivar's eyes narrow slightly, but he doesn't push the issue. Instead, he faces Felix and gives him a nod, a gesture of respect—or, perhaps, resignation. "The cabin is yours if you wish to stay."

Felix regards him coolly, his feline eyes holding an unsettling intensity before shifting back to me. "It was a pleasure, Princess." His voice is smooth enough to be almost mocking. "May you have good fortune in your quest to retrieve your mate."

The words hit me like a punch to the gut, and I can feel the weight of the task ahead settling over me. I give him a quick nod and grab my cloak, fastening it around my shoulders. The familiar snap of the clasp echoes in the quiet room. I take a slow, steadying breath before turning to face Alivar.

It's time to go home.

Chapter Seven

Everly

Nymeria and Anika leap through the portal ahead of us, their movements swift and graceful like shadows passing through the night. I hesitate for a heartbeat, sharing one last look with Alivar. His expression is unreadable, a mixture of concern and something deeper that I can't quite place. But there's no time to dwell on it. With a deep breath, I step into the portal, the air rushing around me as if I've become weightless for a moment.

When my feet touch down, the sensation is jarring, like being pulled from one world to another in an instant.

The war room at the castle unfolds before me, the air thick with tension. The room stands frozen, a mixture of shock and disbelief as everyone's attention lands on Nymeria and Anika, who stand poised and alert, their presence commanding the space.

I take a moment to gather myself, to let the world stop spinning before my eyes sweep across the room.

The large wooden table at the center is strewn with maps and documents, evidence of hurried planning and desperate strategies. I don't recognize most of the faces around the table until my gaze locks onto a familiar figure standing at the head of the table. Raiden. He's holding a stack of papers, his brow furrowed, but the moment his eyes meet mine, everything changes.

The papers slip from his hands, scattering across the table and floor like autumn leaves caught in a gust of wind. His expression shifts in an instant, the hard lines of focus and determination softening into something that makes my chest clench. Relief, raw and unguarded, floods his features.

In an instant, he's across the room, wrapping me in his strong arms. The sudden embrace is overwhelming, and emotions clog my throat, making my nose sting.

"I'm so glad you're back," Raiden whispers into my hair, his voice softer than I've ever heard. I can feel the rapid beat of his heart against my cheek.

I squeeze him tightly, unwilling to let go just yet. "I missed you, Batman."

Raiden pulls back slightly, just enough to look into my eyes. His gaze is intense, filled with a mix of relief, worry, and unspoken questions. "Thank Ainé. Are you okay?"

A tear slips down my cheek. "I'm fine, Raiden."

He wipes the tear away with his thumb, his touch gentle. "We'll get him back," he promises, his voice steady and reassuring.

Before I can respond, the air in the war room erupts into chaos. A cacophony of raised voices, clattering armor, and the sudden scuffle of boots scraping against stone fills the space. I whip around to see what's happening, and freeze.

At the far end of the room, guards and a handful of soldiers face Alivar, weapons drawn, trying to detain him. But they're stopped in their tracks—literally. A shimmering layer of frost creeps across the floor, ice snaking up from their feet, binding them in place. Their faces twist in frustration and shock, helpless as they struggle against the magic that has rooted them to the ground.

Alivar stands calmly amidst the chaos, his hand still outstretched, the faint glow of magic fading from his fingers. His expression remains impassive, but there's a sharpness in his eyes, a cold resolve that mirrors the ice trapping the guards.

The soldiers shout commands at each other, trying to break free, but it's useless. The more they thrash, the tighter the frost clings to their boots. One of the guards lifts his sword, but it's clear he's going nowhere. The rest look to each other in frustration, realizing they're completely at Alivar's mercy.

Nymeria and Anika stand guard between me and the rest of the room, their vigilant eyes focused on the commotion.

"That's enough. Alivar–" Raiden starts.

"Crown Prince–"

Raiden snarls, his wings snapping out as he glares at Alivar, effectively silencing him. Then he locks eyes with the guards and soldiers. "The prince is of no threat. Put your weapons away."

Alivar crosses his arms and raises his eyebrow at Raiden. I can see he wants to say something else. Most probably add fuel to the fire.

Raiden doesn't give him the chance. "Let them go."

Alivar inclines his head, and with a flick of his wrists, the ice melts, disappearing as if it were never there to begin with.

Raiden steps forward, drawing everyone's attention. "Everyone out."

"But, Captain."

"It's okay, Lutin," Raiden says again, more firmly this time.

The young soldier with long blonde hair sends a glare at Alivar, his mauve colored eyes just a shade darker than Kian's, burning with a fire that makes me smile. His eyes shift and his attention lands on me.

"Your Highness," He places his fist over his heart and bows once more, then turns and exits the room with the rest.

Raiden lets out a deep sigh and leans against the table. "Tell me what happened?"

I shrug, feeling a weight on my shoulders as my focus falls to the ground. Seeking comfort, I reach for Nymeria and Anika, burying my fingers in their fur.

"Maxon and Yumekui were fighting. Somehow, she got the upper hand and . . . "

I swallow roughly, my throat dry and my heart heavy with the memory. My eyes fall closed as I try to push back the rising tide of emotions. "She was going to trade me for Maxon. I was going to do it. Maxon knew it. He panicked, and when Alivar showed up." I take a breath, my eyes darting to Alivar. "He demanded Alivar to get me out of there."

"It's a good thing he did, because we wouldn't stand a chance if it were you who had been taken."

I look up at Raiden. "How did the city fare? Was everyone able to get behind the castle walls?"

Raiden's hands land on my shoulders, squeezing. "We pushed back against the hordes, but once you were gone, they retreated." Raiden looks over at Alivar. "We have you to thank for that. Had you not taken her, they would have leveled the city."

Alivar lets out a low noise, crossing his arms over his chest as he watches us closely. Suddenly, the doors open and Tristan and Kian walk in with another man I don't know.

Tristan comes to a halt as soon as he lays eyes on me. "Princess?"

Kian's soft lavender eyes whip up to meet mine, and despite everything, I can't help but smile. For a fleeting moment, it feels like things might be okay. But then his attention shifts, sliding over to Alivar, and something in his expression changes. I watch as a flicker of guilt slithers across his face, subtle but unmistakable, and the realization hits me hard.

It was Kian.

Something cold and heavy settles in my chest, and a prickling sensation moves over my scalp. He was Alivar's spy.

Every chance, every opportunity he had, he used to betray me. He was the closest to me, the one who was always there. Whenever he disappeared or stormed off, I'd brushed it off, never suspecting, never doubting him. But now, with every passing second, the betrayal cuts deeper, and my heart hardens.

Before I know it, I'm standing right in front of Kian, my breath coming in short, sharp bursts. I don't even remember crossing the distance between us, but here I am, my body moving on its own, driven by rage. His eyes widen in shock, the realization dawning on him too late. I hear gasps from those around us, but they're distant, like echoes from another world.

Without hesitation, my arm pulls back, and I deliver a punch to his face. The impact is solid. The force of it reverberates, sending a wave of pain shooting up my arm. Kian staggers back, more from surprise than the blow itself, his expression a mix of pain and disbelief. I moved so swiftly that no one had a chance to stop me, and now the room feels frozen, every eye on us. But the betrayal I feel blocks them out. Right now, it's just Kian and me.

"How could you?!" I scream, my voice raw with anger and hurt. The words tear from my throat, each syllable laced with the sting of betrayal.

What hurts the most is having been so completely wrong about someone I thought I knew. My hand throbs with pain, and I instinctively curse, shaking it to alleviate the discomfort.

"I deserved that," Kian admits, rubbing his jaw.

"Of course you deserve it!" I hiss, poking him in the chest. "You betrayed your king."

Kian drops his head, shoulders slumping.

Tears of anger burn my eyes as I step closer. "You betrayed me."

Raiden steps up next to me, his wings flaring. "Is this true?"

"Yes," Kian replies, lifting his head and looking over my shoulder to Raiden.

So many thoughts bubble up inside of me, and I really struggle not to burst into tears. It's Tristan's low growl that gives me pause, snapping me from the feelings warring inside. Silence falls, blanketing the room in a thick tension.

Tristan's eyes mirror the same sense of betrayal I feel.

Kian raises his palms, his lavender eyes pleading with me, silently begging for understanding. "Can I explain?"

"You fed the Seelie Prince–"

"Oh, *now* I'm the prince," Alivar interrupts with a mocking tone that grates my nerves.

Gritting my teeth, I continue, "You allowed him access to the castle. To my chambers."

Alivar responds, cutting in before Kian can speak. "In all fairness, he didn't know I'd find you naked."

My cheeks flush with embarrassment, heat creeping up my neck. I swing my head around, pinning Alivar with a glare. "Not helping," I snap.

Unfazed, Alivar shrugs. "This all seems like a moot point. All Kian did was keep me updated on your progress and memories. I wanted to know if you were indeed the princess the prophecy spoke of."

"You had a cabin stocked and ready for me. You were planning on taking me at some point and using him to help."

"I was intending to take you. But that was before you mated with Maxon. Seeing his mark on you, I realized it would be a waste of time to take you. Plus, despite what others may think, I'm not that sort of person. I would never break a bonded pair. Especially not fated mates."

I drop my eyes to the ground and take several deep breaths. One thing I know from my short time with Alivar is that he doesn't lie. As for Kian, I'm still pissed off that he would go behind our backs like that.

"Princess," Kian interjects softly, "I only did what I did, so Alivar was aware of your presence. It was for your safety in case something went wrong here."

I look up at Kian, seeing the sincerity in his eyes. The betrayal stings, but I know deep down that he believed he was acting in my best interest. The complexities of our situation swirl around me, making it difficult to see a clear path forward.

"Your safety was my priority," Kian continues. "I never intended for things to get this complicated. I thought if Alivar knew who you were, he could offer some protection, should something happen to the king and things become unsafe for you here."

I sigh, feeling the stress pressing down on me. The prophecy, the Shadoweaver, the bond with Maxon, the spies, Outcasts, Alivar's unexpected involvement—it all seems too much to handle. But I can't afford to crumble now. There's too much at stake.

"What's done is done," I say, my voice steadier than I feel. "We need to focus on what comes next. Getting Maxon back. We need to find a way to navigate this together."

Alivar nods in agreement. "I understand. And I promise, whatever my intentions were before, my goal now is to ensure your safety and see the prophecy fulfilled."

"We don't even know what the prophecy means," I huff, twisting my fingers in my cloak.

"Yes, they can be open for interpretation," Raiden adds.

I flick my gaze back to Kian. "I don't want to be mad at you."

Kian's gaze softens. "I understand if you are."

"I'm fucking furious," Tristan growls. His jaw tightens so much that a muscle pops.

Raiden steps forward, his presence reassuring as his arm lightly brushes against mine. "Look," he begins, his tone calm yet firm, "We need everyone on the same side. When the king returns, we'll deal with it then. But for now, let it go."

Tristan, ever the fiery one, snaps back, "He is no better than Nolan."

Sensing the tension, I make my way toward Tristan. Reaching out, I gently place my hand on his arm, and his intense indigo eyes immediately meet mine.

"It's okay to be mad," I whisper softly, trying to soothe the storm brewing within him. "But let's channel that energy into getting our king home."

Surprising me, Tristan's strong arms envelop me in a hug, providing a sense of security and comfort I've missed. "I'm so relieved you're safe and back home," he murmurs into my hair. "Raiden assured me you'd return, but it didn't sit well with me, having you with *him*."

From behind me, I hear Alivar snort dismissively, but I ignore it. Stepping back slightly, I offer a smile to Tristan, trying to lighten the mood. "I'm glad you're all okay, too. I was so worried, and someone wouldn't pass on any details," I accuse, gesturing over my shoulder with a thumb toward Alivar, catching his gaze.

Alivar's eyes flicker with amusement, but he remains silent. I turn back to Tristan, seeing the worry etched on his face.

"It's been a difficult time for all of us," I continue. "But we're together now, and that's what matters. We'll get through this, and we'll bring our king back."

Raiden dips his head in agreement, his expression resolute. "We need to stay united," he asserts. "No matter what differences we have, our goal is the same: to bring the king home and restore order."

Movement to the side catches my attention, pulling my gaze toward the unfamiliar male who entered the room alongside Tristan and Kian. He stands tall, exuding a quiet confidence, his hand resting casually on the pommel of his sword. His quizzical gaze is locked on me, studying me with an intensity that makes me want to step behind Raiden's wings.

His long black hair is neatly braided into sections that run down his back. The sides of his head are clean-shaven, revealing intricate tattoos etched just above his ears. The sharp, geometric lines of the tattoos only emphasize his pointed fae ears and the chiseled angles of his jawline, giving him a striking appearance. Everything about him, from the precision of his grooming to the silent authority in his stance, speaks of someone who's used to command.

But it's his eyes that draw me in. Unlike the other high fae in the room, whose shimmer with shades of purple, his eyes are a deep, comforting shade of brown.

I barely register Raiden's touch on my back until he steps closer, his fingers press lightly against the fabric of my cloak, a subtle but protective gesture, and I can feel the steady strength behind his touch.

"Everly, this is Fenris. He is my second."

"Nice to meet you," I reply slowly, my mind ticking over.

Why haven't I met him before now, and why are his eyes different? Is he fae or a shifter?

Nymeria and Anika, sensing my unease, cautiously move in closer to the new focus of my attention.

"I've called everyone back to Skora and Vesner so we can regroup." Raiden's words are calm, but laced with the gravity of the situation. "Fenris is usually stationed in Mistbourne, patrolling the borders of the Outlands."

I frown, my brow knitting together. That doesn't seem particularly smart, bringing forces together in one location, but what do I know? I'm an outsider in this kingdom, a stranger to its politics and military strategy. The last thing I need is to open my mouth and say something that reveals just how little I understand. So, I bite my tongue, keeping my thoughts to myself, and instead watch as Raiden exchanges a nod with Fenris.

"It's a pleasure to meet you, Consort," Fenris says smoothly, his voice deep as he gives a slight bow.

I freeze. Consort?

The word hits me like a slap, brutal and unexpected. My cheeks flush, and I feel the heat creeping up my neck as my eyes widen. I've been called many things before—*princess* in jest, *queen* by my people. But *consort?*

That one felt like a punch to the gut. It doesn't carry the same sense of power or respect. Instead, it feels like a diminishment, as if my entire existence has been reduced to my proximity to Maxon.

Fenris might see me merely as Maxon's consort, his mate, but I am more than that. I am a queen in my own right, and I will stand beside Maxon, not behind him.

This title of *consort* doesn't define me. My strength, my resilience, and my leadership do. I have fought battles, made sacrifices, and I will earn my place not just at Maxon's side, but as his equal. I am determined to prove that my worth isn't tied to my relationship with him, but to the power and resolve I hold within. I am not just a decoration or a supporting role; I am a force to be reckoned with.

My own thoughts startle me. I haven't noticed it before—haven't realized that somewhere in the last couple of days, I fully embraced who I am.

Since everyone had first suspected who I was, I resisted. I pushed against the truth, clinging to fears and doubts, convinced that I wasn't enough, that I couldn't carry the weight of who I was supposed to be. The power that hums beneath my skin, the instincts that guide me—it's all part of me.

When Fenris straightens, his eyes drop to my hands, and he frowns.

"Princess?" Kian questions, his voice tinged with worry.

I tear my eyes away from Fenris, suddenly aware of the intense glare I have been giving him. Shit, talk about saying *fuck you* with my face. I drop my focus to the floor, trying to ground myself and regain control of my emotions.

Slowly, my fists unclench, the tension releasing from my fingers. However, my attention is immediately drawn to an odd sensation brushing against the skin of my palms. My hands shake as I lift my palms. The cloak I'm wearing falls to my elbows and a sharp gasp escapes my lips. Hidden beneath my sleeves, vibrant green vines emerge and wrap themselves delicately around my wrists and fingers. Magic dances along my skin, leaving goosebumps in its wake. I can feel my magic expanding, granting me the ability to summon vines from within myself rather than relying on the earth alone.

"That's new," Raiden says, breaking me from my reverie.

Rolling my shoulders, I finally turn to face the others again, finding traces of concern mixed with astonishment etched on their faces.

"It is," I breathe.

"Can you summon a weapon?" Alivar inquires with a hint of curiosity.

I scowl, locking eyes with him, frustration already bubbling beneath the surface. "What do you mean?"

"Like Maxon and I," he clarifies evenly. "Our swords are elemental magic, a part of us. Part of the dragon clan that chooses us."

Weapon. I look down at my hands, the vines now nowhere to be seen. I called them, but not consciously. It wasn't something I controlled.

"I don't know," I reply, my voice softer now.

Uncertainty gnaws at me, memories flickering in my mind—my battle with Yumekui. I summoned those warriors, but they weren't a singular weapon. They were more like extensions of my will, not something I wielded in my hands.

"Too bad everyone who would know is dead."

The words slice through the air like a dagger. My heart stalls, and I snap my attention to Fenris, who leans casually against the wall, his face betraying no emotion. The room goes still, a heavy silence falling over us as I blink in disbelief.

The cruelty of his remark echoes in the quiet, stinging worse than any blade. My fingers dig into my palm, but the anger is drowned out by a deeper ache—a reminder of all that I've lost, of all the knowledge that's been wiped from existence. I open my mouth, ready to bite back, but before any of us can speak, a voice rumbles from the doorway, low and commanding.

"Not everyone."

The air in the room shifts, the tension crackling like a live wire as every head turns toward the door. Standing there, framed by the dim light, is a figure I wasn't expecting.

The vines cast such a spell on us that we failed to notice the door to the war room opening. Nymeria and Anika, my ever-alert companions, even failed to notify us of the presence of anyone else.

"Valric," I acknowledge, staring at my childhood paladin.

The silver-haired fae stands in the doorway, a heavy frown on his face as he stares at Fenris. When his attention shifts to me, his violet eyes soften, and a ghost of a smile tugs at the corners of his mouth. Seeing the scar that runs down his cheek hurts more than I can explain. I know it came from the night my parents died.

"Princess Vera," he replies, with a slight incline of his head.

Alivar pushes himself away from the table, stretching slightly. "That's my cue to leave," he remarks with a casual grin. "I'll be back in the morning. Tomorrow will be a long day. I suggest rest."

I feel a pang of guilt. I know I've been a bit of a brat toward him, despite his efforts to help us. As he turns to leave, I open my mouth, intending to finally thank him. But before I can speak, Raiden discreetly elbows me, a silent reminder. He knows exactly what I was going to say, but he also understands the importance of maintaining my composure. I'm no longer just a human; I'm a queen, and I need to act like one.

Taking a deep breath, I straighten my posture and address Alivar with a measured tone. "I appreciate all your assistance over the last few days," I say, trying to convey the sincerity behind my words.

Alivar's eyes twinkle with mirth, a playful smile spreading across his face. "Anytime, Princess." There's a lightness in his demeanor that suggests he doesn't take my earlier behavior to heart, but I still feel a twinge of embarrassment.

Alivar summons a portal, the shimmering air warping and swirling in front of him. With a final wink in my direction, he steps through, vanishing into the glowing vortex. The portal closes behind him with a soft whoosh, leaving only the faintest ripple in the air where he stood moments before.

"Right, all of you out. I need to speak to Everly and Valric," Raiden's voice rumbles through the room.

His commanding presence leaves no room for hesitation; everyone seems to sense the urgency in his demeanor. I catch a glimpse of his face as he turns toward Fenris, his usual calm and collected expression replaced by something harsher, something edged. His brow is furrowed, and his jaw tightens as he leans in, exchanging hushed words with Fenris.

I can't hear exactly what Raiden is saying, but the low growl of his voice tells me enough. Fenris doesn't flinch under Raiden's intense scrutiny, but I can see the subtle shift in his posture, the hardening of his stance. His eyes narrow, a flicker of defiance crossing his face, but he stays silent, listening to whatever Raiden has to say.

Deep down, I know it's about me.

Fenris may not know me yet, and maybe he doesn't trust me. I can see it in the way he looks at me—quizzical, skeptical, as though he's measuring me against some unseen standard and finding me lacking.

I glance at Fenris one more time before Raiden leads him out of the room. I don't need Raiden to fight this fight for me. I'll earn Fenris's trust, but more importantly, I'll earn his respect.

Raiden strides back over, his footsteps echoing through the room, and closes the door with a resounding thud, pinning Valric with an intense glare. "How did you get into the castle?"

Chapter Eight

Everly

"It's quite easy to get into the palace. I can tell you all your weak points in exchange for immunity," Valric offers, taking a seat at the table. He reaches into the bowl of fruit, snatching up a red apple and taking a bite.

Raiden glares at the leader of the Outcasts with disdain. "I don't trust you."

"Well, you should. Princess Vera is my only concern, her safety is top priority."

I stare at my old paladin and wish for the millionth time I could regain all my memories. My mother definitely hid them well. I've only had flashes here and there of my old life, but I want to remember it all.

"I want you to train me again," I blurt out, unable to hold it in any longer. The urgency in my voice surprises even me. If I have any hope of getting Maxon back, I need to be stronger. I won't be a liability, not again.

"My magic only really shows itself when I'm emotional, and even then, I don't understand how I'm controlling it. I need to understand it."

Valric studies me for a moment, his expression thoughtful, before he speaks. "You always did let your emotions rule you. It's both your greatest strength and your weakness." His words aren't harsh, but they're honest—blunt, even.

I swallow hard and meet his gaze. "Will you help me?"

I need him to say yes.

A smile tugs at the corner of Valric's lips, and he nods. "Of course, Princess."

I exhale, dipping my head in gratitude, but before I can thank him, he adds, "On one condition."

My heart skips a beat, and I look up, confusion and trepidation swirling in my chest. "What condition?"

"If you take your rightful place as our queen." His expression is resolute. "Bring the Outcasts home."

Everything in me stills. Then the air leaves my lungs in a rush.

"What?" I manage, my voice barely above a whisper. This is not what I expected.

Valric's gaze remains steady, unwavering. "Because it's your rightful place. Your people have been waiting for your return, Everly."

The weight of his words crashes down on me like a tidal wave. How could I possibly take on such a role right now? Plus, I'm Maxon's mate—his queen, or I will be, though it's not official yet. But what Valric is suggesting . . . If I were to take up the mantle of queen for my own people, what would that mean? Would the two kingdoms merge? How would it even work?

My head spins with a thousand questions, each one more complicated than the last. The politics, the responsibilities—I know nothing of how to rule.

"I . . . " My voice falters, my thoughts scrambling for some sort of clarity. "But Maxon . . . "

Valric's expression softens, but there's a firmness in his voice when he clarifies, "You can be both. The queen of your people, and his. It's time for you to embrace all that you are, Everly."

I stare at him, my mind reeling. Can I really do this? My attention shifts to Raiden, who stands a few feet away with his arms crossed, a scowl stretched across his face. But when he notices me looking, his silver eyes soften, the hard lines of his expression easing just slightly.

"It's up to you, Princess." His voice remains low and steady, like he's offering me a lifeline—no pressure, just quiet support.

I try to clear my throat. My gaze flicks back to Valric, who is casually munching on his apple like this conversation isn't reshaping the entire trajectory of my life.

"Okay," I finally breathe, the word barely making it past my lips. But it's out there now, spoken into existence. My hands reach for Nymeria, my fingers sinking into the fur at her nape, and the sensation calms me.

Valric grins, his teeth flashing. "Excellent. We'll discuss the coronation after the funeral processions," he says nonchalantly, like it's a perfectly normal thing to toss out amidst plans of a royal funeral. But his words send a cold jolt of reality through me.

Funerals. My heart sinks, the reminder hitting harder than I expected.

"Lavina hasn't been buried yet?" I question.

"We don't bury our dead," Raiden frowns at me. "But no. The former queen and a few others are yet to be sent off, including Rayna."

This is all so much to take in and I understand none of it. A thought flashes through my mind.

"I want to see Nolan," I blurt, my voice cracking slightly.

Valric's grin falters, and even Raiden's usually impassive expression shows a flicker of anger.

"Why?" he demands.

"We need him. And he doesn't deserve to miss Lavina's funeral. If Valric is allowed to roam the castle, and Kian, after everything that was done, then Nolan does, too," I argue.

"He tried to get rid of you," Raiden argues slowly.

I sigh, rubbing my temples. "It's not like he wanted me dead."

"He got people killed trying to get you away from Maxon," Raiden snaps.

"By him!" I yell, pointing at Valric. "His people–"

"Your people," Valric cuts in, earning a glare from me.

"–did the killing," I continue. "Nolan only gave them the information."

Raiden's wings snap out as his anger flares. "I don't think this is a good idea."

"Look, we need all hands on deck here. Nolan has knowledge we may need. He helped raise Maxon, he surely would want his king back."

Raiden growls, running a hand over his head. "I don't like this."

"You don't have to. But we need him. Stick a guard on him if you have to, but we need his input. Whether we want it or not."

Raiden grunts. “Fine, but you’re not going down to the dungeons. I will go myself and get things settled.”

“Thank you.”

Valric stands, his chair scraping across the floor. “Well, I will leave you to it. I will return tomorrow at dawn for the funerals. Then we train.”

Turning on his heels, he slips from the room.

Chapter Nine

The Shadoweaver

I was so close.

So damn close to having that cursed druid in my grasp for the second time. The thought of her slipping through my fingers sends a violent surge of anger coursing through me, a darkness that pulses beneath my skin like venom.

How did she manage to mate in such a short amount of time? It should've been impossible.

I felt her the moment she crossed back into Faerie. Her presence was like a crack in the wall of reality, a ripple of pure, natural power. I sent Yumekui immediately to collect her, but like all my beasts and monsters, she thrives in the darkness, her strength born from shadows and the nightmares that lurk there. By the time she tracked her down, she had been safely hidden in that tree. But the daylight, damn it all, had sent Yumekui into her own hiding.

I watched, of course, as I sent a deadling after her. I saw her run, breath ragged, fear evident in the air around her as the deadling gave chase. She was foolish to believe she could outrun him. He would've done his job, injured her just enough to leave her vulnerable—just enough so that when night fell, Yumekui would swoop in, a savior of sorts, and drag her here, where she belongs.

But no, of course it never goes as planned, does it? The fucking water spirits felt her presence, too. Those meddlesome creatures are always dipping their noses where they don't belong. They drowned my deadling before he could get to her.

My fingers curl inward at the memory—at how close we came to her after all these years waiting.

She was never supposed to know who I am. Not until the moment she freed me from this prison. I'd planned it so carefully, every step laid out like pieces on a board, all leading her to unlock the final seal that keeps me bound here. I would've played the role of the helpless, desperate soul in need of saving.

But then, once free, I would have turned on her. I would have drowned her in my shadows, suffocated her with the darkness that has been festering inside me for centuries. She wouldn't have had time to scream, let alone resist. And her magic—it would've been mine, absorbed into me, fueling my power, binding us in a way that would have made her nothing more than a mindless puppet.

She was always supposed to be a tool, a means to an end. But now? Now, she's something more dangerous. She's aware. And worse—she's mated. That bond has made her stronger, more resilient, more difficult to break. But not impossible.

I will have her. One way or another.

This setback won't stop me. After all, I now have the perfect bait.

Chapter Ten

Everly

Valric leaves, the door clicking shut behind him, and I immediately sag into one of the chairs, rubbing my hands over my face.

"Where is Zaria?" I need to see my friend more than anything.

The back of my throat burns as memories of Rayna being shot with the arrow flash through my mind. My soul cries in anguish, wishing I could have been here to offer my support. Zaria has been suffering alone while I was stuck in the Winter Court.

Every line in Raiden's body goes taut. "She is in the forest."

I frown, attempting to push my hair behind my ears only to hit the pointed tips. My eyes roll at the number of times I've forgotten that they're like that now. "Why?"

"It's a long story."

My spine stiffens. "Tell me."

Raiden hesitates. "I think there are more–"

Standing abruptly, I feel my chest constrict with each breath. "Don't," I warn. "Don't you dare say there are more important things."

I must have a wild look in my eyes, because Raiden narrows his gaze at me. The air between us crackles with tension, and I can feel my pulse quicken.

"Fine," Raiden finally concedes, his voice tight. "After the attack on the city, I went to collect Rayna from the street. I wanted to bring her back to the castle and tell Zaria myself, but when I got to where Rayna was," a muscle in his jaw ticks as he clenches it, tipping his head back as if trying to hold back a torrent of emotions, "Zaria was already there, and when I tried to get near them, she shifted and attacked me. I couldn't get her to calm down. She was completely out of control, and when she realized what she had done, she ran off." Raiden scratches his head where his horns protrude from his head. "I tried to follow, but she . . . she's fast."

"And?" I snap, the frustration building, clawing at my insides.

"Everly, she isn't herself at the moment. We're giving her space to grieve," he explains, his silver eyes meeting mine with a steady gaze.

"What about her parents?"

"They've long since passed."

His words hit me like a punch to the gut, hollowing out my stomach. I feel a surge of anger, my vision tinting red. "Are you telling me that you've left the woman you love out in the forest for days, mourning the death of her sister alone?"

Raiden's silver eyes swirl like liquid metal, a storm barely restrained beneath a surface of calm. The flicker of annoyance in them is subtle—almost imperceptible—but to anyone who truly knows him, it is loud as thunder. His expression is neutral, carved with the same stoic mask he always wears, but there is a tightness to his jaw, a slight narrowing of his gaze that betrays the storm brewing within.

"It's not like I haven't tried!" he snaps, his wings seem to tremble. "She won't let anyone near her—not even me."

I'm too angry to acknowledge the hurt in his tone.

"Not good enough, Batman!" The nickname slips from my lips, my fists clenching at my sides. That familiar, beautiful tingling sensation rises in my chest, spreading outward, magic coursing through my veins like wildfire. My heart pounds, fueling the adrenaline that's already surging through me. "I'm going to get her."

Before he can object, I turn on my heel and storm from the room. I can feel my cloak billowing behind me as I walk, my movements driven by rage. Every step down the hall is a release, my skin humming with power, and magic igniting my senses. The rush of energy pulses through me, and I can sense eyes on me—maids and guards alike gaping at my return. Their expressions are a mix of disbelief and awe, whispers buzzing in the air like static. Some manage to bow, but most are too stunned to move, their eyes wide as they watch me pass.

Ahead of me, Anika and Nymeria lead the way, their presence a silent but unwavering support. They seem to understand my intent without a word exchanged between us, and it's clear they have no intention of leaving my side anytime soon.

"Everly, wait!" Raiden's voice calls out from behind me.

I don't stop. I can't. Not when she's out there, alone and broken, and no one else seems willing to do what needs to be done.

A quick glance behind me reveals Raiden storming after me, his fierce expression hardening the lines of his face. There's no time to think; I act on instinct. With a swift motion, I raise my left hand, channeling the magic that courses through me. In an instant, a stunning wall of ivy erupts from the ground, adorned with vibrant purple flowers. The vines twist and weave together, forming a beautiful yet formidable barrier that stretches across the entire width of the hallway, large thorns protruding from the climbers.

It's an impressive feat, especially considering the hallway is at least twenty feet wide. The flowers' delicate beauty contrasts sharply with the barrier's intent, creating a surreal scene. Just before he is completely cut off from my sight, I see Raiden skid to a stop, frustration and surprise flashing across his face as he realizes he's been effectively blocked.

Excitement surges, not just from the exertion of summoning the wall of vines, but from the sheer thrill of using my powers. It's like sometimes my magic acts on my will and other my emotions. I watch as the green ivy continues to grow, reinforcing the wall, ensuring that it holds strong. Taking a deep breath, the scent of the flowers calms me slightly, even as tension hangs in the air.

"Everly!" Raiden bellows, making me jump.

Shit!

I make a beeline for a set of doors and push out into the garden, the afternoon sun hitting my face. I don't have time to enjoy it though. I need to get to the stables. Racing in that direction, I make my way through the garden toward the training arena. The stables are just beyond that.

Shouts rise in the air from behind, and I can make out Tristan's voice amongst them.

I break into a run, feeling the wind rush past me as I exit the gardens. In front of me, a loud crash comes from the direction of stables and more shouts erupt as Storm gallops through the main doors, racing full speed at me. Elation overwhelms me as I lay eyes on the magnificent war horse, his black coat radiating under the sun's rays. I stop running, his massive form eating up the distances in a matter of seconds.

"Storm," I breathe, my hands reaching for him.

"Everly!" Tristan's voice is closer this time, but I will not be kept from my friend. I frantically look around for something to help me get on Storm's back.

Suddenly a red-haired young boy with bright blue eyes appears. "Need help, Your Majesty?"

"Yes. Yes, please."

The boy intertwines his fingers and bends down, offering his hands for me to put my foot on. With a quick boost, I scramble onto Storm's back, feeling the powerful muscles beneath me.

"Thank you, Gideon."

The young boy's eyes widen. "You remember my name?" he whispers in shock.

I give him a quick smile, gripping Storm's mane tighter as he dances back and forth on his hooves. "Of course."

The boy blinks and quickly bows, his shock of red hair burning like fire in the sunlight.

"Everly, don't you dare!"

I swing my attention behind me and see Tristan, Kian, and Fenris running my way.

My heart leaps into my throat, and I give Storm a nudge. "Storm, take me to Zaria."

Without hesitation, Storm surges forward, muscles coiling beneath me as he breaks into a full gallop. The world blurs around us, the thundering rhythm of his hooves pounding against the earth like the beat of my heart. Within seconds, we burst through the castle gates, the feel of adrenaline coursing through my veins as we dodge the stunned guards.

The meadow opens before us, vast and wild, the tall grass bending in the soft breeze. The wind tears at my hair, pulling it free of its braid, the loose strands whipping against my face as we race toward the forest. My cloak feels like it will tear free any second. I lean low over Storm's back, pressing myself flat against him, my fingers digging into his mane for balance. I can feel the heat of his body through my legs, the raw power in every stride as he eats up the distance between us and the autumn trees. I've never ridden without a saddle before—every jolt and shift sends a shock through my body. My thighs burn from gripping his sides, and the rough motion jars my bones with each leap over uneven ground.

But none of that matters now. The discomfort, the ache in my muscles, the strain of holding on—they all fade, swallowed by the urgency that claws at my chest.

Zaria.

Does she think I abandoned her?

The wind howls in my ears, but it's not enough to drown out the thoughts racing through my mind. I can't stop picturing her alone, vulnerable.

The forest looms closer, dark and thick with the promise of danger, but I don't slow. Neither does Storm. His pace never falters, as if he, too, understands the gravity of the situation. Together, we push forward, breaking into the tree line, the cool shade of the forest swallowing us whole, Nymeria and Anika flanking us.

Chapter Eleven

Everly

Storm slows to a trot as we venture deeper into the forest. The usual sounds of life are remarkably absent, no chirping birds, no fluttering sprites. The silence is unsettling, a stifling stillness that blankets the woods. Only the leaves crunching under Storm's hooves and the occasional snapping of a branch can be heard. Nymeria and Anika are as silent as the shadows, living up to their name: Ghosts of the Evergreens.

My eyes dart around, searching for any sign of movement, but like me, the forest seems to hold its breath. I can feel it, a tingling unease crawling under my skin, like an itch I can't quite reach.

"You sure it's this way?" Nerves stop me from speaking any louder than a whisper.

Storm bobs his head, letting out a loud huff of air.

"Okay. I trust you," I breathe.

Storm is an extremely moody and sensitive horse.

The last thing I want is to offend him and be left stranded here all by myself. Deep down, I know he wouldn't do that. Not now. We've developed a strong connection since my arrival—something unspoken. There's a mutual understanding between us. He reads me as much as I try to read him. And though he's still unpredictable, even dramatic at times, I've learned to respect that part of him.

As we weave through the trees, I watch as orange and brown leaves float from above in slow, methodical motions, gently landing on the forest floor. The Autumn Court is really beautiful. I haven't seen the other courts, only the Winter one, but I think each holds their title and beauty in their own unique way.

A rustle from above sends a shiver down my spine and I lift my gaze to the tangled branches above. The canopy sways, shadows shifting in ways that feel just a little too deliberate. Were there any bellowigs in this part of the forest?

I really didn't want to be fending off one of those carnivorous nightmares right now.

Tightening my grip on Storm's mane and blow out a slow, measured breath, trying to steady my pulse.

I scan the treetops once more. I wasn't in the mood to become someone's evening snack.

The forest grows darker and darker the further we go. The warmth of the sun completely gone. I lift my hood up over my head, hoping to ward away the sudden chill in the air. In this part of the forest, the trees are gnarled and twisted, the thickest dark canopy blocks out all light.

Nervously, I swallow, and my fingers grow stiff the tighter I grip onto Storm's mane. Now that my anger has faded, I'm beginning to regret not having brought someone along for company. This is probably not the smartest idea I've had, but my guilt and loyalty to my friend outweigh all logical thoughts.

The path narrows, the trees growing denser and the underbrush thickening until it becomes nearly impassable. Storm slows, his powerful strides faltering as the ground becomes uneven, tangled with roots and low-hanging branches. Finally, he comes to a complete stop.

I lean forward and pat his neck, feeling the warmth of his skin beneath my fingers. "She's close, isn't she?" I murmur, more to myself than to him. Storm bobs his head in response, his dark mane flicking elegantly with each movement. The simple gesture draws a smile from me. He's always been able to make me smile, even in moments like this.

"Alright then," I whisper, taking a deep breath to calm the rush of nerves that churn inside me. The air is thick with the smell of damp earth and pine, the forest quiet except for the soft rustling of leaves in the breeze. I grip Storm's mane for support as I swing my leg over his back and slide down. My feet hit the ground hard, and I stumble backward a few steps, my legs still shaky from the ride. Nymeria is there, stopping me from tumbling on to my ass.

I wince, steadying myself on a nearby tree, wishing—not for the first time—that I could move with the same effortless grace as everyone else. My movements are clumsy and awkward in comparison. They would have leaped from the horse as swiftly and naturally as a dancer. But me? I've always been fighting to keep up, to make it look like I belong.

I cast a quick glance at Storm, who's watching me with those knowing eyes. I exhale in a rush and straighten, forcing my legs to cooperate as I begin to gather my bearings.

Suddenly, I hear the beat of wings overhead and instinctively look up, though the dense canopy of trees blocks my view. The rhythmic sound is unmistakable; Raiden is searching for me. My breath catches, and for a second, everything inside me stalls—then rushes forward all at once. He's close, but I also know why Zaria chose this spot to hide. The forest here is a labyrinth, its thick foliage and twisted paths make it difficult to navigate, especially for someone of Raiden's size.

I move carefully, each step deliberately placed to avoid making too much noise. The forest floor is a tangle of roots and fallen leaves, concealing potential hazards. I can feel the gentle hum of my magic resonating through my skin, as if it's connecting with the plants and trees surrounding me. It feels as though the ancient magic of the forest yearns for a connection. All around, there is a distinct energy, a gentle hum that resonates in the air.

Nervously, I grip the edges of my cloak and close my eyes, extending my senses to the forest. Instantly, I feel their vibrant life energy enveloping me and gently caressing my own. Waves of magic roll over my body, and I can sense each and every life around me. But among all the heartbeats, there is one specific rhythm I am searching for.

I let my magic glide effortlessly over the rugged rocks and gentle mounds, finally coming to rest at the base of a towering tree a few hundred yards away. The enormous tree stands tall, its gnarled and twisted trunk reaching toward the sky. Like a second skin, its bark is completely covered in a vibrant green moss. In the midst of its foliage, Zaria's glowing amber eyes blink, casting an otherworldly glow in the darkness.

I open my eyes and smile. She isn't far, and I know the path.

"I'll be back soon." I say, giving him a gentle pat.

Storm nudges me lightly, and the sound of his soft breaths fills the air. I immediately feel the tears welling up in my eyes, blurring the scene before me. The sadness in his dark obsidian eyes mirrors the void left by Maxon's absence. Suddenly, as if sensing my distress, Nymeria and Anika trot into the area, their paws creating a soft thud against the ground. They surround me, warm fur brushing against my skin, enveloping me in a comforting embrace.

'We will follow.'

'No, stay with Storm,' I answer.

Like vigilant sentinels, both wolves sit on their haunches, their ears pricked up, ready to react to any sound. My chest fills with a loving warmth as I stare at each of them. "I'll be back soon with Zaria."

Following the subtle pull of my magic, I turn and stride in the direction it guides me. The sensation is both familiar and foreign—like an old friend whispering directions only I can hear.

Out of the corner of my eye, shimmering lights flicker between the branches and leaves, catching my attention. Ethereal trails of fairy dust swirl through the air, drifting like delicate smoke. The tiny creatures flit between the trees, their small, curious eyes focused, sensing the unusual energy that ripples around me. It's as if the forest itself is alive, observing, deciding whether I'm friend or foe.

After the eerie stillness of the ride out here, the sudden spark of life is a relief. I didn't realize how much the silence was bothering me until now. At least out here, in the heart of the forest, there is movement, magic—things watching, shifting. It feels like I'm not alone anymore, and for the first time since entering the forest, I breathe a little easier.

A fallen log in my path has me clambering over it with some effort. As I plant my foot on the other side, the ground beneath seems to rise ever so slightly, catching me before I stumble. I freeze, my heart skipping a beat. It's only now that I notice the subtle movements—leaves rustling when there's no wind, branches shifting to the side, vines parting just enough to let me through. The forest is helping me. Guiding me. My magic must have connected with it, and now the very terrain is bending to assist my passage. I press a hand to the nearest tree trunk, feeling the faint thrumming of life within its bark, an energy that resonates with my own.

I curl my fingers, pressing them into the soft bark, and smile. But then something shifts in the air, and I freeze.

The temperature drops, and an unsettling mist begins rolling toward me, thick and unnatural. I swallow hard, the tension snapping back into my chest. The mist is different—there's something dark about it, something not quite right. I unclip my dagger from my hip, gripping its hilt tightly.

Up ahead, I can just make out the outline of a tree. It's massive—larger than anything I've seen before, its thick roots twisting out of the ground like ancient serpents. This is the tree I saw in my mind's eye, the one my magic has been leading me toward.

"Everly!" Raiden's voice bellows through the trees above, making me jump.

"Seriously, Batman? Are you trying to give me a heart attack?" I breathe, my palm on my chest.

Shaking my head, I cautiously approach the towering tree, my gaze traveling up. How on earth am I supposed to get up there?

As soon as the idea has formed in my mind, a tangled mass of emerald vines bursts from the gnarled roots of the tree. With an audible rustling, they weave a makeshift ladder, reaching skyward, creating a path for me to take.

Swiftly, I sheath my dagger and start climbing, eager to escape from the encroaching mist. I can't explain it, but something feels off about it. Something unnatural.

Goosebumps skitter across my body, and shake them off, climbing quicker. The rough texture of the vines against my palms keep me grounded as my anxiety urges me forward. I do my best to focus on the lush scent of the leaves and the sound of the breeze as it passes. But then the vines stop abruptly. I frown, my hand brushing against a thick knot where the green tendrils cease their climb. My gaze sweeps upward in confusion, but as I look around, I realize this isn't the end of the path—it's a landing of sorts. The branches begin here, weaving together like a network of bridges, forming a natural platform. Nestled within the twist of roots and bark is what looks like a den, a protected hollow shielded from the open sky.

Relief surges through me, and I carefully hoist myself from the vines, crawling onto the wide branch, solid beneath me.

"Zaria?"

A low, menacing growl fills the air, making my muscles tense and tremble in response.

Shit, this is your friend. Pull yourself together.

"Zaria, it's me. Everly. I'm here to take you home." I push to my feet, my eyes searching the dark. "Zaria?"

Pulse thundering in my ears, my vision slowly adjusts to the darkness, revealing two enormous amber eyes peering at me from within the depths of the tree. I halt at the boundary of the shadows, nerves rattling through my body.

"Zaria, please come out," I whisper. "I need you."

The eyes blink and slowly rise. Instinctively, I take a step back and watch in awe as a massive leopard gracefully emerges from the dark depths of the den. Its head is lowered, and a fierce gleam sparkles in its predatory eyes. Fear tightens my throat, and I clench my fist to stop myself from grabbing my dagger. This is Zaria. She is not capable of causing me harm.

Slowly, I reach my hand out, hating how it shakes.

"It's time to go home, Zaria."

Lowering her head, she pins her ears back. A low, guttural noise rumbles from her throat, a menacing sound that is a cross between a hiss and a growl. The air feels heavy as I straighten my shoulders and slowly sit down and cross my legs. My heart pounds in my chest, but I refuse to break eye contact with her, knowing the importance of maintaining this connection.

"Fine, you want to stay here, then I'll stay, too. But just so you know, our friends need us. Our king needs us. Raiden, he needs you. Hiding away won't change what's happening out there, and it won't make the pain disappear. But together, we can face it. You're not alone. You're never alone." I draw in a shaky breath before continuing, "But most of all . . . I need you now more than ever. They have him, Zaria." My voice cracks, but I keep going. "Let's show them that we're not giving up."

A whining sound comes from Zaria, and she seems to crumple in on herself. Everything inside me shatters at the sound, and I scoot closer, pulling her massive head into my lap. She buries her head under my arm, as if trying to get as close as possible. Tears stream down my face, as I cradle her massive head in my lap.

My fingers gently glide over her velvety fur as she trembles and shakes.

God, the lump that forms in my throat swells to encompass my chest. I can barely breathe.

"I'm so sorry, Zaria. Rayna–" I choke on her name, my throat completely closing up.

I tip my head back, blinking away the tears and jolt at the sight of Asrai perched on the branch above. Her dual-colored eyes—one brown one blue—are filled with tears.

Her tiny hands come up and sign, *'She has been stuck in this form since the battle.'*

"Oh, Zaria." I drop my face into her fur and silently cry. My tears soak into her, but I can't stop them even if I wanted to.

I don't know how or when, but eventually, I succumb to sleep, the heaviness of my tears lulling me into oblivion.

Chapter Twelve

Everly

The warm body under me vibrates, a low hiss breaking through my sleep. I jolt awake and Zaria's big brown feline eyes stare at me, then out into the darkened forest beyond.

A sense of foreboding washes over me, catching my breath. Letting it out slowly, a cloud forms in front of my face. It's not normally this cold in the Autumn Court. Moving slowly, I crawl over to the edge of the branch woven platform of the den and peer down. I can't see the ground anymore, only a thick mist that rolls over the forest floor in an unnatural way.

"That can't be good," I whisper, crawling backward next to Zaria.

The sun is sinking fast, its light barely filtering through the thick canopy above. Long shadows stretch like fingers across the forest floor, making the once-serene autumn trees look ominous. I bite my lip, torn between two choices—stick it out here for the night or make a run for it.

Neither option feels safe, but if we're going to leave, now is the time.

My fingers dig into the soft moss covering the tree bark as I think over the options. The wolves and Storm are still out there in the forest, only ten minutes away. I can't leave them out there alone. *Damn it.* Time is slipping away from us.

Movement beside me snaps me out of my thoughts. I glance over at Zaria, her large feline eyes wide with uncertainty. Asrai is perched on her head, her small form trembling, and her wings fluttering with unease.

"What should we do?" I ask, my voice barely above a whisper, trying to keep my fear in check.

Asrai's small frame quivers, her delicate butterfly wings shimmering in the dim light. *'I don't know,'* she signs. *'I'd like to stay until the light returns, but there's something wrong with the mist. It's seeking.'*

An involuntary shiver crawls up my spine. So, I'm not the only one who thinks the mist is unnatural.

"We need to go," I urge, my voice firmer now as the gravity of our situation is mounting. Zaria shakes her head and backs away, her reluctance palpable.

"Zaria, we don't have time for this." I crawl closer to her, trying to break through her fear. "You need to come with me back to the castle. Everything else doesn't matter right now."

I swallow hard, fighting the panic rising inside me.

"Please," I beg, my voice softer this time, a hint of desperation creeping in.

For a moment, Zaria hesitates, her body tense. Then, with a soft exhale, she dips her head and steps forward, nuzzling her face into my chest. Relief floods through me as I wrap my arms around her, pulling her close.

"We're going to make a run for it, okay?" I direct quietly, stroking her fur to calm both of us. "Storm is waiting nearby with the wolves."

Zaria pulls back, her eyes more focused now, and pads past me toward a thick, low-hanging branch. With a powerful leap, she lands on the branch, her silhouette barely visible in the dimming light.

Asrai lands lightly on my shoulder, her wings brushing against my neck.

"Get in my hood," I urge, shifting my hair so she can tuck herself inside. "I'll keep you safe."

Asrai pauses for only a second before crawling into the hood of my cloak. Once she's settled, I turn and take a deep breath, then begin my descent, carefully lowering myself down the rough bark and twisted vines.

I reach the last few feet and pause. The ground below is covered in the thick, menacing mist, its cold tendrils wrapping around the roots and reaching toward me like fingers.

There's no time to lose. I push off the tree and jump, landing in a crouch, the mist curling around my boots. It feels wrong, like something alive and malevolent brushing against my skin as I stand.

I glance up at Zaria, who's already leaped down onto the lower branches, her lithe form barely making a sound as she moves. The sun has completely slipped below the horizon, quickly plunging us into night.

"Come on, Zaria," I whisper urgently.

Her gigantic leopard watches from above with big, unblinking eyes.

Suddenly, a branch snaps to my left. I freeze, my heart leaping into my throat, and Zaria's attention shifts in the same direction. Everything happens in a blur. The mist stirs violently, and from its swirling depths, a deadling emerges. Its twisted, decayed form is barely human, and its milky white eyes lock onto me with an unnatural hunger. I feel a wave of dread rolling over me, freezing me in place.

Before I can even reach for my dagger, Zaria pounces. With a feral snarl, her powerful body collides with the deadling before it has a chance to lunge. Her teeth sink deep into its neck, a sickening crunch echoing through the air as she tears into the creature. The deadling's howl pierces the night, a chilling sound that reverberates through the forest.

"Zaria!" I scream, panic flooding my veins. "Run!"

My body jolts into action, adrenaline coursing through me as I turn and run. The forest blurs around me, branches whipping at my face and tearing at my clothes as I bolt into the underbrush. The world narrows to the pounding of my heart, the rapid beat of my pulse deafening in my ears. I push through the thick branches, the sharp bark cutting into my skin, but I don't slow down.

The sound of the deadling's howls fade behind me, replaced by the deafening rush of blood in my ears and the crunch of leaves under my boots. My breath comes in ragged gasps, each one burning my throat, but the only thing that matters is putting distance between me and that deadling. I don't know how many more might be out there, lurking in the mist, waiting to strike.

My foot catches on a root, and I trip, barely catching myself on a nearby tree. I peer over my shoulder, heart hammering, half-expecting to see more of the creatures emerging from the mist.

But all I see is darkness—the thick, impenetrable shadows of the forest, and the faint glow of the mist curling at the edges of my vision.

Zaria where are you?

I can't abandon her. I grip the hilt of my dagger, still sheathed at my hip, my knuckles white as I weigh my options.

I'm not strong enough to fight those creatures on my own. But I can't just leave her. Turning slowly, I scan the thick shadows between the trees. A shiver erupts over my flesh as I unsheathe my dagger. I flex my fingers around the hilt, and draw in a sharp breath as I take a step in the direction I came from.

"Everly!"

I spin at the sound of my name and almost weep at the sight of Fenris and Tristan as they jog toward me, swords in hand, Nymeria and Anika at their sides.

"Deadling," I breathe.

Fenris's gaze goes over my head into the trees behind me. Then without a word, he moves past, nudging me toward Tristan. "Go. I will stay back and make sure we aren't followed."

"No. We should stay together," I argue.

Fenris gives me a sharp look. "Take your ass back to the castle, Consort."

Anger drives away any fear I was feeling moments ago. It sears along my veins, igniting my temper. "No!"

"No?"

"Zaria is out there. I'm not leaving her behind!" I growl.

Tristan lays a hand on my arm. "You found her?"

"Yes."

Tristan gives a small nod. He knows me well enough to understand that nothing will make me leave until Zaria is safe. I can hear Fenris curse under his breath, and my eyes snap back to him, my glare harsh and unyielding. If he wants a challenge, I'll give it to him, but his attention isn't on me.

Fenris's eyes are fixed on the direction I just came from, his stance going rigid. A low growl rumbles in his throat as two deadlings emerge from the thick shadows of the trees. Their pale, grotesque forms prowl forward, their bodies twisted and unnatural.

Tristan slowly pulls me behind him, his body instantly shifting into a protective stance, his sword at the ready. My wolves lower their heads, their jaws snapping and hackles rising.

The deadlings advance, slow but purposeful, their mouths hanging open in a grotesque mockery of life. Deadlings are vicious—mindless, but relentless. There's no reasoning with them, no way to scare them off. They'll keep coming until either they tear us apart or we stop them.

Anika growls low, the hair on the back of her neck bristling, while Nymeria stalks to the side, her deadly teeth bared, ready to strike. I grip my dagger tightly, my knuckles white around the hilt.

"Stay back," Tristan orders, his voice low and steady, but I can hear the tension beneath it. He knows I won't stay hidden behind him for long, but for now, I do as he says.

Without warning, the deadlings burst forward, with speed I knew they had but wasn't expecting.

I scream, unable to hold it back. Fenris moves, his form shifting ever so slightly as he steps forward to meet a deadling head on. My mouth parts as he moves with efficiency, slicing upward, sending the deadling's head rolling across the ground in seconds. Fenris looks over his shoulder as if checking to see if I'm okay. The dangerous glint in his eyes has my breath catching.

I flex my grip on my dagger, my heart hammering against my ribs. I can't believe this is happening. I thought Raiden said they'd retreated.

As the other deadling lunges at Tristan, Nymeria takes it to the ground, snarls ripping through the air.

I exhale just as two more appear, then another two.

Fenris is moving again, unclipping a dagger from his waist and throwing it into the darkness. There's a thud and the sound of a body hitting the ground meaning it found its mark. He raises his sword, slicing through the neck of another, the sharp smell of blood floating in the air.

I can't seem to look away as he raises his arm and shoves his fist into one of the creature's chest, jerking his arm back sharply. In his hand is something that drips with black blood. Oh my god. Is that its heart?

I can't even begin to process what I just saw.

Fenris is deadly. Cutting through everything in his path.

"Princess!" Tristan yells, drawing my attention away from Fenris.

A deadling drops from the tree above, landing directly behind me. Heart pounding in my ears, I swipe at its face. The blade catches the pale skin, slicing through its hideous features, but it doesn't slow the creature. I duck under its outstretched claws just in time, feeling the icy wind of its attack pass over my head.

Before the deadling can strike again, Tristan's blade flashes through the air. His sword pierces its chest, driving straight into the deadling's heart. The creature lets out a final, sickening gasp, its body convulsing for a brief moment before collapsing lifeless at my feet.

I stagger back, breathing hard. My fingers remain locked tightly around the dagger, adrenaline pumping fiercely through my body. Tristan pulls his sword from the deadling's chest, wiping the blade clean with swift, practiced movements. I give him a shaky smile and survey the scene.

Another comes from nowhere straight at Fenris, but he pivots, grabbing it by the throat and sinking his blade into its chest before I can even draw my next breath. Then he is a foot away. Fenris's nostrils flare as he grips my arm and roughly jerks me around. "Get back to the fucking horse."

Anger rises, sharp and swift, and I rip my arm from his hold. "Don't tell me what to do. I can handle myself, Fenris."

His eyes harden further, if that's even possible. "You're in danger, and we need to leave now."

"No, not without Zaria." My anger is so consuming I can taste it on my tongue.

Tristan steps closer, his voice low. "Everly, we need to get you out of here. It's not safe."

"They won't kill me." Both men blink at my words. "Not when the Shadoweaver needs me."

"But they can do a fucking lot of damage," Fenris spits out.

"You don't think I know that?!"

"Then get to the fucking horse!" Fenris steps closer, towering over me, but I stand my ground. I will not be pushed or bullied into submission. Not anymore.

Nymeria and Anika draw nearer, and Anika pushes between the two of us, but they both surprise me when they don't growl or threaten Fenris as they normally would. They simply seem to want to defuse our fight. I see movement to the side, and a beautiful leopard breaks from the trees.

"Thank goodness." A rush of relief makes me sag. If not for Anika still standing in front of me, I might have collapsed.

"Great! Now let's fucking go." Fenris steps back and pushes past us, heading in the direction of the horses.

I frown at Fenris's retreating form. His stiff, cold demeanor is confusing. Tristan's arm brushes lightly against my shoulder, drawing my attention. I glance up at him, searching his face for some kind of explanation.

"Is he always like this?" I ask, my voice low, though I can't quite keep the frustration from seeping in.

Tristan shakes his head, his expression softening as he looks from Fenris to me. "Before you arrived back here, he was more pleasant. He is quiet in nature and an excellent soldier who climbed through the ranks fairly quickly."

"Well, something has crawled up his ass," I mutter under my breath, hoping to mask the hurt with humor.

A small, amused smile tugs at Tristan's lips, and I can see the worry in his face easing. "Come on, Princess. We'd best get you back to the castle before Raiden has a coronary," he teases.

"Okay."

As we walk, thoughts of Fenris's behavior still nag at the back of my mind. Why does it feel like there's something simmering just beneath the surface with him—something he won't let me see?

Chapter Thirteen

Maxon

A throbbing sensation spreads through my temples, causing my entire head, even my gums, to ache in pain. I tilt my head backward to rest against the stone wall, and attempt to swallow, my throat incredibly dry. Since that deadling found its way in here, knocking over the only source of water I had, I've been left high and dry. No one has come to refill it or even see if I'm alive. I have a feeling that the creature was a test, a way to assess my will to survive. There is no way they'd let a deadling take me out.

I am not even sure at this point how much time has passed. A week? Two? The days blur together in the suffocating darkness, swallowed by the damp walls surrounding me. There is no sun to mark the passing hours, no sound beyond the slow drip of water somewhere in the distance. Just silence. Just isolation.

Except for the comforting hum of the mating bond.

It is the only thing keeping me grounded, the only thread of hope I have left. The bond. Our bond. Faint but steady, a constant pulse reminding me that she is still out there. Still breathing. Still mine.

Everly.

But she is still new to this world, still learning, still finding her place among those who have only just accepted her. I know Raiden and the others will help her, that they will fight for her if it comes to that. But is that enough? Will Alivar return her? Or have I lost her before I even had the chance to truly keep her?

The fear I feel? It isn't for me. It never was.

It is for her.

Because if I were to lose her, if the bond faded into nothing—then the darkness around me wouldn't matter. I would already be gone.

I shift uncomfortably on the stone ground, my breeches stiff with dried blood. I close my eyes, letting my mind conjure up images of her. The look of wonder in her eyes when she felt her magic in the garden that morning before we left for the fourteen-hour horse ride to the Evergreens. My breathing deepens as I let another memory flood in, this one sharper, more visceral. The feel of her body beneath mine as we laid under the enchanted willows, hidden away from the world. Her breathy moans echoing softly through the trees, her back arching into me as I sank my cock inside her. Every sigh, every tremor burned into my mind, a perfect blend of pleasure and need. The way her hands clutched at my shoulders, and her legs wrapped around my waist, the world around us just disappeared.

"Fuck," I mutter under my breath, the raw need surging up inside me. I wish I was there with her now, far from this bleak stone prison. To feel her again, to touch the softness of her skin, to breathe her in.

My ears pick up a slight disturbance in the air, and I know I'm being watched. Keeping my eyes closed, I wait.

"Your queen has emerged from hiding," Yumekui's voice sings from the archway.

Slowly, I open my eyes, my lips peeling back against my fangs. "How would you know?"

If we were in the Outlands, we would be at least a four or five day ride from Vesner through rough terrain. Unless she is using the ravens.

"The Shadoweaver can see through the eyes of those whom it controls."

Unease twists in my stomach, and I stiffen. "What does that mean?"

Yumekui practically vibrates with energy as she smirks at me. "It means that your precious mate decided to leave the safety of the castle unescorted and venture into the darkest parts of the forest to search for a friend. I, of course, had left a few deadlings and imps behind to be our eyes and ears."

My chest aches as I wait for her next words.

"Don't worry, she is fine. That young soldier, the one who guards the veil, saved her."

I lean forward as far as the wyvern bones around my neck would allow, anger and relief bidding for first place. "Stay the fuck away from Everly!" I snarl.

Yumekui walks over to the empty bucket that was holding my water and kicks it. "He is quite handsome, that one."

I freeze at her words, my eyes narrowing. "I won't fall for your games, demon."

"The new moon approaches." The glee in her voice has my hackles raising. "You will both be craving each other's blood. Tell me, what happens if you don't feed?"

A snarl rumbles from my chest, and I can feel my muscles vibrating with rage. If it weren't for these chains, I'd rip out her throat and watch her choke on her blood.

"My, my, look at you. So, savage." Yumekui clicks her fingers, and an older woman shuffles into my cell, snatching up the bucket, and hurries out.

"Now." She gives the air a sniff, her nose scrunching up. "You stink. Like death and rot."

My eyes shift to the dead creature mere feet away. "I would apologize, but . . . "

"You don't care," she finishes.

I stare at her.

The shuffling of feet grabs my attention, and as the woman comes back with a bucket, my mouth instantly longs for a drink. Despite that, I keep my expression blank.

Yumekui doesn't even glance at them. Her gaze remains fixed on me, sharp and predatory, as if I'm some sort of amusement. She snatches the bucket from her hands with a casual, almost lazy motion, as if their presence is beneath her notice. A grin stretches across her face, cold and calculating, and she steps closer, the bucket clutched tightly in her hand.

I barely have time to react before she hurls the water at me. My breath catches in my throat, stolen by the frigid water, and for a second, the world blurs around me, reduced to the stinging sensation of cold slicing through my body.

Yumekui's mocking laughter fills the room as she watches me shudder beneath the water's assault. With a dismissive flick of her wrist, she tosses the now empty bucket back at the woman.

"Another," she orders, her voice dripping with impatience. The words are a command, not a request, and the woman bows once more.

Yumekui turns her attention to the lifeless body slumped in the corner. Her eyes narrow, and she curls her lip in disdain. "And get someone in here to drag this body away for the birds." Her voice is sharp as a blade. Her tone is as cold as the water dripping off me.

Chapter Fourteen

Everly

I give the guards a soft smile as we pass through the gates of the castle, and they bow in return, their fists on their chest. The sight makes me nervous, though Storm seems to somehow stand taller at the gesture making my grin grow wider. I glance down at Zaria's dark, sleek form. She has stayed in pace with Storm the entire journey back to the castle.

"I'll deal with the horses," Fenris's voice cuts through the silence. "Get her inside."

"'Her' has a name," I snap. "And I can brush down Storm myself."

His attention lands on me, and his eyes darken in anger. I return the glare, refusing to back down. With a clipped tone, he says, "Fine," before nudging his horse and trotting ahead, leaving Tristan and me behind.

He disappears almost immediately, slipping away into the shadows.

His abrupt departure leaves a lingering sense of unease in my chest, but I push it aside for now. I don't have the energy to try to sort through how I feel when it comes to him.

Torches have been lit and line the road, light casting long shadows across the courtyard. No sooner have we stopped in front of the stables than Gideon appears with a wooden ladder in hand. A flush of embarrassment creeps up my neck.

"Gideon, how will I learn if you are being so kind all the time?" I chuckle.

The boy's big blue eyes widen, and his mouth opens and closes several times. I cover my mouth to hide my smile. He is adorable.

"What should I do, Your Majesty?" he blurts, and bows quickly.

"Catch me if I'm about to fall." I smile.

Tristan laughs quietly beside me as he dismounts with an easy grace I envy. It's also a little harder because I'm riding without a saddle and have nothing but the mane to grip onto. I shift awkwardly on Storm's broad back, preparing to slide down. Tristan walks over without a word and holds up his hands, ready to help guide me.

"Thanks," I mutter, feeling self-conscious as he catches me around the waist and steadies my feet on the ground.

Before I can say anything else, Gideon cuts in. "Would you like me to take care of Storm, Your Majesty?" he offers, his voice full of nervousness.

Storm stamps his hooves and snorts, sending the boy back a step. I suppress a smile and lift my hand to stroke Storm's neck, my fingers gliding over his sleek, powerful muscles.

"That's okay," I reply gently. "Storm and I need some time together."

Storm nudges my hand with his nose when I stop petting him, a quiet, familiar gesture that tugs at my heart.

"Come on, war horse, let's get you ready for bed," I murmur, giving his flank a soft pat.

Storm stays by my side, his steps matching mine as we walk into the stables. The wolves take their positions near the stable doors, their large bodies lowering to the ground in a silent vigil. Asrai, who is still nestled in the hood of my cloak, flutters out and lands on Zaria's head.

'That was close,' Asrai signs, her tiny hands moving quickly.

"It really was," I agree, my voice barely above a whisper as we step into the dimly lit stall. The familiar smell of hay and earth greets me, bringing a strange sense of comfort after the chaos of the day.

I guide Storm into his stall, taking my time as I brush down his coat, each stroke helping to settle my racing thoughts. Zaria lies down in the corner, her large eyes watching me closely, while Asrai perches on her head, a little sentinel.

My hands run over Storm's shiny black coat, and I draw in a shaky breath. "How is Nova? Have you been taking care of her?"

Storm swings his massive head in my direction and stares at me for a long moment before he snorts, nudging my shoulder.

"I'll take that as an 'Of course, what do you take me for?'" I smile, shaking my head. Storm gives a slow, deliberate nod as if to confirm my words, then lowers his head, tearing into a mouthful of hay.

As I run the brush over his back one last time, a soft voice from behind startles me. "Excuse me, Your Majesty."

Standing just a few feet away is a young man, his shockingly red hair instantly reminding me of Gideon. But as my eyes adjust to the dim light of the stable, I notice the differences—his skin is tinged with a bluish hue, and two small horns protrude from his unruly hair. His eyes, a piercing blue, meet mine hesitantly.

"Yes?" I ask, my curiosity piqued.

"Would you like to see Nova?" His voice is soft, polite, though there's an uncertainty in the way he speaks.

My lips curve into a small smile. "That would be nice."

Placing the brush down on a nearby shelf, I give Storm a final pat on the neck before following the young man toward the stall door.

As we walk, I glance at him, taking in his features more closely. There's something familiar about him, and after a moment, I can't resist asking, "What's your name?"

He slows to a stop and hesitates, shifting his weight from one foot to the other, as if debating whether to answer.

I raise an eyebrow. "I don't bite, you know."

That seems to ease him, and he smiles, though it's small and a bit shy. "I know. I'm Gideon's older brother, Malick."

"Nice to meet you, Malick."

Malick unlatches the door, stepping aside to let me through. But before I enter, I pause, turning to face him again. "Can I ask . . . What are you?"

Malick's smile widens slightly, and there's a hint of pride in his voice when he responds. "I'm a goblin, Your Majesty."

I nod thoughtfully, filing the information away. Goblins. It makes sense now—the bluish skin, the horns. "Thank you, Malick," I say, stepping into Nova's stall, my heart lifting at the sight of her.

The walk back to the castle is wrapped in a comfortable silence, the only sound coming from our footsteps on the stone path. We cut through the gardens, the scent of night-blooming flowers filling the cool air. My magic hums softly at my fingertips, a familiar warmth sparking as I absently trail my hand along the rose bushes, brushing the petals as we pass. A gentle reminder of the magic that runs through every inch of this land.

"I'm surprised Raiden didn't come barging into the stables to scold me." I glance up at the moon, its soft blueish glow much more pronounced here in Faerie. It seems bigger, more ethereal, like it belongs to a different world entirely—this world.

"He did. I intercepted him," Tristan replies.

I stop walking and raise my eyebrow in question. "I can defend myself against Raiden."

Tristan's lips tip up and he rests his hand on the hilt of his sword. "I know that. You've grown quite a bit in your time here, but I was more worried about her reaction." He looks over at Zaria, who is currently pawing playfully at a night lily.

"Oh."

"Come on, Princess. Let's get you to your chambers so you can rest. The next few days will not be kind."

I meet his gaze and swallow roughly, before falling into step with him. His presence is a welcomed comfort as we make our way through the familiar halls of the castle. Zaria pads quietly beside us, her movements graceful and calm despite the tension of the past few hours.

My heart speeds up as we approach the intricately carved doors of Maxon's chambers. They stand tall and imposing in front of us. Too many emotions to name come rushing in like a wall of water, making me inhale sharply. Tristan pretends not to hear and reaches for the doors, pushing them open. Holding my breath, I step inside mine and Maxon's chamber and I'm struck by the stillness that fills the space beyond. The room is dimly lit by the soft glow of a few candles, casting flickering shadows on the stone walls.

"Thank you, Tristan."

He bows. "It's good to have you home, Princess."

"It's good to be back. I was so worried while I was in the Winter Court."

Tristan smirks. "About us?"

"About everything," I whisper, unclipping my cloak, and slipping it off my shoulders.

"Our king is strong."

My eyes lift to his, and it takes me a moment to reply. "I know."

Running a hand over his dark scruffy hair, he takes a step closer. "I want to apologize for everything that happened with Kian. He was my partner, and I should have picked up on what he was doing."

Going back a month, Tristan would never have apologized to me. When we first met, he didn't like me very much. He especially didn't like the fact I had slipped past him on a couple of occasions.

"None of this falls on you. Kian acted on his own for his own reasons. Though I don't completely understand them, I am willing to push them aside for now."

Tristan narrows his gaze. "But he betrayed your trust. The Seelie Prince used him to get inside information. Not to mention, he allowed the prince access to the castle. More specifically, these chambers."

"All valid points." I sigh, looking over to where Zaria is now curled up on the bed sleeping. "I'm not saying what he did is right, but you need to find a way of pushing the anger aside."

Tristan looks ready to argue, but I hold up my hand. "You were here in this room with me when Alivar showed up. I was ready to storm the castle when I realized someone was betraying Maxon, that they had allowed an outsider access to these chambers. I will keep an eye on him, on everyone but for now we are all on the same side."

Tristan draws in a deep breath, his expression hardening. "Why did Alivar take you to the Winter Court and not back to his castle?"

"To hide me," I grumble, crossing my arms. "He had my magic and presence concealed. Didn't want anyone knowing where I was, in case it got back to the Shadoweaver or his pet."

Tristan's eyes sharpen with suspicion, and he steps closer, his voice low. "Did he?"

My brow furrows as I blink at him, unsure what he's implying. "Did he?"

"Make a move on you. Try to steal you away from the king with his silver tongue," he clarifies, his gaze never wavering.

Heat rushes to my face at the suggestion, and I snort despite myself. "I don't think he would've had much of a chance with all my yelling and complaining."

Tristan visibly relaxes, the tension leaving his body as he exhales. "Good," he breathes out, relief softening his features.

Chapter Fifteen

Everly

Stepping from the bath, I wrap a towel tightly around myself, the warmth of the water lingering on my skin as I pad across the cold stone floor. I make my way to the mirror, wiping my hand across the fogged glass until my reflection begins to take shape. My eyes immediately trace over the mating mark on my temple. The intricate vines weave together in an elegant, almost delicate design, intertwining like living threads of magic. The mark is unmistakable—a perfect replica of Maxon's.

I reach up and trace the outline with my fingers, a lump forming in my throat.

"I hope you're okay," I whisper, a tear falling down my cheek.

I quickly swipe it away and draw in a ragged breath. I need to stay strong. I can't allow myself to fall apart, because if I did, I'm not sure I could put myself back together.

"I miss you," I whisper down the bond, hoping he can hear me.

I finish drying and slip on a nightdress before running a brush through my hair. It's really grown over the last month, and now my blonde locks sit at my waist, thick with a slight wave.

Slowly, I open the door, tiptoe over to the large bed and sit down, pulling a pillow into my lap. Asrai nestles on my pillow and is now fast asleep, completely exhausted. Nymeria occupies the lower half of the bed, while Anika rests on my right side and Zaria on my left. It's impossible to ignore the beauty of Zaria's leopard as I carefully reach out and run my hand over her sleek fur. A loud purr rumbles from her chest and her ears twitch.

"I'm sorry I wasn't here for you, but I'm here now. We are, after all, 'Anam Cara,'" I whisper softly in my native tongue.

The words meaning soul friend roll off my tongue by surprise.

I'm struck by a feeling of déjà vu when I hear those words, and I make an effort to capture the sensation, hoping it will trigger another memory, but it fades away before I can recollect that familiar feeling. I let out a heavy sigh, placing my hands in my lap and leaning back against the headboard. The engagement ring Maxon gave me catches the light, and a knot forms in the back of my throat. It's only been four days since the city of Skora was attacked, since my mate was taken from me, but it feels like an eternity. I lift my hand and tilt it back and forth, watching the gems sparkle and shimmer in the light. The sight is both beautiful and painful, a reminder of what I've lost and the uncertainty of what lies ahead.

Nymeria lifts her head and whines, looking over at me. *'I sense your heartache. What can I do?'*

"Nothing to be done, but I will find Maxon, and I will bring him home."

Nymeria shifts closer, nudging my hand with her cold, wet nose. A silent request for comfort—or, perhaps, reassurance. I give her a faint scratch behind the ear, and with a quiet sigh, she lays her head back down on her massive paws.

With a heavy heart, I sink deeper beneath the blankets, though warmth is hardly an issue with two giant wolves and a leopard curled up beside me. Their steady presence forms a living barrier, shielding me from the emptiness that gnaws at my chest. I press my face into Maxon's pillow, inhaling the faintest traces of his scent still clinging to the fabric. A shuddering breath escapes, tension unraveling at the edges.

I don't expect sleep to come easily, but I'm caught off guard when the gentle tendrils of exhaustion wind their way around my mind, pulling me under without resistance. The steady rise and fall of the others' breathing becomes a lullaby of sorts, rhythmic and grounding. The warmth surrounding me is almost smothering, yet it cocoons my body in a fragile sense of safety.

And for the first time in what feels like forever, I let it take me.

I blink against the soft sunlight filtering through the curtains, feeling the gentle warmth of the breeze as it floats in, making the fabric dance. A sense of contentment fills me as I lie here, soothing the jagged edges left by Maxon's absence. It's good to be home, but I won't truly feel at peace until Maxon returns. I've only been in Faerie for a month at most, but it has quickly drawn me in, and I can't imagine ever leaving. I miss my friends dearly and know they'll be heartbroken, but I hope Nero was able to deliver my message to them. My hope is that they find some comfort in knowing that I'm safe, even if I never return.

Rolling over, I startle and quickly sit up. "Zaria, you're back."

Zaria is sitting up beside me, her legs crossed as she plays with her sleeve. Those warm brown eyes lift to mine, and I see tears threatening to spill over. Hastily, I reach out for her, pulling her into my arms. Zaria's arms hook under mine, her hands quivering as they grip my shoulders. A gut-wrenching sob tears through her body, the sound reverberating in the air and slashing at my heart.

"She's really gone," Zaria cries, her soft voice breaking under the weight of overwhelming grief. The sound of her pain rips through me, each sob pulling at my heart.

Her body trembles in my arms, and I feel utterly powerless, like I'm standing on the edge of an abyss with no way to pull her back.

"I'm so sorry, Zar," I whisper, my voice thick with my own sorrow, though the words feel woefully inadequate. What can I possibly say to make this better? Nothing I offer will ease the ache or fill the void that's tearing her apart.

"She was so young . . . She didn't deserve her fate," Zaria's voice cracks again, and I can feel her pain, raw and unfiltered, pouring into every word.

Zaria's shoulders heave with sobs, and I tighten my grip around her, as if holding her close can somehow shield her from the hurt threatening to consume her.

"No, she didn't," I reply, my voice faltering as emotions I've been trying to bury rise to the surface. My throat tightens, and I struggle to hold back the tears threatening to spill. The loss is too much, too sudden, and I feel it clawing at me just as fiercely as it is at her.

Zaria buries herself deeper into my arms, her body shaking violently now. I press my cheek against the top of her head, feeling the strands of her brown hair tickle my face as we cling to each other. When her sobs finally quiet down, she lets go of me, her hand reaching up to wipe the tears from under her eyes.

"I can't believe I just cried all over you."

"I'm sorry I wasn't here when you needed me."

"That was out of your control."

My shoulders slump, and I drop my gaze to my hands, to Maxon's ring. The stress and anxiety of the last few days bubbles to the surface. Zaria reaches over and grips my hands.

"We will get him back." Her voice is firm, filled with quiet conviction.

I bob my head up and down, but I can't bring myself to look at her or to speak. The words feel hollow, like I'm just going through the motions, too lost in my own despair to believe them.

"We will," she repeats, squeezing my hands tighter. "The whole kingdom has come together. They want their king returned. They will fight for it."

My chest tightens at her words, a mixture of anger and guilt swirling inside me.

"She took him because she couldn't get to me," I murmur.

"I know," Zaria replies softly.

I finally lift my gaze, staring into Zaria's big brown eyes. "He's blocked the bond." The words were barely audible, as if speaking them out loud makes it too real. "I can't feel him anymore."

"He's trying to protect you." Sympathy edges Zaria's voice.

"I just want to know he's okay," I admit, my throat tight with unshed tears. "But that's stupid. Of course he isn't okay." Anger wells up in me, and I swipe at the tears that have escaped my eyes. "This isn't about me right now."

Zaria stays quiet, her hands still wrapped around mine, offering silent comfort. I take a deep breath and glance at her, trying to find something else to focus on—anything to pull myself out of this spiral. My eyes land on her hair, and a small smile tugs at the corners of my mouth as I reach up and tug on it gently. "You shifted."

"Yeah." Her lips curve into a faint smile. "I got stuck for a bit, but you got through to me. I still wasn't able to fully shift back into my regular form." She gestures toward her ears, which still have a distinctly feline shape.

"I like you like this," I assure her, my smile growing a little wider.

"Yes, but having a tail can be awkward," she quips, a hint of humor creeping into her voice.

I squeeze her hands, feeling a flicker of hope. "Do you think you can shift back into your leopard?"

"I don't know."

Taking in the assortment of food in front of me, I reach for a pastry. Bringing it to my lips, I take a small bite, expecting a burst of flavor and the buttery pastry to melt in my mouth but instead it tastes like cardboard. I can't help but cringe as I force myself to swallow the bite. Everything has lost its taste. With a heavy sigh,

I place the pastry back on the cart, and brush the crumbs off my fingers. Backing away from the food, I turn to the balcony and take in the breathtaking view of the garden.

Without warning, a tiny figure darts through the sheer curtains, soaring into the room, stopping less than a foot away from my face.

"Nix! Where have you been? Are you okay?" I ask.

"I'm fine. But I feel like that's something I should be asking you," Nix replies, flying forward and flicking me on the forehead.

"Ouch. What was that for?"

Nix shrugs and looks around the room. "Raiden said you found her."

"Yes."

Her big sapphire eyes shine with sadness as she meets my gaze. "How is she?"

"She is doing better than I expected." I sigh, looking over my shoulder at where Zaria disappeared into the bathroom.

Nix's wings droop, and her tiny shoulders slump. Seeing her dip in the air has my heart skipping a beat, and I quickly reach out, my hands cupped and steady, offering her a place to land. She shoots me a grateful look, her usual spark softened by weariness, and gently glides down, her delicate feet landing in my palm.

Nix pulls her long brown braid over her shoulder, cradling it in her hands as she rests her cheek against it. "It was complete mayhem that day. I saw the smoke and heard the screams from here, but there was nothing I could do." Her words prick at me like tiny needles.

"I've never seen anything like it. All those deadlings." I shiver.

"The Shadoweaver is making a move," Nix states. "And they will use Maxon to get to you."

CHAPTER SIXTEEN

Everly

A pounding on the door makes me jump, and I frown, making my way over. Swinging it open, I find Raiden standing there, looking worse than I've ever seen him.

"Batman?"

"How is she?" he asks immediately, his voice taut with concern. "I wanted to come earlier, but with everything–"

I raise my hand, cutting him off. "She's okay. She's shifted back this morning and is taking a shower."

"Right. Okay." He exhales sharply. "The Seelie Queen is due to arrive within the hour, and we need to meet before she gets here. There are things to go over."

"Okay. I'll get ready now–"

"Raiden?" Zaria's voice whispers from across the chambers.

Raiden tenses, his attention riveted on Zaria as she stands in the doorway of the bathroom.

She's dressed in a clean maid's dress, her long, thick chestnut hair dripping wet.

Tears well up in her eyes, and her hands cover her mouth. "I'm so sorry I attacked you," she cries, her voice trembling.

Raiden is past me and across the room in seconds, scooping Zaria into his massive chest. He holds her tightly, his face softening as he murmurs reassurances. Wanting to give them a moment, I motion for Nix to follow me, and we slip from the room, closing the door behind us.

"Don't you have to get dressed?" Nix raises an eyebrow.

"I still have some clothes left in my chambers. I haven't had the chance to move all the remaining items Zaria bought for me into Maxon's chambers."

"Isn't that the maid's job?"

I don't know why, but I bristle at her words. "I have two able hands, and I can move my own stuff."

Nix shrugs. "You're weird."

"What? Why?"

"The other high fae wouldn't move their stuff. It's beneath them."

I stop walking, placing my hands on my hips. "I'm not them. I think the system needs to change. I hate the way shifters are looked down on."

Nix grins, her sapphire eyes sparkling with mischief and her razor-sharp teeth on full display. "I knew I liked you."

I huff out a laugh and reach to open the door to my chambers, but before I can touch the handle, it swings open. Eve stands there, startled, and halts in her tracks.

"Your Majesty," she blurts, quickly bowing her head.

"Is everything alright, Eve?" I ask, catching a glimpse of her slightly red, glassy eyes.

"Oh, I'm fine." She forces a tight smile. "I was just checking everything was in order here, just in case the room was needed."

"That's fine, but are you sure you're okay?"

"It's just been a long few days, and with the funerals . . . " Her voice trails off.

"You and Lavina were close?" I ask softly, sensing her hesitation.

Eve looks up at me, surprise flickering in her deep brown eyes. "Yes, she took me in after . . . " Her voice falters.

I frown, curiosity stirring. "After what?"

Eve's gaze drops to the floor, her hesitation hanging heavy in the air. Before she can respond, Nix speaks up from behind me, her voice quiet but pointed. "Queen Lavina took Eve and her son in after the attack that killed your parents. Eve lived in the Evergreens castle with you, as your mother's lady-in-waiting."

The words hit me like a physical blow. My mouth falls open, and I feel as though the ground beneath me has crumbled.

"What?" I breathe, disbelief clouding my thoughts.

Lavina had always been close to my mother, her most trusted friend. It makes sense that she would offer Eve refuge. But why didn't I know? Why hasn't anyone told me? I didn't even find out about Lavina's relationship with my mother until it was too late.

Eve's eyes lift to meet Nix's, confusion mingling with a flicker of anger reflected there. "How did you know that?" she demands.

Nix shrugs. "I'm paid to find things out."

I stare at Nix, my mind spinning. "Why didn't you tell me?"

"I didn't want to rush your memories," Nix explains. "Your mother didn't make it easy for those memories to return."

"Honestly, I don't think she ever wanted you to come back to Faerie," Eve whispers, pushing some of her dark hair back from her face.

Tension snaps in the air as her words hang between us. I can practically feel Nix's emotions flaring beside me, her face turning the shade of a ripe tomato as her temper boils over. "Do you even know the pain she was in when she went through her Renascitur?" Nix demands, her voice sharp, biting.

I cringe at the memory of the agony, the searing pain that had nearly broken me when the magic and transformation had overtaken me. If it hadn't been for Maxon, and the bond we shared, I might not have survived it.

Eve's composure cracks, her voice rising defensively. "If Everly hadn't returned, it wouldn't have been an issue."

"Her suppressed magic would've torn her apart eventually!" Nix snaps back, her tiny figure radiating fury as her sharp teeth flash in warning.

"Not if she had been able to recharge in nature," Eve counters, her voice steady, though hostility bristles in the air between them.

My head spins with this flood of information and I step between them, raising a hand to silence the bickering.

"Stop. Both of you." The firm authority in my voice surprises me. Eve drops her head in respect, but Nix, true to her fiery nature, pokes her tongue out at the shifter. I can't help but roll my eyes at her antics.

"Look," I sigh, my voice softening as the weight of responsibility presses down on me once more. "I need to get ready for the arrival of the Seelie Queen." *And the funerals,* I add in my head. I still hate the thought of Maxon not being here to say goodbye to Lavina.

Chapter Seventeen

Everly

When I open the door, Tristan and Kian stand there, both in their formal black soldiers' uniforms. The gold and red dragon emblems on their chests shimmer in the low light, standing out against the dark fabric. This uniform marks them as elite members of the Unseelie Court Legion.

Their faces are unreadable, but I can sense the tension radiating between them. Something's off, though they're trying their best to mask it.

"Princess," they greet me in unison, bowing slightly, their hands resting on the hilt of their swords.

I glance between them, my brows furrowing. "I thought Raiden was coming to get me," I note, stepping out into the hallway with Nix perched on my shoulder and Zaria following closely behind.

Kian's eyes flick toward Tristan, as if waiting for him to answer.

"Raiden's been delayed. He sent us to escort you instead," Tristan explains.

I study them for a moment, noting how Kian's jaw clenches ever so slightly, and how Tristan stands just a bit too stiffly.

"What's going on?" I ask.

Zaria steps up beside me, her black dress rustling softly as the golden pleats peek through the flowing fabric with each step. Her gown is simple and delicate, contrasting with my more regal, dark green gown. The corset of my dress pulls me upright, and the flowing skirt brushes against the floor with every movement. The long tight sleeves loop over my middle finger, and the neck is square with soft trims of lace around the edging.

"Nothing." Kian's tone is clipped, eyes narrowed slightly, as if measuring his words.

Nix makes a soft sound, and I see her cross her arms from the corner of my eye. "You two haven't kissed and made up yet?"

Zaria glances at me, curiosity sparking in her brown eyes. I haven't told her yet—it was Kian who fed Alivar information about me. That he somehow bypassed the wards and granted the Seelie Prince access to the castle. And honestly, now isn't the time to get into it.

"Well, Kian can grovel later." My nerves for what is coming are eating me up on the inside.

Without Maxon here to help me navigate all this, my anxiety is through the roof. I smooth my hand over the soft silk of my full skirt, taking a deep breath as we start to move down the hall.

When we turn left at the end of the hall instead of right, I stop. "Where are we going?"

"Raiden asked to bring you to the war room," Tristan answers.

"Why?"

"He went to get Nolan from the dungeons." Tristan's voice is calm, too calm.

"On your orders," Kian adds, and I can hear the question behind the words.

I pull my shoulders back, squaring off against Tristan and Kian, my gaze locking onto Kian first. "If you're free to walk around," I begin, narrowing my eyes, "then it's only fair that he is as well."

Kian's eyes widen in shock at my bluntness, and I catch the subtle shift in Tristan's posture—his spine straightens, the muscles in his jaw clenching slightly. I can feel the tension radiating from him, his unease evident, though he tries to hide it. Behind me, Zaria's hand slips into mine, her fingers squeezing gently before letting go. Her support is silent but steady, yet I can sense the questions brewing in her mind. She knows there's more to this conversation.

No one speaks for a long moment.

Finally, I break the silence, my voice low but firm. "Look, Nolan has information we need. Information I need to run this court. He was the closest to Lavina, and we can't afford to keep him locked up if he's willing to help us. He's not our enemy." My gaze flicks to Kian, then back to Tristan. "And you know it."

There has been so much deceit that it's hard to keep track of friend and foe. My head spins with each lie and betrayal, building a tangled web of mistrust. Every step forward feels like stepping on glass, sharp and cutting, leaving a trail of open wounds. I was so mad, so furious when we first realized someone close to us had been leaking information to the Outcasts and then to the Seelie Prince. But I don't have the luxury of holding grudges. If I have any hope of getting Maxon back, I need everyone's help, whether I like it or not.

My heart clenches painfully, anger still simmering beneath the surface, but it's a dull throb now, not the burning inferno it once was. I take a slow breath, steadying myself. I can't let this cloud my judgment. Not when so much is at stake.

"I haven't forgiven," I whisper, the words escaping my lips like a confession, heavy with the truth. "But I will let it lie. If any of you deceive me again, I will not hesitate to toss you in the dungeons and throw away the key."

My words seem to thrum with magic, a silent warning rippling outward like a stone cast into still water. The air is charged; the tension crackling around us like static, prickling my skin. I brush past them and continue down the hall.

Nix tugs lightly on my hair. "Well said," she remarks, her tone laced with something I can't quite place. Approval, maybe? Or, perhaps, a hint of mischief. "I think you're stepping into your role nicely."

The comment catches me off guard. A flicker of warmth rises, gratitude welling up at the unexpected praise. I'm about to thank her when she continues, her words sharper than before.

"For someone who thought she was a weak human."

"Thanks." The word slips out before I can filter the sarcasm from my tone. "I think."

As we near the heavy wooden doors of the war room, I close my eyes, finding that thread deep in my chest.

My bond. My mate. My love.

I let my mind brush against it, hoping for any flicker of response, but there's nothing. It remains dormant, blocked. The silence from the other side of the bond feels like a weight pressing on my heart, a reminder of everything I've lost and everything I still have to fight for. I feel a tear slip down my cheek, hot and unbidden, but I don't bother wiping it away. It's a quiet release, a momentary crack in the wall I've had to build around my emotions to keep going.

My magic stirs in response, sweeping gently over my skin as if trying to soothe me, a soft hum of warmth and comfort that's more instinct than intent. I take another deep breath, letting it settle me, and open my eyes, determination filling the hollow ache that's been building inside of me.

Nolan, Valric, and Raiden stand to face me as I enter the war room. Raiden stands at the head of the large wooden table, his arms crossed, his expression unreadable, though his silver eyes flicker toward Zaria the moment she steps in behind me. He gives her a slight nod, one of silent understanding, or perhaps, reassurance. It's hard to tell with Raiden—he guards his emotions like a vault.

Hearing the soft creak of the door, I peer over my shoulder and see Tristan and Kian closing it behind them. For a brief moment, I catch sight of Nymeria and Anika trotting down the hall toward us, their large forms moving with a fluid grace.

My hand raises instinctively. "Stop."

Kian and Tristan pause, and I point into the hall. Both draw open the doors wider, allowing the wolves access. The others' eyes are on me as the two wolves enter, their powerful forms brushing past me as they circle, each one pressing close before sitting down on either side of me. Nymeria's white fur shines faintly under the dim light, while Anika's coat seems to be covered in dust or dirt.

"What have you been in?"

Anika's golden eyes lift to mine, and she tilts her head in question.

'Me?'

"Yes, you're filthy."

Anika blinks, as if thinking. '*The chicken coop.*'

I feel my eyes widen at her response, but before I can answer her, Nolan's snotty voice cuts through the air.

"Is she speaking to the wolves?"

My gaze snaps up, and I pin him with a glare. "That's none of your business."

There is a long, tense silence before Nolan steps forward. Every eye in the room is on him, waiting for what he has to say. He drops to one knee and bows his head.

"I want to apologize for the disloyalty I have shown toward my king," Nolan begins, his voice rough. "I'm at your service, and I thank you for releasing me from the dungeons. For allowing me to join you today."

There's a beat of silence, and then Nix's voice cuts through like a knife.

"Bet that was hard to get out, old man," she snickers, her wings giving an amused twitch.

I bite down on the inside of my cheek to keep from laughing. The tension shifts, lightening for just a moment. Nolan rises slowly, his eyes narrowing into slits as he turns his glare on Nix, but he holds back from responding.

Nix's grin widens, thoroughly enjoying the reaction, but she doesn't push further.

"Right," Raiden says, clapping his hands together. "The funeral rites will be held on the edge of the Elysium Bluffs, as per usual."

At my confused look, Nolan adds. "Royal and high-ranking fae are sent there."

"Why?"

"There are special trees there that absorb the dead," Nolan explains.

My mouth drops open in horror as I stare at him. "You can't be serious."

Nolan rears his head back, as if I've offended him. "I can assure you I most certainly am."

"Absorbed? By a tree?" I splutter.

Nolan's brows furrow. "What exactly do you not understand?"

"Everything," I breathe, shaking my head.

Nolan rubs his forehead and looks at Valric and Raiden.

Valric steps forward. "You were too young to grasp the concept as a child, but when a high fae dies, there is a special tree with golden leaves that absorbs our souls."

"You don't just . . . bury them? Or . . . set them on fire?"

Valric shakes his head. "We need to give back to which we were made."

"I'm not following."

"The first fae were born from the tears of the fae gods," Nolan explains, his head tilting to the side. "You really should know this."

Valric cuts him a sharp look and steps forward, his voice dipping into a somber, almost reverent tone. "The first fae were born from the tears of the gods. It was Morrigan, the Great Goddess of War, and her consort Dagda, the All-Father, whose grief and love for the world flowed into the earth. Their tears fell upon the seeds of ancient trees. And from those seeds, the fae were born." Valric continues, his voice taking on a deeper cadence. "It is said that Morrigan wept not only for the bloodshed she witnessed on battlefields, but for the fragility of all living things. Dagda, in his wisdom, wept with her, not from sorrow, but from the joy of creation. And so, their tears did not merely water the land—they gave it life. They infused the trees with power, a sacred bond between the fae and the natural world."

"As the trees grew," Valric explains, "they took on a dual purpose, acting as both sentinels and guides. When a fae passes from this world, their body is returned to the trees. The trees absorb our souls, reuniting us with the universe, releasing the souls through their leaves."

I swallow hard, struggling to take in all this information. It doesn't help that Nolan is looking at me like I'm already failing.

"Okay. I think I get it," I whisper.

"You'll understand better when you see it for yourself," Valric assures me.

"You have a lot to learn. Your time away from Faerie and your lost memories will make this difficult," Nolan adds, though the softness in his voice surprises me.

"There is one more thing." Valric lifts a small brown satchel over his head and places it carefully on the table. Curious, I step closer, my heart beating a little faster as I watch him reach inside.

His hand emerges slowly, and when he turns toward me, holding the object, my breath catches in my throat. Instant tears flood my vision, blurring the world around me.

"How?" I whisper, my voice trembling, barely audible. My hands instinctively reach out, but I pull them back, too overwhelmed to touch it.

Valric's eyes soften, his face full of understanding. "Before the soldiers came and looted the castle, a few of us—myself and some loyal followers—managed to save a few things of great value. I have been keeping them safe for when you returned to us." His words are calm, but they carry the weight of everything we lost, everything we had to leave behind that night.

I swallow hard, running my tongue over my teeth in a feeble attempt to stave off the tears, but it's no use. My eyes are fixed on the crown in his hands—my mother's. The sight of it is like a punch to the gut, the kind of pain that's both sharp and deep, yet tethered to something beautiful. The green jewels catch the light, exact replicas of her eyes—the same eyes I now see in the mirror every day. The gold is intricately twisted, woven into delicate vines that resemble the marks of the mating bond on my skin. It's almost as if the crown has always been a part of me, waiting for this moment.

Valric steps closer, his eyes never leaving mine as he lifts it. "May I?" he offers gently, as though he knows the weight of this moment, not just for me, but for everyone who remembers her.

I can't find my voice, so I simply nod, a single tear slipping down my cheek. The room is silent, and I can feel everyone's eyes on me, but all I can focus on is the crown in Valric's hands.

He smiles softly and places it on my head with reverence, his fingers brushing through my hair to adjust it. His touch is light, but it sends waves of emotions crashing through me, memories of my mother flooding my mind. When he steps back, I lift my eyes to meet his, and I'm surprised to see his own are glistening with unshed tears.

"You look just like your mother," he remarks, tone thick with emotion.

A quiet sob threatens to escape, but I manage to hold it back.

"Thank you," I whisper as I reach up, my fingers grazing the cool metal. The sensation is almost surreal, like a part of her is here with me now, watching over me, guiding me.

In this moment, everything else fades—the room, the people, even the pain—and for just a second, I'm a little girl again, standing beside my mother, feeling the warmth of her presence as though she never left.

Chapter Eighteen

Everly

"The seelie royal court has arrived, Princess," Nolan says, stepping into the room. I didn't even see him leave. Everything feels surreal, and I'm struggling to keep up. "We will greet them in the courtyard so we can leave with the funeral procession and make it to Elysium Bluffs by sunset."

Nervous energy thrums through me, which seems to be a constant hum beneath my skin. I wish Maxon were here—not just to calm my nerves, but to say goodbye to his aunt. The ache of his absence hits harder now. He deserves to be here.

I push up from my chair and round the table. As I pass Raiden, he lays a hand on my shoulder, the weight of it both grounding and comforting. Our eyes meet, and in that moment, a thousand unspoken emotions flicker between us—grief, understanding, a quiet promise to see this through together.

Tristan and Kian pull open the doors, and we step into the corridor, my heart pounding a little faster as the anticipation of what's to come settles in my bones.

Lutin's mauve eyes catch mine as we exit. He bows low in his black soldier's uniform, a picture of respect, but it's the woman beside him who draws my attention.

Someone new. Someone I don't recognize.

I know I've stared too long when she steps forward, raising her fist to her heart in a formal salute.

"My name is Senka, Your Majesty." Her voice is low, measured. Her black hair, sleek and midnight-dark, is pulled back in a tight ponytail, accentuating the sharp lines of her face. Her eyes, a soft shade of periwinkle, catch mine—an unusual shade that means she's lower on the magical scale. But I sense strength in her all the same.

Lutin steps forward, mimicking her gesture. "The two of us are to escort you to the bluffs, along with Tristan and Kian, Your Majesty."

"Thank you." I bow my head slightly in acknowledgment. It feels like the proper thing to do, but when I lift my gaze again, I'm met with wide eyes. Looking around the group, I see varying degrees of amusement on their faces.

"Too naïve and kind for your own good, Princess Vera," Valric murmurs as he strides past me, his words half a warning, half a tease. I shoot him a look, but he's already gone, disappearing down the hall.

I turn to Zaria, who only smiles and slips her arm through mine, pulling me forward. "We shouldn't keep the Seelie Queen waiting," she says in a hushed, conspiratorial whisper. "Who knows how many people she'll offend while we dawdle."

A weak laugh bubbles up from my throat despite the tension curling in my chest. "Let's hope the list is short today."

Stepping out of the castle's main doors, I'm immediately greeted by the sight of horse-drawn carriages lining the courtyard, their ornate designs glistening in the pale morning light. Fae from various courts have gathered. Gowns flow in the breeze, a mix of colors and textures. It's like Maxon's coronation day all over again, only this time, the atmosphere is far heavier. There's tension in the air, a sense of anticipation that gnaws at my nerves.

The women are adorned in gowns that range from extravagant and shimmering to more practical yet elegant attire, but all carry an air of formality. Each dress seems to reflect the identity of their respective courts—some bright and elaborate, others dark and muted. I can identify the Summer and Spring Courts easily, their colors brighter and hair color lighter. The males are a similar mix, their clothing ranging from formal coats to soldier's uniforms and casual breeches paired with tunics, though even the casual ones seem carefully chosen for the occasion. They stand tall, their postures rigid.

As my attention sweeps over the crowd, it strikes me how unfamiliar they all are. No faces stand out, no names surface. It's as though I've walked into a gathering of strangers, each of them more alien to me than the last. The cobblestone path that cuts through the courtyard is barely visible beneath the press of bodies, horses, and carriages, leaving me feeling even more out of place.

Then, my eyes catch on a cluster of fae with pale blonde and white hair, their presence like a beacon among the crowd. My attention focuses, and I spot Alivar standing among them. His tall figure is unmistakable, his posture a blend of strength and calm. Next to him is a woman whose pale blonde hair almost glows in the early morning sun, cascading down her back in perfect waves. Her deep purple eyes catch the light and hold a sharpness that demands respect. There's no mistaking her—Queen Anwyn.

She stands with an air of authority, her presence commanding even in the sea of fae. The way she holds herself, regal and unyielding, leaves little doubt that she is a force to be reckoned with. Alivar leans slightly toward her, speaking quietly, his expression unreadable from this distance.

I hesitate for a moment, feeling so out of place and completely unsure.

Crap. I can feel my anxiety creeping in, tightening in my chest.

Just as the panic threatens to take over, I feel a gentle pat on my arm. The touch pulls me out of my head, snapping me back to reality. Turning my head, I find Zaria beside me, eyes warm with understanding. She says nothing, just offers a quiet presence that somehow helps steady the storm inside me.

I manage to muster a small, grateful smile, though I know it doesn't quite reach my eyes.

"Alivar won't let his mother step out of line," she whispers in my ear.

"Really?"

"He might not say it, but I can see the way he is looking at you right now, and he cares for you."

My heart thumps hard, and I feel a sickening sensation wash over me. It takes all my strength not to look over at him. "You're wrong."

Zaria shrugs and gives me a soft smile. "I might be, but he will protect you. We all will."

Nix suddenly materializes, landing on my shoulder, breaking me from this uncomfortable topic. "I have something for you."

"What is it?"

With a graceful leap from my shoulder, she hovers in front of me, her wings beating so quickly that golden fairy dust trails behind her, shimmering in the early morning light. She's like a streak of liquid sunlight, the sight is breathtaking.

But the sparkle in her eyes dims as she crosses her arms, a pout forming on her lips. "Well, after the whole tiara thing, it just feels . . . stupid," she mutters, looking away.

"Don't be silly, Nix," I say gently. "What is it?"

Nix huffs, her tiny cheeks puffing up as she releases a frustrated sigh. "I made you a jewel, like you asked," she finally grumbles, though there's a hint of pride in her voice.

"Wait . . . You actually did?" I blink, genuinely surprised.

She holds my gaze, her pout slowly giving way to a small, shy smile. "Yes, I did."

After a long pause of just staring at her, curiosity gets the better of me. "Can I see it?"

"Right." Her eyes light up as she waves her tiny hand. In a soft shimmer, a delicate rose quartz appears in her hand, no bigger than a penny, attached to a fine gold chain. The stone catches the light, glinting softly with hues of pink.

"It's gorgeous, Nix," I say, softly.

I reach out to cradle the pendant in my palm. It feels cool and smooth, almost like it's humming with a faint magic all its own.

Nix preens a little, looking pleased with herself, though she tries to hide it behind a modest shrug.

"It has a purpose," she adds cryptically.

I fiddle with the clasp and clip it around my neck with the crystal sitting in the middle of my chest.

"What do you mean?" My fingers run lightly over the crystal.

"Well, if you go missing, I can find you, so long as it is on your body."

My eyes widen, and my mouth drops open. "You made me a tracker?"

Nix shrugs and grins, her razor-sharp teeth on full display. "I won't be taking any chances with our soon-to-be queen."

With those parting words, she flies off, heading back inside the castle.

"Is she not coming with us?"

"Raiden asked her to stay and keep watch," Zaria replies as we descend the stairs, heading in the direction of the carriages.

Tucking some wayward hair behind my ear, I peer up at Asrai, who's perched atop Zaria's head. She's watching me closely, her fingers moving in a fluid rhythm as she signs, *'Nix is the best at finding things out. I'm actually surprised she didn't know about Kian.'* Her dual-colored eyes blink thoughtfully.

I pause, letting go of Zaria's arm, my hands moving carefully to respond. '*Me too,*' I sign back, holding Asrai's gaze. *'But we all trusted him.'*

Asrai's expression shifts, something hesitant flickering in her eyes before she continues, *'Do you still trust him?'*

Her question hangs heavy in the air, and I feel the weight of it settle over me. I exhale slowly, forcing myself to give an honest answer. My hands move a little slower this time. '*If I reply emotionally, I'd say, definitely not. But if I'm honest—if I put my anger aside—I do trust him.*'

Asrai studies me for a moment, her intense gaze softened by an understanding I didn't expect.

"I wish you could teach me how to communicate with her," Zaria says, her voice wistful.

Several gasps ripple through the gathering, drawing our attention. Looking around, my gaze lands on Queen Anwyn and Alivar, who stand only a few feet away, flanked by two high fae women and a male who stands a little taller than the rest. The queen's deep purple eyes are fixed on me, narrowed with suspicion and maybe . . . a little curiosity.

"Are you speaking to that Willowroot?" Queen Anwyn demands, her tone sharp enough to cut through the air like a whip.

Caught off guard, I falter, stumbling over my words. "I– I . . . " I glance at Zaria, confused by the sudden scrutiny. "Yes?" I manage to answer, unsure if that was the right thing to say.

The male fae, who is staring at me with an air of detached superiority, tilts his head slightly, his nostrils flaring ever so subtly. "I heard the druids could communicate with nature spirits and other species," he remarks, his voice cool and aloof. "But I've never witnessed it firsthand."

His nose lifts higher as he speaks, as if he's trying to distance himself from the concept, like the very idea of communicating with something as wild and untamed as nature's spirits is beneath him.

I squint my eyes at him, my annoyance bubbling to the surface. I don't like his tone, the way he says *druids* as if we're some sort of disgrace.

"Yes, communicating has never been an issue for me," I reply, lifting my chin slightly in return.

There's an arrogant curl to his mouth that makes my lips twitch to say something more, but I bite my tongue, knowing this isn't the time to pick a fight.

Alivar steps forward then. "Come now, Uncle. No need to be jealous," he teases.

The man splutters, his brow furrowing. "Jealous!"

Alivar ignores him entirely and steps forward, bowing deeply, his hand extending toward mine as he rises. His fingers are warm as they curl around mine, and he places a gentle kiss on the back of my hand. Instantly, my cheeks flush, and Zaria's words echo in my mind.

"Princess," he says smoothly, a smirk tugging at the corner of his lips.

"Alivar," I reply, mirroring his smirk, but not letting my guard slip.

The sound of several gasps cut through the moment, loudest from the two high fae women standing by the queen.

What have I done now?

"How dare you address the Crown Prince so casually," one of them snaps, her voice dripping with indignation,

Alivar turns toward them, unbothered. "It's okay, Aunt. We are friends, aren't we, Everly?" His eyes gleam with amusement, as if he's daring me to contradict him.

Keeping my focus on Alivar, I nod slowly. If I met any of their eyes, I'd probably lose whatever calm I'd managed to gather.

"Yes," I reply, clearing my throat. "Friends."

Queen Anwyn steps closer, her presence imposing, and Alivar reluctantly releases my hand.

"We haven't been formally introduced," she begins, her voice carrying the weight of authority. "I am Queen Anwyn of the Seelie Fae."

My mind scrambles as I quickly sink into a curtsy, hoping this is the proper etiquette. Nolan should have been here to handle introductions—and to prepare me for . . . well, all of this.

Rising, I muster a polite smile, despite the heat rising to my cheeks. "It's a pleasure to meet you, Your Majesty." I meet her gaze. "Though better circumstances would have been preferred."

I'm about to introduce Zaria, but she has taken several steps back to stand almost in line with Lutin and Senka, and has her head bowed.

"It is just terrible what happened to the former queen, and to think the king was taken from his own court. Do you have plans to–"

"Mother, now isn't the time to talk about this. We should get in the carriage," Alivar smoothly cuts in.

The second those words leave his mouth, Malick stops beside me. "Your Majesty, the carriages are ready."

Alivar's lips curl into a smirk as he winks at me, a flash of mischief in his eyes before he turns, extending his arm to Queen Anwyn. "Come, Mother, we mustn't keep the dead waiting any longer."

I watch them go, my gaze tracking the small group of seelie fae as they make their way toward the carriages. Zaria steps up beside me, her expression inscrutable as she keeps her eyes fixed on the retreating figures. There's an unspoken tension in the air, a sense of wariness that seems to ripple through everyone present. Lutin and Senka shift slightly, their bodies tense, as if they want to keep the seelie in their line of sight, alert to any sudden movements.

Finally, I spot Kian and Tristan as they approach, leading two horses behind them. Their expressions are blank, the usual warmth in their eyes replaced by a cold alertness.

"Where are Storm and Nova?" I ask, frowning as I take in the horses they lead.

Kian and Tristan trade a look—one of those silent exchanges that tells me they've already decided something without my input.

"In the stables," Kian answers, his tone careful but firm.

My frown deepens. "Why?"

"You're taking the carriage, Princess." Tristan gestures toward the second one in the procession.

I bristle at the implication, my pulse quickening, and my voice a little sharper than intended. "I don't want to take the carriage."

Being confined in that small space, away from the open air, it already makes me feel trapped. Feelings of claustrophobia rise to the surface and I do my best to keep my breathing even.

Kian sighs, stepping closer. "Trust me, it's going to be a long day of riding, followed by a night of rituals, and then we'll be traveling back at dawn. You'll be dead on your feet before we even finish."

I cross my arms, still not convinced. "I can handle it."

"Not in that dress," Kian murmurs, trying to disguise his words with a cough.

Tristan shakes his head, a soft smile tugging at his lips. "I know you can. But Lutin and Senka will be with you and Zaria in the carriage, and it's not just about you being tired. It's about safety. We need to make sure you're well-rested and protected."

My attention flickers over to Lutin and Senka, who remain silent, their stoic expressions betraying nothing.

"What about Raiden?" I counter, searching for some argument that might let me ride with the others.

"He's leading the convoy with Fenris." Kian's tone leaves little room for negotiation. "And I'll be riding alongside your carriage with Tristan. You'll be safe, I promise."

"It's not that," I whisper, and if I was honest with myself, it isn't just my fear of small spaces. Unease twists my stomach at the thought of leaving Storm here.

If I can't have Maxon with me . . . he is part of Maxon.

I start pacing, trying to get my feelings under control. My chest grows warm with the telltale signs of my magic burning brighter by the second.

Maxon.

My mate bond sits silent, making my throat tighten with the urge to scream—to rage at the heavens for the sheer injustice of it all.

A warmth at my fingertips begins to spread, and I glance down, startled to see delicate flowers sprouting from the ground where I stand. Petals of every color push up from between the stones, their beauty mocking the storm brewing inside me.

Shit, Everly, pull it together.

"Princess?" Kian's voice cuts through the maelstrom, but I barely hear him.

A low growl escapes my throat before I can stop it, a warning more primal than I expected. Once again, my magic flares up, reacting to my emotions as I struggle to maintain control. I was perfectly fine just a moment ago.

I can sense the fae around me, their shock and uncertainty evident in the way they subtly shift away. Suddenly, Kian's face fills my vision, his gentle touch sending a comforting warmth coursing through my body as his hands gently settle on my shoulders.

"You're okay, Everly."

But I'm not okay.

Magic swirls within me, a tempest ready to break free. The air crackles with energy, my hair standing on end. Kian's touch anchors me, but I can sense his concern, his fear. The ground trembles beneath us, making my heart pound harder against my chest.

"I can't leave Storm here." My voice trembles, and with it, the ground beneath us shifts, as a wave of magic surges outward, rolling over the ground like a storm cloud.

"What was that?" Tristan asks.

I blink, feeling the magic withdraw and curl back into the recess of my chest as if it just threw a temper tantrum. Two loud howls pierce the sky, followed by the unmistakable sound of hooves pounding the earth in the distance like thunder.

We all turn, eyes wide as the sound grows closer.

Nymeria and Anika round the gardens into the courtyard, followed by Storm.

Storm's black coat gleams like polished onyx, his powerful strides thundering against the ground.

Kian curses under his breath, his jaw tightening as his gaze shifts to me. Commotion spreads, murmurs rising around us in a low hum of disbelief. I somehow forgot about the audience surrounding us. Shit. This was supposed to be my chance to prove myself, and so far, I am definitely not making the best impression.

"Did you just . . . call to them?" Zaria mutters under her breath, leaning into me, her eyes locked on the wolves and Storm.

I shake my head, confusion stirring inside me. "I don't know."

Then, before I can work out a response, Storm stops in front of me, his large, dark eyes meeting mine with a calm intensity. He nudges me gently with his nose, his touch surprisingly comforting, and I instinctively reach out, steadying myself with a hand on his head. The familiar feel of his mane under my fingers eases some of the panic threatening to rise.

Taking a deep breath, I look up, my gaze moving from Storm to Kian and Tristan, all watching me closely. My pulse is pounding, but I stand a little straighter, forcing myself to meet their stares head-on.

"I told you. I can't leave him behind."

Kian shoots me a look, but it's mixed with something that almost resembles respect. "You're impossible, Princess." His tone carries a hint of exasperation, though his lips quirk into a small smile.

"I'll take the carriage," I declare, turning back to Kian with a fierce glare. "But If I decide I want to ride, I will ride."

He opens his mouth to argue, but then seems to think better of it. He just shakes his head, a rueful smile playing on his lips. "Stubborn as ever."

Chapter Nineteen

Maxon

Even with my eyes closed, I can sense the shadows in my dungeon growing darker, deeper, pressing in with a suffocating weight. This whole place breathes darkness and despair, like it's alive and feeding off my anger and exhaustion. I know Yumekui is watching me. Her gaze is sharp, lingering—a prickling sensation that crawls over my skin, settling like an itch I can't scratch.

If only I could get these bone chains off. Just for a second. One second is all I'd need to cause enough damage to leave a mark she'd never forget.

"You look like you could use a pick-me-up, Your Majesty," Yumekui's voice weaves around me like wisps of smoke.

I force my eyes open, glaring into the shadows that seem to pulse with her presence. "I don't know why you're keeping me. You should just kill me. I'm of no use to you. Everly isn't coming for me. My men won't allow it."

The shadows shift, and she steps forward in her beast form. Her black coat glints like polished obsidian, scruffy yet formidable, her size dwarfing even Nymeria and Anika. She's massive, a hulking wolf, a pure predator, one that carries both elegance and danger with each and every movement.

"If that's truly what you wanted," she murmurs, her voice soft but sharp as steel, "you wouldn't have killed the deadling that snuck in here hoping for a little taste of royal blood."

Her voice lingers in the air, low and ominous, yet her beast stands before me, messing with my mind. Exhausted, I let my head fall, my filthy, matted hair draping over my face, shutting out her sharp gaze.

I sense her magic snaking through the air, then the sound of her footsteps drawing closer, slow and deliberate. Back in her human form, she crouches in front of me, close enough that I can feel the heat of her presence.

"See, I think that's a lie. Which is interesting, since high fae are unable to lie. You still hold out hope that you will see your precious mate again. You don't want to die."

I lift my head just enough to meet her gaze, fighting to keep my expression blank. "Go the *fuck* away."

Yumekui's lips curve, a flicker of dark amusement lighting her eyes. That wicked gleam—the one that promises she's about to dig her claws into something painful—settles into her expression. "I just thought you'd like to know," she purrs, every word soaked in satisfaction, "the former queen is being taken to the Bluffs for her rites."

The words hit like a blow, and the dungeon around me shrinks, pressing in as my mind stumbles to catch up. I search her face, looking for a crack in that twisted smile, a sign she's toying with me. But she isn't lying. Lavina is dead.

When did . . . Everly's words the day of the attack come rushing back.

Oh my god, Maxon, I'm so sorry. I'm so sorry. I didn't see it coming and she, she . . .

My mind spins, grasping at fragments of memories, of Lavina's fierce smile, her steady voice—a force that kept me grounded after the death of my parents. Now she is gone. A hollow ache claws at my chest. And Everly . . . She's out there, facing this storm alone, forced to navigate betrayal, power struggles, and enemies closing in, all without me by her side. The thought coils tight in my gut, a searing resentment that burns hotter with every second I'm trapped in these cursed chains. I hate this—this helplessness, this cage, and most of all, the distance keeping me from protecting her.

"I can see you need time with your thoughts," Yumekui snickers.

Chapter Twenty

Everly

Tristan and Kian were right; the journey to the Bluffs is long. We left in the morning and have been traveling all day, and I can see the sun is close to setting. The convoy has grown steadily as we've traveled through Skora, with mourners joining along the road, all coming to say their goodbyes to their former queen and to those of noble descent who had passed with her during the battle. Rayna, too, will be honored among them. True to his word, Tristan has kept to the carriage's side, Kian on the other, while Storm and the wolves stay at the rear, a quiet but ever-watchful presence.

Zaria's head rests on my shoulder, her breathing deep and steady, the rhythmic sway of the carriage having lulled her into a fitful sleep. Gently, I reach over, giving her a soft shake. "We're here, Zar," I whisper.

Her eyes blink open, disoriented, before she sits up straight, her cat-like ears twitching. She looks ahead, her expression shifting as she takes in the reality of our destination.

The carriage slows, finally coming to a halt. Lutin and Senka, who have been seated across from us, stand and step out, their faces somber. Lutin extends his hand to help guide me down the steps. I reach out and take it as I climb down, feeling the press of the silent crowd surrounding the convoy, their faces drawn, eyes lowered.

The Elysium Bluffs stretch out before us, vast and steep, with the mist swirling up from the cliffs, giving the entire landscape an ethereal, almost haunting feeling.

As soon as my feet touch the ground, a feeling of pins and needles shoots up my legs. "Oh my god, my ass is numb," I mutter under my breath.

After ten long hours cramped in the carriage, every bone in my body aches. The endless jolting over uneven roads, the constant rattle of wheels, and the close quarters are more than enough to drive anyone mad. A part of me is almost tempted to find Alivar as soon as possible and beg him to transport me back home tomorrow.

The thought of his magic whisking me away from this claustrophobic box on wheels, straight to the familiar comfort of my own chambers, is extremely tempting.

Kian swings a leg over his horse, dismounting. He hooks his arm in mine and smiles warmly down at me. My chest aches as I look at him and I give him a weak smile.

"I'll just keep a hold of you until your legs are steady. I wouldn't want the future queen to cause a scene."

Tristian takes Zaria's arm, giving her hand a reassuring pat. "Let's go and give your sister the sendoff she deserves."

The hush in the air is heavy, thick with anticipation and respect. The wind blowing across from the cliffs seems to absorb even the faintest sounds. My attention drifts forward to the front, where Raiden and Fenris sit atop their horses, standing watch with the stoic grace of seasoned warriors. Raiden's eyes meet mine, and he gives a subtle nod before his gaze moves to Zaria.

With Anika and Nymeria flanking Kian and me, I peer over my shoulder, catching a glimpse of Storm munching on grass beside the rumbling carriage.

Movement catches my eye—the Seelie Court, gliding forward toward the heavy mist. As they approach, towering trees rise from the haze like something out of a dream. I feel my breath catch, a quiet gasp escaping as I take in the scene.

"Oh, wow," I murmur, mesmerized.

The massive oak trees have leaves that are a stunning, burnished gold, their bark the deepest, richest brown I've ever seen, as though they've been soaked in magic for centuries.

There's a pulse in the ground beneath my feet, a hum of ancient magic thrumming softly, guiding us forward. The golden leaves seem to catch and hold the light in ways that defy reason, casting a warm glow that fills the misty expanse, an ethereal path leading us deeper into the grove.

With a deep breath, I begin to move toward Alivar and Queen Anwyn, my steps careful yet purposeful.

To my left stands Nolan, while on the other side of him are Alivar and Queen Anwyn. On my right is Kian, followed by Zaria and Tristan. I haven't caught sight of Valric since we left the war room, leaving me unsure if he even came along.

The sun is getting low. I know the rites are about to begin, but I have no idea what to expect. I watch as fae move some of the bodies to the base of the ancient trees.

My mouth drops open in silent awe as the mist rises from the earth, swirling up to shroud the figures placed at the base of the ancient trees. The mist moves with purpose, as though it is alive, wrapping around the bodies and swallowing. The trees tower above us, immense and powerful, their golden leaves pulsing with life. Then leaves begin to shift, turning from gold to a deep, fiery red that ignites the sky above, casting everything in a crimson glow, as if setting the world on fire.

One by one, the high fae are honored as we stand witness. The air thickens with reverence, every soul here held captive by the solemn beauty of the ritual. The sky darkens over the cliffs, the sun setting on the horizon.

Then Raiden steps forward, carrying Rayna in his arms. He holds her with such tenderness. The sight has my heart clenching in my chest like someone is quite literally squeezing it.

Stepping from the line of soldiers, he moves with steady, measured steps. Rayna's light blue gown drapes over his arm, the fabric fluttering gently, her head nestled against his massive chest as if she were only sleeping.

Oh, how I wish she were just sleeping.

My vision blurs as tears sting my eyes, the lump in my throat making it hard to breathe. Rayna—bright, bubbly Rayna—is truly gone.

Zaria steps forward, Tristan steady at her side, his arm still looped through hers in a quiet act of support. Raiden kneels on the ground, placing her gently at the base of the tree. And for a moment, she looks peaceful, almost as if she might wake and smile at any moment.

Then Zaria begins to sing. Her voice rises, light as the breeze but resonant, filling the air with a haunting melody that carries sorrow and memory, grief and loss. The song is gentle yet filled with aching heartbreak, a sound that seems to echo in the very roots of the trees. The crowd stirs, silent, listening as the melody weaves through the branches, wrapping us all in its embrace.

Raiden's silver eyes swirl with grief as he moves toward Zaria. As her voice fades, he reaches out, cupping her face in his hands. His forehead dips to hers, a quiet, shared solace passing between them. Tristan steps back, releasing Zaria's arm, giving them this moment.

The mist thickens, and the tree's leaves seem to shimmer, the crimson light casting a warm glow over Rayna's body. And then, almost reverently, the great branches bend, dipping low, as if offering their own farewell, as the mist rises, covering her completely.

Zaria takes her place between Kian and Tristan as Raiden, flanked by five other soldiers, walk with solemn purpose toward the ornate cart brimming with flowers. Their faces are set, expressions stoic and unyielding. The cart is a burst of color and beauty, seeming almost at odds with the weight of the occasion, but somehow fitting—a final tribute for Lavina.

The sky has darkened fully now, a deep, pitch-black void empty of stars, with no moon to offer even the faintest glimmer of light. It is as if the heavens themselves mourn her passing. A low wind sweeps through the trees, carrying with it an icy chill that cuts to the bone.

Raiden and his soldiers take their places by the cart, then the entire procession begins to sing, their voices rising in a mournful, chilling harmony.

The song echoes across the ground, the haunting melody slipping into the empty spaces around us. It's a sound that seems to come from the depths of the earth, raw and ancient, reverberating against the trees.

Images flicker in my mind, my mother and other druids dancing around a fire. A fire that burns tall and bright as if reaching for the heavens, and their singing lulling me to sleep. My mouth opens, and I begin to sing with the rest of the procession, the words once forgotten pouring out of me and into the open air.

Once it's all over, everyone turns as one, walking in the direction of the cliffs. Kian pats my arm and tilts his head in that direction.

"We need to follow," he whispers.

I linger at the back, content to keep my distance. Maxon's warm violet eyes fill my mind, and I sigh, wishing more than anything that he was here, his arms around me. But with every step forward, the ache of his absence deepens. It's only been five days since he was taken, since the battle that left Skora in ruins, but it feels like an eternity.

Suddenly, a gust of wind tears through the procession, forceful and unexpected. It tugs at my clothes, nearly making me stumble. Kian's arm tightens around mine, steadying me, and I focus forward, eyes widening as we reach the cliffs.

"Oh my god," I whisper, breath stolen by the sight. The bright, fiery red leaves from the towering trees float on the wind, swirling like embers against the dark sky. They drift toward the cliffs, carried upward before disappearing over the edge, mingling with the gray-blue waves crashing far below. The ritual of farewell feels final as the last leaf vanishes from sight, and slowly, the fae around me start to turn, heading back toward the horses and carriages.

As we pause, a sharp pain blooms in my cheek, radiating through my jaw and up into my ear. The dull, rhythmic pulse at the base of my neck throbs in time with my heartbeat. I wince, reaching up to rub my cheek.

Kian's gaze sharpens as he glances down. "Are you okay?" His steps slow to match mine.

"Just a headache," I murmur, trying to shake it off.

"A headache?" He doesn't sound convinced.

I let out a low moan, my eyes falling shut for a brief moment, hoping the throbbing will ease.

Kian's voice softens with concern. "That's not normal. We should see a healer."

"Don't be silly," I wave off the concern, forcing a small smile. "I'm fine."

As we approach the line of carriages, my steps slow, attention drawn to the large, dark blue tent set up further away from the road. Banners flap softly in the breeze, bearing our coat of arms.

"What's that?" I inquire, looking back at Kian.

He inclines his head. “That, Princess, is for the feast—reserved for nobility only. A chance for you to rest and refuel for the ride back.”

I frown, casting a quick glance around as I notice commoners already beginning to gather belongings, dispersing into small clusters to start the journey back on foot.

“It seems a little unfair. Shouldn’t everyone have the chance to eat?”

Kian shrugs, unconcerned. “It’s just how it is.”

“But it shouldn’t be.” I frown at his lack of compassion.

The throb in my jaw makes itself known again, and I grimace.

Before he can respond, a familiar figure steps up beside me. “Are you all right?” Tristan’s violet eyes catch mine, assessing.

“Yes,” I answer quickly.

“She’s got a headache,” Kian cuts in, “and she keeps rubbing her cheek.” He gestures to me in a way that draws Tristan’s scrutiny immediately.

I shoot Kian a pointed look, folding my arms over my chest. “I said I’m fine.” My eyes move over the crowd that’s dispersing, and a frown pulls at my lips. “Where’s Zaria?”

Tristan’s gaze lingers a moment longer, suspicious. “Raiden took her to the carriage.”

“Your Majesty,” Lutin speaks up, his tone quiet but firm as he glances at the people still nearby. “We should keep moving.”

Reluctantly, I give a nod, exhaustion taking the fight out of me. “Okay.”

Chapter Twenty-One

Everly

The conversation around me is nothing more than a low hum as I take a seat at the long table set up in the center of the massive tent. The air inside is alive with a quiet, magical energy that seems to pulse in time with the glowing orbs floating above us. They drift lazily through the space, their soft, golden light casting a warm, enchanting glow over everything.

The air is thick with a mixture of tantalizing aromas and underlying tension. I'm sitting at the head of the table, not my choice. This was the last place I wanted to sit. To my left, Raiden settles into his chair, his presence a comforting anchor. To my right, Alivar sits with a relaxed demeanor, a glass of elixir in his hand, and his mother next to him. Her violet eyes are sharp and calculating, and it makes my skin prickle with unease. Her entourage surround her, their expressions as inscrutable as her own.

Nolan is seated a bit further down the table, his face a mask of unreadable calm. These noble fae are extremely good at remaining aloof. It's like nothing fazes them.

A few other nobles, whom I haven't had the chance to meet, are scattered along the length of the table, engaged in quiet conversations.

I can't shake the feeling of being watched, scrutinized, as if every move I make is being carefully evaluated. The queen's presence is especially unnerving. Her poised elegance seems to conceal a simmering hostility, and the glances she occasionally throws my way are far from friendly.

Raiden leans in slightly. "Stay calm," he murmurs softly, his voice barely audible above the clinking of cutlery and murmur of voices.

Tristan and Kian stand behind my chair, barely a few feet away, their presence making me increasingly nervous. They have stayed within arm's reach the entire time.

Leaning closer, I whisper under my breath, "How is Zaria?"

Raiden's silver eyes meet mine. "She is sleeping in the carriage. I gave her a tonic from the healers to help her rest. Lutin and Senka are watching over her."

Sadness and guilt gnaw at my insides.

"I see that look, and it wasn't your fault," Raiden says softly.

"She was coming for me." Anger and hurt edge my words, and the reality of what happened stabs me in the chest.

"Rayna took her own risks," he counters firmly.

"But if I had been quicker . . . "

My words linger in the air between us. Raiden's hand lands on mine, where it rests on the table, and he leans in closer. "Don't start down that path, Everly. There will be more losses to come. You must not let it weigh you down."

Before I can respond, Queen Anwyn's voice cuts through the air, sharp and tinged with false sweetness. "You two seem incredibly close," she remarks, a fake smile playing on her lips. Her comment makes me straighten in my chair, my cheeks flaring with heat at her implication.

"We *are* close. Raiden has been like the brother I never had."

Raiden's large hand envelops mine and squeezes, and I watch the queen's eyes track the movement.

"I see. Well, it's a little misleading the way you whisper between yourselves."

"What I do isn't of any concern to you. Do not make up lies in your head. I love my mate, and I will be getting him back."

Queen Anwyn's eyes widen, but before she can answer, there is a commotion by the tent's doors. Immediately, Raiden is on his feet. Wings flared to cover me. Kian and Tristan draw their swords, their eyes sharp and wary, as they begin to slowly pull me out of my seat.

"Nero, what is the meaning of this?" Raiden's voice booms, the sound making me jump.

Nero?

Pulling my arm free from Kian's grip, I move out from behind Raiden, curiosity overriding caution. As soon as I see who has entered, a gasp escapes my lips, my hands flying to my mouth.

"Everly!?" two voices I have missed dearly yell out in unison.

I choke on a laugh, emotions clogging my throat as I sprint toward my friends. I trip on the hem of my dress, lifting the silky material to keep from falling. Scarlett and Mia close the distance, and we all embrace, tears streaming down our faces. Scarlett pulls back first, her wild red hair a mess of curls. She grips my cheeks, tilting my face side to side as if to confirm I'm real.

"It is you!" she breathes, her green eyes wide with disbelief and relief.

"It's me," I cry, barely able to get the words out. "How did you get here?"

"He brought us." Mia points to where Nero stands calmly to the side.

I'm acutely aware of the audience around us, but for a moment, all that matters is that my friends are here. Mia grips my hands tightly, her blue eyes searching mine for any sign of injury or distress.

"Are you okay?" Concern is etched into her features.

"Of course she's not okay!" Scarlett shouts, her fiery temper flaring. "Who tattooed your face? I know you wouldn't have done that willingly." She pushes up her sleeves, looking around the tent with a fierce expression. "Whose ass am I kicking?"

The tension in the room escalates as Scarlett's defiant stance draws the attention of everyone present. Raiden steps forward, his wings still partially spread in a protective gesture.

"These are my friends," I explain quickly, my voice wavering with emotion. "They mean no harm."

Raiden's gaze softens slightly, though his posture remains tense. He nods to Kian and Tristan, who reluctantly put away their swords but stay close.

Nero steps forward, his expression unreadable. "You have extremely stubborn friends, Everly."

I swallow hard, overwhelmed by the flood of emotions. "I know."

Mia and Scarlett flank me, their presence comforting.

"I promised I'd bring them here to see that you're safe and sound, but given the news I received since returning, it looks as if you might need them here."

I stare at the dark-skinned warrior in front of me, his golden eyes kind and understanding, the tattoos that cover his body swirling with magic. A tear spills, running down my cheek.

"They took him."

Stepping forward, he cups my shoulders. "I have no doubt in my mind that you will find him again."

"How can you be so sure?"

"Because you, Everly, are the druid heir, the promised one, and you will not break."

His words sink in, lingering in the quiet spaces inside me.

"No, I won't break," I repeat.

"Okay, girl, you have a lot to catch us up on," Scarlett cuts in. Her voice is light, but I can hear the concern.

"Yes, we do," I agree, wiping away the tears.

Mia tilts her head as she stares at me. "Like how your eyes are a different color."

"Or the fact you have a tattoo on your face."

I grin. "You're really hung up on this tattoo, Scar."

"Well, yeah," Scarlett says in utter exasperation.

Nero clears his throat and bows deeply. "I have to return to the human realm for a bit, but I will be back in a few days to assist in any way I can."

"Thank you, Nero."

He gives me a wink. "You got this, Your Majesty." His golden gaze goes to my friends next. "Behave. Don't make me regret bringing you here." With that, he turns and leaves.

Scarlett and Mia's hands tightly grasp mine. "Your Majesty?" they echo, making me chuckle.

"Like you said, there's a lot to catch up on." I turn to face the dining table. "I apologize for the interruption, but I must leave. I appreciate you coming to show your respect for our former queen and those who lost their lives in the attack."

"This is unacceptable." Queen Anwyn stands from the table. "You can't leave halfway through the meal."

"Now, Mother, it's been a very long night. Let the princess rest," Alivar urges, taking a sip of his wine.

Queen Anwyn's face hardens as she turns to her son. "If you'd have found her first, then we wouldn't even be here."

"No, it would probably be you that was dead." Alivar downs the last of his wine and stands. He shoots me a wink that has my stomach fluttering before staring at his mother. "Everly is exactly where she needs to be. If it were I she was destined to meet, then I have no doubt we would have."

My heart melts at his words, and for some unexplainable reason, I want to throw my arms around him.

Nolan also stands, straightening out his coat, his cool gaze landing on the Seelie Queen. "After the stunt you pulled in the human realm, sending your nephew to kidnap that young girl, you have no right to criticize anyone, Your Majesty."

Nolan's words send a gasp through everyone gathered, and my attention goes to Alivar, but by the look on his face, he had no idea about this.

"I don't answer to you or anyone else in this room. I'm leaving!" Queen Anwyn declares.

"Don't let the door hit you on your way out," Scarlett mutters under her breath, unaware that the fae have extremely good hearing.

Queen Anwyn's sneer deepens, her lip curling as she looks over my friends with barely concealed disgust. There's a glint in her eyes, something cold and calculating, and though I have no idea what her magic can do, I can tell she's weighing her options. My instincts kick in—I take a smooth, measured step forward, cutting off her view, drawing her attention away from my friends.

"I would leave now while you're still in my good graces," I warn, my voice calm but filled with warning.

The room goes still at my words, tension tightening in the air. Everyone is frozen except Nolan, who, unfazed, steps forward with a formal bow. "Let me escort you out, Queen Anwyn," he urges, his tone polite but firm.

Queen Anwyn's violet eyes flash with spite, her gaze flickering over us one last time, cutting and scornful, before she turns to follow Nolan, her entourage trailing behind her. My heart races, though I keep my face impassive. I know better than to think this is over; Queen Anwyn doesn't seem like the kind to take defeat easily. The look she gave me as she left made one thing clear—I'll need to stay vigilant.

Alivar saunters over, the amusement clear in his gaze, his smirk unmistakably smug. "I'm proud of you," he murmurs, voice laced with a lazy drawl. "Not many would stand their ground against my mother."

My cheeks flush, but I manage a small smile. "Like you said, it's been a trying day. I'm done with drama for now."

Alivar's expression softens, and, to my surprise, he reaches for my hand. His fingers curl around mine as he lifts it to his mouth, his lips brushing my skin with a teasing gentleness. My pulse skips at the low growl from Raiden, who steps closer, his expression thunderous. "Don't test me, Alivar."

Alivar's smirk widens, a wicked gleam in his eye. I can see he's reveling in riling up my friends, enjoying the tension he's stirring. With a sigh, I slip my hand from his and step back, putting some space between us. Alivar doesn't miss a beat, his attention moving to my friends.

"These must be your friends from the human world I was told about." Alivar's tone is smooth but laced with intrigue. A knot tightens in my stomach as his attention shifts from me to the others.

"Yes, this is Mia," I reply, gesturing toward her, "and Scarlett."

Alivar inclines his head in acknowledgment, but his gaze lingers on Scarlett, a glint of curiosity sparking in his eyes. He takes a step closer, hand slowly reaching toward her fiery red hair. Scarlett's eyes narrow, and before his fingers get close, she jerks back. "Don't even think about touching me."

A slow, deliberate smile spreads across Alivar's face, dark and appreciative. "Such lovely creatures," he murmurs, the words almost a purr.

I step forward, narrowing the gap between us. "Will I see you tomorrow at training?"

"Why the rush, Princess?" he responds, tilting his head.

"You know why, Alivar," I growl, the heat of my temper rising, flushing my face. "I will not leave Maxon in the hands of that demon."

"SOOO much to talk about," Mia notes, her eyes flicking between me and Alivar.

A lump forms in my throat. God, I am tired. Mia and Scarlett—they're my safe space, a connection to something good and untouched by this world. But bringing them here feels like exposing them to dangers they don't even know exist.

Alivar stares at me for a moment longer, something unreadable in his gaze, then he turns on his heel.

"I will be back when I can," he says over his shoulder. "Though I have a feeling my mother will make things difficult for me. But I made you a promise, and I intend to keep it." With that, he strides out of the tent.

Kian leans closer, his lips quirking up. "Things have certainly turned interesting since you arrived, Princess," he muses with a hint of humor.

"Understatement," Tristan snorts.

Scarlett steps away from me, turning to take in the others, her gaze landing on Raiden. Her eyes widen as she takes in his towering form. Arms crossed over his chest, Raiden raises an eyebrow, an amused smirk tugging at his lips. I bite down on mine, stifling a laugh; I know exactly what she's seeing. The first time I met Raiden, I had the same reaction. His sheer size—broad and muscled, with massive, leathery wings folded at his back—is enough to make anyone pause. Two swords crossed on his back, and the sharp horns curving from his hairline only add to his formidable stance.

"Scarlett, Mia," I begin, gesturing toward him, "this is Raiden. He's the General of the Unseelie Armies, and a close friend of mine."

Scarlett stares a moment longer, then blurts, "You're huge!" Her cheeks flush as she claps a hand over her mouth.

Raiden's laugh rumbles out, rich and warm. He grins down at her, inclining his head in a mock bow. "Why, thank you."

I roll my eyes, stepping between them to link my arms with Mia and Scarlett. "And over here," I gesture to the others, "are Kian and Tristan."

Each of them nods in turn, their gazes assessing but welcoming.

Chapter Twenty-Two

Maxon

I jolt awake, frigid water slapping me in the face. Gasping for air, I struggle against the tight grip of the wyvern bones, feeling my breath being cut off as they constrict around my neck. I know I have to still my movements or they will continue to tighten, but it isn't easy to do.

A sharp, sinister laugh rings out through the small cavern, bouncing off the walls. I take deep, measured breaths, my chest rising and falling with each lungful.

When my vision finally clears, I see Yumekui standing just a few feet away, her arms crossed and a mischievous grin on her face. Next to her stands a small, hunched-over woman clutching a wooden pail in her hands, most likely the culprit who doused me with water under the instructions of the bitch demon before me.

"I can't have you getting rest, Maxon," she tsks.

A deep snarl rumbles from my throat, breaking free. The menacing sound resonates in the small space, making the small woman shrink back with a gasp.

Yumekui's light chuckle sends an unsettling shiver down my spine, like nails on a chalkboard. Her piercing red eyes scan me with unnerving precision. There's a glint in them—part amusement, part something darker, something ancient. She doesn't blink. Doesn't look away. Just watches.

A subtle curl tugs at the corner of her mouth, not quite a smile, more like the shadow of one. It's the kind of expression predators wear when they already know how the hunt ends.

Stepping forward, she delicately removes a kanzashi from her hair, causing her long, ebony locks to cascade around her. The kanzashi is long and sharp, its menacing edge still fresh in my memory from the day before.

"The Shadoweaver wishes to see you." She smirks.

A spasm runs through me tightening my muscles. "Good for him," I mutter. "Is he coming to me? Oh, wait. He can't."

"I know this must be difficult for you." Yumekui lets out a sigh, absently flipping her kanzashi between her fingers. "But it could be your beloved soul mate here instead. You know I had a taste of her blood, her magic. It was exquisite. I bet you are craving it, aren't you?"

The heat radiating from the fire in my chest intensifies, matching the fierce flames of my anger. I can feel my heartbeat pounding in my temples as the suppressed magic surges through my veins, yearning to be unleashed. The power I inherited from the dragons embedded in my core hums with an energy that threatens to consume me. Every breath I take feels like fire, as if my very existence is a catalyst for combustion. I grit my teeth, the pain coursing through me as the magic within me demands an outlet. It twists and turns, like a caged beast desperate to break free.

"It's burning you up from the inside, isn't it?" Yumekui tilts her head, eyes alight with fascination. "I can feel the dragon's fire flowing beneath your skin."

I take a deep breath, feeling the burden of each inhalation. "Fuck you."

"I wonder if this sudden flare in your dragon's power is due to Everly's return." She muses, tapping her chin with the kanzashi.

I stiffen, hands curling into fists as my eyes track the kanzashi. I want nothing more than to stab her in the eye with it.

"My magic was growing before she returned!"

Yumekui laughs softly. "Well, then, maybe the dragons are waking from their millennia-long slumber. Perhaps they sense the building tension, the darkness that is leaking across the plains."

The air crackles with an eerie sense of awareness as her words hang in the air.

"Perhaps," I mutter.

According to ancient folklore, these dragons are not mere beasts, but revered beings of immense wisdom and strength. The presence of dragons is a symbol of prosperity and protection, their very existence a sign of divine favor upon the kingdom.

"They had once aligned themselves with the royal families, creating a bond that was both mystical and unbreakable," she smiled, her gaze sweeping over me. "But where are they now?"

The alliance was marked by a shared magic, a unique power that flowed between the dragons and those of royal blood, granting them extraordinary abilities.

Yet, despite their grandeur and significance, the dragons vanished without a trace. No one could remember the exact moment they disappeared or the events that led to their sudden absence. It was as if one day they were there, soaring above the mountains and valleys, and the next day they were gone, leaving behind only legends and a lingering sense of loss. The magic that had once flowed so freely in the veins of the royal bloodline faded with their departure, diminishing over the centuries to a faint echo of its former glory. Alivar and I seem to be the first who possess the unique ability to harness the dragons' magical elemental energy in generations.

Some believed that the dragons had been betrayed by the very families they had sworn to protect, driven away by greed and corruption. Others thought they simply went into hibernation. But no one knew the truth, and the dragons became nothing more than myth, their stories slowly fading into darkness.

If the dragons are awakening and returning, it would mean the dawn of a new era—one that could reshape the world as we know it. I can feel Yumekui studying me, silently evaluating the extent of my knowledge. Those crimson eyes searching, looking for a crack in my shields.

Suddenly, her face transforms, and a mischievous grin spreads across her lips. "Right, better not keep the master of darkness waiting."

Before I can register her movements, a harsh blow lands to the side of my head and the world abruptly plunges into an inky blackness.

Chapter Twenty-Three

Everly

The next night, I lie in my bed, the exhaustion from the long journey settling heavily into my bones. The headache from yesterday has returned, along with the throbbing in my jaw. Maybe I should see the healer and get a tonic to help me rest. Since Maxon was taken, I've barely been able to get more than a few restless hours a night. I sigh, rolling onto my back as I stare at the ceiling. The lantern beside my bed flickers softly, casting shadows along the walls, but my mind is still too restless to succumb to sleep.

During the ride back, I filled Scarlett and Mia in on everything that had happened. I can still picture their wide-eyed stares, their barely restrained questions. They were both captivated by Zaria and Asrai. Both demanded to stay with me until all this was over. I didn't expect them to react that way. If anything, I thought they'd be trying to drag me home.

But as I recounted the story, they leaned in, absorbing every detail.

Then came the questions I'd been half-dreading.

"You're not . . . human?" Scarlett asked, her voice quiet, as though the words were almost foreign on her tongue.

I gave a half shrug, feeling the weight of the truth settle in. "Apparently not. But I still don't remember much from my past—just fragments here and there. It's like trying to grasp fog."

Mia reached over, squeezing my hand reassuringly. "We'll help you piece it together."

Despite the heaviness in my heart, her words kindled a spark of gratitude. I don't know if I'll ever uncover every piece of my past, or if I even want to.

Now lying in the dim light, my thoughts grow heavier and more suffocating by the second. Maxon's absence gnaws at me, leaving an emptiness that throbs like an open wound. Time seems to stretch in the fae realm, and although I have only been here briefly, it feels like a lifetime due to the multitude of events that have unfolded.

My thoughts become a relentless tide, consumed by him, every sense sharpened as if to conjure his presence. I try my best to push it away, but my mind betrays me, replaying the smallest details—his voice, smooth and captivating, echoes through my head like a melody I can't silence. His scent lingers faintly on the pillow beside me, drawing a fresh ache to the surface, and the urge to cry presses hard against my chest.

"Maxon, please let me in."

Every inch of my body yearns to be intertwined with his, to feel his weight pressed against me. The mere thought of his hands exploring my skin sends shivers cascading down my spine, igniting a fire that burns low in my belly.

I squirm against the sheets. The indescribable need that rushes through me is raw and visceral, a primal force that demands to be acknowledged.

Closing my eyes, I focus solely on our bond. I follow the thread that binds us together, determined to reach him. My hair trails behind me as I float through the ominous darkness.

In the depths of my mind, fear gnaws at me, but I grit my teeth, casting it aside and pressing forward. I clutch the golden thread and gently pull on it, observing how it softly glows and shimmers in the darkness. A heartbeat, pulsating in the distance, travels down the thread and reverberates within the depths of my core.

Maxon!

I surge forward, following that golden thread, hope pounding in my chest. Suddenly, I'm stopped in my tracks, the impact knocking the wind from me as I collide with an invisible barrier. My fingertips gently glide along the cool surface, trying to find a weak spot.

What the hell?

I can see the thread, our thread. It's visible in the distance, taunting me with its presence, yet I'm unable to move any closer.

Tears well up in my eyes, stinging and blurring my vision, as I angrily slam my fist against the wall. "Maxon, let me in!"

A flicker of light dances along the thread, and a surge of hope washes over me.

"Maxon!"

The wall trembles under my palms, and I know he can hear me. The wall begins to give way, and pressure builds behind my eyes.

I take a step forward and the wall trembles as it allows me closer. Then, out of nowhere, an intense, vibrating pain courses through the bond. I double over as the pain steals my breath, leaving me gasping for air. Just as quickly as it fell, the wall reinforces itself, cutting off my access to him.

"No!"

I'm suddenly sucked from the void, and I jerk upright in bed, a light sheen of sweat covering my body. I rub my hand over my chest, a sob working its way up my throat.

What are they doing to him?

Chapter Twenty-Four

Maxon

I wake to the disorienting sensation of being tugged upright. The sack that has been placed over my head is suffocating, filling my nose with the stench of damp fabric, making it hard to breathe.

As I stand, my legs feel like they might give out at any moment, and my head is throbbing intensely, like a war drum. My wrists are now cuffed tightly behind my back, with the bones pressing into my skin with unyielding force. These bones are worse than any iron I've come in contact with. The fact that they tighten periodically is a fucking nightmare, draining me of my sanity.

"Move!" Yumekui's voice slices through the muffled darkness, her tone harsh and biting.

I barely have time to steady myself before she shoves me in the back, the force making me stumble forward.

My boots scuff the stone floor, the uneven ground making it hard to navigate blindly.

As we walk, the air gets colder, heavier, and it smells different—like iron, like blood.

Hunger gnaws at me, making my gums ache, and stomach tighten. I need food, or preferably blood, so I can heal. My mouth is dry, my throat raw, and I can't shake the ringing in my ears. I stumble again, but this time, I catch myself, a growl escaping my lips as I grit my teeth. Yumekui's hand clamps down on my shoulder, steadying me with a mocking laugh.

The walk feels like it goes on forever, the sounds around me are muted but revealing—a door groans open heavily, distant footsteps create echoes off the cave walls, and the clinking of chains can be heard in the distance.

"Here we are," Yumekui purrs, and with a quick yank, the sack is pulled from my head.

Before I can get my bearings, she kicks the back of my knees, and I go down hard, pain shooting up my legs. Breathing through the agony, I clench my jaw, feeling my muscles tense. Being unable to heal, my injuries amplify every sensation of torture coursing through my body.

Adjusting to the light, I blink a few times, trying to clear the blurriness from my eyes. Kneeling in the expansive cavern, Yumekui looms behind me, gripping the chain that tethers me like a degrading leash. I glare over my shoulder at her, and she is slow to smile, her eyes betraying her unease. Despite her strong posture and outward stance, I can see the fear lurking in her eyes.

I direct my attention back in front of me and survey the immense cavern. Torches line the walls, their warm glow illuminating the room and highlighting the peculiar carvings etched on its surface. I don't see anyone else. Is this where the Shadoweaver is imprisoned?

The silence reigns around me, and I shift my position, earning a tug on the chain. I take a deep breath and wait, opening up my senses. I can feel movement in the cavern and slowly look around. I notice a flicker in the torches to my left, and shadows seem to amass there. I don't look toward the disruption, instead keeping my gaze fixed straight ahead.

"Prince Maxon," a disembodied voice murmurs from the dark shadows that are slowly creeping closer. "Or should I say king?"

I grind my teeth together, remaining silent.

"So good to have you here. How are you enjoying your stay?" The mocking voice fades on the air with a laugh.

The shadows around the cavern move unnaturally, making my pulse quicken. A surge of apprehension pulses in time with the pounding in my chest as the air grows colder, thicker.

The mass of shadows begins to take form, solidifying from the darkness into something far more menacing. At first, it's just a swirling black fog, but then it starts to stretch and twist, growing arms, legs, a silhouette that looms over me like a dark god.

The Shadoweaver.

I heard stories about him when I was just a child. Tales meant to frighten, to keep us in line. *Stay out of the woods at night or the Shadoweaver will come for you.* Back then, I thought he was just a myth—a terrifying cautionary tale. I knew there was truth to the tales, but never in all my nightmares did I think I'd ever face him. The monster from the dark, the one who devours souls and leaves nothing but hollow, broken husks in his wake.

I blink, trying to get my eyes to adjust. His form has taken on something almost human in shape, but there's nothing remotely human about the evil radiating from him. Eyes—if you could call them that—glow faintly from the shadowy mass, two slits of pale light that pierce through the gloom, staring right at me, into me. My skin prickles, and an icy chill grips my spine, freezing me in place.

An oppressive darkness pulses outward from him, rolling like waves of ink, suffocating every bit of light in its path.

And then he steps forward. Only—it's not him.

The shadows cling to the figure's footsteps, swirling at their feet like dark tendrils, but the silhouette that emerges from the inky blackness isn't the monstrous form I've been bracing for. It's . . . a woman.

My mind stutters to a halt, momentarily scrambling to process what I'm seeing. This isn't what the legends said. The Shadoweaver is a man—an ancient, faceless creature born of the darkest corners of the world, not—this. Yet here she is, stepping through the thick veil of darkness as if she commands it. As if the shadows themselves are woven into the very fabric of her being.

Her figure is tall and slender, draped in dark, flowing robes that ripple like smoke around her as she moves. Her hair is a cascade of midnight, blending into the shadows, and her eyes—those eyes—glow with a faint, eerie light, watching me with an intensity that makes my skin crawl.

My heart pounds in my ears.

"Surprise," she taunts with a wicked, almost playful smile, her voice dripping with a sinister amusement that makes my blood run cold.

Her arms sweep out to her sides in a grand, theatrical motion, the darkness shifting and swirling with her as if the shadows themselves are bowing to her command. Her dress clings to her body like a second skin, each curve and line accentuated, though there's nothing remotely alluring about it. The dress covers every inch of her from the neck down, excluding her hands. It shimmers in the low light, catching faint glints of silver and shadow, its surface rippling like water with every slight movement she makes.

With a twisted smile, her eyes lock onto mine, and the icy chill that follows sends a shiver down my spine. There's something in her gaze, something that flickers just beneath the surface—control, power, dominance.

"Cat got your tongue?" she teases, stepping closer, reaching for my face.

I jerk back, my eyes narrowing on her. "Why the charade? Why make everyone think you were male?"

"Everyone just assumed." She shrugs. The movement seems odd on her, almost unnatural, like she is trying too hard to seem unbothered. "I never corrected them because males seem to hold more power and respect. You're one of the lucky few to see my true form. Most only see the shadows."

"Lucky me," I mutter.

The Shadoweaver narrows her gaze on me, her form flickering. She is weakening. Her display earlier was a show, but I can feel it now—her magic is dwindling.

"I have a bone to pick with you, young king."

I raise an eyebrow, waiting for her to continue.

"You ruined my carefully laid plans."

"How so?"

"The night you rescued the druid, my beast was lying in wait to snatch her up. Yumekui was tracking her, just like before. But you stole her before we could get to her. I need her. Her blood is the key to unlocking the tomb. You know that."

I cast a quick look over my shoulder to see Yumekui kneeling, her head bowed. That's why she's being so quiet. "If it was just her blood, you would have had it by now."

The Shadoweaver's eyes flicker with light, her lips pursing.

"You know, back when I was free, I ruled all of Faerie. There was none more powerful than me." She walked at a slow pace around me as she spoke. "I ruled over all of Aos sí."

I frown at her use of the ancient word. We haven't been called the Aos sí in centuries.

"You all descend from the Tuatha Dé Danann. You were whispered to be the most powerful of the fae. Well, it was those strongest of you, the druids and Guardians, who saw fit to use their magic to overthrow me, trapping me in this tomb. They handed Faerie over to the other Aos sí, in which a dual monarchy was born, two courts, the Seelie and the Unseelie Court. Almost every Aos sí member belonged to one of the courts and held a title. Those, like the druids, that decided against a court, went off on their own, separate from the court system. The Guardians also refused to fall into the court system, abandoning the Aos sí, taking the dragons with them, vanishing into the mists like they were never there at all. Their departure left chaos among the courts, uncertainty in every corner of the realm. The druids, ever so cautious, retreated to their sacred havens, hiding behind their ancient wards. It took centuries of waiting for the perfect moment to arise." Her voice is steady, calculating, as she speaks, the shadows swirling around her like serpents ready to strike.

"I had felt her before any of you did," she continues, her tone darkening with satisfaction. "When her magic first began to stir, to blossom. The way it surged, wild and untamed, it called out to me. She was the key—the one who could get me out of this prison, so I could reclaim what was rightfully mine. My throne."

She pauses, her eyes narrowing as she watches for a reaction. But I don't give her one.

"Finally, I could make my move. With the Guardians gone and the druids in hiding, I turned my attention to the Aos sí, to the kings and queens who thought they were safe behind their walls and titles." Her lips curl into a sly, malicious smile. "It was easy, really, poisoning their minds. They were so desperate for answers, for control, that they didn't even notice the shadows slipping into their courts, whispering doubts, twisting loyalties. Fear makes people so . . . pliable."

There's a glint of triumph in her gaze, as if she's already won. She takes a slow step forward, her black dress clinging to her like a second skin.

"But your father—ah, he was a different story," her voice drops to a low, dangerous purr. "He was harder to break. Stubborn, like a rock standing against the tide. I expected nothing less from him, of course. The proud king, the protector. He didn't fall as easily as the others. Oh, no. He put up a fight. A real one."

Every word she says feels like it's dripping with venom, each syllable sharp and deliberate, designed to wound. There's a flicker of something behind her eyes—amusement, maybe, or perhaps just cold satisfaction.

"That was you? You made them all turn on the druids?" I growl, letting my words rumble.

"Yes, it was the perfect plan. Have them all kill each other, and I could swoop in and rescue the princess, but that druid queen had to send her daughter through a Sidhe gate and ruin everything."

"You're delusional."

Suddenly, I'm lifted from the floor, my body sailing through the air and slamming into the cave wall with jarring force. I hit the ground hard; the wind knocked from my lungs.

As I lie here, a thought hits me. "You need her willing. That's why you tried to orchestrate having Yumekui rescue her under false pretense to bring her here."

The Shadoweaver's eyes snap to mine. "Clever boy. Yes, I need her to willingly unlock the tomb using her blood and magic combined."

Chapter Twenty-Five

Everly

I open my chamber doors and step out into the corridor. Nymeria and Anika immediately push past me, bounding down the hall, their tails flicking as they disappear down the staircase. I smile faintly, watching them vanish before I catch sight of Lutin and Senka standing a few paces away.

"Your Majesty," Lutin greets me, surprised. "What are you doing up so early? It's barely dawn."

"I couldn't sleep," I reply, letting out a sigh.

Senka glances at me, her gaze soft yet cautious. "Can I fetch something for you?"

I shake my head, closing the chamber doors behind me. I'm dressed in my training clothes, the snug material wrapping comfortably around me, allowing for movement while providing protection. The leathers overlaying the fabric gives an added layer of defense, and my daggers are strapped securely to my hip and thigh.

"I need to start my training," I reply, pushing my long braid over my shoulder.

Lutin and Senka exchange glances, their concern evident, but I ignore it, setting off down the hall. My boots echo in the stillness, a surge of determination coursing through me.

"There's too much at stake, and I can't afford to waste a single moment," I murmur, my fingers curling into my palms as I walk.

Without a word, Lutin and Senka fall into step beside me, and we silently make our way through the castle.

A few maids and guards give us curious looks but say nothing as we head outside.

"Do you wish to train in the gardens or in the arena?" Lutin asks.

"The arena."

My magic stirs as we walk through the gardens, the flowers waking from their slumber and blooming around me, filling the air with an intoxicating sweet scent. As the sun peaks over the horizon, my magic responds to the vibrant energy surrounding me, and an array of colors burst across the sky, turning it from dark blue into a canvas of pink and orange. Every step forward fills me with a sense of purpose. I am going to get better. I have to get better. I will make myself stronger—not just for my sake, but for everyone who's counting on me. For those who have already sacrificed so much.

I can't afford to let fear hold me back.

I can't let hesitation or self-doubt keep me from doing what needs to be done.

Too many people are relying on me, and I will not let them down. Now, more than ever, I need to step up.

The arena is eerily quiet when we arrive, with just two soldiers engaging in a practice duel, their movements the only sign of life.

I feel somewhat disoriented without Kian by my side. However, both he and Tristan are currently serving as Mia and Scarlett's bodyguards at my request.

Biting my lip, I move toward the weapon area, taking in the impressive selection. Archery might be a good choice for today. I haven't done it since that one time at school, and from what I remember, I wasn't too bad at it.

Senka approaches and stands beside me.

"You need to get used to holding a sword," Senka says, her tone matter-of-fact. "Personally, I find wielding two at a time easier than just one."

"Really?"

Senka shrugs and flips her dark ponytail over her shoulder. "It balances me."

An idea sparks, and I can't help but ask, "Would you spar with me?"

Her eyes widen slightly as she glances over at Lutin, who's watching with an amused grin.

"Go on," he encourages. "Help our future queen become a warrior."

Senka considers me for a moment, then inclines her head. "Alright."

Lutin strides over to the weapons rack, picking out two straight, double-edged practice blades. He hands them to me, his grin widening. "Just focus on blocking. Nothing fancy."

"Got it," I say, dipping my head, but my stomach twists with nerves. I've been in a battle, and I've trained with Kian, yet something about sparring one-on-one with Senka feels intimidating.

I turn to face her, watching as she removes her jacket and readies her twin blades, gripping them with an ease that speaks to years of practice. Her stance is confident and balanced.

We begin circling each other, our eyes locked. There's a flicker of challenge in her gaze, and I feel myself rising to meet it. With a quick, fluid motion, she steps forward, her arm slicing through the air. I instinctively raise my left arm, intercepting her blade just in time. The clang of metal rings out, and for a moment, I think I've managed to hold her off.

But Senka doesn't retreat. She smoothly swings her other sword, stepping in closer, leaving me with no time to adjust. The second blade is arcing toward me from the side, and I realize I have to move fast.

I twist, angling my other sword to block her strike. The force of the blow vibrates up my arm, but I hold my ground. Senka smiles, her gaze sharp with approval. There's no time to savor it; she's already shifting, pressing forward with a series of rapid attacks, testing my reflexes and forcing me to move, to react without hesitating.

I try to mimic her fluidity, focusing on blocking each strike as she presses me backward. My eyes follow each movement.

"Try to predict where she is going to strike before she does," Lutin calls out. "If you can read your opponent, you'll have the advantage."

But her movements are swift, relentless, and I feel my muscles burning as I adjust to her pace. I manage to deflect another hit, stepping to the side, and for a split second, I think I see an opening.

Taking a deep breath, I lunge forward, aiming a cautious strike toward her side. But she anticipates the move, twisting gracefully out of reach and countering with a quick swing of her blade that I barely manage to parry.

"Not bad," she remarks with a smirk, but there's a hint of pride in her eyes.

My heart is pounding, and adrenaline courses through me as I continue to match her strikes. I can feel my confidence growing with each block and counter. Senka's pace slows just a fraction, her movements a little more deliberate now, guiding rather than overwhelming. She's pushing me to think, to adapt to her rhythm.

"Good," she praises. "Stay focused. Don't let your guard down, not even for a second."

I nod, breathing hard, my senses sharper than ever. The thrill of wielding the blades, of holding my ground against someone as skilled as Senka thrums through me. We continue, the clash of steel filling the air, until finally, Senka steps back, lowering her swords.

"That was impressive," she remarks, her tone genuine. "You've got potential."

I can't help but smile. The praise fills me with joy. "Potential?"

"Yes. You need to work on your footwork. It's sloppy, but I'm surprised with how well you can handle a sword."

"Thank you for sparring with me."

Lutin claps from the sidelines. "You're getting there, My Queen."

I turn to smile at him, and a flash of red hair catches my eye as Gideon barrels into the arena, skillfully dodging around soldiers who are deep in their sparring. How have I not noticed the arena filling up?

Gideon's face is flushed as he stops in front of me, bowing slightly before speaking.

"Your Majesty, the blacksmith is here to see you," he pants, catching his breath as he straightens up.

"Me?" I wipe the sweat from my forehead with the back of my hand.

"Yes, Your Majesty," he confirms.

"Can you bring him over?"

Gideon nods and immediately hurries off, his red hair disappearing behind the edge of the training grounds as quickly as he'd appeared.

I walk over to the table and grab a glass of water, savoring the coolness as I take a long drink. The sun is high now, and the birds are singing, the garden calling to me, but I'm determined to get in as much training as possible.

The sound of footsteps draws my attention, and I turn to see the blacksmith approaching, his broad shoulders silhouetted against the bright sunlight. His face is a mixture of purpose and reverence as he walks toward me with two fae boys in tow, each holding the handle to a large trunk between them. I set down my water glass and take a step forward, my curiosity piqued.

"Your Majesty," he greets me with a respectful bow, one hand fisted of his heart.

I blink in surprise. "You're a faun," I blurt and slap a hand over my mouth, embarrassment heating my cheeks. "I apologize."

A boisterous laugh rumbles from the blacksmith, his hazel eyes shining with mirth. "No apologies needed, Your Highness. I'm the blacksmith in Skora."

"Yes. George, right?"

It's his turn to look surprised. "You know my name?"

"Maxon took me into Skora, and we passed by your forge. It had some beautiful pieces. You're very talented."

George's eyes grow wide. "That truly means a lot, coming from the Druid Heir." He bows.

I smile, a warmth invading my cheeks at his kindness. "You wanted to see me?"

"That I did. I have something for you. When I saw you at the king's crowning, I had a vision."

I tilt my head to the side, the faint scent of pine needles tickling my nose as he steps closer.

"A vision?"

"Yes." He turns and gestures for two young fae boys to approach. The markings on the wood give me pause. They are mine and Maxon's marks. My hand drifts to my face, tracking over the markings there, as the two of them place the trunk on the ground. Out of the corner of my eye, I notice Lutin and Senka step closer as George opens it.

He pulls out a chest plate with a heart-shaped neckline, adorned with dark green metallic plating that mimics the intricate look of leaves. Delicate, twisting golden vines are embossed along its surface, weaving gracefully across the chest and down the torso, blending seamlessly into a layer of detailed leaves that appear almost alive. The leafy embellishments extend along the edges of the armor, giving it a natural, forest-like aesthetic, as if it were crafted from living plants.

"The design is both elegant and formidable, blending the essence of nature with the unyielding strength of armor," he declares.

I'm completely speechless. Stepping forward, I glide my fingers over the golden vines, feeling their smooth, intricate texture beneath my fingertips.

"This is stunning," I whisper in awe.

George beams with pride. "It is a gift."

He gestures for the men to bring forward more pieces. One of them holds up a set of shoulder guards, spiked and angular, adding an edge of fierceness to the enchanting armor. The other presents a pair of forearm guards, each crafted with the same exquisite ornamental metalwork that ties the set together.

"This is too much," I breathe, words lost in my astonishment. "How much do I owe you?" I glance up at George, still in disbelief at the beauty of the armor.

"Nothing. This is my gift to you," he replies warmly.

Before I can protest, he steps forward, lifting the chest plate with gentle hands. "Let's try it on."

I hand my glass to Lutin, who takes it without a word, his eyes also fixed on the armor. George carefully fits the chest plate around my torso, adjusting it with care as I lift my arms slightly. The shoulder guards are fastened next, and then the arm guards. Each piece fits perfectly, as though crafted to match my form alone.

"It's so light." I move my arms and marvel at the weightlessness of the armor. "It doesn't even feel like I have anything on."

George's grin widens. "Exactly. That's the magic of it."

I return his smile, feeling an overwhelming sense of gratitude.

"One more thing," George says, his voice tinged with excitement. He turns and bends down, reaching into a chest beside him. When he stands again, he holds a sword, its silver blade gleaming in the sunlight. He turns back to me, holding it in my direction. "The king came by and asked that I make you a sword as a wedding gift."

Emotion wells up in my throat, nearly overwhelming me as I take in the craftsmanship, the blade reflecting rays of light like liquid silver. Golden symbols matching the design of our mate mark are etched along the length of the blade. The hilt gleams with a burnished gold finish, adorned with an intricate crossguard.

The gesture from Maxon, and from George, means more than words can express, and I feel a lump forming in my throat. I reach out to take the sword, feeling its weight, its power, as I cradle it in my hands.

"That is a gorgeous sword," Senka marvels in awe.

"Fit for a queen," Lutin agrees.

Tears line my eyes, and I glance up at George. "I don't know what to say," I whisper.

I never grew up receiving gifts, especially for no reason, but this is overwhelming.

"All I ask is that you wear this when you slay the Shadoweaver."

Chapter Twenty-Six

Everly

"Your Majesty, you've been out here for three hours. I think you should eat something," Lutin weaves a careful mix of concern and formality into his words. There's a faint crease of worry in his brow as he watches me wave goodbye to George.

The thought of food sends a wave of nausea through me, twisting my stomach into knots. Everything tastes different since Maxon was taken. The once-appealing flavor of sweets now holds no allure for me.

"Okay, you're probably right. Besides," I continue with a faint grin, "I should probably save Tristan and Kian from my friends."

At this, Senka and Lutin exchange confused looks.

"Faerie is in for a shock with those two," I add as I start walking toward the castle.

Tristan thought I was trouble. Oh, he has no idea.

Scarlett is a force of nature—a fiery whirlwind of confidence and biting retorts.

If she hasn't already cornered him in an intense debate about something trivial, I'd be surprised.

And then there's Mia. Sweet, diplomatic Mia. She's the voice of reason, the one who steps in to smooth things over when Scarlett inevitably crosses a line or takes things too far. Kian might be faring slightly better than Tristan, but only because he's the more adaptable of the two.

As we leave through the gates, a few guards and soldiers bow or nod in greeting as I walk past. Their expressions are a mix of deference and curiosity.

I return the gestures, a little awkwardly, feeling my cheeks heat in the process. The attention is still something I'm getting used to, and while their respect is appreciated, it's also slightly overwhelming. I quicken my pace, seeking refuge in the familiar serenity of the garden.

The moment my feet touch the soft paths winding through the greenery, I feel the tension in my shoulders ease. The garden is alive with quiet energy, a harmony of scents and sounds that always manages to ground me.

"E!" Scarlett's voice cuts through the tranquility, vibrant as ever. My head snaps up, and I spot her and Mia walking toward me.

Trailing slightly behind them are Kian and Tristan, and I have to stifle a laugh at their expressions. Kian looks amused, his lavender eyes sparkling, whereas Tristan looks decidedly disgruntled, his usual composed demeanor replaced with a faint scowl.

I grin, unable to hide my amusement and head toward them. My fingers trail lightly over the leaves and petals of the plants lining the path. Each touch sends a ripple of connection through me, magic pulsing in gentle waves. The garden responds to my presence, the faint hum of life growing louder in my mind as my body and spirit attune to the nature surrounding me.

By the time I reach them, I can feel the subtle buzz of energy dancing at my fingertips.

"Having fun?" My grin widens as I glance from Scarlett's mischievous smirk to Tristan's unimpressed glare.

"Oh, absolutely," Scarlett replies, her tone dripping with mock innocence. "We were just getting to know your friends here."

"Fascinating company," Mia adds with a soft smile.

Kian chuckles under his breath, clearly enjoying whatever torment Scarlett has inflicted, while Tristan mutters something too low for me to catch but enough to make Scarlett's grin grow sharper.

I laugh, shaking my head as I step closer. "I see you've made quite the impression."

Scarlett winks. "Naturally."

Tristan sighs, pinching the bridge of his nose as if summoning patience. "Princess, your friends are . . . unique."

"Unique is one word for it." Kian smirks.

"Why aren't you training?" a low growl comes from my left. The tone is piercing, clipped, and unmistakably angry. "Valric is waiting for you in the grand hall."

I turn abruptly, startled by the voice, and find Fenris storming toward me. His strides are long and purposeful, his dark eyes blazing with irritation. My heart races, a blend of anxiety and my own irritation. But I stand my ground, crossing my arms and lifting my chin. Princess or not, I will not tolerate being spoken to in such a manner.

"He never informed me he would be here," I reply defensively, the edge in my voice matching the heat rising in my cheeks.

Fenris halts just a few steps away, his gaze narrowing. "Well, I'm informing you now. So go."

"Excuse me?" I growl, my voice low and challenging. My magic stirs faintly beneath my skin, as if deciding it doesn't like his tone either.

His eyes flash as he takes a step closer. "Are you hard of hearing?"

Before I can reply, a flash of red streaks into my vision, cutting between us like a blade. Scarlett plants herself squarely in front of me, her fiery hair blazing in the sunlight like a warning, her posture tense and brimming with protective energy.

"Hey, buddy," she warns, her voice sharp enough to cut. "Who the fuck do you think you are, talking to her like that? I hear she's your princess, not your slave."

A mix of exasperation and gratitude bubbles up inside me.

Fenris bristles, his jaw tightening as he looks down at Scarlett. "This is none of your concern, human," he snaps, his tone low and dangerous.

Scarlett doesn't so much as flinch. Instead, she crosses her arms, mirroring my earlier stance, and leans forward slightly. "Oh, I think it is. You see, Everly happens to be my best friend. And I don't take kindly to anyone—especially some arrogant fae prick—talking to her like she's dirt."

For a moment, Fenris looks utterly stunned, clearly unused to anyone standing up to him.

"And she has been training in the arena since dawn," Lutin pipes in, earning a sharp glare from Fenris.

Fenris's dark brown eyes pierce mine as he stares at me over Scarlett's head. There's flashes of violet flickering in his irises, he must be really powerful. I can see why they have him patrolling the borders of the Outlands.

"Scarlett," I interject softly, placing a hand on her shoulder. "It's fine. I can handle this."

Her head turns and her eyes linger on me for a second before she huffs and steps aside, though she doesn't go far.

I take a step forward, closing the space between Fenris and me. "You don't get to storm over here and bark orders at me, Fenris." I keep my voice steady despite the adrenaline coursing through me. "I'll meet Valric when I'm ready, not when you decide."

Having his full attention fixed on me has my fight or flight response in high gear, and I do my best not to fidget under his intense gaze. After a tense moment, he turns on his heel and stalks off, leaving the charged air behind him.

Scarlett immediately breaks the silence with a low whistle. "Damn, E. That was badass. Who knew being in Faerie would give you the courage to stand up to a bully?"

I exhale, letting the tension leave my shoulders. "Thanks."

"You're welcome." Scarlett grins. "But if that guy keeps pulling this crap, I'm decking him. Royal guard or not."

I look over at Tristan, whose face is etched with worry as he watches Fenris storm off. His vibrant purple eyes meet mine, confusion clouding their depths, and he shrugs.

"I'm starting to think I cursed his family or something," I mutter.

"Don't take it personally, Princess," Kian says. "Since the attack, he's been distant and cold with everyone."

My gaze falls to the ground, and with a sigh, my fingers work their way through my long braid, undoing it. "I really wanted to go into Skora today to help repair the village."

“Really?” Senka’s voice pipes up, shocked.

I turn my head to the side and frown at her. “Yes. They need help, right?”

“Well, sure, but you're a princess,” she continues slowly.

My frown deepens at the unexpected response.

“How about Scarlett and I go into the village to see what help they need, and you go do whatever this Valric is wanting?” Mia suggests, her hand finding mine and squeezing.

Chapter Twenty-Seven

Everly

"Your magic is instinctive, driven by your will and emotions," Valric explains, his eyes steady on mine. "It has always come naturally to you, which is lucky, because you were never one to sit and focus on spell work or incantations as a child."

I snort softly, unable to help myself. "I can't imagine most children would focus on spell work."

His lips curl into a small, knowing grin. "Perhaps not. But you were different. By the age of two, you were already showing signs of powerful magic. Your magic and the natural world around you were deeply intertwined, almost inseparable. Your parents did their best to keep it under control, to shield you—and themselves—but people talk. By age four, you could do just as much, if not more, than your mother."

I blink, my mind racing back to distant, fragmented memories. "I remember that day in Pinehelm," I admit quietly, almost to myself. "The entire forest came to my aid." The words catch in my throat, and I quickly swallow the lump threatening to form.

Valric nods, his expression softening, but his tone remains firm. "You were brave. Your actions saved you that day."

"But I condemned my parents."

His eyes glimmer with sympathy, but he doesn't flinch. My eyes drift to the scar running down the side of his face—a silent reminder of his own sacrifices that night.

After a long pause, he speaks again. "Druids have always been deeply connected to the earth, the plants and animals. You are the last of the royal bloodline, your magic is deeper, stronger than you think. I know you feel it, especially when you're outside, that tingle of magic under your skin."

My head bobs, my fingers gliding over the smooth, emerald-green silk of the dress. The rich fabric shines faintly in the light, a welcome contrast to the gritty sparring clothes I just discarded. I hadn't wanted to meet Valric looking like I'd just crawled out of a battlefield. Magic demands focus, and it's hard to concentrate feeling like you reek of sweat and exhaustion.

The dress isn't extravagant, its design simple yet elegant, cinching just enough at the waist to flatter my figure without being restrictive. Practicality still rules my choices. And there's something about the deep green that makes me feel powerful, connected.

"But unlike other druids, you have been more in tune with the animals, yes, some could understand animals and other species, like your mother, but for you it came naturally, you bonded with almost anything that crossed your path. Then you took it a step further and were able to work with natural elements. You created a connection with the wind and water spirits. Which is extraordinary for a child, as this was something that isn't learned until adolescence."

I frown, brushing a loose strand of hair behind my ear. "The elements?"

"Yes, water, air, earth. But you only ever displayed a talent for water and earth. The water spirits took a liking to you, but you've never been able to wield fire. I think it is because of its destructive nature. That was never you."

My mind goes back to when I summoned that wall of water in the bathroom, and the shock I felt when I realized it was my magic causing it.

I take a deep breath, memories stirring—both exciting and terrifying. All the times the breeze and wind have guided me since arriving back here, the gentle brushes across my skin as if soothing me, was that the air spirits trying to connect with me?

"Tell me what you have managed to do with your magic since returning, and what you were feeling when it happened?"

I settle into one of the plush chairs around a small table, sinking into the soft cushions as I think of where to start.

"Well, the first time I really noticed anything happening was when the Vuriens attacked me. I created a dome of vines," I begin, my voice soft. "It encased Maxon and me. I just wanted them to stop hurting him, to protect us both. And then—" I shake my head, struggling to put the experience into words. "I didn't even think about it. The vines just . . . responded."

Valric's head dips, silent encouragement urging me on. "And what else?"

I hesitate, skipping over some of the more personal memories—the bond with Maxon, the Renascitur, those private moments. Instead, I let my mind drift to the intensity of the battle in Skora.

"In Skora, during the battle, I commanded the earth and the plants, with a single thought," I tell him, feeling the pulse of that moment as if I'm reliving it. "It's like I knew exactly what I wanted to happen, and the earth responded. I feel more connected with the earth." My eyes return to Valric. "When Yumekui took me, I remember struggling to keep hold of my magic. At one point, I thought about warriors with bows and arrows. It was a fleeting thought, a flash of an image, four figures standing strong beside me. And then . . . they came to life. Four women, made of sticks and vines, each with a bow and arrow drawn, all ready to protect me." My eyes find Valric again. The realization of it is still raw, almost surreal. "I hadn't meant to summon them."

"You said you had trouble keeping hold of the magic. What do you mean?"

"It was . . . I don't know, like I was drained, like I'd used too much all at once. There was barely a spark left by the time Maxon arrived and took over the fight. I could hardly stand, let alone wield anything powerful enough to make a difference. I was useless—I couldn't save him or Rayna. And I was terrified because . . . because I thought it was gone." I swallow over the lump in my throat. "I thought I'd lost it for good when I was in the Winter Court, but it wasn't that. It was Felix. He'd been blocking my magic the whole time."

Valric's eyes are lined with sympathy. "You haven't used your magic in a long time. It was locked away from you in the human world. Remember, you and your magic are one and are slowly becoming reacquainted. It will take time, but you never need to force your magic to rise. It's more coaxing it to life."

I nod, leaning against the table and tracing the patterns on the surface of the wood. Valric stands and opens the balcony doors, and immediately a soft warm breeze enters, wrapping around me as if trying to comfort me. I close my eyes and smile, feeling the stir of magic under my skin.

"Show me something," Valric implores in a soft voice.

My fingertips tingle as the sweet smell of roses infiltrates my senses. I envision a riot of vibrant roses, their petals unfurling and reaching, transforming this room into a fragrant paradise. Shadows dance over my vision, as if something large and gentle were shifting across the sun, and I open my eyes with a gasp.

The balcony has been transformed. Brilliant pink and purple roses bloom everywhere, hanging from creeping vines that spill into the room and arch across the ceiling. Each blossom seems to pulse with a soft, inner light, casting faint glimmers like stars over the ground.

At the center stands Valric, his full attention focused on me. Then he lifts his hand, and a glimmer of sapphire blue flutters into view. A beautiful butterfly, its wings shimmering like stardust, lands on his outstretched palm. Valric's expression is calm, almost reverent, as he holds the butterfly up to his face.

"I've never seen this species before," he marvels.

With a blink, I stand up to round the small table, and approach him. More butterflies emerge from the roses, each a vibrant blue like the first.

"When you're calm and at peace, so is your magic."

I nod absently as I crouch down, running my fingers over the rose petals. I draw a deep breath, hands trembling just slightly.

The doors to the room creak open, and I look over to see Alivar stroll in, his usual effortless grace on full display. His footsteps falter slightly as his eyes sweep over the room, taking in the rose bushes now invading the area.

"Doing some remodeling?" He quirks an eyebrow, a faint smirk tugging at his lips.

I stand, brushing my hands down the front of my dress. "Something like that," I reply lightly. "What are you doing here?"

Before Alivar can respond, Valric answers for him. "I thought the Seelie Prince could be useful in getting you to train magically."

I blink, my grin faltering. "But I thought you said it's all instinctive. I just need to channel it better, right?"

"Under pressure," Valric clarifies, folding his arms. "Instinct is powerful, but it's raw. I want someone who can push your buttons, someone who can bring out the emotions driving your magic."

I snort, crossing my arms over my chest. "Bring Fenris in here, then. He's got a stick up his ass about something, and would love a chance to wipe the floor with me."

Out of the corner of my eye, I catch Valric flinch, just the slightest twitch of his shoulders.

I tilt my head, narrowing my eyes. "What was that?"

"What was what?" he replies, avoiding my stare.

"That look," I press, stepping toward him. "You know why Fenris is so pissed at me, don't you?"

Valric sighs heavily, running a hand over his head, clearly debating how much he wants to share. "He's angry about a lot of things, Princess."

"That's not an answer."

Alivar watches the exchange with obvious interest, leaning casually against the wall. "Whatever it is," he says, his smirk returning, "I'm sure it'll come out eventually. Fenris isn't exactly subtle with his emotions."

I give Alivar a dry look. "Helpful as always, Your Highness."

"You're welcome," he replies, utterly unbothered.

Valric clears his throat, drawing my attention back to him. "Right now, your focus should be on your training." His voice is firm, though there's still a hint of discomfort there.

"Fine," I relent, my shoulders drooping. "Where do we start?"

Valric rises from his chair, his gaze lingering on me. "I think that will do for today." His tone leaves little room for argument, and I frown, my eyes flicking to the window. The sun has disappeared beneath the horizon, its golden glow fading into deep purples and blacks of night.

"Have you even eaten?" Alivar inquires, his voice tinged with concern. "I heard you were at the arena at dawn."

My attention snaps to him, my frustration bubbling to the surface. "I don't have time, Maxon–"

Valric's low growl cuts through the air, silencing me. Instinctively, I recoil as I swivel to face him.

"What?" I demand, more defensively than intended.

"Do you think Maxon would want you working yourself to death? Starving yourself like this?"

Anger flares, hot and bitter. "I can't eat," I retort sharply. "I can't sleep. I need to keep busy." My voice cracks, betraying the storm raging within me. I glance between them—Valric's unyielding stare, Alivar's quiet concern. Their judgment feels suffocating, even if it comes from a place of care.

"I need to learn," I continue, my voice rising. "I need to train. To make myself better, so no one ever has to sacrifice themselves for me again."

Alivar tilts his head, studying me with calm patience that only fuels my irritation. "You're forcing something that will come in its own time. Magic isn't something you learn to control overnight."

"No shit!" I explode, throwing my hands in the air. "But I'm still going to try!" My voice reverberates in the quiet room, the words heavy with desperation.

Valric and Alivar exchange a glance, their expressions unreadable.

Finally, Valric speaks, his voice gentler now but no less firm. "Trying is one thing. Endangering yourself in the process is another. If you really want to honor Maxon, you need to survive this. Not just endure it."

I know he's right.

I also know that if I have any chance of getting to Maxon, I need my strength. My heart squeezes painfully. I wish I could reach him, see if he's okay.

"We have set your coronation for a week's time."

A jolt of surprise shoots through me, making my heart pound in my chest. "A week? Why so quickly?"

"At a time like this, the kingdom needs something to come together for. Bringing your people home and uniting them will do that. For too long, they have been scattered, living in shadows, hiding from the fear of what might happen to them. You—your coronation—represent hope."

Hope.

The word lands like a stone, sinking deeper with every second. I shake my head, trying to muster some sense of control over the emotions threatening to spiral out of me.

"But I'm not ready. How am I supposed to lead a kingdom when I can barely keep myself together?"

Alivar steps forward. His hand lands on my shoulder and squeezes gently. "You're already their queen. This just makes it official."

My throat tightens as his words sink in. Nerves swarm through my body, twisting my stomach into knots and sending a hum of energy rippling under my skin.

"It feels like everything's falling apart," I whisper.

"It's not," he says firmly. "It's falling into place."

Chapter Twenty-Eight

Maxon

It's been two days since the Shadoweaver revealed herself, and I haven't seen another living soul. The oppressive darkness of this place seems alive, shifting and breathing as though it means to swallow me whole. Faint shuffling sounds come and go without warning, and whispers echo in the shadows—just on the edge of comprehension. They're maddening, like distant voices mocking my isolation, or perhaps my sanity.

No food or water has come.

My bucket ran dry yesterday, even though I rationed what little I had.

The ache in my gums and the gnawing void in my stomach are constant companions now, relentless in their torment. Yet, they pale compared to the aching within my chest. The longing I feel.

Fuck, I miss her.

I close my eyes, letting her memory bloom in the darkness. Her golden hair, as radiant and warm as sunlight itself, cascading over her shoulders in waves that seem woven from starlight.

The way her golden aura shines so brightly it could light up the darkest corners of the world—and it does. For me.

I can almost feel her, her warmth against my fingertips, soft skin beneath my touch. My breath hitches as the memory sharpens—her lips parting in a breathy moan as I pressed into her, the way she clung to me, her nails raking my back as she cried out my name.

A traitorous heat floods through me, my cock stiffening against the rough fabric of my pants. It's obscene, this response amidst such dire circumstances, but I can't stop it. The hunger for her is primal, a fire burning hotter than any physical starvation. It's not just her body I crave, but her presence, her light, her everything.

I shake my head violently, trying to dispel the image, but it clings to me, taunting. My breathing quickens, echoing too loudly in the oppressive silence. The whispers grow louder, their cadence almost rhythmic now, like a chant. My heart pounds against my ribs, and I can't tell if it's from the memory of Everly or the unrelenting pressure of this cursed place.

The shadows deepen, their edges shifting unnaturally. Something is watching. I can feel it.

Chapter Twenty-Nine

Everly

Mist clings to the earth, swirling beneath my feet as I make my way across the grass. I don't remember leaving my room, nor how I got down to the garden. My hands instinctively reach out, brushing along the leaves of various plants as I pass, heading deeper into the gardens.

A flicker of movement catches my eye, and I freeze. My heart beats a frantic rhythm against my ribs. Slowly, I turn toward the movement, but nothing is there. I let out a shaky breath, my bare feet sinking into the dew-covered ground as I approach an overgrown bramble bush. Pushing my way past the bush, my night dress snags on the branches, the sound of the delicate fabric tearing. Emerging from the other side, I see something up ahead. I squint at the pale figure that seems to merge with the mist. Flowing white robes float around them, and flashes of silver hair reflect off the moonlight.

"Hello?" my voice trembles as I call out, cold sweat slicking my skin despite the night's chill.

In response, singing fills the air. The haunting melody comes from every direction, as though the very wind carries the voices, whispering in a language that is familiar but also completely alien. I stand frozen for a moment, my heart pounding in my ears. Slowly, I begin to turn in a circle, searching for the source, but what I find makes the hairs on the back of my neck stand on end. Several ghostly figures materialize from the mist, their faces obscured by swirling fog. They hover at the edges of my vision, the song growing louder, more hypnotic, until I feel my body swaying, almost involuntarily, to the eerie rhythm.

"Who are you?"

"We are the White Witches," comes the reply, the voices overlapping in a strange harmony, as if they're all speaking as one.

"The guardians of the land," another voice adds, this one deeper, more resonant.

The magic feels both ancient and powerful as it moves over me, prickling my skin and sending shivers down my spine. The air feels thick, charged, like the calm before a storm.

Something feels wrong.

How did I even get out here?

A creeping unease twists in my stomach, and I instinctively take a step back, gripping the fabric of my nightdress tightly in my fist.

"Why are you here?" I ask, my voice barely a whisper, more to steady my own nerves than to demand an answer.

Tendrils of mist begin to snake their way up from the ground, curling around my ankles like icy fingers, reaching for me before they dissipate, floating away into the night like autumn leaves caught in the wind. The figures don't move closer, but their presence presses down on me, heavy and foreboding.

"It is you who seeks us, druid," the voices reply softly.

I blink, confusion flickering through my mind.

Me? Seek them?

My breath catches in my throat, and I can't seem to form a coherent response. I tighten my grip on my dress, feeling the cool fabric damp with dew as my pulse quickens.

"Everly!" Raiden's voice shatters the spell, booming through the night with a force that makes me jump.

My pulse skitters wildly as I spin around, nearly losing my balance. My feet slip on the wet grass, and for a heart-stopping second, I think I'm going to fall. I manage to catch myself, but the ghostly figures are gone, swallowed by the mist as if they were never there. Only the faint echo of their singing remains, fading into the night, leaving me alone in the eerie silence.

"Everly!" more voices now ring out into the night.

Several torches flicker into view, their warm light breaking through the thick darkness. I let out a deep sigh, running my hands over my face, trying to ground myself after what just happened. The bramble bush behind me rustles, and I turn to see Kian stepping through, holding up a torch, his silhouette familiar and steady.

"Princess?" His voice carries a mixture of relief and confusion.

"I'm here." My answer is quiet, almost embarrassed by the situation.

Kian's eyes sweep over me, and even in the dim light, I can see his brow furrow. "I can see that, but why are you out here in the dead of night . . . barely dressed?" His tone is teasing, but there's concern laced in it.

I glance down, suddenly realizing the state I'm in. The sheer nightdress, pale pink and almost translucent in the moonlight, leaves little to the imagination. My heart skips a beat, and I feel the heat rush to my face, my ears burning with embarrassment. I cross my arms, trying to cover myself, but it does little to help.

Kian steps forward, placing his torch on the ground. Without a word, he shrugs off his soldier's jacket and drapes it over my shoulders. The fabric is rough but warm, the scent of leather and the forest clinging to it. He helps me slip my arms into the sleeves, tucking the jacket snugly across my chest, making sure I'm covered completely.

"Thank you," I whisper.

He grins, his usual charm returning as he looks down at me, the dimple in his cheek making an appearance. "Did Nix teach you nothing?" he teases lightly, but there's an affection in his voice that makes the words feel like less of a rebuke and more of a gentle reminder.

"Look, I can't help it. In my world–"

"This is your world," Kian cuts me off, his tone suddenly serious. The reminder hangs in the air between us, heavy with meaning.

I open my mouth to respond, but before I can say anything, another figure emerges from the bushes, moving with purpose. Fenris. His eyes lock onto mine, sharp and filled with anger, the torchlight casting harsh shadows across his features.

"What are you doing out here?" he snaps, his voice colder than the night air.

I square my shoulders, my embarrassment quickly turning to frustration. "None of your business," I snap back, meeting his gaze head-on. There's a challenge in my voice, a stubborn refusal to be scolded like a child, especially not by him.

Fenris's jaw tightens, and for a moment, the air between us seems to crackle with tension. I can see the barely-contained fury simmering beneath the surface, but I refuse to back down. Kian, standing between us, glances from one to the other, his smile fading as the atmosphere shifts. Fenris's gaze drops as he takes in Kian's jacket, his posture stiffening. Sending Kian a chilling look, he turns, walking back the way he came.

"The whole castle is looking for you. Get your ass moving," Fenris snaps over his shoulder.

Chapter Thirty

Everly

I'm still wrapped in Kian's jacket, the fabric heavy and warm against my skin, though it does little to calm my nerves as I pace the war room. The others watch me in silence—Raiden, Tristan, Fenris, Kian, Zaria, Scarlett, Mia, and Nix—all positioned around the table like sentinels, their eyes tracking my every movement.

The air is thick with tension, as if the walls are closing in on me, and I can feel their unspoken questions, their anticipation for an explanation. Yet, I find myself unsure if I even have one.

Raiden is the first to break the silence. His voice is steady, but I can hear the edge of concern beneath it. "Tell us what happened."

I stop pacing and turn to face them, bringing my thumb to my mouth, biting down on the nail. The weight of their stares makes my skin prickle, and my heart races as I try to gather my thoughts.

"I don't know how I ended up in the garden," I admit, my voice sounding too loud in the stillness. "I was asleep in bed, and then . . . I was outside. I don't remember waking up or walking there. It was like something magical was pulling me deeper into the garden. I was being led somewhere."

"By whom?" Tristan probes, his arms crossed over his chest.

I hesitate for a moment, my mind still piecing together what I saw. Finally, I force the words out. "They called themselves the White Witches. The Guardians."

The room goes deathly still.

Everyone freezes, their expressions shifting from confusion to something darker, something wary. The silence stretches, thick and heavy, as they exchange uneasy glances.

"What?" I ask, my voice barely above a whisper, though I'm not entirely sure I want to hear the answer.

Scarlett and Mia look just as confused as I feel by their reaction.

Nix flies forward, her features filled with something that looks like awe—or fear. It's hard to tell with her. Her voice is hushed, reverent when she speaks, "You saw the Witte Wieven?"

The name sends a chill down my spine, and I glance around the room, searching for some hint of explanation, but everyone looks equally unsettled.

"Maybe?" my voice shakes slightly. "Who are they?"

Kian, still standing close by, clears his throat, his face unusually serious. "The Witte Wieven are . . . not to be trifled with. They're powerful spirits—guardians, some say—but others believe they're something far more dangerous. They've existed for centuries, tied to the land, to the ancient magic that flows through it."

"And you saw them," Raiden adds, his voice low, his eyes narrowing as if trying to piece together the gravity of what this means. "That's no small thing, Everly."

I can feel my pulse accelerate. "But they didn't harm me . . . They just–"

"Just called to you," Fenris interrupts, his tone cutting through the room like a blade. His jaw is clenched, and there's a flicker of something odd in his eyes. "Do you know what that means?"

I shake my head, feeling more confused than ever. "No . . . I don't."

Nix steps closer, her big blue eyes wide with childlike fascination. "They don't just call to anyone. The Witte Wieven—they seek out those who have a connection to the ancient magics."

"Those who seek answers. Did you call to them?" Zaria questions, earning a warning glance from Kian.

"Well, not that I'm aware of. I'm only just learning who they are, but they did say I was the one to seek them out."

Raiden sighs heavily, running a hand through his hair as he turns back to me. "We need to figure out why they called you to them or why they answered your call. But whatever this is . . . it's not something we can ignore."

"I wish I could tell you more, but I have no idea who these beings are or why any of this happened," I reply, running a hand over my head. "Why are you guys so wary?"

I look around the room for answers, and it's Fenris who responds, his demeanor still radiating a harshness I've grown to expect from him.

"The White Witches are ancient elven guardians who protect sacred places. They travel through the veil and realms through stone monuments."

Nix flies closer, hovering in front of me, her blue orbs shining in wonder. "They are said to be beautiful beyond words, full of sorrow and wisdom. Prophecy and foresight. I wish I could have met them."

I tilt my head, considering the memory. "They were beautiful . . . but haunting too. Will they return?"

Tristan rubs his hands over his face and sighs heavily. "It's possible."

A chill runs through me at the thought. I wasn't expecting that answer.

"You need someone to guard you while you sleep," Raiden adds.

"I already do," I reply. There have been guards outside my doors since I arrived in Faerie.

"In your room," he insists, his gaze steady and voice firm.

Scarlett suddenly stands, drawing everyone's attention. "We can stay with her."

I smile, grateful for her loyalty. Holding out my hand, she takes it, standing by my side. A moment later, Mia rises and crosses the room, her eyes flashing with the same resolve, as she, too, takes her place beside me.

"We can watch over her at night," Mia challenges confidently, her tone leaving no room for debate.

Fenris, however, doesn't seem convinced. His voice is cold, condescending as he pushes off the wall and straightens up. "Don't take this the wrong way, but you're human. What good are you in a fight?"

The words hang in the air like a slap, and I feel Scarlett and Mia stiffen beside me. The tension in the room shifts, before I can utter a word in defense of my friends, Mia releases my hand

and marches straight over to Fenris. Her small frame is dwarfed by his towering presence, but she doesn't falter. She plants herself in front of him and pokes him hard in the chest.

"Humans have heart and compassion," she retorts, her voice filled with fire. “We're stronger than you think.”

Fenris glares down at her, his eyes narrowing in irritation, but Mia doesn't back down. The sheer audacity of it catches everyone off guard, and the room falls silent at their standoff.

Raiden clears his throat. “Right. Well, Mia and Scarlett will stay in Everly's chambers, along with Lutin and Senka guarding outside. I will also set up patrol of the gardens, in case Everly manages to slip by. Tristan and Kian, you will also be stationed nearby, just in case she slips past.”

As a murmur of agreement goes around the room, I notice Mia walking back toward Scarlett and me, her soft features still lined with anger. I glance past her and see Fenris, observing Mia with a slight frown. Suddenly, his eyes snap to mine, narrowing in on me. A flush spreads over my skin, and once again, I'm grateful for Kian's jacket.

Chapter Thirty-One

Everly

I don't bother trying to go back to sleep after quietly slipping back into my chambers.

The events of the night still swirl in my mind, leaving me restless, my thoughts too unsettled to find peace. Instead, I decide I'm going to draw a hot bath, hoping the heat will help ease my tension and clear my head.

Mia and Scarlett climb onto the bed that Maxon and I share, and nestle into the blankets, settling in as if they own the place. It warms my heart to know they decided to stay here with me and be my support.

"I'm going to take a bath," I say, hoping to dispel this chill that has settled over me.

"Okay," Mia replies. "We will be waiting."

I pause at the bathroom door, my fingers curling tightly around the cool wood of the door frame.

My attention is on Nymeria and Anika as they weave their way through the room. They're alert, ears perked and tails stiff, each movement deliberate, searching.

A prickle of unease slides down my spine. The way they move—silent, focused—it doesn't feel casual. It feels like something is *off*.

'Is everything alright?'

Nymeria's head turns my way, her golden eyes glowing. '*There was someone unfamiliar here.*'

Goosebumps scatter across my arms, and my scalp tightens with awareness. '*Can you tell what they were doing?*'

Anika trots over and nudges my hand, and I reach up, stroking her soft fur. '*No, but we can't sense any danger. We will keep watch.*'

I frown. These chambers are heavily warded. Maybe it was a new maid?

The wolves pad over to the daybed by the balcony doors, curling up together and resting their heads on their paws, keeping watch over the room.

I slip into the bathroom, the cool tiles greeting my bare feet, and shut the door behind me with a heavy sigh. Reaching for the taps, I turn them slowly, the warm water begins to flow in a steady stream. It splashes against the porcelain with a rhythmic patter, swirling and rising steadily. I uncork the small bottle of lavender soap from the shelf. As the water deepens, I pour a generous amount into the bath. The soap clouds and blooms like ink in water before soft white bubbles begin to form, gathering at the surface and clinging to the edges of the tub. I peel away Kian's jacket and my nightdress, letting them fall to the cool tile floor without care. The air kisses my skin, cool against the warmth rising from the bath. A breath escapes me—slow, steady—before

I place one foot in, then the other, easing myself into the waiting heat.

The water welcomes me, curling around my legs and back as I lower myself deeper, until it cradles me fully. The heat seeps into my muscles, loosening the knots of tension, but my jaw and gums still ache, a dull, throbbing reminder of the stress I can't seem to shake. I clench my teeth, then force myself to relax, sinking deeper into the bath. The ache subsides slightly, soothed by the warmth, though a part of me knows the discomfort is rooted in something far deeper than fatigue—a gnawing worry that no amount of rest can chase away.

I close my eyes, letting the warmth cradle me, trying to wash away the weight that's settled so heavily on my chest. The quiet hum of the early morning settles around me, its gentle rhythm offering a fleeting sense of calm. The soft murmurs of my friends nearby should be enough to ground me, their presence a reminder that I'm not alone. But even their comforting voices can't fill the gaping void left by Maxon's absence. It's like an ache buried deep, festering, consuming. Every second he's gone is another thread unraveling from whatever fragile control I have left. I can feel it building, this wild, feral need to act. To tear through every obstacle in my path, to reduce everything standing between us to ashes. If I don't keep a lid on these emotions, I might just snap. It terrifies me—this rage, this desperation—but it also fuels me. A quiet, trembling part of me knows I've never been this close to the edge before. Not even during my time in foster care, when my life was a cycle of abandonment, uncertainty and cruelty, did I feel so out of control. Back then, I had mastered the art of invisibility. I was a wallflower, blending into the background, doing everything I could to avoid drawing attention to myself.

Survival meant silence. It meant shrinking away from the world, pretending not to feel anything at all.

But now? Now, I want the world to notice. I want everyone to understand the lengths to which I will go. I want them to see just how far I'm willing to go to bring my mate home. The thought of Maxon out there, in the hands of the Shadoweaver, makes my blood run hot. He's my anchor, my safe place, and I refuse to let him be taken from me.

I know the others can see it, the fracture lines splintering beneath the surface of my carefully crafted exterior. I take a deep breath, trying to focus on the gentle hum of the morning again, but it's no use. Every beat of my heart feels like a countdown, urging me to move, to act, to fight.

For Maxon, I'd burn the whole world down. And right now, I just might.

I storm out of the bathroom, in a worse mood than when I went in. My hands shake as I rip open the wardrobe, the hinges creaking in protest. Behind me, I hear the shuffle of movement—Mia and Scarlett sitting up in bed. Their groggy murmurs barely register over the roar in my head.

"What are you doing?" Scarlett groans, her voice heavy with sleep.

I don't answer, too consumed by the storm raging inside me. My fingers fumble as I pull on my underwear and reach for the tight pants I had made to go under my dresses. My movements are harsh, hurried, like I'm trying to outrun the ache that's steadily building.

"I need to train," I bite out, strapping my daggers to my thighs with practiced precision.

"But you've barely had any rest," Mia argues, her tone laced with concern.

I ignore her, grabbing the wrap-around dress and yanking it into place. The fabric clings to me as I tighten the belt around my waist, the high slit in the front giving me the freedom to move the way I need to. My hands are steady now, the methodical process of dressing, a brief reprieve from the chaos in my mind. With a swift motion, I slide my feet into my boots and tighten the laces.

Then I see it—the long sword. It rests where I left it; on the small table, its blade glinting faintly in the dim light. I pick it up, my fingers running over the hilt, tracing the intricate carvings I've come to know so well. It's Maxon's. The pang hits me in the chest like a blow, and for a moment, I can't breathe.

God, I miss him.

Tears prick the corners of my eyes, and I blink them away quickly, refusing to let them fall.

"You need rest, E," Mia urges gently, her voice closer now. She's standing, her worry palpable as she watches me.

I snap, the words spilling out before I can stop them, "No, I need my mate." My voice cracks, raw with emotion, and the room falls silent.

For a long moment, I can't meet their eyes. The vulnerability is too much, too exposed. Instead, I grip the sword tighter and walk toward the door.

"I'll be in the arena," I say over my shoulder and slip out the door.

Chapter Thirty-Two

Everly

I've been out here since the first light of dawn, the sun climbing lazily over the horizon, painting the training grounds in soft golds and pinks. The air is cool and crisp, but sweat clings to my skin, dripping down my back as I move. Senka and Lutin linger on the sidelines, their shadows a quiet presence. I think they understand I need this space, this solitude. Neither of them say a word, simply standing watch as I throw myself into my drills, my dagger slicing through the air in precise arcs.

The straw dummy bears the brunt of my frustrations, its tattered surface already scarred from repeated strikes. I focus on the techniques Kian and Tristan have drilled into me: perfect form, calculated strikes, speed over brute strength. My body moves on autopilot, each movement a desperate attempt to quiet the restless thoughts swirling in my mind.

At some point, Senka disappears, but I don't stop.

The steady rhythm of my strikes, the repetitive motion—it's the only thing holding me together. My breathing comes hard and fast, my muscles burn, but I can't let up. Not yet.

It isn't until I catch movement from the corner of my eye that I realize Senka's returned, and with Kian in tow. Kian's tall frame is unmistakable. His lavender eyes lock on me as he closes the distance. Concern flickers across his features, softening the angular lines of his face.

I freeze mid-strike, my dagger poised inches from the dummy's chest.

"At it early again, Princess?" A note of worry lies beneath his usual calm.

Straightening, I wipe the sweat from my brow with the back of my hand. "I couldn't sleep," I admit, my voice hoarse from exertion.

His gaze softens as he studies me, his eyes searching mine as if he could see straight through the facade I'm clinging to. "That doesn't mean you should push yourself until you break."

"I'm fine," I retort too quickly, the words defensive enough I know he doesn't believe me.

Kian doesn't reply immediately, though he does step closer, making me tip my head back. "You've got nothing to prove, Everly," he says quietly. "Not to me, not to anyone."

His words hit harder than I want to admit. I look away, my grip tightening on the dagger in my hand.

"I can't stop," I murmur. "If I stop, the thoughts . . . the memories . . . they'll take over."

Silence stretches between us, then he dips his head. "Then let's train."

For a moment, I don't trust myself to speak. Instead, I nod, the knot in my chest loosening.

Out of the corner of my eye, I notice Mia, Scarlett, and Tristan stepping into the training grounds. Mia's eyes light up when she sees me, and she waves. Scarlett has a smirk tugging at the corner of her lips while Tristan nods. I wave back, already curious about what has brought them here. Before I can call out, Tristan turns to Senka, who is adjusting the wraps on her hands, and gestures for her to come over. Senka dips her head, brushing a loose strand of hair from her face before making her way over. She is one of the best fighters here. She has sharp instincts and swift counterattacks. My friends gather around as she and Tristan begin demonstrating some basic defensive stances. My heart warms instantly. Tristan wants to ensure my friends are ready for anything.

My attention shifts back to Kian then to the dagger in my hand.

"Ready to go again?" Kian asks.

"Yes," I reply, flipping the dagger in the air.

Kian's grin returns, the dimples showing in both cheeks.

"Right."

I focus on his voice and the steady rhythm of his directions. Even now, after everything, he moves with that same effortless grace, his tone calm and patient as he corrects my stance or adjusts the angle of my strikes.

Despite it all—despite the betrayal—I can't bring myself to hate him. When Kian told Alivar things about me, things he never should have, it felt like a dagger to the back. But time has softened that wound, if only slightly. I still think of him as a friend—a good one—even if he's a stupid one who made a dumb, reckless choice.

And despite my anger, I know in deep down he'd do anything for me. Just like I'd do anything for him.

There is a bond between us, and it might be strained under the weight of disappointment, but it's still there, steady and resilient. I trust him, even now. Perhaps that makes me foolish, but I can't shake the certainty that Kian's mistakes were born from a place of care, however misguided.

"Focus," Kian's voice cuts through my thoughts, pulling me back to the present. His lavender eyes meet mine, a hint of a smirk tugging at his lips. "Unless you plan on daydreaming your way through this fight."

I roll my eyes, but there's no real heat behind it. "Just thinking about how much trouble you are."

He chuckles, a soft sound that eases some of the tension knotting in my chest. "Good to know I'm still living rent-free in your head."

"Don't flatter yourself," I shoot back, but a small smile creeps onto my face despite myself.

"She isn't going to learn shit if you keep babying her," a harsh, rough voice cuts through the air. I swipe the sweat from my forehead and frown, turning to see Fenris leaning against the wall, his arms crossed, expression unreadable.

Kian tenses beside me, his jaw tight. "I'm not babying her," he snaps.

"Looks like you are to me," Fenris drawls, his gaze steady and challenging. "You're just taking it easy on her, hoping she'll forgive you for betraying her."

Kian's face hardens, and he takes a step toward Fenris, fists clenched at his sides. A shot of adrenaline moves through me, and I quickly sidestep in front of him, grabbing his arm to stop him.

"Hey, stop it. Both of you," I command firmly, throwing a warning glance at each of them.

Fenris's eyes flicker down to me, and his gaze narrows. The piercing intensity in those dark eyes makes my stomach twist uncomfortably.

"You're a shit fighter," he accuses, his voice cold and direct.

I bristle. "Why are you being such a jerk?"

Without answering, Fenris steps forward, scooping up one of the training swords from the ground. He flips it over with practiced ease, his movements smooth and controlled. When his eyes meet mine again, there's a spark of challenge in them. He tosses the sword in my direction, and my pulse jumps as I barely manage to catch it.

"Fight me." His tone leaves no room for argument.

"What? Why?" I sputter, caught off guard by his sudden demand.

He doesn't waste time answering. In a flash, he's charging at me, closing the distance before I can even think about reacting. The next thing I know, I'm on the ground, the impact jarring as the air rushes out of my lungs.

Shit, that hurt.

I roll over, trying my best to hold in the groan, as I force myself onto my hands and knees before struggling back to my feet.

"Was that necessary?" Kian growls.

But Fenris isn't paying attention to him. His eyes are locked on me, a sharp edge to them, as if daring me to give up.

I swipe up the sword, planting my feet firmly in the dirt as I raise it in front of me, my grip tightening.

"Again?" Fenris taunts, his voice dripping with mock amusement.

"Bring it on," I fire back, refusing to back down.

A grin spreads across his face, and before I can prepare, he's moving faster than I've seen anyone but Raiden or Maxon move. His speed is a blur, and I barely manage to raise my sword before he's on me, his blade knocking mine aside with an almost effortless flick. The next moment, he's behind me, and I feel the cool edge of his dagger poised at my throat.

"Too slow," he breathes against my ear, his voice low and chilling as he shoves me forward, dismissing me like a child who barely put up a fight.

Frustration bubbles up, and I whirl around, a low growl escaping my lips. I lock my eyes on him, my body tense and ready. My grip shifts, my fingers curling with renewed determination. He just watches me, his expression unreadable, his eyes flicking over me as if calculating my every move.

I know I don't stand a chance against him, but some part of me feels like I have to at least try. Losing might be inevitable, but I can't let him think I'm weak or too scared to fight back.

"Let's make this fun." There's a dangerous glint in his eye as he stalks toward me. He closes the distance, and I instinctively straighten, bracing myself, unsure of what he's planning.

Then his hand reaches for my waist. I freeze, every muscle coiled and ready, but I force myself to hold my ground, determined not to flinch or back away. His fingers graze my side, sending a shiver down my spine as he reaches to unclip the dagger from its sheath. With a calm, practiced movement, he lifts it and holds it out, offering it to me.

"Here," he offers, his voice low, daring me to take it. His eyes bore into mine. For a second, I hesitate, wondering if this is a trap, some trick to catch me off guard again. But his gaze doesn't waver, and neither does his grip on the hilt. I snatch it from him, with a glare.

Fenris steps back, a slow smirk curving his lips as he raises his hands, ready to fight.

"You want to fight me with no weapon and let me keep both of mine?" I ask, narrowing my eyes.

He tilts his head, that infuriating smirk never faltering, and shrugs casually. "You won't land a hit."

A spark of irritation flares through me, and the arrogance in his voice makes my teeth clench. "How can you be so sure?" I growl, the simmering anger in my chest stirring my magic. It hums along my skin, a living, breathing force that demands to be unleashed.

Fenris doesn't answer. He just stands there, calm and poised, like he already knows the outcome. It's maddening.

I let my magic flood every corner of my being, filling me with raw power. The air around me shifts, charged with electricity, and the ground beneath my feet trembles in response. My glare locks onto him, unwavering, and I feel the moment his own magic stirs—a glow forming behind those deep brown eyes, sending streaks of purple lightning through them.

Without another thought, I charge forward. The ground answers my call, buckling under his feet as I unleash my power. The earth shifts violently, propelling me forward with a speed that takes him by surprise. My dagger slices through the air, fast and precise, aimed directly at him.

But Fenris moves like water—fluid and graceful. He bends backward, narrowly avoiding the strike, and steps smoothly out of the way, regaining his footing with ease. If I wasn't so pissed, I'd be impressed.

I land hard but pivot quickly, my sword swinging wide in an arc meant to catch him off guard. This time, he ducks, his movements completely controlled. Before I can adjust, he surges up, his fist slamming into my midsection with enough force to knock the breath from my lungs.

I stagger back, gasping, and glare at him as I clutch my side. Fenris steps away, giving me just enough space to recover but not enough to feel in control.

"You're never going to be ready," Fenris goads, his voice cold and cutting. His words are a challenge, his tone dripping with disdain, and it grates on my last nerve.

"Says you?" I snap back, my hands curling into fists at my sides.

"Says me," he agrees, the smirk on his face only fueling my anger. He crosses his arms over his chest, the picture of arrogant confidence, and I swear, if looks could kill, he'd be a smoldering pile of ash.

"You're being a jerk." I glare up at him, resisting the urge to scream.

"I'm not being a jerk," Fenris argues dismissively. "I'm just stating facts."

"No, you're not!" The words burst out of me, louder than I intended, my voice trembling with emotion. "Something is bothering you. You've been nothing but an ass since we met, and I don't know why. So why don't you enlighten me?"

The anger wells up inside me, hot and consuming, but it's the frustration that breaks me. Tears burn at the corners of my eyes, and I hate it—I hate that I feel this vulnerable, this raw in front of him. Of all people.

Fenris's expression darkens, his smirk fading as he takes a step forward, closing the space between us. His movements are almost predatory, and for a moment, I feel the weight of his anger matching my own. But before he can get any closer, Kian steps into the space between us, his presence an unyielding barrier.

"That's enough." Kian's voice is low, like the rumble of distant thunder. His lavender eyes lock onto Fenris, daring him to push further.

Fenris halts, his jaw clenching. "Out of my way."

"Calm the fuck down," Kian volleys back.

They are standing so close, and it's only now that I realize how much bigger Fenris is compared to everyone else. I step out from behind Kian, ignoring the way his hand twitches as if to pull me back. Facing Fenris, I keep my voice level, refusing to let the hurt seep through.

"What did I ever do to deserve your hatred?" I whisper, the words barely audible.

Fenris freezes, his body going impossibly still. His eyes burn with anger, as they lock onto mine, and for a moment, I think I see something else—something deeper. But then his expression hardens, the fury in him flaring to life like a spark catching fire.

The next moment, his body ripples with raw, untamed magic. I barely have time to react before he transforms, his shift so sudden and violent it sends Kian stumbling to the side. All around me, shouts erupt, distant and muffled in the haze of disbelief.

I stare, dumbfounded, at the massive wolf now standing before me. Fenris's gray and black fur bristles with tension, each strand catching the light like steel. His sheer size is overwhelming—easily a foot taller than Nymeria and Anika. He prowls closer, his movements fluid and deliberate, the low, menacing growl rumbling from his chest reverberating through the ground beneath my feet.

The dagger in my hand feels laughably inadequate. My fingers tighten around the hilt, but I know it's useless against him. The sheer power radiating off his form is suffocating, a force I can't hope to match head-on.

I force myself to take a deep breath, steadying the wild rhythm of my heart. But as I do, his scent hits me. Notes of leather, star anise, and olive blossom flood my senses, overwhelming and oddly familiar. The recognition slams into me like a physical blow, stealing the air from my lungs and leaving me momentarily paralyzed.

A memory surfaces, unbidden and vivid.

"You can't catch me." I giggle, running across the grass, my bare feet sinking into the damp earth.

"Wanna bet!" Fenris shouts from behind me.

I look over my shoulder and squeal when I see him shift, his wolf form racing after me. Excitement and adrenaline pulse through my veins. The heat of my magic flowing through me as I run. Barely ten seconds later, Fenris barrels into me, knocking me over. Laughing, I roll onto my back and sit up, only for Fenris to nudge me with his nose, his fur warm and soft.

"I wish I could shift into a wolf." My hand glides over his thick coat.

Fenris shakes, sending me tumbling back, and I laugh even harder. Around us, fireflies scatter, their tiny lights flickering as dusk settles in, creating a magical aura.

Fenris shifts back into his human form and sits next to me, his eyes twinkling with amusement. "It is pretty cool," he admits.

"If I could shift, then you'd never catch me," I tease, still breathless from our play.

Fenris meets my gaze, his eyes reflecting a depth far beyond his years. "I will always catch you, Vera. You are mine to protect. Once I'm old enough, my father will pass on Paladin duties to me. I will be by your side as long as you want me there. I promise."

His words, so sincere and filled with determination and strength, make my heart swell. I grin at him, feeling a warmth spread through my chest. "You won't get sick of me?" I ask, half-joking but also seeking reassurance.

"I might." He nudges my shoulder playfully, a smirk tugging at his lips. "But you'll have to work really hard to make that happen. We are Anam Cara."

We sit there for a moment, the world around us fading into the background. The fireflies continue their dance, the twilight sky casting a gentle glow over us. Fenris's presence is comforting, a steadfast promise of protection and friendship. I lean into him, feeling the truth of his promise, knowing that whatever the future holds, we will face it together.

"Mother is taking me into the village tomorrow. Want to come?"

Fenris looks away, focusing on the setting sun. "I can't. I have to train."

I can't help but sigh at the thought of him not being able to accompany us. "You're always training," I complain.

"Someone has to protect you."

I smile. "I will bring you back those pastries you love."

Fenris's eyes light up, and he grins. "You better."

"I will, I promise."

"You shouldn't make promises, Vera," Fenris says sternly.

I grin over at him. "I promise you and I will be best friends forever and ever."

Fenris's growl deepens, a warning that drags me back to the present. My legs feel like lead, and I gasp, blinking back tears as I focus on the wolf pacing back and forth in front of me. The memory that overwhelmed me was of us, just two days before my parents were killed and I was sent to the human realm.

"Fenris," I breathe, emotions well up at the thought of the pain my childhood friend must have gone through. He had to endure my sudden disappearance, and worse, my return with no memory of him.

I'm about to take a step forward when Eve suddenly blocks my way. Her hand snaps out, flicking Fenris on the ear with surprising authority.

"Boy, you should know better than this," she scolds.

Fenris stops pacing, his wolf eyes meeting mine with a mixture of sorrow and longing.

"Eve, it's okay," I say, my voice shaking.

Valric appears at my side, his arms crossed over his chest. "It's not. We can't have him letting his emotions control his actions. I taught him better than that."

Fenris shifts back to his human form, his eyes locked onto mine. "Do you remember now?"

"Yes," I breathe. "I'm so–"

"It wasn't your fucking fault!" he yells, the sound ripping through the air.

I hear footsteps approaching from behind, but I can't tear my eyes from Fenris. Despite his outward display of anger, his eyes reveal a deep sense of hurt and anguish. He has been keeping it bottled up since he got here. My chest splinters as I imagine the pain he must be feeling.

"Boy, you need to take a walk!" Valric barks, striding over to him.

"Don't speak to me, old man. You left; you have no right."

Confusion clouds my brain as I blink, trying to make sense of what he said. I watch as Eve cups Fenris's face gently in her hands. Then, like a lightning strike, realization hits me. Eve is Fenris's mother, and Valric is his father. That is the reason why his eyes are a combination of violet and brown, and even though he's a shifter, he has pointed ears.

A hand slips into mine. I look over my shoulder to see we have an audience. Zaria squeezes my hand, understanding reflecting in her eyes. She heard what was said. Scarlett stands with Mia behind Kian and Tristan. All the other soldiers training have also stopped to watch the scene unfold.

"What is going on here?" Raiden's voice booms through the arena.

I take a hesitant step toward Fenris. I don't care about the questions or the looks from those around us—I care about him. I see it now, the truth I should have recognized all along. He doesn't hate me. The anger, the coldness, the distance—it wasn't about me. It was about what happened to me, about the pain and helplessness he couldn't bear.

"Fenris," I whisper, my voice barely audible over the blood rushing in my ears. I want to reach for him, to ease the torment written in every tense line of his massive form. But as I take another step forward, his head snaps up, and he shakes it, a silent plea for me to stop. His bright eyes are conflicted, swirling with emotions I can't quite name—regret, pain, guilt.

Now I understand. Nymeria and Anika never saw him as a threat because he wasn't. He was family, bound by ties deeper than blood or magic. And though his actions often felt like anger, they were rooted in something far more complex—something protective, something broken.

A tear slips down my cheek, hot and unbidden. The lump in my throat grows as Fenris takes one last, lingering look at me before turning and storming out of the arena. I watch him go, his massive frame disappearing into the shadows, and my chest aches with the weight of unspoken words.

The moment he's gone, Raiden's shadow falls over me, his presence as always, solid and grounding. "Everly?" His voice is softer now, though the edge of his authority remains.

I blink, brushing the tear away quickly, though my throat still feels tight. "I'm okay, Batman," I choke out, forcing a weak smile.

Raiden isn't fooled. He crouches, bringing himself to eye level with me, his silver eyes piercing through my walls. "You don't look okay," he says, his voice low but filled with a quiet, simmering fury—not at me, but at the situation.

I look up at him and give him a watery smile. "I just got another memory back."

Understanding fills his eyes, and he reaches out, drawing me into his arms.

"I need Maxon. I can't do this without him," I whisper into his chest.

Raiden makes a low noise and pulls back, cupping my shoulders. "You are stronger than you think."

Chapter Thirty-Three

Everly

I move swiftly through the secret tunnels in the walls, my fingers gliding along the rough, cool stone. It's almost soothing, the way the chill seeps through my fingertips and into my bones, keeping me centered, keeping me aware. Since my Renascitur, my senses are sharper than I ever imagined—sound, scent, sight.

The darkness of these tunnels no longer holds the same danger it once did. Now, shadows are mere wisps that my gaze pierces with ease. And the scents—they layer over one another, a blend of old moss, earth, and stone.

As I near the end of the tunnel, the faint aroma of the garden reaches me, growing stronger with every step. The familiar fragrance of wild lavender, night lily, and roses, the dewy scent of untouched grass, it all calls to me.

A deep sigh escapes my lips; my body knows what I need even before my mind does.

I need to get out of this stone labyrinth and into the open air.

I need space, distance, and a sky stretching endlessly above me. I need the solace only the garden can offer away from people.

I know I don't have long. The alarm will sound soon, and they'll come looking. But just for a moment, I want to be alone. I quicken my pace, slipping through the final corridor, each footfall silent, a skill I've honed since the transformation. The thought of the fresh air, the feel of it on my skin—it pulls me forward.

Stepping out into the open air, I tilt my face to the sky, the light sprinkle of rain kissing my flushed skin.

I make my way quietly through the garden, taking my time, savoring the solitude. My fingers trail over every petal, lingering on the delicate textures—silken rose petals, the faint fuzz of lavender leaves, the feather-light touch of daisies that lean toward me as I pass. The storm clouds darken the already fading light as I follow the narrow path leading down to the lake.

My heart pounds a little faster as I approach the lake, remembering the last time I was here. Maxon had taken me under the shelter of the gorgeous weeping willow, hidden away from the world, just the two of us bound together in solitude. My cheeks warm at the memory of him pulling me close, of his fingers weaving through my hair, his hands on my skin. The feeling of him moving within me was like nothing I'd ever known—a dizzying blend of pleasure and connection that sent me tumbling into bliss, every sense heightened, every breath stolen.

Our bond was immediate, magnetic, pulling us together the moment our eyes met. In those early days, I didn't understand it, didn't understand him. I was lost then, unsure of what any of it meant. Now all I feel is a yearning that cuts deeper every moment he isn't near.

A dull ache rises in my jaw, pulsing upward into my ear. I wince, pressing a hand to my cheek, trying to will it away. Not again. It's been happening more often lately, these strange pangs that echo through my head. Maybe it's part of the Renascitur, some lingering effect. Whatever it is, I wish it would stop.

The lake is silent, stretching out before me like a mirror, smooth and still. I slip off my jeweled slippers, letting them fall softly onto the grass at the edge of the shore. Stepping forward, I feel the cool, soft earth beneath my feet as I wade out into the water. My red dress trails around me, floating on the surface, swirling in dark, shadowy waves as I venture deeper.

The cold water rises past my ankles, then my knees, sending a chill over me, but I barely notice. My emotions are overriding everything else. I can't even begin to put words to what I feel. It's like everything is tangled inside me. My anger, grief, longing, and a hollow ache that won't leave. The weight of it drowning me as memories of Maxon flicker in my mind. I feel his absence like a wound, raw and open.

Then there's my friends' sudden arrival in Faerie, the Shadoweaver's haunting presence always lingering in the edges of my awareness, the coronation with all the expectations, and Fenris, who brings his own ghosts and complications. I'm stretched thin, pulled in too many directions, and it's too much.

I press my palms to my eyes, squeezing them shut as the first tears slip free. I try to stifle my sobs, to keep the anguish locked inside, but the quiet of the lake only amplifies it, and the tears spill over in silent, unstoppable waves. My breathing is shaky, the air catching in my throat as I fight to keep control, but I'm losing.

Suddenly, there's a ripple in the water, gentle yet undeniable, moving close enough that I can sense it. Startled, I drop my hands from my face, blinking to clear my tear-blurred vision as I look out over the water. The clouds part just enough that the moonlight streams through, reflecting off the lake. The surface shivers, breaking the moon's reflection into scattered shards, and my breath hitches.

I stand very still, barely daring to breathe as I watch the water shift, something unseen moving beneath.

Before I have time to comprehend what is happening, a figure emerges from the water, and I watch in awe as droplets of crystal liquid spin around the figure in slow, lazy swirls. The beautiful spirit, made entirely of water, stops a few feet in front of me. A soft blue glow surrounds her, and I can make out every feature of the liquid body as she moves closer. Her head tilts to the side and she reaches for my face, her hand cool and surprisingly soft, brushing the tears from my cheek.

'Don't cry, chosen one.'

The voice that fills my head is so tender and sweet, it makes the tears fall faster.

'I can't help it. I feel so lost,' I reply.

'You only need to follow your heart. If you do, you can regret nothing.'

Her words settle in my chest, soothing the crack that has formed from Maxon's absence.

'I miss him so much,' my voice breaks with the admission. '*I don't know how to get him back. I don't know what I'm doing.'*

The water spirit's expression softens, her shimmering form radiating a quiet strength. '*You are stronger than you think,'* she replies gently. *'I've been watching you since you arrived, and you've grown. Your magic is returning, along with your memories.'*

I blink, startled, unsure how to respond. How could she see strength in me when all I feel is this aching emptiness?

'You can reach him,' she continues.

My heart leaps with hope, even though doubt shadows my thoughts. *'How?'*

'Listen,' she urges.

'To what?'

'Listen. Your hearts are one. Your souls are one. If you truly listen and follow that connection, you'll find him.'

I swallow hard, wrestling with the desire to believe her. *'I've tried that. It . . . it didn't work.'*

She shakes her head slowly, her gaze never leaving mine. *'You'll need each other very soon. If you don't feed within the next few days, your strength will wane. You'll likely fall ill.'*

'Feed? What do you mean?' I ask, panic tightening in my chest.

'The headaches. It's your fangs coming through. Once mated, you are required to feed from each other every new moon. It keeps the body and bond strong. This pull to feed, it will consume you.'

I stare at her, dumbfounded. Why didn't anyone bring this up before?

'They likely didn't know that druids require the same as the high fae. And didn't want you fretting over Maxon any more than you already are.'

My eyes dart to hers. Did she?

'Yes, I can hear your thoughts. They are very loud.'

'Sorry?'

The water spirit laughs, and the sound is like tiny chiming bells.

'What is your name?' I ask, curiosity getting the better of me.

'Faelynn.'

'That's pretty.'

She grins and a shimmer of light moves through the water, lighting up her form even more.

I hear the sound of approaching footfalls, and sense Anika and Nymeria drawing nearer with someone.

The water spirit must sense them, too, because she moves closer, taking my hands in hers.

'You just need to truly listen,' she explains, placing her hand over my heart.

'I'll try.'

I swallow over the lump in my throat. I know she's about to leave, and for some reason, I don't want her to go. I don't want to face the world right now. As if understanding, she leans closer, her forehead resting on mine for only a moment. Droplets of glowing crystal water float around us as a calming sensation moves over me.

'I believe in you, Queen Vera.'

Then, with a sudden roar, the water collapses. Waves surge around me, splashing up against my body. The force of it catches me off guard, and my foot slips on the muddy lakebed. I feel myself falling, the cold rush of water waiting to swallow me whole, but before I can hit the surface, strong arms wrap around me, pulling me up and out of the cold water.

I gasp as I'm cradled against a warm solid chest. Fenris. His arms hold me, my soaked dress clinging to me like a heavy weight, dripping and pulling me down even as he holds me firmly against him.

"What are you doing out here? And without a guard? Do you want the Shadoweaver to find you, is that it?" Fenris's voice is clipped and hard, but each word is laced with a protectiveness I don't think I deserve.

"Put me down," I whisper, pushing at his chest.

Fenris grunts and continues to the shore. Once we are completely out of the water, he lets go of my legs, letting them swing down, but he doesn't let go completely, his other arm is still around my back as he curls me into his chest. I look up, startled. My breath catches. His gaze pins me—unblinking, intense—his eyes shadowed darker in the moonlight. The warmth from his body sends a pang of longing through me, and I gently push away from him. His arm drops, slowly lowering my feet to the ground, but he grabs my hand.

"I'm sorry for earlier," he says, his voice rough.

"It's fine. I can't imagine how hurt you were when you found out I had returned but had no memory of my life before." I drop my gaze to the ground, letting my hair fall around me. Fenris's other hand reaches for my chin, tipping my face up to his.

"You were my world from such a young age, and I vowed to find you again. I searched everywhere."

Tears immediately spring to life again, bringing with it that dull throb in my jaw. I squeeze my eyes close. "I'm sorry for the pain you had to endure."

He steps closer, and I open my eyes. "You were my best friend. I never should have treated you the way I did. You didn't deserve it."

"It's fine."

"Stop saying it's fine. It's not. Nothing is fine."

Startled, I step back until Nymeria and Anika flank me, their warm bodies pressing against me.

Fenris drops his head, shaking it. "We need to get you back to the castle. You shouldn't be out here alone."

I gather up my wet skirts, bundling them around my hips so I can walk without tripping. With each step, the damp fabric sticks to my legs and makes it harder to walk, but I don't care. Silence stretches between us, heavy and awkward, as we make our way back toward the castle. The only sounds are the crunch of gravel beneath our feet and the faint drip of water from my drenched clothing.

When we reach the castle grounds, I see Raiden on the terrace, his arms crossed tightly over his chest, a dark frown etched into his face. His eyes are fixed on me, piercing and intense. Even from a distance, I can feel the weight of his concern mixed with irritation, and it sends a fresh wave of nerves through me. Why do I feel like a naughty child?

He doesn't move as I get closer, watching every step with that brooding expression. His wings are half-spread behind him, like he's ready to launch himself into the air at any moment. The tension between us is palpable, and I can't quite bring myself to meet his gaze directly, the guilt settling in my stomach.

"What the hell, Everly! How are we supposed to protect you when you keep walking off?" he all but growls.

The hairs on my neck stand on end, and something wild and angry sprouts inside of me, and before I can tame it, I'm standing directly in front of him, poking him in the chest. "I don't need someone watching me all the time. I am capable of handling myself."

Raiden just stares, his jaw clenched, waiting for me to explain. I hear Fenris behind me scoff, and I spin on him, my glare cutting through the space between us.

"I'm not completely defenseless!" I lash out.

"Just untrained with no memories."

Hurt seeps into my chest before I can stop it, and Fenris must see, because a pained look flashes across his face. He steps forward.

“I didn’t–”

I hold up my hands. “You did.”

With a sigh, I turn back to Raiden, ready to explain everything. But as soon as I open my mouth, a sharp pain pierces my head, stabbing through my jaw in a way that’s nothing short of excruciating. It feels like something is cracking open beneath my skin, like the very bones in my face are rearranging.

"Fuck," I gasp, dropping to my knees, my fingers tangling in my hair as I press my palms against my skull, trying to force the pain away. But it only intensifies, throbbing in time with my heartbeat, a pulsing agony that blurs my vision.

Raiden is immediately in front of me, crouching down, his hands firm on my shoulders. “Everly, are you–”

“Why didn’t you tell me?” I manage, the words coming out through clenched teeth, each one a struggle against the pain radiating through my jaw.

He blinks, looking genuinely alarmed. “What?”

“That we need to feed,” I grind out, half-accusation, half-desperation.

A flicker of realization dawns in his eyes, widening them as panic sets in. “Shit,” he mutters, his voice low, tense. "You’re getting your fangs?”

“I think so,” I reply hoarsely.

My head spins, making his hands tighten on my shoulders, steadying me. “Listen, you’re going to be okay. Just focus on breathing.”

I try, but the pain refuses to subside, relentless and consuming. I grit my teeth, but that only makes it worse, like pressing into raw nerves.

"Why didn't you tell me?"

He looks down into my eyes, guilt shadowing his features. "I thought . . . I thought you'd have more time. That maybe you didn't need to feed."

I let out a pained laugh, half a whimper. "Well, so much for that."

Raiden stands and scoops me into his arms. "Why are you soaking wet?"

"I went for a swim."

Raiden's attention moves from me to Fenris.

"I found her in the lake." Fenris shrugs.

Raiden lets out a weary sigh as he carries me through the castle, each step sending a jarring pain through my head. Finally, we enter my chambers and Zaria, Mia, and Scarlett are there waiting.

Scarlett rushes over. "Is she okay?"

Suddenly, Nix is in my face. "What's wrong with you?"

"Fangs," I croak.

Nix grins and flies down to my face, trying to lift my lip. I push her away and she laughs. "You're getting your fangs? This is great!"

"Doesn't feel that great," I grumble.

Raiden places me down on the daybed and opens the balcony doors, allowing a soothing breeze to come in. "It's not great!" he fumes. "It means she will need to feed."

Mia takes a seat next to me, grabbing my hand in hers. "What does that mean?"

Zaria settles beside me, her cool hands lifting my face to meet her gaze, her eyes full of concern. "Are you okay? I can get some tonic for the pain if you need it."

Uncertain, I give a slight shrug. The pain has lessened, but something else has replaced it—a strange, tingling awareness in my mouth. Almost instinctively, I run my tongue along my teeth, only to freeze as I graze the sharp points of my canines. Startled, my hand lifts to touch one, and I flinch as my thumb comes away with a small bead of blood.

“Oh, wow,” Scarlett murmurs, crouching in front of me, her eyes wide with fascination. “Show me.”

Feeling suddenly self-conscious, I lift my lip, revealing the newly formed fangs. Both Scarlett and Mia lean in closer, their eyes widening.

“You’re a vampire!” Mia giggles, a hint of awe in her voice.

“She is not!” Raiden growls, his tone rough enough to make us all go silent, staring at him in surprise. He’s pacing now, one hand running over his head as if he’s trying to think through a problem he can’t quite solve.

“What’s wrong with the big guy?” Scarlett mutters as she stands and crosses her arms.

Raiden’s jaw tightens, but it’s Zaria who answers. “The implications of Everly developing fangs are severe. If she doesn’t have her mate here to feed from, it could lead to . . . It could lead to her falling ill or even going mad.”

Mia’s eyes dart to me, worry clouding her face. “Can’t she just . . . feed from someone else?”

Raiden’s silver eyes meet mine. “No. It has to be her mate. That’s the only way to stabilize her.”

“Okay, so what do we do then?” Mia asks.

Raiden starts pacing, muttering under his breath. I don't think I've seen him like this, and it doesn't exactly fill me with confidence.

"How long do I have before I need to feed?"

Raiden turns and stares out the open balcony doors. "The new moon is in two days."

I stand up and walk over to the balcony doors, pushing the sheer curtains aside. "How long does the new moon phase last?" I whisper, trying not to let distress seep into my voice.

"The moon goddess graces us three days of each moon phase. But that does not mean the need to feed from Maxon will pass with the phase, it will only get worse. As will the headaches," Zaria explains softly.

"And what do I do?" I look over my shoulder, my fingers gripping the curtain tightly.

"We will have to lock you in here when the new moon comes and hope for the best. You will be a danger to yourself and everyone around you."

Zaria stands, her tail whipping back and forth. "I will stay with her."

"I just want him back. I want this nightmare over with."

Once Mia and Scarlett leave with Raiden, I retreat to the bathroom, locking the door behind me. The silence feels heavy, pressing down around me as I peel off my wet clothes and drop them onto the tiled floor with a soggy thud. The shock of everything that just happened—the pain, the fangs, Raiden's tense reaction—buzzes through me, a reminder of just how out of control things have become.

I don't tell anyone about Fenris or Faelynn. My complicated past with Fenris isn't something I'm ready to share, and meeting the water spirit . . . Well, that felt too strange, too personal. I can still hear her words echoing in my mind: *You'll need each other very soon.*

I step into the shower, letting the hot water pour over me, washing away the lake's chill. My hands scrub the last remnants of mud from my skin, letting the sweet bubbly scents calm my thoughts. As I step out of the shower, I catch my reflection in the fogged mirror—a small, almost imperceptible hint of fangs peeking from beneath my upper lip. My heart thrums faster, making my hands tremble as I run a finger over one of the sharp points again, feeling the sting as it pricks my skin. A reminder of the transformation that's begun, and the future that awaits me if I don't find a way to reach Maxon. Faelynn's words float through my mind again. She seemed to think there was a way.

Chapter Thirty-Four

Everly

Confusion clouds my mind as I look around. I'm in the garden again, that familiar tug pulling at my chest. It is so dark, and the silence that surrounds me is thick, pushing in from all sides like a physical force.

Slowly, I walk forward until an old abandoned well comes into view. I stop a few feet away, looking at the moss-covered stones, each etched with strange symbols, shimmering in the moonlight.

"Everly . . . " the voice calls again, soft and melodic, like a lullaby drifting through the air. It seeps into my bones, familiar and haunting. My breath hitches, and I can feel the tremor move through me as I step closer to the old well. Something pounds inside me, fierce and frantic, each thud echoing in my ears, the thudding so loud I'm sure the entire forest can hear it.

Slowly, my hands land on the edge of the old well, fingers curling around the cold stone.

The moss is damp and soft beneath my touch, but under that is the rough, jagged rock, a sharp reminder of where I am—teetering on the edge of something unknown, something dark. I swallow hard, forcing down the rising panic that swells in my throat. Fear prickles across my skin, but something is pulling me closer, a force I can't resist.

Holding my breath, I lean over the edge to peer into the inky depths of the well. Even though I'm outside in the open air, feelings of panic tighten my chest as if I'm alone in an enclosed, dark space. My pulse pounds, making spots dance in front of my eyes. Dizziness swamps me and I feel like I'm about to tip over and fall into that abyss.

Another gust of wind whips through the air, ruffling my hair and sending it across my face, momentarily blinding me. Pushing it back with shaking hands, fingers trembling against my skin, I notice the mist—thick, swirling around me, closing in like a ghostly shroud. It wasn't there before. I'm sure of it.

The voice comes again from deep within the well.

"*Everly . . .*"

It sings my name with a sweetness that makes my stomach twist. There's something wrong, something lurking beneath the surface of that melody. It sounds too kind, too soft, like a predator luring its prey.

I step back, but the mist curls tighter around me, tendrils of fog slithering over my skin like icy fingers. The mist feels alive, as if it's trying to pull me closer, to draw me into the well's grasp.

"Who are you?" My voice cracks, little more than a whisper swallowed by the rush in my ears. It's like a drumbeat surging through me, loud and relentless, drowning out everything but the throb of panic rising beneath my skin. But the well doesn't answer. Only silence follows, suffocating, as the mist thickens, making it harder to breathe.

My hands grip the edge of the well tighter, knuckles white, nails digging into the moss and stone. The air feels heavy, oppressive, as if the world itself is holding its breath. I can feel the pull again, the compulsion to look down, to listen, to fall.

"Everly," the voice sings once more, but now it's darker, more urgent, wrapping itself around my mind, squeezing.

I take another step back, but the mist shifts with me, closing in like a noose tightening around my body. My legs feel weak, and I stumble, the ground slipping beneath me. My heart is in my throat, fear coursing through my veins. I can't tear my eyes away from the well, from the blackness inside, from the voice that keeps calling my name, pulling me deeper into its spell.

Magic bursts from my chest, pushing away the fog. My entire frame sags, and I gasp for air. I lift my head and stare at the well, anger burning like a fire through my veins. Lifting my hands, thousands of vines shoot from the ground, encasing the well in a dome. The singing abruptly cuts off, leaving me in silence, the only noise my harsh breath.

'That wasn't very nice,' a melodic voice chides from behind me.

I spin, slipping on the damp ground, my heart leaping into my throat.

'We only want to show you the secrets you seek.'

"What secrets? What do I seek? Because it feels ominous as shit and not at all friendly!" I snap.

The woman standing before me in white robes that float on the air just shrugs. *'That's your interpretation. We simply answered your call because your magic comes from the earth. The druids are our distant relatives.'*

I eye the White Witch in front of me with distrust. "Why should I believe you?"

Her white-orbed eyes flare in anger. *'We never lie.'*

"Then tell me what you think I seek to know."

She opens her mouth, but before she can answer me, I hold up my hand. "I'm not getting in that well, so forget it."

The White Witch hums thoughtfully. *'Why are you scared?'*

Flashes of my childhood bombard me, and I realize it's her flicking through my memories.

"Stop that!"

'That boy should be strung up for the cruelty he inflicted on you,' several voices echo in my head at once.

I shake my head, trying to dislodge the memories of my foster brother. His wicked, cruel smirk as he shut the door of the closet, locking it and leaving me there for days at a time.

"It was a long time ago."

'But it still affects you greatly,' she prods, floating closer.

I narrow my eyes in warning. "Doesn't matter anymore."

'I beg to differ. If you don't face your fear, how do you expect to rescue your mate?'

Her words have their desired effect. I freeze, my breath stalling. "Do you know where he is?"

'We do. But to get there, you will need to traverse several cave systems. It's the only way.'

A sudden gust of wind tears through the clearing, whipping my hair across my face and biting into the thin fabric of my nightdress. The cold gnaws at my skin, making me shiver. I'm really going to have to start sleeping in my fighting gear.

Swiping the hair out of my face, I gasp. The witch stands mere inches from me, her pale features illuminated by the faint moonlight.

“What–” my words barely form before her cold hands shoot forward, grasping either side of my face.

A scream rips from my throat as a searing, unbearable pain stabs into my skull. It's as though her fingers are sinking into my mind, prying it apart. My vision blurs, knees buckling beneath me as agony radiates through every nerve.

"Through caverns deep and shadows wide, the Skythari Nomads dwell where beasts do hide. To earn their trust, a bond must form, in Ethereal Peaks where magic storms. The beasts will guide your path they know, but only through trust can you truly grow. To reunite with what you've lost, seek the creatures, no matter the cost. Shadow's hand will search in vain, for only the beasts can break the chain."

The witch's grip tightens, and images swiftly start to invade my mind. They flash like broken shards of glass, each one sharper than the last. Snow-capped mountains tower before me, their icy peaks bathed in an eerie, otherworldly glow. I see figures standing atop the ridges—fae with skin so pale and icy blue it almost blends with the snow, but the white markings etched across their faces still stand out. Their eyes are an unnatural, glacial blue, so clear they seem to pierce straight through me. Their long, white hair falls in thick ropes, dreadlocks that whip in the wind.

Then, as if pulled by some unseen force, my vision shifts. A massive, winged beast appears, its wings the color of snow, feathers gleaming in the pale light. It lets out a roar that echoes across the mountains. My pulse quickens, and I try to pull away, but the witch's hold remains unrelenting.

The next image crashes through my mind with a brutal force, making everything inside me constrict painfully. Maxon. He's chained to a cavern wall, his arms pulled taut above him, his chest rising and falling with shallow, labored breaths. Blood drenches his front, seeping from countless cuts and gashes that mar his skin. His face is pale, eyes barely open, pain and exhaustion clearly weighing heavily on him.

A scream rips from my throat, more raw and primal than anything I've ever heard myself make. The air around me quivers, vibrating with my fear and anguish. I try to reach for him, to break the chains, to do something, but I'm helpless, trapped in this nightmare vision.

The world around me pulses, growing darker, the images distorting and flickering, until everything is swallowed by the void. All that remains is the endless darkness and the crushing reality of my own helplessness. Then, silence.

Chapter Thirty-Five

Maxon

I lift my head, ears straining at the faint echo of a scream that carries through the damp air of the cavern. I'm on my knees, arms strung above my head and wyvern bones wrapped around my wrists and neck, a pool of blood steadily growing beneath me.

My heart stutters, then picks up pace. That scent—roses, night jasmine, and sugar—Everly. It can't be. My pulse races, and I thrash against the chains, making them bite deeper into my wrists, bones shifting and twisting, puncturing skin as they constrict around me like a snake strangling its prey.

"What's gotten into you?" a bewildered voice snaps from the darkness, with a hint of cold impatience.

I freeze, turning my head as much as the bone chains allow, glaring into the darkened doorway. There, standing like a shadow within shadow, is the old woman I've seen in the company of the demon.

The edges of her mouth tug downward into a frown as her eyes roam over my body.

"Does she have her?" I snarl, my voice rasping with desperation. My whole body tenses, awaiting her answer.

The woman's eyes widen, and she shakes her head, her voice trembling when she speaks. "You would know if the Shadoweaver had the druid."

I grind my teeth, annoyance bubbling under my skin. I can't trust her, not entirely, but the thought of Everly in that creature's hands makes the chains around me feel like they're crushing my bones.

"I hear them," I press, forcing my voice low and dangerous. "The march of many feet, moving further away."

The woman's lips press into a thin line as she nods, shifting nervously on her feet, glancing around as though even the walls have ears.

"Where is she sending them? Where are her armies going?" My tone is pleading now, a raw edge creeping into it. The scent of my blood drips steadily from the wounds at my wrists, pooling on the stone beneath me. I'm weak, but if I can learn something—*anything*—while I'm still lucid . . .

Her eyes dart around, frantic, as though shadows might betray her. She shifts again, hands trembling. "The dark has ears. The shadows carry secrets. I should not be talking to you."

"Tell me."

Her eyes flicker back to mine, wavering. I have her attention, but it's slipping, and I don't have long before the blood loss makes me delirious again. The chains creak as I shift, pain radiating through my body, but I ignore it, focusing on the woman in front of me.

She shifts closer. “The Shadoweaver has sent–” her words cut off, eyes bulging as blood spills from her mouth. I sag against my chains, disappointment crashing through me. I was so close to gleaning some information.

The woman's body falls to the floor in front of me, her eyes wide open. Yumekui steps around the body, crouching in front of me. I put my head down, but her fingers grip my hair, forcing my head back. Those crimson eyes gleam as she tilts her head, studying me.

“Look what you made me do,” she goads with a sly tilt to her red lips.

“I didn’t make you do shit!”

The demon hums softly as she releases her grip on my head, her nails trailing coldly down my skin before she steps back. Slowly, deliberately, she begins circling me. Each step is measured, her movements lazy, as if she’s savoring this moment of control.

“You’ve been thrashing about.” Her voice is smooth yet razor-sharp, like the edge of a blade. “And bleeding more than we’d like. What good is bait if you’re dead?”

I bite back a retort, my body trembling with the effort to stay upright, but I can’t help the words that slip from my lips. “No one will come for me.”

If they have any sense, they’ll stay far away. Coming after me would only sign their death warrants.

The demon’s smile widens, amused. “On the contrary,” she purrs, her voice taking on a mocking lilt, “your soldiers have amassed, gathering allies as we speak. They seem to be preparing for something.”

A chill runs down my spine, making my breath catch in my throat. They're coming? I clench my fists, fighting the surge of emotions that threaten to overwhelm me.

The demon's laughter is cold and mirthless. "All for you. How touching." She pauses, standing in front of me now, her gaze burning into mine. "But what they don't realize is that they'll be marching straight into a trap."

I grit my teeth, refusing to show weakness, but inside, my mind is racing. I never wanted this. I never wanted them to risk their lives for me. And now, they're walking into something they can't possibly understand.

"You're lying," I spit, trying to keep my voice steady. "They wouldn't be that foolish."

"Oh, wouldn't they?" The demon's smile widens, her eyes glowing with dark amusement. "Your people love you. They'll die for you if it means bringing you back. The druid will happily follow if it means getting her mate back."

Her words twist like a knife in my gut.

"Let them come," the demon whispers, leaning down so her lips brush against my ear. "I'll be ready."

Pulling back, she dips her fingers into the blood pooling beneath me, her movements slow and deliberate. Her lips part as she begins to whisper, her words a strange, ancient language that slips between syllables too quickly for me to catch. The accent is unsettling, like the rustling of dry leaves in a storm, a sound that doesn't belong.

My muscles strain, instinct urging me to move, to resist, but my body betrays me—weak, bound, utterly powerless. The chains holding me in place bite into my skin.

She leans closer, her breath hot against my skin as her fingers move in intricate patterns, smearing my blood across my skin. I can't see it, but I know what she's doing—drawing runes. Demon runes.

Her crimson eyes flash with a spark of dark magic, the glow intensifying as she draws another rune, her pace quickening. The tip of her finger grazes my forehead, the wetness of my own blood cold against my burning skin as she draws the final symbol there. The sensation is nauseating—a slick, crawling feeling as the magic seeps into my flesh.

My heart pounds hard, as I try to cling to consciousness, my breaths shallow and fast, vision blurring. But it's no use. Whatever spell she's casting, it's taking its toll. I can feel the weight of it crushing down on me, like a vice tightening around my soul.

The room spins, darkness creeping in at the edges of my vision. I've been bound and weakened for too long, my strength drained with every drop of blood spilled. All I can do is watch, helpless, as she marks me for whatever fate she has planned.

Then, just as suddenly as it began, she stops. The room goes deathly quiet, the weight of her magic hanging in the air like a thick fog. She leans back, her glowing eyes locking onto mine, a wicked smile curling at the edges of her lips.

"That should be sufficient."

Chapter Thirty-Six

Everly

Warm hands grip my shoulders, shaking me gently. "Everly," a familiar voice calls, thick with worry.

Distantly, I hear the rustle of clothing and the unmistakable sound of Raiden's wings snapping open.

"Is she okay?" someone inquires, their voice strained.

"I don't fucking know," Raiden snaps, irritation lacing his words.

A low whimper reaches my ears, soft but unmistakable. I can sense them—Anika and Nymeria are close by, hovering. My head pounds relentlessly, but that seems to be a normal thing at the moment.

Without warning, I'm scooped into someone's arms and cradled against a warm solid chest. The scent of leather, pine, and whiskey surrounds me. Raiden.

"How did she get past all of us?" Tristan's voice cuts through my hazy mind.

Fenris's rough voice answers, a snort of resignation in his tone. "If the Witte Wieven want her, we can do nothing to stop them."

Raiden's chest rumbles beneath my cheek, his anger barely contained. "She's so cold," he mutters, his arms tightening around me protectively.

Two wet noses push against me. *'Mother?'*

'I'm okay. I just can't move yet.'

Their warm heads nuzzle against me. Though I can't move, I'm not scared. More than anything, I'm relieved the pain is over, and I know what our next step is.

"The Witte Wieven wouldn't hurt her," Nix assures as I feel her land on my knee. "The Guardians and the druids are closely related. It doesn't make sense for them to wish her harm."

"Everly is in danger, now more than ever," Fenris growls.

"What do you mean?" Tristan questions, and I hear him move closer.

"She is the key to releasing the Shadoweaver from his prison. A lot of fae won't want that to happen, and the only way to truly prevent it . . . "

"Is to kill her," Raiden finishes.

"Exactly," Fenris agrees darkly.

Their words send a shiver down my spine, and I want nothing more than to curl in on myself, to shrink away and make myself small. It's the same instinct I felt all those years growing up in foster care, back when I learned that hiding could keep me safe, unseen.

"I will fly her back," Raiden's voice cuts through my thoughts, firm and final. I don't hear a response before we're airborne. My stomach drops as we ascend with each powerful flap of his wings, and though I can't open my eyes, I can imagine the ground swiftly shrinking away beneath us.

"You really gotta stop leaving your bedroom, Everly," he quips, half-amused, half-scolding. "I'm going to need to put a bell on you."

I wish I could get my mouth to work to reply, but every muscle in my body is locked in fear. Being unable to move is terrifying. Still, I push the panic down. Raiden's got me, and I trust him with my life. Whatever happens, I know he will keep me safe.

Back in my room, I feel the faintest stirrings of movement returning to my limbs, like a slow, tingling current. Raiden gently lays me down on the daybed, his touch careful, as if I might shatter. I'm vaguely aware of a blanket being pulled up over me, its weight a soft, comforting pressure that anchors me as my senses start to clear. I think about everything I just saw and what the Witte Wieven told me. That verse has been burned into my brain.

The verse seems straightforward, almost deceptively so, but if there's one thing I've learned during my time here, it's that nothing is ever simple. Every word, every phrase, could have layers, like hidden traps waiting to be sprung. I turn the verse over in my mind, again and again. With a soft breath, my eyelids flutter open, and the relief I feel is immediate. It's like my body was so overloaded with what the Witte Wieven had done that it shut down momentarily.

The door to my chambers opens, and I hear Zaria whispering to Raiden. I turn my head to the side and see her worried expression.

"Is she okay?" Zaria whispers harshly.

"I'm okay," I croak, trying to sit up, but my head protests the movement.

Zaria's warm honey brown eyes land on me, and relief softens her features as she quickly crosses the room and helps me sit up.

"Oh, thank Morrigan. I was worried when the others said you were unconscious."

At the mention of the goddess's name, a strange feeling surges through me—an odd, fluttering jolt I can't explain. I've heard of her, and Valric mentioned her once when he spoke of the funeral rites. But there is no reason for her name alone to have this effect on me.

Zaria opens her mouth, but I hold my hand up, magic washing over my body, and I abruptly stand. The world around me fades and shifts. Suddenly, I'm standing at the elegant fountain outside my castle at the Evergreens. Water laps playfully around my hand as I skim it across the surface. I catch my reflection only to see the five-year-old version of me.

Another memory? A vision?

I sense someone's presence, a subtle warmth that makes the hair on the back of my neck prickle, and I turn, glancing over my shoulder. A beautiful woman stands there, a soft, serene smile on her face. Her honey-brown hair cascades down her shoulders, impossibly long and glittering like spun gold, and her amber eyes radiate a kindness and wisdom that draws me in, making me feel oddly safe.

"Who are you?" I whisper, unable to tear my gaze away.

The woman steps forward, her movements as graceful as the wind. Reaching out, she traces a gentle path down my cheek with her fingertips. Her touch is warm and soft, and a profound sense of calm settles into my bones.

"I'm Morrigan," she answers softly.

A flicker of recognition surges through me. "Hi, I'm . . . I'm Princess Vera," I manage, suddenly feeling small under her gaze.

Her smile widens, warm and knowing. "I know, Vera. I am the one who blessed your life in your mother's womb. You are destined to do great things, my child. But there is one thing you must remember—it's very important."

I stare completely entranced by her presence as her words settle over me like a protective veil.

"Trust your heart, you can do no wrong if you follow your heart."

I tilt my head, the weight of my golden hair cascading over my shoulder. A soft smile graces Morrigan's lips as her hand reaches out, fingers like feathers gliding through my hair, the touch light and ethereal.

"And one more thing," she whispers, her voice gentle. "If you try to do it all by yourself, your heart will crumble into dust. There are allies everywhere—people willing to stand by your side, some even willing to give their lives to help you fulfil your destiny."

A pang of fear twists in my chest. "But I don't want anyone to die," I object softly.

Morrigan's eyes soften, a gentle sadness mingling with her wisdom. "Death is not the end, Vera," she murmurs, her words filled with a promise I don't quite understand. "Those who choose this path understand its cost. Remember, they will find peace in purpose, and their spirits will always walk beside you."

"I don't understand."

"Your birth stirred something ancient and dark. The Shadoweaver, long bound in slumber, felt the ripple of your magic echo through Faerie. It awakened her. Drawn to your power like a moth to flame. She knew you were the one that could free her, and she has been hunting you ever since. Your mother understood the danger that your presence posed, not just to you, but to all of Faerie. That's why she made the impossible choice—to send you away, to hide you beyond the veil of this world, far from the Shadoweaver's reach. It was the only way to protect you. But the moment you returned to Faerie, everything changed. Now, her gaze is fixed on you. Whether you find and free your prince or not, she will not stop. Not unless you face her. Because even if you win this battle, there will be another. The Shadoweaver will keep coming, again and again—until she claims the crown that was never meant to be hers."

A cold rush of realization washes over me—I haven't even considered that. Every ounce of my focus has been on getting Maxon back. But that's just the beginning.

She wants out.

And she won't stop until she's free.

My mind trips up for a second as the word slams into me. "Wait. She?"

Morrigan nods and leans down, pressing a light kiss to my forehead, and I feel warmth blossom there, spreading through me like sunlight. "You are not alone. Trust your heart, and trust those who choose to walk with you."

As she pulls away, her form begins to fade, dissolving like mist.

Then I'm standing in my chambers again with Zaria's big brown eyes filling my vision.

"Seriously, Everly. You must stop doing that!"

"Sorry," I reply, rubbing my temples.

"What did you see?" Raiden gently takes my hand, guiding me over to the sofas, his touch steadying. I sink down, feeling a comforting weight settle over me as Zaria drapes a blanket around my shoulders. I smile up at her, grateful.

"I'm going to get you some tea," she murmurs softly, brushing a hand over my shoulder.

"Thanks," I reply, watching her go before turning back to Raiden. He sits beside me, his silver eyes meeting mine, their usual calm replaced by a storm of emotion swirling within them, flickers of worry and something deeper. I can tell he's been holding back his own anxiety, and I give him a half-smile, trying to lighten the tension.

"Sorry, Batman."

Raiden sighs, shaking his head, his tone softer now. "It's not your fault."

I take a steadying breath. "Should we wait for the others before I tell you what I saw . . . and what the Witte Wieven shared with me?" I ask, searching his face for guidance.

He considers for a moment before nodding. "Probably, unless there's anything you don't want them to know," he replies, his voice gentle but curious.

"No, we'll wait." I pull my legs up, crossing them beneath me, and tighten the blanket around my shoulders, feeling both anticipation and a sliver of dread settle over me.

A few moments later, Nix bursts into the room, her energy loud and brash, exactly as expected. "Do you know what time it is?" she shrieks, crossing her arms and fixing me with a look that would intimidate anyone but me. "How are we supposed to get any rest when you keep disappearing all the time?"

"Nix," Raiden growls, his voice rumbling through the room, instantly silencing her outburst. There's a protectiveness in his tone, and his eyes flash with warning.

I sigh, looking down as guilt coils around me. "She's right," I admit.

My friends are here trying to protect me, and I am making it hard for them. Although, admittedly, not on purpose.

Fenris strolls into the room, and I freeze when I catch the look on his face—worry, raw and unguarded. I'm so used to seeing that stoic, simmering anger in his expression that the concern takes me by surprise.

Without a word, he strides over to me, and in one smooth motion, scoops me up off the sofa and into his arms. I gasp as he pulls me close, tucking my head under his chin, his arms holding me tightly, almost like he's afraid to let go.

"Fuck, Vera," he murmurs, his voice rough, the words rumbling through his chest.

Just for a moment, I relax in his hold, savoring the warmth of his body.

A throat clears behind us, and I feel the heat of embarrassment rise to my cheeks. Fenris sighs and slowly sets my feet on the ground, but he doesn't step away. His gaze remains fixed on me, his brown eyes softened by flickers of violet. For a moment, we just look at each other, the silence heavy with unspoken feelings I can't quite decipher.

But then Raiden speaks, breaking the quiet. "Want to explain?" His voice is tense, anger tightening his words, though I can tell it's not directed solely at me.

I take a steadying breath, pulling the blanket tighter around my shoulders as I turn to face everyone.

Kian and Tristan stand there, their brows furrowed in confusion, scanning the scene before them.

"Yeah, only one day ago you were both ready to tear each other apart," Kian agrees.

Nix flutters a few feet away, her arms crossed, as Zaria places a tray of steaming tea on the small table.

This is it—the moment to confess all, to spill the beans, to share everything I've been holding back.

I clear my throat, the sound echoing slightly in the quiet room, and gesture to Fenris. "We were best friends growing up. It's not romantic."

Fenris snorts. "I would never betray my king like that."

Raiden's eyes dart back and forth between us, a flicker of uncertainty in their depths.

"He was going to be my paladin, take over from Valric when he was old enough, but then the attack happened . . . " I fade off. "I remembered Fenris in the arena, that was the memory. He is like a brother to me, a confidant when I was young."

Raiden lets out a low grunt, his shoulders slumping as he sinks back onto the sofa. "Alright, tell us what happened tonight."

I have no idea how he finds sitting like that comfortable with his massive wings. Settling beside him, I glance around as the others find their places, the air thick with anticipation. Nix lands on my lap, while Zaria takes the spot next to me. Perched atop

Zaria's head, Asrai tilts her head, watching me with those big bright, knowing eyes.

Across from us, Kian settles into the armchair, folding his arms as his assessing gaze fixes on me. Tristan takes the other armchair, his expression unreadable, though I can sense the intensity in his watchful silence.

Fenris, on the other hand, stalks over to the balcony, his gaze directed outward as he stares into the night, his silhouette tense against the faint glow of moonlight.

With everyone settled, I take a deep breath, steeling myself.

"The Witte Wieven told me and showed me what I have to do next." I take a deep breath and repeat what they said. "*Through caverns deep and shadows wide, the Skythari Nomads dwell where beasts do hide. To earn their trust, a bond must form, in Ethereal Peaks where magic storms. The beasts will guide your path they know, but only through trust can you truly grow. To reunite with what you've lost, seek the creatures, no matter the cost. Shadow's hand will search in vain, for only the beasts can break the chain.*"

Everyone is silent, a mixture of expressions flickering across their faces.

"That's really fucking vague. Did they say anything else?" Raiden grunts.

I bite my lip. "They showed me the snowy mountains and a great white, winged beast, fae with skin so pale it was an icy blue. I think . . . I think I need to find these Skythari Nomads and gain their trust so they can either help us or give the location of these beasts that can lead us to Maxon."

"What did these beasts look like?" Fenris asks, not turning around.

"They looked like giant white lions, but with massive, feathered wings. Two horns jutted out from their white manes. They were . . . incredible."

Asrai, who is perched quietly on Zaria's head, suddenly bursts into flight, her wings a blur as she flits before me, her tiny hands signing furiously. *'Luxaryn!'*

"What?" I feel the confusion rippling through me.

'Luxaryn!' she signs again, emphasizing each letter. '*Creatures that have wings that crackle with lightning and protect mountaintops from intruders. They're the Light Bringers, a winged beast with feathers that shine brightly, illuminating dark places.'*

"What did she say?" Zaria's brows knit together as she reaches out to cup the small Willowroot in her hands.

I meet her worried gaze. "She said they're luxaryn."

Raiden's expression turns dark as he leans forward. "The luxaryn are extinct."

"Or maybe . . . not," I argue, letting the possibility sink in.

Raiden stands abruptly, rubbing a hand through his hair, his steps becoming more agitated with each pass. "What about before?" he demands, his voice tight. "What else did you see?"

I swallow hard. "Morrigan."

The name hangs in the air, heavy as a storm cloud. Zaria and Nix suck in sharp breaths, and Kian's jaw drops slightly, his disbelief visible.

"No way," he says under his breath. "No one has seen the gods since the dragons left."

I frown, the words escaping me before I fully realize what I'm saying. "The dragons didn't leave."

"What?" Nix's eyes widen.

"How do you know that?" Raiden's voice is low, challenging, as he studies me with open intensity.

I open my mouth to answer, but no words come. How do I know that?

"The Witte Wieven, the druids, and the dragons . . . they were all guardians of this land, right?" I begin slowly, piecing it together as I speak.

Murmurs of agreement fill the room.

"Well, the Witte Wieven pulled away first. The druids did the same. The dragons simply followed suit. They didn't leave—they're waiting. If the right person calls, they will answer."

The weight of what I'm saying sinks in, a revelation that shakes even me. Tristan's eyes go wide as he leans forward. "So, you're saying, if we free Maxon, he could call the dragons back?"

I nod, feeling the enormity of it press down on me. The room falls silent, each of them processing what this could mean. A prickle of awareness moves over me, and I stand, moving to the doors and opening them. Nymeria and Anika trot inside, both jumping straight on the bed.

"Okay, so we have the verse to guide us, kinda," Kian acknowledges, "But what did Morrigan say?"

"She advised me not to do this on my own. That I will need all the help I can get."

Chapter Thirty-Seven

Maxon

I can feel it—a gnawing hunger, a deep, primal need clawing its way to the surface. It's everywhere, an ache that reverberates through my entire being. It's a hunger gnawing at my soul, demanding her presence, and only the depths of our bond can appease it.

The new moon is drawing closer. Despite the darkness, I can sense its approach like a predator senses its prey, a subtle shift in the night's energy. The pull usually wouldn't be this bad, but my body is screaming for replenishment, for the chance to heal. The dull, throbbing ache in my gums worsens, spreading with each passing second. My body is demanding my mate to heal it. I look down at the deep, gaping cuts across my torso and see the once-crimson flow of blood from my wounds has now reduced to a sluggish seep.

Yumekui's last visit left a mark on me far beyond the physical. My mind remains a haze of fragmented and scattered pieces of a puzzle I'm too weak to assemble. I remember the feeling of her presence, cold and consuming, like a shadow that lingered long after she was gone. I remember the sharp, searing pain, the way her touch drained more than just my strength. And then, nothing—just the fog, oppressive and unrelenting.

I close my eyes, trying to push through the hunger, to resist the primal urge clawing at the edges of my sanity. But the ache doesn't fade; it deepens, growing more insistent. It's not just hunger. It's need—raw, unfettered, and terrifying in its intensity. It's a need that only my mate can fulfil.

Chapter Thirty-Eight

Everly

I stand on the balcony looking out into the garden. Tonight is the first night of the new moon, and I've been locked away in my room with Zaria. The others have been kept away from me for their safety and mine.

The urge for Maxon's blood burns through me, setting alight a fiery hunger coiled tight in my chest. It isn't just the thirst—it's the need. But that need is dangerous, and I know it. Zaria said if I let it consume me, I could fall ill—or worse, lose myself completely to madness. Neither option is appealing.

Fenris offered his blood, but I declined immediately, recoiling at the thought. It isn't about him—it isn't about anyone but Maxon. No one else's blood can quench this. No one else can calm the storm raging inside me.

I force my attention to the garden stretching out before me.

The soft rustling of leaves in the breeze offers a temporary reprieve from the chaos in my head. My eyes drift across the courtyard, catching sight of the guards in their sage-green uniforms patrolling the grounds.

And then, like a whisper carried on the wind, I hear it.

'Listen.'

The word is soft, almost tender, yet unmistakable. I blink and glance around, searching for the source.

No one's near me. The guards are too far away to have spoken, and none of them seems to have noticed anything unusual. Yet the word lingers in the air, tugging at something deep inside me.

A warm breeze curls around my body, brushing against my skin. It sends the loose long-sleeved, light blue night dress floating around me.

'Listen and follow. He will be waiting.'

Instinctively, I close my eyes and find the thread connecting us. I reach out slowly, running my fingers softly over it, feeling its warmth.

'Well, I'm listening, but for what?'

I feel like I've done this a million times. It's always the same. I feel the bond. It's here but silent.

What does she mean?

Steadying myself with a deep breath, I do something I haven't done before. I slowly open my end of the bond. I let down every wall, every defense, peeling back layer after layer of my guarded heart until all that remains is the bare essence of who I am and what I feel. I send wave after wave of love, warmth, and longing into the space between us, pouring everything into the bond, hoping it reaches him, that it's enough.

'Maxon?'

The silence lingers, thick and oppressive, until I feel a tremor—a faint, electric pulse. And then, like a soft whisper, his voice stirs, faint but unmistakable.

"Everly."

Elation swells, a rush of joy and relief surging through me, pulsing louder with every breath.

"I'm here." The words tumble out in a rush, as if he might slip away if I don't say them fast enough.

There's a pause, and then his voice again, warm and achingly familiar. "Everly."

The sound of my name on his lips, a calling meant only for me, unlocks something deep inside. I let everything else fall away—every worry, every fear, even the hollow ache that's been weighing me down. I surrender to the pull of his voice, letting it guide me forward, deeper into the connection. I drift completely weightless, pulled through the endless space between us.

And then, suddenly, I'm jolted, and my feet hit solid ground, my eyes fly open. The bond buzzes, alive now, vibrating faintly.

Confused, I look around, my breath halting in my lungs as a wave of awareness skates across my skin. The thick darkness of the night surrounds me as I stand in the middle of a meadow. I swallow roughly, turning in a slow circle.

How did I get here? Where is here? Am I dreaming?

I swear I was so close to reaching him. I do my best not to let the crushing weight of disappointment settle over me.

Then a soft, indistinguishable noise reaches my ears, and I freeze in fear, my feet rooted to the spot.

Knees trembling, I take a small step forward in the long grass, sending thousands of fireflies scattering into the cool night air.

Someone is watching me. I can feel it in every inch of my body. I strain, listening for movement or any sound.

"I know you're there!" I call out. My fingers flicker over the place my dagger is usually strapped, and once again, I'm only in a light silk night dress.

Shit.

"Everly?"

My heart stalls at the sound of that voice, then a warmth blooms through me. Excitement flows like liquid fire, filling my veins as I look out into the darkness, adrenaline coursing through me.

"Maxon?"

Movement catches my attention as a figure walks toward me. I hold my breath as they approach, doing my best to push down the uncertainty that's rising. After the Witte Wieven, I'm not sure what to expect.

Fireflies swirl around the grass, their golden glow illuminating the darkness in gentle, pulsing waves. The entire field seems to breathe with light, as if the stars themselves have drifted down to dance around us. Their delicate brightness is just enough for me to see who is approaching from the shadows. I stand completely frozen, my breath caught on an inhale as the figure steps closer. It is him.

Maxon moves with quiet, deliberate steps, his white tunic and black pants looking immaculate even in the dim light.

He stops just in front of me, close enough that I can feel the warmth radiating from him. My heart is beating so damn hard I swear I will pass out any minute. His presence is overwhelming, commanding the space between us. I'm rooted in place, unable to look away. Slowly, he raises his hand. His fingertips brush my cheek, and I shiver as he cups my face, his touch both firm and tender.

His thumb glides across my cheek, leaving a trail of warmth in its wake.

"Don't cry," he whispers.

I choke on a laugh. I didn't even realize I've been crying. He draws closer, and the warmth radiating from his body slides over my exposed skin. My hands land on his chest as I search those deep violet eyes I love so much.

"Are you . . . Is this . . . " I can't seem to get the words out. "Is this real?"

A grin tugs at his lips before his mouth drops. His lips brush mine, unhurried. My body leans in, unconsciously drawn to him, and I feel the strong, steady beat of his heart beneath my palm. A soft whimper escapes me, and Maxon's grip tightens, his arm sweeping around my waist. In one swift motion, he pulls me flush against him, our bodies pressing together as if we were made to fit this way. His kiss deepens, and I melt into it, surrendering completely to the intensity of his touch.

My mind is a haze, every thought drowned by the intoxicating taste of him. Our kiss grows more urgent, more demanding, his tongue finding mine in a rhythm that feels like it could set my very soul on fire. I can't get enough of him—his warmth, his strength, his very presence envelops me, grounding me in a moment that feels both fragile and infinite.

How can this be real? This is him. He is here. But how?

Logic slips away, lost in the heat between us. If this is a dream, I am determined to live every second of it, to drink in every sensation before it fades. My fingers twist into the fabric of his tunic, pulling him impossibly closer, my need for him growing with a desperation I've never felt before. I press myself against him, aching to erase every inch of space between us, to feel nothing but him and the fire blazing between us.

Maxon carefully eases us down onto the billowing waves of tall grass, the sensation of the soft blades tickling our skin as we continue to kiss. I gasp as he sucks my bottom lip into his mouth before trailing kisses down my neck and across my collarbone. My body is on fire, my core like liquid heat as he trails his hand up my body, cupping my breast. I lose my breath as he slips the strap of my nightgown down over my shoulder, his lips following its path, exposing my breast. My fingers thread into his hair, and I anchor him to me, as his mouth latches onto my nipple.

My back arches and I rock my hips upward, needing to feel him even closer. In desperation, I tear at his tunic, needing it gone.

"Maxon, please," I beg.

Lifting his head, those violet eyes flicker with a heat I've missed dearly. He slides his palm down my stomach and between my legs, his eyes never leaving mine as he presses two fingers inside me. My breath rushes out and I tip my head back on a moan. Maxon pauses his movements and leans closer to my face.

"You have fangs," he breathes.

"Huh?" I reply, confused.

His hand leaves me, but before I can protest, his mouth is on mine. He kisses me, long and deep, his tongue sliding over my teeth.

"You do have your fangs," he says wickedly as he pulls away, the words making my stomach flip.

"Raiden said something about having to feed on the new moon. Can we? Is it possible?"

Maxon's eyes light up. His hands slide up my thighs, bunching the thin fabric of my nightgown at my waist. Without hesitation, his mouth finds its mark, covering my most sensitive spot. A deep, primal growl escapes his throat as his tongue begins to swirl, teasing and tormenting before he draws me fully into his mouth, the sensation both electric and consuming.

"Oh . . . holy–" My mouth drops open as waves of endorphins flood my body, sending every nerve in my body on fire.

Maxon growls, the vibrations shooting through my core, as he presses his fingers inside me, curling them and rubbing along my inner walls. He sucks and thrusts in the perfect rhythm, making my head spin.

My hips jerk and words tumble from my mouth as he continues as if he were starving for me. Heat engulfs my body as my orgasm rips through me, lighting up the air around me with golden sparks.

Oh, fuck . . .

I scream, my fingers digging into the dirt beneath me as I struggle to catch my breath. Suddenly a violent searing pain radiates from my inner thigh, and a strange pulling sensation washes over me, sending my orgasm into overdrive. My entire body is shaking uncontrollably, as my back bows. I glance down, seeing Maxon's mouth locked onto my inner thigh, his fangs sinking deep into my flesh. The sharp puncture sends a jolt through me, but it's the slow, deliberate pull of my blood that overwhelms my senses. Each drag of his lips draws my pulse in a thunderous rhythm, the sound pounding in my ears. A wave of arousal floods me, making my muscles tremble, thighs shaking beneath his grip. I can't stop the whimper that escapes me, the heat growing unbearable as my own fangs ache, needing release.

Maxon's violet eyes flick up, catching mine, and the raw hunger in his gaze sends my body reeling. My head grows lighter with each pull, my breath hitching as I fight to stay grounded, though I feel like I'm drifting—losing myself in him. The line between pain and pleasure blurs as his mouth lingers, drawing deeper, tasting me.

Maxon keeps drinking, each pull of my blood making my head swim. My vision blurs, and the world tilts as I try to hold onto some sense of balance. "Maxon," I slur, barely recognizing my own voice. The sound of my pulse is deafening, pounding in my ears as if it's trying to escape.

His mouth releases me abruptly, and I hear a violent curse burst from him, filled with tension and something close to regret. The absence of his bite leaves a strange emptiness in its place, and before I can process it, I'm being lifted, my body moving as if I weigh nothing at all. I'm cradled in his lap, my cheek pressed against the warmth of his chest, while his arms wrap around me.

His grip tightens, one hand cradling the back of my head, and I can feel the rapid rise and fall of his chest.

"Stóirín, drink from me." He guides my head to his neck, wrapping my legs around his waist.

My mouth trails slowly over his shoulder to his neck, the smell of him making my mouth water.

"I shouldn't have taken so much, but the damage to my body . . . " He trails off with a sigh.

A tremor runs through my body, quick and sharp, at the regret in his voice. It isn't his fault. My eyes flutter and the urge to taste him overrides all other senses.

My mouth clamps over the spot where his neck meets his shoulder, and my fangs slide into his skin effortlessly. Immediately, warm liquid fills my mouth, the taste of his blood coating my tongue. It's coppery with a burst of citrus. I moan, drawing deeper, his blood and magic filling my veins.

"That's it, Stóirín, drink," Maxon murmurs, his hand running through my hair.

I feel him grow hard beneath me and wriggle on his lap. Maxon hisses, his fingers digging into my hips, rocking me against his cock.

I release his neck on a moan and slowly run my tongue over the bite mark. I reach up, gripping each side of his face as I slam my mouth down on his, nipping hard at his bottom lip. Maxon's groan spurs me on, and I lift slightly, his cock sliding through my wet heat. His hot, rough hands grip my ass cheeks and squeeze, rocking me over him. His growl is possessive and feral when he feels how wet I am.

Lights dance behind my eyes as he pushes in. My breath catches. I forgot how big he is. I whine as he stretches me, our panting growing louder. I want to sink down on him, but I need to adjust.

"Relax," Maxon murmurs in my ear, sending goosebumps scattering across my skin. I drop my head to his shoulder as he lifts his hips, working his way deeper. I do as he says and melt into him, sinking down further.

"That's my girl," he says, rocking into me, this time pushing in all the way.

Panting, I pull back just enough to steady myself, my hands still gripping his shoulders as we move together in a slow, rocking rhythm. His body feels like it's on fire beneath my palms, every muscle tense and coiled with barely contained hunger. My gaze locks onto his face, and for a moment, I lose myself in the intensity of his violet eyes. They glow in the dim light, but something shifts—flickers of red flames dance there, bright and consuming, as if something far more primal stirs within him.

"Beautiful." His voice is a husky growl, roughened by desire. He reaches up, tugging gently on a strand of my hair, his fingers curling into it.

Before I can reply, before I can even catch my breath, he moves, shifting with predatory grace. His strong hands grip my waist, and in a fluid motion, I'm on my back, the world spinning as he presses me into the grass. Then, with a restless desperation, he thrusts into me, driving so deep it steals the air from my lungs. The force of it tears a scream from my throat, a raw sound that echoes in the air as the overwhelming mix of pleasure and pain collides.

I'm spiraling, tumbling into the sensation, my body quaking beneath him as each thrust pushes me closer to release. The dizzying pleasure builds and builds until it feels like I might shatter, my nerves on fire, my senses drowning in him.

Suddenly, the world narrows and stars explode behind my eyes, blinding in their brilliance, and for a moment, I can't tell where I end, and he begins. Pleasure crashes over me, violent and consuming, dragging me under until all I can feel is him.

Chapter Thirty-Nine

Everly

I shoot up in bed, gasping, the throbbing in my core still pulsing. My body is covered in a sheen of sweat. Oh my fucking god, did I have a sex dream?

Was it real? It felt real.

I don't even remember going to bed. The last clear memory I have is standing out on the balcony, the cool night air brushing against my skin as I stared at the moonlit garden below. Did Zaria bring me inside?

My gaze sweeps across the quiet room and lands on the daybed in the corner, where Zaria is sprawled out, her head resting on one arm, her long dark hair cascading over the pillows.

Curled up beside her are the wolves, their silvery white coats blending into the plush cushions. Asrai is nestled on a pillow just beside Zaria's head. Both of them are sound asleep.

I throw the covers off and stumble to the bathroom, fumbling as I turn on the tap. I splash cold water on my face and look up at the large mirror in front of me and gasp. My eyes are feverish, skin flushed, my hair mussed.

"Holy shit," I whisper. "I look thoroughly fucked."

Surprisingly, the headache that's been plaguing me is gone, and my gums aren't aching anymore. I lean in closer, looking at my teeth, and see they are back to normal.

Exhaling a weary sigh, I turn toward the shower. "What the hell was that?" I mutter.

Slipping off my nightdress, I kick it to the side and step under the warm stream of water, tipping my head back.

I take a small amount of soap, put it in my hand, and breathe in the scent. The smells in Faerie are so powerful and vivid. Even before my transformation they were intoxicating. I lather my body with a sweet, citrusy soap, the scent of lychee and summer fruits swirling around me. My hand brushes my inner thigh, and I flinch, feeling a wave of unexpected anxiety. Snapping my eyes open, I peer down, bending slightly to get a closer look at the mark on my leg.

"Holy shit," I breathe softly, tracing the bite mark. "It wasn't a dream."

My heart soars, a rare feeling of pure happiness and contentment flooding through me. The memory of last night lingers, warm and vivid, sending a soft flush across my skin. We were together; we shared each other's blood. I don't feel the cravings anymore, or the tiredness from before.

I finish washing, the cool water doing little to temper the heat still radiating within me. My movements are quick but deliberate as I dry myself.

As I push open the door and step into the room, my eyes are immediately drawn to Zaria. She's sitting up on the daybed, her eyes half-lidded with a mix of alertness and laziness, like a predator basking in the first light of dawn. Her tail sways lazily behind her, brushing against the soft cushions in a rhythmic motion that seems to match the calm energy of the room.

She looks up at me, and there's a faint smile on her lips.

"You're up early," she notes.

I chuckle softly, running a hand through my damp hair as I cross the room. "Couldn't stay in bed. Too much energy," I admit.

Zaria's tail flicks once, her eyes narrowing slightly, a hint of worry there. "Energy, or restlessness?" she teases, her tone light but edged with curiosity.

"Maybe a bit of both," I reply, sitting down on the edge of the bed.

"You look . . . lighter," she remarks slowly.

I blink at her, and a smile tugs at my lips. "Maybe I am," I whisper quietly, more to myself than to her. "I saw Maxon. The bond opened for me."

Zaria's brown eyes widen. "It did?"

"Yes, we fed from each other," I admit softly, unable to hide the mix of emotions swirling within me. "I can feel the effects of it already. My muscles aren't sore, my head feels clearer, and our bond—it's stronger than ever."

Zaria practically radiates excitement, her energy bubbling over as she claps her hands together. "That's amazing!" she exclaims, a grin lighting up her face.

Before I can say anything else, she strides over to the wardrobe with purpose, throwing open the doors. Her hands move swiftly as she rummages through the array of garments until she pulls out a vivid blue dress. It's simple, understated even, but before I can fully appreciate it, she pulls out an overcoat to pair it with.

My breath catches as I take it in. The overcoat is nothing short of stunning. Its long, flowing design exudes both power and grace, the different shades of blue blending seamlessly into a masterpiece.

"Did he tell you anything we should know?" Zaria inquires casually as she holds up the dress for me.

My cheeks heat instantly, and I avoid her gaze as I slip my arms into the dress. "We . . . didn't do much talking," I mumble.

Zaria pauses, then turns to me with a soft, knowing smile playing on her lips. She doesn't say anything, but the glimmer of pleasure in her eyes says enough.

"Here." She holds up the long overcoat. I slide my arms into it, the luxurious material hugging my skin like a second layer. As I turn to the mirror, I pull my hair free, letting it cascade down my back.

Zaria steps behind me, her arms wrapping around my waist to fasten a black belt that sits snugly, holding the floor length coat in place. The buckle catches my eye—a gleaming symbol of the sun and moon, intricate and beautifully detailed.

I freeze for a moment, my breath catching in my throat. The design . . . it's strikingly similar to my birthmark.

Zaria doesn't seem to notice my sudden stillness, or if she does, she doesn't comment. She steps back, letting her hands brush against the material of the coat as she admires her handiwork.

The overcoat's collar stands tall, framing my neck with regal elegance. The deep V-neck plunges to my waist, balanced by the long sleeves that fit snugly, the velvet-like fabric soft and luxurious. The subtle gradation of blues, from deep sapphire to shimmering azure, adds a regal elegance to the ensemble.

"Wow," I breathe, turning slightly to take in the full effect. "This is . . . stunning."

Zaria's grin widens, and she folds her arms, clearly pleased with herself. "It's one of my own designs," she says with pride. "I was aiming for something elegant and intricate, something that exudes sophistication and nobility."

"You've definitely succeeded," I murmur, still turning in front of the mirror, the fabric catching the light with every movement. "I feel like I'm ready to command an army or walk into a royal court."

Zaria laughs lightly. "Good. That's exactly the energy I want you to carry. You're meant for greatness—might as well dress the part."

Chapter Forty

Maxon

I wake groggy, my mind thick with confusion. The world around me spins as I blink into the shadowy surroundings, my mouth dry as sandpaper. But something's different—something is missing. The constant hunger, the gnawing emptiness that's plagued me for days, is gone. It takes a moment to register, the absence so strange that I instinctively brace for it, expecting the sharp pang to return. It doesn't.

I take stock of my body, and my pulse stammers, then surges, sending a jolt of alarm through me. I look down, scanning for the familiar aches and pains, the bruises, the cuts—broken bones and gashes I've come to accept.

But they're not there.

It can't be.

My skin is smooth, unmarked. Every wound, every trace of the torture I've endured is gone.

I run my hand over the spot where a deep gash marred my ribs, my fingers brushing over nothing but smooth skin. The disbelief nearly chokes me. The pain that crippled me mere hours ago—it's vanished. Healed as if it never happened.

Was that dream . . . Was it real?

I reach up, my fingers run across my lips. Her kiss lingers there, a ghostly memory. My soul still hums with the connection; that pull I felt when we met in the veil of dreams. It was real. Somehow, through the impossible, we found each other, our souls colliding in that strange place, while our bodies remained distant. I shake my head, trying to grasp the logic, the mechanics of it, but nothing makes sense.

"You've been a busy boy," a voice slithers from the shadows, low and mocking, sending ice through my veins.

I drop my hands to my lap, the movement making the wyvern bones tighten slightly.

"The Master will not be happy about this," Yumekui singsongs.

She steps into view, a whip coiled in her hand as she saunters closer. Stopping a few feet away, she taps the whip on her chin and stares down at me. A cruel smile tugs at her lips.

"Should I punish you now or wait until the Master has seen you?"

"Do whatever the fuck you want," I snap.

My magic and fire burn beneath my skin, begging to be free of these bones so I can burn her alive.

"How did you do it?"

I narrow my eyes, and a growl slips from my throat.

"You've completely healed. The only way that could happen is if you fed. Who gave you their blood?"

Sensing her frustration, I smirk, but remain silent. As she leans down, her crimson eyes dart between mine, trying to read me.

"Tell me which one of my fucking handmaidens I need to kill," she hisses, her fingers sliding into my hair and ripping my head back.

The wyvern bones tighten around my neck in protest.

"Fine, have it your way." She steps back, clicking her fingers.

I watch as the two trolls lumber in, their footsteps echoing against the cave walls. They aren't like the maidens—they have strange, jagged markings etched into their gray skin. My eyes trace the lines, and a sick realization settles over me.

Slave markings.

Not everyone here serves by choice. I wonder how many others wear their chains on their skin as these trolls do.

Without a word, they unhook the wyvern bones from the wall. My muscles scream in silent protest, stiff and sore from being in the same position for days on end. The trolls grip me roughly, dragging me across the cold stone floor toward the center of the room.

One of them lowers a chain from the ceiling, the cold metal rattling as it unspools. It takes both of them to haul me up, their combined strength lifting my body effortlessly. I feel the strain in my shoulders as they grab the chain between my wrists and loop it over the ceiling's hook, suspending me above the ground. The stretch—painful and tight—also brings a strange sense of relief. After being forced to sit on stone for so long, I need to move. Even like this, it feels like a reprieve, however fleeting.

I know what's coming next.

The trolls retreat to the entrance, their faces emotionless, as if they've been conditioned to care about nothing beyond their orders. I try not to think about them.

Yumekui's touch is featherlight as her fingertip glides down the length of my back, tracing the curve of my spine before curling around my torso. My muscles tense beneath her touch. She comes to a stop in front of me, her eyes gleaming with that twisted mixture of amusement and cruelty she always wears so well.

"Last chance," she whispers, her voice laced with dark promise.

I bare my fangs in response, a guttural growl tearing from my throat. The sound bounces off the cave walls, deep and feral, echoing back to me like a challenge—a warning. My body trembles with pent-up rage, fury simmering just beneath the surface.

Chapter Forty-One

Everly

The main sitting room is alive with energy, though not the kind I need. Everyone has joined me under the pretense of helping me practice my magic, but I know they want to keep a close eye on me because of the new moon. Other than Zaria, Scarlett, and Mia, I haven't told a soul what happened last night.

Taking a deep breath, I try to block out their bickering and let the tension in my shoulders melt away. My eyes close, and I feel the magic swirling around me, warm and vibrant. The noise and distractions fade into the background as I let the energy flow, concentrating on the spell I've been struggling with.

When I open my eyes again, a small orb of water hovers in front of me, pulsing softly with light. For the first time all day, the room falls completely silent, everyone's bickering forgotten as they watch in awe.

"There," I utter more to myself than anyone else. "That's what I was trying to do."

"Did you hear me?" Tristan grouses.

"Oh my god, there is no need to repeat yourself. I ignored you just fine the first time," I grumble, rubbing my temples. The water orb sloshes back down into the small water feature.

"Rude."

"What do you want?" I ask, trying to keep my voice calm and level.

Tristan folds his arms and stares at me, long and hard.

"Don't be dramatic," I huff.

"Honestly, it's a wonder she hasn't accidentally wrapped the lot of you in vines yet, with all the noise you're creating." Zaria laughs from her spot by the balcony doors.

The room goes quiet, all eyes turning to her. I can't help the small smirk that tugs at my lips at her comment.

"Don't tempt me," I quip, waving my hand as a small tendril of energy sparks in the air. The faint golden glow dances around my fingers before fading away, but it's enough to make them all pause.

Scarlett's expression softens. "Sorry, E." She gives me a sheepish grin. "Didn't mean to make it harder for you."

Kian strolls over, drawing my attention, his lavender eyes narrowing on me. "Something is different with you. What happened?"

My face instantly heats, and I take a step back. "Nothing."

"You're lying," Tristan accuses.

"Fae can't lie," I respond, my defenses rising.

"With you, that's debatable," Kian argues, raising his eyebrow. I narrow my eyes at him, his lavender eyes searching mine for answers.

"Didn't you have something to tell me?" I deflect, rounding on Tristan.

"Well, I only wanted to say Coraline is here to see you and drop off some of her specialties."

Surprise has my eyes widening. "Really?"

"Who's Coraline?" Mia walks over, her fingers sliding through her long, dark brown hair to braid it over her shoulder.

"She is a purple-haired pixie who bakes the most delicious treats." I bite my lip as my mouth begins to water. "I hope they taste good."

"Coraline's baking always tastes good." Kian's frown looks personal.

I hold my hands up in surrender. "I'm just saying, since Maxon's been gone, everything tastes like cardboard."

"What's cardboard?" Tristan asks, wrinkling his nose.

"Never mind." I sigh. "It would be good to see her."

"I'll get Lutin and Senka to bring her up," Tristan offers, turning for the door.

I watch as he pokes his head out and speaks to Lutin, I'm assuming, and then shuts the door. My attention goes to Kian, who is staring at me oddly.

"What?"

His head tilts and steps closer. "How's the headache?"

His question takes me by surprise, even though it shouldn't. He's always been attentive. And being the first day of the new moon, I should be crawling out of my skin, right?

Taking a breath, I glance to the side at Mia. She just looks at me expectantly.

"They have gone," I reply carefully.

Kian takes another step closer. "The jaw pain?"

"Also gone."

His eyes move over my face and trace the mate mark. "What happened last night?"

Mia steps between us, her hands on her hips. "What's with the questions?" she snaps.

"Yeah. If you want to ask her something, don't beat around the bush," Scarlett adds walking over and opening up the balcony doors.

"Beat around the bush?" Tristan echoes.

Kian ignores everyone else in the room, his intense gaze locked on me, sharp and probing. "Did you feed?" His voice is low, but there's an edge to it that makes my heart race.

Heat floods my cheeks, my mind flashing back to the memory of last night. I can't hold his stare any longer, so I drop my eyes to the ground.

"Don't do that," he snaps.

My fingers curl into fists at my sides, nails biting into my palms.

"Do what?!" My response is harsh, my voice trembling with a mix of embarrassment and rising frustration.

"Hide!" Kian bellows, his voice echoing through the room.

"Hide?" I echo, staring at him for a moment. "Why are you getting so worked up?"

"He thinks you fed from another." Zaria sighs.

My eyes widen. "Not that it's any of your business, but I had a dream last night, okay? But I think it was real!"

"What do you mean?" he demands, his voice quieter now, but no less intense.

"I woke up in a meadow." My voice shakes as the memory rushes back. "Maxon was there. We . . . " My breath hitches, and I force myself to keep going, my pulse pounding in my ears. "We had sex. And we fed from each other."

The room goes deathly silent at my confession. Tension hangs in the air like a storm about to break.

"Are you sure?" Tristan's voice breaks the tension, his frown deepening as he steps forward, concern etched across his face.

I swallow hard, my throat dry. "I don't know. It felt real. I could feel everything—the blood, the connection, him . . . It was too vivid to just be a dream." I glance between Tristan and Kian, my mind still spinning. "And I have his bite mark on me."

"Show me," Kian demands.

Embarrassment surges through me, heating my skin until it feels like I'm burning from the inside out. I shake my head vigorously, taking a step back. "Nope, not happening."

"Why?" His eyes narrow, suspicion threading through his voice.

I shoot a desperate glance at Mia and immediately, she jumps up, hooking her arm through mine.

"Talk's over," Mia declares. "She doesn't have headaches anymore, her jaw pain's gone, and she had an amazing sex dream with her mate. It's done. Let's move on."

Her bluntness makes my cheeks burn even hotter, but at the same time, I can't help but feel a wave of relief wash over me.

"I've never heard of those kinds of dreams. We should ask Nolan or Raiden," Tristan muses.

"No!" I don't know why I am so embarrassed about this, but the thought of talking about my time with Maxon with others just makes me uncomfortable. "Look, if it happens again, I will find out, but for now, just forget it."

Before either can argue, there is a knock at the door. Scarlett skips over, red hair bouncing behind her, and swings the door open.

"Come in. You must be Coraline." She steps back for her to enter.

Coraline flutters into the room. Her wings are just as beautiful as I remember, with their rainbow hues catching the light. Her pink, jewel-like eyes lock onto mine as she gracefully takes flight toward me. She's no bigger than Nix, but her aura makes her feel bigger.

"Your Majesty. I'm so sorry to hear about the king. I bought some of my most popular sweets to try to lift your mood."

I smile softly at her, remembering how fond Maxon is of her. "I appreciate it."

Mia shrieks and jumps back as Nix comes flying into the room through the balcony window like a bullet.

"Coraline!" Nix yells, with excitement, colliding with Coraline in a burst of fairy dust. Both fairy and pixie are laughing when they pull back.

"I haven't seen you in so long. Where have you been hiding?" Coraline asks, cupping Nix's face like a mother would.

"Lurking in the shadows, biting unexpecting people." She grins, flashing her teeth.

"I believe that," I mutter.

"What brings you to the castle?" Nix asks.

"I brought Her Majesty some of my baked goods, to lift her spirit."

Nix's eyes light up, reminding me of the last time she had sugar, and I cover my mouth to hide my smile at her excitement.

"I love your sweets," Nix whispers, her hands folding under her chin.

"I've brought plenty for everyone," Coraline replies, smiling at us all in turn. Scarlett and Mia walk over to the wooden crates Lutin and Senka brought in and placed on the table before slipping back out into the hall.

Scarlett sniffs the air. "They smell divine."

"Are they made with magic?" Mia lifts what looks like a slice of strawberry cake from the crate.

"Yes. I pour my love and magic into everything I bake. Sometimes potions, too, depending on what the customers want."

"Like love potions?" Scarlett snorts, taking a bite of a chocolate croissant.

"Exactly."

Scarlett's green eyes widen, and she chokes, looking at me for clarity. Giving her a shrug, I turn to thank Coraline, but jump in surprise as she hovers less than a foot away from my face.

"Do you have a plan?" she questions, her voice quiet and urgent.

I frown, caught off guard. "A plan?"

Her eyes flash with a desperation that's almost painful to see. "To get the king back. You must have a plan."

Something pulls inside me at the vulnerability in her gaze. I force myself to nod, keeping my voice steady even as it softens. "Yes, I have a plan," I whisper, trying to put conviction behind the words.

Her pink eyes shimmer, and with a gentle touch, she traces the mate mark on my face, her fingers lingering. Eyes return to mine, steady and full of conviction. "You two are fated mates. You're in each other's blood, bones, heart, and soul. You will always find each other. I believe that."

Her words wrap around me, a balm for the gnawing doubt that has been tearing at me.

"I sure hope so," I murmur, my voice catching.

Her fingers slip away from my face, leaving a warmth that lingers.

"Well," she continues, her expression softening slightly, "it's past the time of the new moon, and you're not in a cell being driven mad with the need to feed from your mate, so I take it you found each other when you needed to."

Her words hit me like a punch to the gut, and I draw in a sharp breath. "How do you know that?"

She gives a small smile, one filled with centuries of knowledge. "I'm over five hundred years old, Your Majesty. I know a few things."

I blink, my mind spinning with the weight of her words. "Do you know of the Skythari Nomads?" I blurt, the question slipping from my lips before I can stop it, too desperate for answers.

"Everly!" Tristan snaps from the corner, cutting through the tension. "Raiden will be pissed if he finds out."

I ignore him and look pleadingly at Coraline.

"Yes, they dwell deep in the Ethereal Mountains. They also cannot be found unless they wish to be. Why do you ask?"

I bite my lip, anxiety bubbling up as I glance between Mia and Scarlett. They both give me a subtle shrug, neither of them offering advice. It's clear—this decision is mine alone. Should I share what the Witte Wieven told me? Can I trust Coraline with that kind of information? Maxon is fond of her, sure. But trust doesn't come easily for me, especially not now. I chew on my lip, bringing my gaze back to Coraline, who is patiently waiting.

"I was given some information," I offer cautiously, my voice tight with uncertainty. "And I need to find the nomads."

Coraline's eyes narrow, a subtle movement that somehow makes her pink irises glow even brighter. "Information by whom?"

"Everly," Tristan snaps.

My heart races, my pulse thudding loud in my ears.

"It doesn't matter who told me," I reply.

Coraline's stare doesn't waver. "Then what did they tell you?"

Too late to back out now.

I swallow hard, the words burning at the back of my throat. The verse, cryptic and haunting, has been burned into my mind since the moment the Witte Wieven whispered it to me. Every syllable, every twisted word has taken root, growing in the deepest corners of my thoughts.

"Through caverns deep and shadows wide, The Skythari Nomads dwell where beasts do hide.

To earn their trust, a bond must form, In Ethereal Peaks where magic storms.

The beasts will guide your path they know, but only through trust can you truly grow.

To reunite with what you've lost, seek the creatures, no matter the cost.

Shadow's hand will search in vain, for only the beasts can break the chain."

Coraline's eyes expand the longer I talk, and her wings sag. "That's a lot of information that can be interpreted in many ways, Your Majesty."

"I know," I whisper.

"Well, the clearest thing is the Skythari Nomads. If you're able to find them and gain their trust, they possess beasts that are unwaveringly loyal. They will be the key to finding our king."

"So, what are we waiting for? Let's go!" Scarlett comes to stand next to me, bumping my shoulder.

"Yeah, I want to meet this amazing mate of yours." Mia grins.

"I think you're all forgetting that Everly is being crowned queen tomorrow," Tristan snaps angrily.

"And we aren't simply knocking on someone's door, this will be a long journey through the snowy mountains, looking for a race that doesn't allow any outsiders," Kian adds.

Coraline flits up to my face, her small form radiating confidence as she taps my nose lightly. "I believe in you," she says, her voice unwavering and full of faith. "You've got this."

Her words settle over me like a cloak, warm and steady, banishing the chill of doubt that's lingered in my mind. I take a deep breath, pushing down the last remnants of fear, and straighten my back, feeling my resolve harden. "You're right. It's time to stop waiting and start acting."

I turn to Tristan and Kian, who stand nearby wearing expressions that are a blend of anticipation, concern, and something close to admiration.

"Tristan, let Raiden know I want to meet in the war room in thirty minutes." Tristan's eyes flash, and he gives a sharp nod before he strides off.

I turn to Kian, who's watching me closely. "Kian, go find Fenris. Tell him I want him there as well."

Dipping his head, he leaves the room without a word.

Chapter Forty-Two

Everly

I pace the length of the war room, my thoughts crashing into one another like waves in a storm. Mia and Scarlett sit at the long wooden table, absently picking at the baked treats I had Lutin and Senka bring in, silently watching me. Zaria went to find Nix, promising to return soon.

My body thrums with annoyance, making me twitchy and irritable. I am not leaving this room until we have a solid plan.

The double doors push open with a creak, and Raiden strides in, a heavy frown etched into his features. His skin glistens with a sheen of sweat, and his breath comes in sharp exhales. "What's going on?" he growls, his silver eyes sweeping over me, assessing. "I'm training the new recruits. This couldn't have waited?"

Stopping mid-pace, my hands fly to my hips as I face him. "No, it couldn't."

Raiden studies me for a beat longer, his gaze searching my expression before he raises an eyebrow. "How are the headaches?"

Heat floods my cheeks, and I shoot a quick, pointed look at Tristan, who is taking a seat at the table.

"Fine," I grit out through clenched teeth. "Gone."

"Hmmm." Raiden's eyes narrow slightly as he crosses his arms over his chest.

"Look, that's not what I want to talk about," I continue, pushing the topic aside with more force than necessary. "We need to make a plan to leave for Ethereal Peaks immediately after my coronation tomorrow."

Raiden's silver eyes flash with something unreadable before they harden. "Not happening," he refuses flatly, the authority in his voice unmistakable.

"Raiden," I growl, feeling the tension ratchet up between us.

"You cannot leave the safety of the castle," he continues, his tone brooking no argument. "I will send men–"

"No!" I shout, the power thrumming just beneath my skin responding to the surge of anger. Magic hums along my arms, sparking in the air. "I need to do this myself. I need to build trust with the nomads."

Before Raiden can reply, the door swings open again. Kian and Fenris enter first, their presence commanding as usual, followed closely by Zaria and Nix.

"What's going on?" Fenris's focus moves between Raiden and me.

"We are leaving for Ethereal Peaks the day after tomorrow," I inform him.

"We are?" Fenris pries, looking at Raiden's stiff posture.

Raiden's jaw clenches, but he doesn't answer Fenris.

"Okay, what's happening here? Raiden looks like he is going to blow a horn and you look like–"

"Like what?" I demand.

"A queen."

His words stall all my thoughts, and I blink.

Raiden shakes his head. "Everly, we can't risk the Shadoweaver getting his hands on you."

"The Shadoweaver won't know I've left."

"How do you figure that?" he growls.

"After the coronation, we say I'm sick. That the absence of my mate has left me weak, and I've been put on bed rest. Then we slip into the forest at nightfall. We stay off all the roads and cut through the Feyglades and into the mountains."

"You've been planning," Fenris mutters. "What makes you think we will agree?"

I take a deep breath, squaring my shoulders. "I'll go alone if I have to." If it's me against the world, so be it. Since I was abandoned in the human world, learning how to survive is all I've ever known. "I will not wait any longer. I know in my heart we can find the nomads and rescue our king."

"What makes you so sure?" Raiden asks.

"Because I'm not afraid. The Shadoweaver thinks she has the upper hand that he can use Maxon as bait, that I'm weak and will give myself over but she is wrong. I'm stronger than she thinks, and I will set her world on fire. I will not let her take anymore from me." My voice grows stronger, firmer the longer I speak.

They all trade looks as I struggle to rein in my magic. I see shadows move across the windows and jerk my head toward them, but it's only the vines of wisteria that grow along the castle walls reacting to my magic.

"Wait, you said she?" Raiden questions.

Then remember I haven't told them what Morrigan had said.

"The Shadoweaver is a woman," I murmur.

There's a beat of silence before Fenris speaks. "Why do you say that?" His tone is careful, but alert.

I hesitate. The memory of Morrigan's words linger.

"Morrigan told me when we spoke," I admit. "Even Maxon mentioned it—offhand, but still."

There's a sharp sound, like a growl torn from deep in Raiden's chest. My head snaps up to meet his glare.

"Why are you only telling us this now?" he demands, anger riding his words.

I frown, tilting my head slightly, confused by his intensity.

"What does it matter?" I ask. "Does the Shadoweaver's gender really change anything?"

"It changes everything," he snaps. "We need to know *everything*. Every thread of truth, every hint of what we're facing. This isn't some borderland skirmish—this is *the fucking Shadoweaver*. We've spent years thinking it was a man. Everyone has. If we walked into a room and saw a woman standing there, we wouldn't even blink. We'd *underestimate her*."

I bristle the words. He's right, in a way I hadn't considered. In assuming it wasn't important, I may have missed how much *perception* could matter in this war.

I open my mouth, then close it again.

"Male or female, it doesn't matter," Zaria interjects sternly. "Either way the Shadoweaver is evil and needs to be destroyed."

"She's right," Fenris agrees.

"And who have you planned to accompany you?" Kian says, casually.

I have a feeling he is trying to defuse the situation I've caused. I send him a grateful look, he winks and reaches for a pastry as he takes a seat next to Mia.

Fenris stiffens when Kian smiles at Mia, and I frown, tilting my head to study him before answering.

"I was thinking–"

There's a knock at the door and Raiden turns abruptly, ripping it open. "Fucking hell." He steps aside, allowing Valric to enter.

Valric looks around, his eyes lingering on Fenris. "Should I be offended that I wasn't invited?" he asks lightly.

"Not at all," I quip.

"What are we discussing?" Valric speaks slowly as he reads the tension in the room.

"Everly here wants to go to Ethereal Peaks to search for the Skythari Nomads," Raiden huffs.

Valric tilts his head, and I can see the gears turning. He's considering it. Hope rises in my chest.

"What's your plan?" he inquires, looking directly at me.

Relief floods me, and I rest my hands on the table, looking down at the map.

"While everyone is celebrating my coronation, I will pretend to fall ill. Nolan will inform those gathered that I've been put on bed rest. Then a small group of us will leave, slipping into the night. We stay off the roads and head through the forest to the Feyglades." My finger trails over the map. "There we will enter the mountains."

I look up, meeting each and everyone's eyes one by one. "Fenris will stay behind and take the army to Escalle. It's the closest place to set up a base to enter the Outlands." I meet Fenris's gaze. "There you will wait for us to meet you."

He runs a hand over his face and lets out an exasperated growl. "I don't like this."

"Agreed," Raiden says, his silver eyes swirling.

Everyone starts talking at once, making my magic rise, humming along my skin, and I see tendrils of vines creeping down my arms under the sleeve of my overcoat.

"Would everyone shut up!" Fenris's voice rises over the group.

"Maybe you could shut up," Scarlett shoots back, not missing a beat. "Everly doesn't need a lecture right now."

"I don't need you all fighting," I mutter under my breath, clenching my fists to keep my magic from flaring in response to my rising frustration. The tension in the room feels like static electricity prickling at my skin, making it harder to focus.

"I don't like this," Fenris repeats.

"Too bad. It's happening."

Valric leans on the table across from me, his dark purple eyes trailing over the map before looking up at me. "It's been two weeks since the king was taken, and now is the time for action. I'm in agreement with you, but I insist on coming with you."

A smile spreads across my face, and I nod, my heart overflowing with gratitude. "Tristan and Kian, you'll both be coming with me."

"I think the humans should remain at the castle. Or be taken back through the gate," Fenris advises, interrupting me.

I straighten up, opening my mouth, but he holds up his hand. "I'm not saying this to be a prick, but they have nothing to offer and will only get in the way. Plus, they are fragile."

"Sounds like you're being a prick to me," Mia mutters, and Scarlett snorts in response.

"And how do you think she'd feel if you got killed?" Fenris snaps, his body vibrating with rage as he flings his arm at me.

I walk around the table and stop next to Fenris, putting my hand on his arm to draw his attention away from my friends. His deep brown eyes meet mine and flicker with an emotion that looks a lot like regret.

"You're right, and you're wrong," I whisper, emotions riding my words.

His face turns into a severe frown, and my lips tip up as I shrug. "I'd be devastated if I lost any of you."

Fenris blinks, his head dipping in acknowledgement of my words, but then he turns to me fully, crossing his arms over his chest. "If they are to remain in Faerie, then I think they should stay at the castle."

"You're not our keeper," Scarlett argues, standing from her chair.

"He's right though." I turn to face them, my hand dropping from Fenris's arm. "If you disappear, people will become suspicious. I need you here to keep up the ruse. I don't want anyone outside of this room knowing our plan."

Mia slowly stands, her gaze flicking between me and Scarlett. "You want us to stay?"

"Yes." This isn't ideal, but there are few options left.

Scarlett huffs and plops back down in her seat, crossing her arms with a dramatic sigh. "Now I don't like the plan."

I can't help but let out a soft breath, half a laugh despite the tension in the air.

"Are you sure about this?" Mia asks again, her worry deepening. Her usual calm demeanor is slipping, and I can see the unease in her eyes.

"It's the best way," I reply as calmly as I can, though even my own doubts claw at me.

"Everyone will think I'd want you close. So, if you're here, they will think I am, too."

Mia hesitates, then slowly lowers herself back into her seat. Her gaze drifts to Fenris, and I can't help but notice the subtle blush that creeps up her cheeks. I bite my lip to keep from smiling. Fenris always manages to get under her skin, and as much as she tries to hide it, I can tell she isn't immune to his good looks.

"Nix will stay with you," I continue, shifting the focus back to the plan. "She will keep an eye on things here. I will speak to Alivar tomorrow and see if he is still willing to aid us." I look over at Fenris. "Fenris, you will gather the soldiers and lead them to Escalle. The rest of you are with me."

Raiden stiffens beside me, his jaw tightening. "Zaria should stay." His tone leaves no room for debate—except that Zaria has never been one to follow his orders without a fight.

Before I can even respond, Zaria steps forward, her gaze cutting sharply toward Raiden. "I'm coming," she asserts, her voice steady. "Everly wants me with her. I'm coming. I can shift now, so I'm not helpless."

Raiden frowns, but before he can protest, Tristan blurts out, "You can shift? Like completely, without getting stuck?"

Zaria just smiles, and with a swirl of magic, she transforms in front of us, her body rippling into the sleek, powerful form of a leopard. She slinks around Raiden, the movement fluid and graceful, before shifting back in another flash of magic. Her grin is wide, proud.

"I've been practicing," she says, a hint of satisfaction in her tone.

"But you still have your cat ears and tail?" Scarlett points out.

Zaria shrugs. “I’ve grown used to this form and prefer it.”

Raiden grabs her shoulders, spinning her to face him, his expression troubled. "Are you sure?"

"I’m sure," she declares. "I can handle myself. I’m not the girl you need to protect anymore, Raiden."

Raiden exhales sharply, a mixture of pride and reluctance crossing his face. “I will always protect you, whether you need it or not.”

His silver eyes swirl as he studies her, then dips his head. “Okay.”

Zaria grins widely, her warm brown eyes dancing with purpose as she glances at me. "So, two soldiers, a shifter, a paladin, Batman, and a druid," she says, almost giddy. "Sounds fun."

"Sounds like the start of a joke," Scarlett mutters dryly from beside her, her arms crossed but with a hint of a smirk tugging at the corner of her mouth.

I can’t help it—a soft laugh slips out, and I shake my head, feeling a moment of unexpected lightness amidst the tension of what’s to come. Grinning, I look to each of them.

"Maybe we’re all just one big punchline."

Chapter Forty-Three

Everly

My eyes remain fixed on the ceiling as I lie in bed, trying to calm my mind. Mia and Scarlett are fast asleep on either side of me, their soft breaths the only sound in the quiet room. Tomorrow, I'll be crowned queen, and then, under the cover of night, I'll slip away to find the people who can help me locate Maxon. I close my eyes, willing myself to rest, but sleep feels impossible. Instead, I focus on the thread, the invisible connection that ties me to Maxon. I reach for it, my fingers metaphorically tracing its path, following it as I've done so many times before.

But I hit something—an all-too-familiar barrier, the one he's placed between us. It usually feels impenetrable, a solid wall keeping me from him. But as I rest my hands against it, I feel it tremble. With a forceful push, the barrier shatters like glass, cascading down like a waterfall. I stumble through the breach. Pain instantly rips through me, sharp and all-consuming.

My knees buckle, and I double over, gasping as agony claws at my body.

What the hell is this?

My hands press into my knees, my breath coming in ragged bursts as I try to steady myself.

When I lift my head, everything is dark—so dark I can barely see anything around me. A creeping sense of unease settles in, but I fight it back.

"Maxon," I whisper, my voice shakes as my fingers dig into my legs.

Then, a sound—a soft, broken voice. “Everly?”

I freeze, my heart pounding. His voice. The pain in it is unmistakable, cutting through the darkness like a knife. Forcing myself upright, I stretch out my hands in front of me, stepping forward through the blackness.

“Maxon, I’m here.” I keep moving, spotting a small patch of light up ahead. As I draw nearer, everything inside me freezes, the pain fading over my panic.

Maxon is kneeling on a stone floor, a pool of blood beneath him and his hands are hauled above his head, as he hangs there, limp.

“Maxon!” I breathe in horror, running forward.

Dropping to my knees, my soul shatters at the sight of his tortured body before me. My hands tremble as they cup his face, brushing strands of hair from his blood-streaked skin.

“A chroí. Please look at me,” the words leave my lips in a sob, my voice thick with desperation, but he doesn’t move.

My eyes sweep over him, taking in the blood. It's everywhere.

“What happened?” I whisper, my voice barely audible.

His face twitches, and for a moment, hope flickers within me. His violet eyes flutter open, meeting mine, and I nearly break, a sob tearing from my throat as I press my forehead against his, the relief overwhelming.

“Everly?” His voice is weak, labored.

“Yes,” I breathe. “I'm here. I'm here.”

“You need to leave. It's not safe,” he murmurs, his breath ragged and pained.

“I'm coming for you,” I tell him, the conviction in my voice stronger than the terror coursing through me.

“No, you mustn't, she'll stop at nothing to get you. She knows you're visiting me, it'll be a trap.”

“Maxon, I'm coming for you. I'm not leaving you here.” His head lolls to the side against my hand tenderly cradling his cheek. “I'm not afraid to fight for you. I love you, not just with my heart, or my mind, but with my soul. We are fated mates, and I will always find you.”

His violet eyes lock onto mine, and in them, I see a flicker of that fierce fire I love. “You promise to fight?” His voice is a rasp, but the fire in his eyes strengthens.

“I promise.”

“Don't you die on me, Stóirín,” he whispers, his words firm.

“Ditto,” I choke out, my voice thick with emotion, a strained laugh escaping despite the fear curling around me like a vice.

I reach to wrap my arms around him, but his body suddenly bows in pain, a ragged gasp tearing from his lips. My blood runs cold as I see the chains—bones—around his neck tighten, drawing more blood.

“What the . . . ” I stand, horror twisting inside me as I slowly walk around him. Bile rises in my throat, and my hand comes up to cover my mouth as my eyes trace over his back. Fury ignites in my chest. I push the sob down, gritting my teeth fiercely. His flesh is torn, flayed down to the bone, the brutality of it almost too much to bear. I sense it then, the hatred that begins to seep into my soul, fueling my rage.

I jolt up in bed with a gasp, the kind that rips through your chest when you're desperate for air, as though you've been drowning and have finally breached the surface. My lungs burn, my body trembling as if I just fought my way out of some unseen force trying to drag me under.

I'm covered in a sheen of sweat, my clothes sticking to me uncomfortably. My heart is racing so fast I can barely think straight. Panic claws at me, making the room feel smaller, the shadows pressing in closer, suffocating. Without another thought, I throw off the covers, scrambling from the bed like it's on fire.

My legs wobble as my feet hit the floor, the cold stone grounding me for a moment, but I'm still shaking, still horrified by what I just witnessed. It clings to me like my sweat-drenched clothes.

Mia and Scarlett are out of the bed in seconds, their movements quick, almost frantic.

"What happened?"

"What's going on?" Scarlett's words overlap with Mia's as they both rush toward me, eyes wide with alarm.

I don't answer right away, my hands already fumbling with the armoire door. I throw it open with more force than necessary, my fingers shaking as I sift through the clothes hanging there, searching for my fighting gear.

My mind races, panic pulsing in my veins, and I can feel their eyes on me, feel their worry thickening the air between us.

The soft hiss of a match being struck cuts through the silence, warm light flooding the room as one of them—Mia, maybe—lights a lantern. Scarlett steps closer, her bare feet silent on the stone floor as she reaches out, her hand hovering near my arm.

"You're scaring me, E." Her voice is softer now, more vulnerable. "What's going on?"

I don't respond, and Scarlett's hand lands on my shoulder, halting my movements.

"Everly?" she whispers, and I make the mistake of looking up into her soft green eyes.

A sob tears from my throat, and I collapse in her arms. Mia is suddenly there, her arms around me, too, holding me up.

"He . . . He . . . " Oh my god. Something inside me is breaking. Getting air into my lungs becomes harder. "They are torturing him. I can't wait any longer. We have to go now."

Scarlett and Mia pull back, worry etched in their faces. I quickly swipe at my face, brushing the tears away, then scoop up the fighting gear I dropped. I storm toward the bed, throwing them down, and rip my nightgown over my head, tossing it aside. From the corner of my eye, I see Scarlett open the chamber door to whisper to either Lutin or Senka before closing it back again.

Mia wraps her arms around her middle. "Are you sure this is a good idea?"

"He is my mate," I whisper harshly, tugging the leather pants over my hips and doing them up. "I won't leave him there."

“We aren’t asking you to,” she says, gently. “But this isn’t part of the plan.”

"Screw the plan!" I bellow, shoving my arms into the tight, dark-blue long-sleeved tunic. The leather corset is next, my fingers fumbling for only a second before I manage to lace it up at the front. I grab the leather cuffs, strapping them tight around my wrists as I stride toward the trunk where my daggers and the sheaths are kept.

A soft knock at the door jerks my attention, and I glance up to see Scarlett standing by the door, biting her thumbnail.

"I asked them to get Raiden," she whispers, voice hesitant, like she’s trying to gauge how close I am to snapping completely.

I let out a heavy sigh, dropping my head and pulling out the weapons I need from the trunk, feeling the weight of each blade in my hands. “You shouldn't have,” I mutter, my voice flat, exhausted.

The door creaks open and Raiden steps in, taking a careful stock of the room before his eyes settle on me. “What's going on, Everly?” he says gently, soothingly.

I laugh, a harsh, humorless sound, the kind that feels like it’s scraping its way up my throat. I can feel the sting of tears gathering at the corners of my eyes, but I refuse to let them fall. Instead, I glare at him over my shoulder. “What’s going on is they’re torturing him,” I croak, my voice breaking on the last word.

Raiden's eyes soften as he steps toward me, his movements slow, deliberate. He grabs my shoulders and turns me to face him fully. His touch is firm, grounding, but it does nothing to stop the storm raging inside.

“He's strong, Everly.”

Like that's supposed to fix everything.

"You don't think I know that?" I cry, yanking myself out of his grip. Of course Maxon is strong, but strength has limits, and I'm terrified he's close to reaching his.

Raiden doesn't flinch at my outburst. Instead, his hands cup my face, his thumbs swiping away the tears. "I see that fire in you," he assures quietly. His gaze locks with mine, anchoring me back. "And we're going to use that fire to get him back. But we have a plan; your plan."

I clench my fists, my nails digging into my palms. "Screw the plan! Every second we waste is another second he's suffering."

My magic flares and lashes out around us. Sparks crackle in the air, the force of my power surging like a storm barely contained. I glare at him, but he doesn't so much as flinch. Wave after wave of magic ripples through me, striking him with all of my fear, but still, he holds on. His eyes lock onto mine, calm and unyielding, like he's bracing himself against a tempest but refuses to move.

"You think I don't know that?" his voice cracks with a rare flicker of emotion, raw and honest. "You think I don't want to tear this entire world apart to bring him back to you?"

I stop, the weight of his words sinking in. For the first time, I see the tension in his shoulders, the shadows under his eyes. He's fighting, too. But he's right—we need more than rage. We need a plan.

"I can't lose him, Raiden," I mutter, voice breaking again. "I can't."

"You won't," he promises, his grip tightening just slightly. "Not if we do this right."

I take a shaky breath, but the fire in me doesn't dim. "Then we do this now. Raiden, he is hurting and I can't bear it."

"The people need to see you tomorrow. They need to know you'll fight for them—fight for your king." His eyes search mine, filled with an urgency that makes my chest tighten. "If we slink into the night, if we leave without them knowing where you stand, they'll turn on you, Everly."

I bite my lip, the words sinking in, heavy and suffocating. He drops his hands from my face and my body slumps as the weight of it all crashes down on me. The thought of standing before them all tomorrow when Maxon is still out there suffering . . . It feels impossible.

Raiden's arms come around me, pulling me into him before I can fall apart completely. I bury my face in his chest, my arms wrapping around him on instinct.

He doesn't say anything more, doesn't offer false comfort or make promises he can't keep. He just holds me, his grip firm and steady, like he knows that I need this, to be reminded that I'm not alone in all of this. I'm not the only one carrying the burden.

"I don't want to wait," I murmur against his chest, my voice muffled. "I can't stand here and pretend everything's fine when he's out there, Raiden. I can't–"

"I know." His breath ruffles my hair as his hand runs soothing circles on my back. "I know. But the people need to believe in you. They need to know you'll fight for them. After that, we'll go. We'll get him."

His words are like a lifeline, a fragile thread of hope I cling to, even though my heart and soul ache with every second that passes. I nod against him, the movement small, almost imperceptible, but it's enough for now.

Chapter Forty-Four

Everly

My breath catches at the sight of my reflection in the mirrors. The dress Zaria created for my coronation is nothing short of breathtaking—a masterpiece woven from dreams and stardust. The gown is a soft, shimmering white with delicate green accents that trace through the fabric like vines. Layers of silk and chiffon fall gracefully around me, the flowing skirt adorned with scattered diamonds and jewels that catch the light, each one sparkling like stars. Every movement sends a cascade of glimmering light around me, making the gown feel alive, like a piece of magic brought to life.

The bodice is an intricate work of art, embroidered with green vines that trail gracefully over my torso, curling around my shoulders and creating a soft, delicate look. From my shoulders drapes a sheer, gossamer fabric that flows all the way to the floor, its surface dusted with glitter, casting a soft, ethereal glow.

It's as though I'm wrapped in moonlight, every detail carefully crafted to bring out the magic of my heritage.

My birthmark is visible, displayed proudly, along with my pointed ears and the mate mark etched on my temple. There's no makeup, just the rawness of my features. My hair is styled half-up, soft tendrils framing my face, allowing my fae heritage to shine through fully and unapologetically. The woman staring back at me is not the woman who stepped through that faerie door a couple of months ago.

I smile down at my arm, slowly gliding my fingers over the birthmark as my thoughts turn back to the day I woke after my Renascitur.

"It's funny, back at the Evergreen Castle, I thought that we were reminiscent of the sun and the moon, and this mark always looked like a unique combination of a sun and moon to me, together in a winding pattern of vines. It was us all along. Marking me as a druid and you as my mate."

Maxon's hand reaches out, gripping my wrist, bringing it to his mouth and kissing it softly.

"Entwined together by fate," he whispers against my skin.

I blink out of the memory to see Scarlett and Mia coming up behind me, their eyes shining brightly.

Scarlett's voice is barely above a whisper when she speaks. "You look so beautiful."

"I can't believe this is real," Mia adds, fanning her face with her hand.

I turn, pulling her into a hug. "I don't know how many times I said that myself when I first arrived," I murmur, my voice tinged with the bittersweet memories of my own uncertainty back then.

When I step back, Scarlett reaches out, her fingers gently twirling a strand of my hair. "How are you holding up after last night?" she asks, her tone soft but searching.

"Rough," I admit, my gaze dropping as my hand brushes over the intricate details of the gown.

Scarlett lets out a sigh. "I know it sounds hollow, but you'll get him back. Somehow, I just know everything will work out. It has to."

I look up, giving her a small, grateful smile. "Thanks, Scar. Will you both be okay here?" I look between them. "If not, I can take you to the gate. I don't want you here if things get . . . complicated."

"No way in hell are we leaving you here in the middle of this shit show," Scarlett's green eyes light up.

"Yeah, we'll hold down the fort while you're gone."

Scarlett grins. "Keep these men in line."

The soft creak of the door opening catches our attention, and we all turn as Zaria steps quietly into the room. She's no longer in her usual maid uniform; instead, she's dressed in a stunning light pink satin gown that flows around her like a gentle blush of dawn.

"You look amazing," I breathe.

Zaria's cheeks flush, the delicate pink spreading up her neck making her brown skin glow. "Thanks."

I beckon her over and hook my arm in hers, and we all face the mirror. Scarlett is a striking contrast standing next to me, wrapped in a deep emerald green gown that clings to her form in all the right ways. The color brings out the brightness of her fiery red hair, which tumbles around her shoulders like living flames, wild and fierce.

"We look gorgeous," Scarlett notes, flipping her hair over her shoulder.

"We really do," Mia adds. Her dress is royal-blue chiffon that wraps around her small frame. The color complements her dark brown hair which has been elegantly braided over one shoulder. Tiny flowers have been woven into the braid, each petal a small pop of color against her deep brown locks. Nix's handiwork, no doubt—though as usual, she's nowhere to be found.

"I wish Maxon could see me," I murmur, a deep longing tugging at me.

"Me, too," Zaria replies.

My eyes meet hers and the emotions there make me want to cry. "I don't want you to put on that maid's uniform again."

Startled, she blinks at me. "What? Why?"

"You are not my maid or my servant. You are my friend, my confidant, and will be treated as such."

Zaria's big brown eyes widen almost comically, and if I wasn't feeling so emotional, I'd laugh.

"As of today, you are no longer my maid, okay?"

Zaria blinks a few more times. "Okay."

In that moment, I feel an overwhelming sense of gratitude and pride to have them by my side, their loyalty and friendship wrapping around me like armor. With them, I feel ready for whatever lies ahead.

Chapter Forty-Five

Everly

As we step out of my chambers, a hush falls over the hall. Raiden, Tristan, and Kian are standing there waiting, but the moment they see us, their conversation dies. They stare openly, their eyes sweeping over each of us, clearly taken aback. A few paces away, Lutin and Senka, who have been standing with their backs to us, go rigid, sensing the sudden shift in energy. Slowly, they turn to face us, their eyes widening in surprise.

Kian is the first to recover, stepping forward with a deep bow. "You all look stunning," he says, his gaze full of admiration. "But, Princess, you look like a goddess."

"More like a queen," Tristan adds, his tone warm as he follows Kian's lead, bowing.

A blush creeps up my face, the heat rising as I feel the intensity of their gazes on me. I'm not used to attention like this. "Thank you."

Raiden, however, hasn't said a word. His eyes remain fixed on Zaria with an intensity that he doesn't even try to hide. There's something in his expression—approval, maybe even awe—that makes me want to laugh.

I can't help myself. "Righto, Batman," I tease, stepping forward to give him a gentle pat on the chest. "You can drool on your own time."

He blinks, pulled from whatever trance Zaria has him in, and the look of surprise on his face is priceless. The girls break into laughter, their voices ringing through the hall, and even Kian and Tristan can barely contain their grins, their shoulders shaking as they try to keep straight faces.

For a moment, the tension dissolves into laughter and lightness, a rare and welcome reprieve. With my friends and allies around me, I feel stronger, more grounded, ready to face whatever this day holds.

"Shall we?" I suggest, taking a deep breath.

Raiden nods, holding his arm out for me. I slip my arm into his and we start walking down the hall.

"There is a huge turnout. I think it's even bigger than Maxon's."

"Great," I murmur through the nerves already buzzing around my stomach.

"You'll be fine. I have every soldier and guard on high alert. You won't be alone for a second. Valric is waiting with Nolan at the dais we've set up in the gardens."

"In the gardens?"

"Yes, we thought that would be a fitting place to crown the Druid Queen." He winks down at me.

"Thank you," I whisper.

"You are bringing the Outcasts home. They don't have to hide anymore. I heard talk of the Evergreens being restored."

"Really?" My excitement makes the word come out louder than intended.

Lutin and Senka stop and wait, their hands resting on the handles of the doors leading out into the gardens.

Lutin's eyes meet mine. "Are you ready, Your Majesty?"

"No," I admit, a weak laugh slipping free.

His smile is soft and understanding. "You will do great. The king would be proud."

His words knock some of the air from my lungs.

"I will take Mia and Scarlett to the private platform," Tristan prompts, and the girls step forward, each giving me a hug and whispering words of encouragement that I don't seem to hear over the buzzing in my ears and the trembling in my knees.

Shit, I'm terrified.

Raiden steps up next to me again and we face the doors together. "Thank you for being here, Batman."

"Anytime, Everly Baker."

I laugh, slipping my arm through his, drawing strength from his steady presence. Lutin and Senka bow to me before swinging the doors open. The bright light from the garden floods in, and I immediately feel the weight of hundreds of eyes turning in my direction.

Raiden wasn't exaggerating—the place is packed. Fae of all shapes and sizes fill the gardens, their colorful wings and vibrant attire a dazzling display under the morning sun. An aisle has been cleared, leading up to a large, raised dais where a woman in flowing white robes stands alongside Valric and Nolan. Their expressions are serious yet welcoming, their postures straight and proud. But the sight of all those faces turned toward me, expectant, hopeful, is overwhelming. Panic flares, consuming me, and I attempt to take a step back.

I can't do this. I can't–

Without warning, Fenris is in front of me, appearing out of nowhere like he always does. His unusual, piercing eyes hold mine, grounding me, drawing me out of my spiraling thoughts. He bows deeply, pressing a fist over his heart. His voice is a quiet murmur, meant only for me. "I will guide the way. Just keep your eyes on my back."

I take a deep, shuddering breath, the panic beginning to ebb. His words echo in my mind, steady and reassuring, and I nod, feeling the first stirrings of courage return. As Fenris turns, I let my gaze settle on him, focusing on his familiar form, and take my first step forward.

With Raiden by my side and Fenris leading the way, I feel the pressure of the crowd around me beginning to ease, and in what seems like no time at all, I'm making my way up the stairs. Nolan and Valric bow. Then Valric steps forward, taking both my hands in his as Raiden steps away.

"You look every bit like the queen I imagined. Are you ready?"

I shrug, my eyes widening. "Do I have a choice? Because I feel it's a bit late to back out now."

Valric's eyes brighten, and he grins. "This is your destiny."

"Figured."

Valric shakes his head and leads me over to the woman in the white robes, her features are stern, but she looks familiar.

"Princess Vera, this is our high priestess, Elowen," Valric explains.

We both incline our heads in greeting before Elowen begins speaking, her voice clear and steady as it carries over the crowd. I try to focus on her words, but something feels . . . off. My magic, usually a subtle, comforting hum beneath my skin, is surging, rising higher and higher, until the familiar tingling becomes overwhelming. My breath hitches as an unsteady feeling overtakes me, like I'm on the verge of losing control.

A spike of panic twists in my chest, and I glance over at Valric, hoping for some kind of reassurance. But he's frowning, his eyes narrowing as he studies me, clearly sensing that something isn't right.

The ground beneath the dais gives a low, ominous rumble, and a ripple of murmurs spreads through the crowd. People are glancing around in confusion, some looking fearful. But the priestess, unperturbed, continues her speech as though nothing has happened, her voice as steady as ever. I wonder if this is normal, a part of the ritual perhaps, but my instincts scream otherwise.

My magic surges again, stronger this time, pushing against my control. I try to steady my breathing, to center myself, but it's no use—whatever is happening inside me is too powerful to be contained. My arm where my birthmark is burns, and I drop my gaze to see it glowing like the sun.

I feel Raiden's hand brush my hand, his touch anchoring me just enough to keep me from completely unraveling.

"Breathe," he whispers softly, his voice barely audible over the priestess's words. I cling to the sound, trying to focus, trying to push the magic back down.

The priestess steps forward, holding a crown crafted from delicate golden vines. At its center sits a sun and a moon, their jeweled surfaces catching and refracting the light in mesmerizing patterns. As I look up at it, an unexpected calm washes over me, soothing the wild magic still churning inside. I close my eyes, bowing my head instinctively, feeling my golden hair spill forward over my shoulders.

The crown settles onto my head, its weight both grounding and electrifying. A new wave of awareness ripples through me; a quiet, powerful force that feels like it's connecting me to something ancient and vast. The world feels sharper, more vivid, every breath filling me with an unfamiliar but welcome sense of clarity and strength. The magic from moments ago settles, and I breathe a sigh of relief.

The faint shuffle of feet and the rustling of fabric brings me back, and I lift my head, glancing around.

I freeze, a soft gasp slipping from my lips. Everyone has dropped to one knee. Raiden, Fenris, Valric, Nolan, and even Zaria, Mia and Scarlett. It's only the priestess and me who remain standing, the only two figures upright amid a sea of bowed heads.

The sheer gravity of the moment catches me off guard. This isn't just a ceremony. It's a vow. A new path I am choosing to walk, one that others have placed their faith in.

Elowen comes to stand in front of me, taking both my hands in hers.

"As queen, you hold command over the druids, respected guardians of nature and ancient lore, and the fae who, by choice, follow your path. You are the bringer of light, a radiant force of healing and hope in a world beset by shadows.

"Prophecies foretold your coming, naming you the one to unite the realms of nature and spirit. Through your connection to the land, you draw on powers both fierce and gentle, representing the balance of all life.

"You are the last of the royal druids, the last true blood heir to a lineage as ancient as the stones and as enduring as the rivers. Your rule is not marked by force, but by peace. A peace woven through respect for all life, and through your deep understanding of the natural order. Creatures of the forest bow as you pass, and the trees themselves lean closer, eager to offer their strength and shelter.

"Under your guidance, the bond between the druids and fae grows stronger, woven with trust and mutual respect, their shared purpose clear. To safeguard the realms and bring balance to a world forever shifting."

"Long live the Queen," echoes after the priestess, the words resonating through the crowd.

Goosebumps make all the hair on my body rise at the chants, her words hitting me harder than I expected.

As everyone rises to their feet, my eyes scan the crowd, looking for familiar faces among the sea of fae. At the very front, Alivar catches my gaze and, with a grin, gives me a playful wink. His light heartedness steadies me somehow, reminding me that I'm surrounded not only by allies, but also by friends who believe in me. Though I do notice his mother isn't here.

I see Gideon's vibrant red curly hair and his brother Malick standing to the side. Both offer me bright smiles.

I take a deep breath, centering myself before I address the crowd. "I do not take this role lightly," I begin, my voice ringing out over the gardens, strong and resolute. "I will do my best to be a fair and just leader, to see us through this hard time. But I want you all to know, I will banish the Shadoweaver from this realm and reclaim what is ours. Our king will be returned to us. That, I promise."

As the words leave my lips, a faint ripple seems to pass through the air.

Suddenly, there's a flash of movement, and two snow white forms leap onto the dais—Nymeria and Anika, but their demeanor gives me pause. Their heads are lowered, hackles raised as they snarl at an unseen threat.

I step forward to reach out for them, but a scream cuts through the silence. My head snaps up, gaze sharp, but before I can react, Raiden is in front of me, his massive wings unfurling in one swift motion. They stretch out wide, creating a protective barrier that blocks my view of the crowd. A tremor runs through my body, quick and sharp. My magic flares in response, a searing heat that churns beneath my skin as opposed to the gentle tingling hum I'm used to.

Another scream echoes, followed by the unmistakable whistling of arrows slicing through the air. Then, one after another, I hear the dull thuds as they strike the ground. I barely have time to register what's happening before reality crashes down.

We are under attack.

A cold fury rises within me, fueled by the instinct to protect. I glance around Raiden's wings, catching a glimpse of my friends, who are already moving. Tristan and Kian have their swords drawn, ushering them from the viewing platform. Valric's blade is drawn, his gaze focused on our surroundings, while Fenris's eyes flicker with the beginnings of his own magic, his expression fierce and deadly.

Raiden's wings shift slightly, and he glances back at me, his jaw set. "Stay behind me," he orders, his voice low but firm.

But I'm not about to just hide. My hands tingle with power, my magic swirling like a storm ready to be unleashed. "I'm not hiding, Raiden."

He hesitates, but only for a second, giving me a quick nod. "Just stay close," he murmurs, his voice softer but still edged with urgency.

As the next wave of arrows hurtles toward us, I raise my hand, letting my magic rise fully this time. An invisible shield forms, shimmering faintly as the arrows hit it and fall harmlessly to the ground. The power surges through me, this is not the gentle magic, this is my true magic, the one those fae were told to fear.

Chapter Forty-Six

Everly

Rose vines shoot up from the ground, thick and twisting, to form a protective canopy over the crowd. The lush tendrils stretch and intertwine, creating a living shield against the storm of arrows. Commanding the vines, I build an arch of woven greenery, a path leading straight to the castle's towering doors.

"Get to the castle!" I shout, my voice cutting through the cacophony.

Alivar doesn't hesitate to begin ushering the frightened villagers forward, his commanding presence spurring them into action.

"Move! Stay together!" he barks, propelling them toward the sheltering arch.

My gaze flicks upward to the castle walls. Shadows dart across the balconies, and I spot several archers drawing their bows. They are positioned strategically, their vantage points giving them a clear line of sight of the dais.

"The perimeter wall!" Kian's voice rings out, urgent and clear.

I turn my head, following his gesture toward the wall on the left. More figures are rushing toward us—fae rebels, their movements swift and predatory. One of them nocks an arrow, the sharp tip glinting menacingly in the sunlight.

Instinct takes over. I raise my hand, summoning a gust of wind with a sharp flick of my wrist. The arrow veers off course, spinning harmlessly to the ground. The archer stumbles, caught off balance by the force of the wind.

Another arrow slices through the air, this time aimed directly at Alivar. Without thinking, I sweep my arm sideways, sending a blast of wind that shatters the arrow mid-flight.

The crowd runs to the castle for cover, guards and soldiers swarming the gardens.

A familiar voice shouts out from behind us, full of panic. Quickly, I turn to see Gideon being ripped from Malick's side, and roughly shoved to the ground by a rebel.

"Gideon!" the cry tears from my throat before I realize I'm moving. Adrenaline surges through my veins as I dash down the stairs of the dais.

"Everly!" Raiden's voice booms, but I don't stop.

The ground trembles under my feet as I run, sending a column of earth spiraling skyward, crashing into the rebel who stands towering over Gideon. The impact sends him flying, his body crumpling against the nearest tree with a sickening thud. Malick is holding his own against the other rebel, his movements sharp and precise. For a moment, I think he has the upper hand—until I catch the glint of a dagger slipping from the rebel's sleeve, aimed low and fast.

Fury sears through my veins like wildfire.

I thrust my hand forward, drawing from the earth beneath me. A column of dirt erupts from the ground, slamming between Malick and his attacker with a thunderous crack. Before the rebel can recover, I summon a gust of wind that howls like a living thing, sweeping him off his feet and hurling him backward.

I reach Gideon, dropping to my knees beside him. "Are you hurt?"

He shakes his head, dazed but uninjured. Malick is already there, pulling him to his feet and shielding him with his broad frame.

"We need to move," Raiden growls.

The sound of soldiers fighting with rebels snaps me back to the present. "Get him inside," I tell Malick, my voice steadier than I feel.

Raiden inclines his head, his eyes swirling pools of silver. "I'll cover you. Go with them." His jaw is set, his blade already in hand

"Nope," the word escapes my lips before I even think about it. I push past him, his surprised look barely registering.

The air seems to thicken, and then the red haze descends. It's like stepping into a storm; the sharp edge of fear fades, replaced by the roaring heat of my own magic. Rational thought vanishes, swept away like leaves in a gale.

The magic from before rises swiftly, and this time I don't hold it back. My hands lift in front of me, trembling, not with fear but with power. The sensation swells—hot, vibrant, alive. Magic flows outward, unrestrained, like a dam finally broken. The earth responds to my call, and the vines surge forth.

They snake across the ground with impossible speed, weaving past our soldiers and lashing toward the rebels. The scent of disturbed soil fills the air, sharp and earthy as the vines break free from the garden's edge.

Thick as pythons, they wrap around legs and arms, yanking the rebels off their feet. Their bodies hit the hard-packed earth with dull, bone-jarring thuds. A few manage shouts of warning, but it's too late—the vines are ruthless.

I curl my fingers inward, and the vines obey, tightening their grip. High-pitched cries of panic mingle with angry roars. The rebels thrash, clawing at the tendrils that hold them, but the more they fight, the tighter the vines constrict.

With a flick of my wrist, I command them to drag their captives toward the outer wall of the garden. The vines pin them there, pressing them into place like insects trapped in a spider's web. The vines pulse beneath my control, waiting for my next command.

Raiden's voice cuts through the noise. "What the hell?"

I turn to him, my breath heaving, the heat of the magic still burning in my veins.

Behind him, the remaining soldiers glance at me with wide eyes, their weapons slack in their hands.

Chapter Forty-Seven

Everly

"Your Majesty, maybe you should retire for the day." Lutin's voice is low but insistent as his footsteps quicken to keep pace with me.

I don't respond, my gaze fixed on the doors to the great hall. I reach them first and push through with a single-minded purpose.

Inside, Raiden has arranged over two dozen fae rebels in two rows, their hands bound behind their backs, their heads bowed, forced to kneel on the cold marble floor before the throne. A murmur runs through the room as I enter, though it dies as quickly as it began.

Nolan sees me and rushes over, his face taut with concern. "Your Majesty, this is no place–"

I raise my hand sharply, silencing him. Fenris and Raiden both turn to face me, their expressions shifting from surprise to something unreadable.

Alivar, as usual, is a study in indifference, leaning casually against one of the marble pillars. With a flick of his fingers, he conjures a small flurry of snow, the flakes swirling idly in his palm.

Fenris runs a hand over the side of his head, his tattoos flexing as his muscles ripple with the motion. His eyes burn with barely contained fury; he looks like he's about one wrong word away from tearing someone apart. Raiden, on the other hand, stands in complete contrast—calm and composed. He crosses his arms, watching me as I draw nearer, a small, knowing smile playing at the edges of his mouth.

"Your Majesty," he says in a voice as steady as steel.

"General," I reply, drawing to a stop in front of him. I want these rebels to know who they are dealing with. Though I'm sure everyone in Faerie knows Raiden. "What's their excuse?"

Raiden turns, beckoning me to join him as we walk around the group until we are standing in front of them. Fenris follows, his dark presence making the kneeling fae shrink back.

I glance directly at one of the rebels, and his eyes widen at my attention. Then I slowly let my gaze travel over the others. Some seem fearful, while from others a deep-seated anger emerges.

Before Raiden can speak, one of them spits at my feet, a sneer twisting his face. "You must die before you ruin us all."

Another shouts, "It's the only way to ensure the Shadoweaver doesn't escape."

Fenris shifts in an instant, his menacing black wolf towering over the rebel, jaws snapping at his face.

"You think if you kill me the threat will be over?" I question.

"Yes. It's your blood that unlocks the prison."

Nolan storms forward, his hand lashing out and hitting the fae man across the face. “You’re a fool. You're all fools.”

“We are thinking of the realm!”

“You should be killing her, not crowning her!” another shouts.

My pulse kicks up and I frown, my eyes traveling over the group of rebels.

Nolan looks about ready to explode, but it’s Alivar who steps in.

“The old man is right. You're all fools.” There’s a calculated look in his eyes as he moves down the row of rebels. “The queen will be the one to bring peace, not destruction.”

“But her–”

Alivar’s hand reaches out, the ice sword forming in his hand poised over the man’s throat.

“The Shadoweaver cannot simply use her blood to unlock the prison. She must be willing.”

My eyes widen as the realization sinks in. Willing? What the hell does that mean? I feel a surge of frustration and confusion.

“Wait, what?” I blurt, stepping forward in disbelief, but Raiden’s hand lands firmly on my arm, holding me back.

Alivar inclines his head, his long white hair falling like a curtain over his face, hiding his expression for a moment. When he finally looks up, it’s with a predatory gleam in his eyes, focused on the rebels who kneel in front of us, bound and utterly bewildered. They stare back at him, their expressions shifting from defiance to uncertainty.

“You should know all the facts before mounting an attack against the crown.” Alivar’s voice is as cold and menacing as the snow flurries swirling around his sword. The air around him seems to grow even colder, and the rebels shiver, visibly unnerved.

A ripple of murmurs spreads through them as they exchange uneasy glances, doubt beginning to overshadow their initial bravado. They've realized, perhaps too late, that whatever plan they'd devised was missing a crucial detail—one that could change everything and tip things in our favor.

I turn to Nolan. "Did you know this?"

Nolan rubs his temples. "I did."

I frown. "Then why not tell me? It seems like something I should know."

"I happen to agree with her." Raiden's wings flare out in a quick display of irritation. "If this is a choice, then we don't have a problem."

Nolan scoffs, shaking his head dismissively. "She is weak," he argues, the words laced with disdain.

The insult hits me like a slap, and I rear back, my fingers flexing at my sides as I fight the urge to lash out.

"Weak?" My voice cuts through the room, and I can't hide the disbelief in my tone. Vines of ivy encircle my arms, snaking down to my wrists, their leaves brushing lightly against my skin.

"Yes," Nolan presses, his gaze unwavering. "You still have the mentality of a human."

A ripple of tension runs through the hall. Fenris, who has shifted back into his human form, steps forward, his expression hardening.

"Not here," he growls, his tone low and dangerous. It's a warning—a barely veiled threat to keep a lid on this rising conflict before it spills over somewhere anyone could hear.

"He's right." Raiden's gaze shifts over the kneeling rebels, calculating and calm. "Take them to the dungeons."

At his command, the guards stationed around the room close in, forming a tight formation around the rebels. Alivar steps away, his sword vanishing in a flash of light, as if it were never there. He watches the rebels, his cold expression betraying no sympathy, no pity.

"Fine," I snap, the decision coming fast and furious. "I want answers, and I want them now. Meet me in the war room in ten minutes." I turn on my heel, my steps carrying me swiftly out of the hall. I can feel my anger thrumming through the air, a force so intense that even the ground beneath my feet seems to tremble, as if it, too, can sense the storm forming inside me.

Chapter Forty-Eight

Everly

Nymeria and Anika press in on my sides, their presence a warm, grounding comfort. Nymeria leans in on my right, her big amber eyes watching me with a fierce kind of protectiveness. On my left, Anika nudges me gently, her soft fur brushing against my hand as she glances up with a gentleness that eases my tension.

I stand at the head of the long table in the war room, both Kian and Tristan silently watching me. Usually, I'd be bothered by that, but I need time with my own thoughts. I sigh, looking over the table. The map of our territories, peppered with strategic markers, lies open across its surface, but my mind is far from military logistics at the moment.

The heavy oak doors swing open, and Nolan, Fenris, and Raiden stride in, their expressions guarded.

I don't waste a single second; the instant the doors shut, sealing us inside, I lock my gaze on Nolan. "Explain. Now."

The force of my voice echoes in the stone chamber, ringing with all the authority I can muster.

Nolan inclines his head and takes a seat.

"The Shadoweaver's prison is absolute," he begins, his voice calm, calculated. "The only way for the spell to be broken is by choice. It requires free will—your willing blood—to break the seal."

"And you thought this detail wasn't worth mentioning until now?" I bite out, fury lacing every word.

Nolan scoffs, folding his arms. "Weakness," he mutters. "Your human mind is still clouded with emotion and fear."

I make a sound in the back of my throat, anger boiling over. "Weakness? Do you even hear yourself?"

Nolan's gaze hardens. "Yes. You're still thinking like a human, like someone who doesn't understand the stakes of what we're facing. You let your emotions rule you. We need a ruler who is cold and calculating. Someone who won't run to her mate and give up everything to save him."

My fists clench, but before I can retort, Kian speaks up, his voice calm. "Enough. Everly has grown, and if this is a choice, there is no way that she would willingly break that spell." He casts a sharp look around the room.

"Agreed," Tristan murmurs. "Everly's heart may be big, but she isn't foolish."

Fenris and Raiden share a look that immediately has my defenses up.

"What?" I demand.

Raiden sighs and runs a hand through his horns. "Look, I have complete faith in you . . . "

"But?" I press.

"But I know how much you love Maxon, he is the other half of your soul. If the Shadoweaver uses him as leverage–"

"She already is!" I shout.

"I know–"

"If I was as stupid and naive as you say, I'd have walked into the woods with my arms wide open. I haven't because I know Maxon would be furious, because he knows and trusts that I can see the bigger picture. I'm not stupid. If I give in and give myself over, that's it. You will all die or be under the rule of that monster." My breathing is ragged, as the words spill from me.

"We have a plan. The Witte Wieven told me what needs to be done. I will fight, I will not just give in. You may think my human emotions are a weakness, but they're not!"

Fenris steps forward, his hands raised. "Okay. If it's any consolation, you've always been emotional." His lips quirk up. "Always had a big heart." His eyes drop to my wolves. "You'd never let anyone suffer, especially if there's something you could do about it. Forgive us for thinking that you'd do something foolish to save your mate."

I swallow over the lump in my throat and drop my gaze to Nymeria and Anika. "I would do anything for him, but releasing the Shadoweaver has never crossed my mind," I admit.

The doors open, and Alivar and Valric stride in, looking around the group.

"What did we miss?" Alivar asks with that easy smirk on his face.

I sit down, suddenly feeling exhausted.

Raiden fills Alivar in, his voice steady as he outlines the plan to find the Skythari Nomads. He spares no detail, explaining each step with the precision he's known for. Alivar listens carefully, his face impassive, but I can feel his gaze resting on me the entire time. I keep my own eyes lowered, fingers tracing patterns over the map in front of me, feeling the faint lines of rivers and mountains beneath my touch. I'm careful not to look up; too aware of how everyone's attention seems to land on me.

When Raiden finishes, Alivar finally speaks. "Okay. If that is the plan, then I will hold up my end."

A relieved smile slips across my face, and I incline my head in thanks. "If that's all sorted, then I'm going to get ready to leave."

Raiden dips his head slightly. "Yes, we'll meet at your chambers at midnight."

I step around the table, heading for the doors with the wolves on my heels. Now with the plan in motion, my sense of frustration at the lack of action eases. Before I make it two steps, the large oak doors bang open, with Zaria, wide-eyed and breathless, stumbling into the room.

"What happened?" I demand, already moving toward her. A jolt runs through me at the fear in her eyes. I catch the tremble in her hands as she reaches out, and a glistening of tears teeters on the edge of her lashes.

"It's Nix," she chokes out, thin and strained.

My blood turns to ice, and I fight the instinctive dread clawing at me. "What about Nix?"

Zaria's hands grip my arm, her gaze dropping to the floor as she shakes her head. Her voice is barely more than a whisper. "Nix . . . she was poisoned."

The room falls silent, and the weight of her words slams into me like a physical blow.

Chapter Forty-Nine

Everly

"There's a flower that grows at the base of the ghost trees," Zaria explains in a hushed voice. "It's golden, and its petals will absorb into the skin, clearing the poison from the bloodstream."

"Where?" I demand, my pacing relentless as my gaze flickers to Nix, lying unconscious on the bed. Anger punches through me every time I look at her pale face, her wings limp and lifeless against the silken pillow. Zaria moved her into my chambers, where the wards will protect her, but it feels like a hollow measure if I can't save her.

Zaria hesitates before whispering, "The Outlands."

I stop in my tracks, my eyes narrowing as I take in the look on her face. "Where the Shadoweaver is?"

"Yes," she admits softly, and I see her wince, as though saying it out loud makes the situation even worse.

I can feel the blood slowly draining from my face. "How the hell are we supposed to get that?"

"I don't know," she sighs.

"Who would have poisoned her?" I snap, my voice rising despite myself. My hands clench at my sides, the helplessness swirling within me making my magic ebb and flow faintly in the air.

"Maybe she found something, and someone had to keep her quiet." Zaria's tail sways behind her, the only sign of her own agitation. She steps closer. "Someone in the village might have some. I can leave right away," she offers, gripping my hands firmly in hers.

Asrai peers down at me from her perch in Zaria's thick, dark waves. The worry in her small, luminous mismatched eyes breaks my heart.

"Okay," I accept finally, nodding. I bite down hard on my lip, my mind racing.

Before I can say anything more, Scarlett rises to her feet, her fiery hair catching the light as she moves toward us. "I'll go with her."

I open my mouth to protest, but before I can respond, there's a soft knock at the door. It creaks open, and Raiden, Fenris, and Alivar step inside.

Raiden's gaze immediately goes to Nix, his expression darkening. "How is she?" he questions, clipped but tinged with concern.

"Not good," I answer, my voice thick. "The healers can't do anything. They tried, but nothing. We need a flower that grows at the base of the ghost trees to save her."

Raiden stiffens, his jaw tightens as his eyes flick to Zaria. "The Outlands," he says in a flat tone.

Alivar crosses his arms, his golden eyes narrowing. "That's Shadoweaver territory. Dangerous for anyone, especially now."

"I'm going into Skora to see if any merchants have some, but if they don't, we might need to make a decision," Zaria says.

Alivar steps forward. "If it comes to that, then I'll go." His voice is quiet, but there's a resolute edge to it that makes everyone look at him.

"No," Fenris snaps. "You are too important to go. I will."

"You have an army to lead," Alivar snarls back. "I can portal in and out before the Shadoweaver knows I'm there."

"Doubtful," Raiden mutters, rubbing the back of his neck.

"Why do you even care enough to risk your life?" Scarlett asks, and I have to admit, I'm curious about that one, too.

Alivar's violet eyes flash with icy blue for a split second as his attention shifts from Fenris to Scarlett and settles on me. "Nix is important to you. If we can prevent casualties in the coming weeks, we should at least try."

Without thinking, my feet carry me across the room and I wrap my arms around Alivar, feeling his muscles stiffen under my hold as the smell of honeysuckle and salty summer air fills my senses.

"Thank you," I whisper.

My anger and frustration are doing a good job at holding back the tears, but now with Alivar's offer, they are right here, ready to spill over.

Alivar relaxes, and his arms come around me slowly. "It's my pleasure to assist, Everly."

"If something goes wrong?" Scarlett interrupts, her voice dripping with sarcasm. "Something always goes wrong, wolf boy."

I release Alivar and turn to see what I missed.

"We need that flower. The question is, how do we get it with the least amount of risk?" Fenris snaps back, his piercing glare focused on her.

"Yeah, and if Zaria can't get the flower in the village, then what?" she argues, her temper rising to match her hair.

There's a tense silence before Fenris speaks up. "I'll go with Alivar. Two warriors are better equipped to handle the Outlands than just one."

Alivar tilts his head slightly, a faint smirk playing at his lips. "It's not the first time I've faced something dangerous, and it won't be the last."

"At least let me go into Skora first," Zaria says softly. "This might all be a moot point."

"You have two hours. If you can't get any, we will leave immediately," Fenris replies, then his attention shifts to me. "This won't interfere with you leaving. Alivar and I will do what we must, and we will meet you in Escalle with the armies."

I let out a deep breath, my eyes sliding over to Nix again. "I want to know who did this."

"Don't we all?" Raiden runs a hand over his head in defeat. "She was here as my spy, she is good at gathering information. If someone has done this on purpose, it means Nix found out something important."

The idea of there being someone in the castle who hurt Nix makes my stomach tighten in fear. Was it the person who was in my chambers the other night? The unfamiliar smell Nymeria and Anika detected?

"I better go; we're running out of daylight." Zaria looks over to Scarlett. "You coming?"

"Of course," Scarlett replies without hesitation. She turns to me, wrapping me in a tight, fierce hug. When she pulls back, her emerald eyes bore into mine. "Chin up. You're a queen now."

Her words are meant to bolster me, to remind me of my strength and position, but instead, they feel like a weight pressing down on me. Dread claws its way through my stomach, twisting and churning.

I nod numbly and watch as they head toward the door.

"Tristan, go with them," I call out.

He hesitates for only a moment before bowing deeply. "As you command."

Without another word, he slips from the room, following Zaria and Scarlett.

The door closes softly behind them, and silence falls. I turn to find Mia still seated on the edge of the bed, hands clasped tightly in her lap as she gazes out at the open balcony. Her brown hair catches the light, but her face is pale, the usual warmth replaced with a somber stillness. She hasn't said a word since we got here.

"Mia?" I say gently, stepping closer.

Her head turns slowly, and when her eyes meet mine, I see the glistening tears welling within them.

I tense. "What's wrong?"

She hesitates, blinking rapidly as if trying to force the tears away. "I just . . . I hate this," she whispers finally. Her voice trembles, and she looks back toward the balcony, as though the view of the horizon might steady her.

"Hate what?" I ask softly, sitting beside her.

"All of this," she says, motioning vaguely at the room, but clearly meaning more. "The danger, the uncertainty . . . the constant what ifs. Not knowing if everyone will come back."

Her words hit me like an arrow, because they echo the fears I've been trying to suppress.

"I feel so powerless," she continues, her voice breaking. "I want to help, but I don't know how. I don't have magic or abilities. All I can do is watch, wait, and hope—hope that you will survive whatever lies ahead."

My stomach drops, filling me with a sickening sensation, and I place a hand over hers, squeezing gently. "Mia, I understand," I murmur quietly. "I feel it, too. Every decision I make feels like a gamble, and every time I send someone out there, I wonder if it'll be the last time I see them. But we can't let fear control us."

Her eyes glisten as she looks at me, a single tear slipping down her cheek.

I take a deep breath. "You do help, Mia. More than you know. You're the calm in the storm, the one who keeps me and Scarlett grounded. And right now, I need that. I need you."

"Thanks," she whispers.

I glance up and catch Fenris watching her, a deep frown etched across his face. His sharp features are softened by a flicker of something I can't quite place—curiosity, perhaps? His head tilts ever so slightly, and I notice the way his hand unconsciously drifts to his chest, rubbing over his heart as though trying to soothe an ache he doesn't understand.

A small smile tugs at my lips. Despite his gruff exterior and his disdain for humans, I can see the cracks forming in that icy demeanor. His frown deepens as Mia shifts, wiping away the remnants of her tears, and I watch as something softens in his expression. He doesn't say a word—he rarely does unless it's to criticize or growl out an order—but his actions speak louder. The way his hand lingers over his chest, the way his eyes stay on Mia, tells me more than his words ever could.

I tuck this small observation away, a tiny spark of hope warming my chest.

Raiden steps forward, his tone all business. "We'll prepare supplies for our trip. You should get some rest until then."

Chapter Fifty

Everly

Every step is charged with impatience and frustration as I pace my chambers. Today spiraled into one disaster after another, and the thought of spending another night in this castle without Maxon is unbearable. Zaria has returned unable to find the mystery flower that grows in the Outlands. So now we wait for Alivar and Fenris to get back, and pray to Morrigan they return.

"Sit down, E," Mia urges from her spot on the daybed where she's sitting with Anika curled up beside her, watching my frantic pacing.

"I can't," I reply, shaking my hands out in front of me, feeling the tremors running through them. I'm unable to tell if it's nerves or adrenaline fueling me, but the restless energy keeps building, threatening to spill over.

Scarlett drops into the chair next to Mia, letting out a sigh. "We need alcohol."

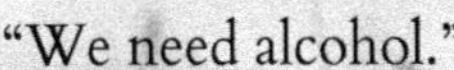

The suggestion snaps my attention to her. "You know, that actually sounds like a good idea."

I turn toward the drink cart tucked in the corner, eyeing the bottles of faerie elixir and wine that I've never even considered tasting before.

Scarlett laughs, a note of disbelief in her voice. "I was joking. You've got a horse to ride tonight. Probably best not to do that drunk."

Her words pull me back to reality. She's right; as tempting as it is to drown out the anxiety clawing at me, the last thing I need is to be impaired for what's coming. I turn back to face them, drawing in a steadying breath.

"Alright, no alcohol," I agree reluctantly. "But something has to give. I feel like I'm coming out of my skin waiting like this."

Mia's expression softens with understanding. "We know. We're here with you, E. Just breathe. Tonight will be the first step toward getting him back."

A gentle knock sounds at the door before Raiden, Zaria, Tristan, and Kian enter one by one.

My pulse quickens, a wave of anxiety washing over me as I watch them all. The tension in my body grows at their fierce expressions. Taking a deep breath, I try to compose myself, willing my emotions to subside. A sharp mix of frustration and anticipation course through my veins.

"Wait. Let Lutin and Senka in," I tell Kian before he can shut the door.

His lavender eyes widen, but he steps out the door before returning with both Lutin and Senka. Kian closes the door behind them, walking around them and taking a seat in the armchair.

"So, tonight is the night," Tristan breaks the tense silence that hangs heavy over the room. "Are you ready?"

I meet his gaze. "I'm more than ready."

Raiden lets out a low grumble, his brows furrowed in concern. "I've told Malick and Gideon to prepare the horses discreetly. They'll have them waiting outside the castle grounds, near the grove. We'll slip out quietly, but we have to be swift."

A voice from behind interrupts. "Sorry, but what exactly is happening tonight?" Lutin steps forward, a puzzled look on his face. Senka stands at his side, her sharp eyes curious.

We all exchange glances, before I turn back to face them. "I'm leaving tonight."

They stare back at me, their wide eyes mirroring the shock and confusion that lingers in the air. Senka opens her mouth to protest, but I raise a hand to stop her. "I'm going to get help. I can't wait here, hoping for something to change on its own. I need to bring our king back, and to do that, I have to gather allies and prepare for a real fight. But I can't do it alone."

Lutin's face softens as he places a fist over his heart in a gesture of loyalty. "Whatever you need, My Queen."

Senka follows suit, her own hand pressing firmly over her chest. "We'll do whatever you need."

"Thank you," I whisper, emotions rising and clogging my throat. "I need you both to pretend I'm still here. Spread word that I've fallen unwell, weakened by my mate's absence. Let them believe that I'm confined to my chambers, too heartbroken to be seen."

Senka nods, understanding immediately. "You don't want anyone knowing you've left. Smart."

"Exactly. I can't have anyone suspecting my departure until I'm well out of reach." I take a deep breath, looking each of them in the eye. "I trust you both with this. Keep the truth hidden. And protect my friends and this castle in my absence."

"We will," Lutin promises, his expression fierce and resolute.

Senka opens her mouth but seems to hesitate before speaking. "Forgive me for asking, but . . . " she trails off for a moment. "Why aren't you suffering like most bonded mates would be after two weeks without their other half, especially with the new moon just past? I mean . . . if I'm not mistaken, your fangs look new. Doesn't that mean you need to feed, like we high fae do after mating?"

I give her a small smile, though the question strikes me right in the heart, a bitter pang of longing echoing through me. "I am suffering, Senka. Being without Maxon . . . it's like trying to breathe underwater. Every second apart feels like I'm drowning, like I'm missing a part of myself that I can't live without."

Senka's brow furrows, the concern on her face deepening, but I continue. "I've been able to see him, in a way. We actually dream-walked together during the new moon." A soft warmth rises in me as I remember that night. "We shared each other's strength . . . and fed off each other, too."

Senka's eyes widen slightly in understanding, and she gives a respectful bow. "That explains it. The connection would sustain you both, for a time at least."

I absently rub a hand over my heart. "Yes, it helps. It soothes the worst of the longing . . . but it doesn't erase it. I can still feel his absence like an open wound." I pause, inhaling deeply to steady myself, and feel the comforting hum of our bond, even though it's muted. "Maxon and I, we're bonded in every way. And while that connection gives me strength, it also makes it impossible to forget how far away he is. It's . . . agonizing."

Lutin shifts on his feet, drawing my attention. "Forgive me, My Queen, but can I ask something?"

"Go ahead," I reply, wanting them to be open with me.

"How is the king? Is he okay?"

My lip's part on an exhale, and I hear Raiden grunt and turn away. My mind flashes back to what I saw last night, a shiver running down my spine. Lutin's eyes dart around the room, and with each face he looks at, his own expression turns grim.

"The king isn't in good shape. They are torturing him." I swallow roughly, pushing my tears down. "I fear he doesn't have much longer before the darkness takes him, but he is strong, and he won't give up without a fight. He has fire in his heart, and it still burns brightly."

Lutin's face turns pale as he nods slowly.

Nymeria and Anika suddenly leap off the bed, flanking me protectively. Their low growls resonate like a warning bell through the room sending goosebumps scattering over my body.

"What is it?" I whisper, my voice tight with unease.

Nymeria's ears twitch, her eyes locked on the door. *'We don't know, but something smells off.'*

Before I can question further, the tingling sensation of magic prickles through the air, sharp and unmistakable. A loud, echoing bang on the door jolts me. Lutin spins, his movements fluid and controlled, his hand reaching instinctively for the hilt of his sword. His eyes flash with readiness as he grips the handle.

Without hesitation, he rips open the door, sword half-drawn. Alivar and Fenris stumble inside, both disheveled and battered. Their clothes are torn, streaked with dirt and blood, and gashes crisscross their exposed skin. My breath catches, and my hands fly to my mouth as I gasp.

Despite their state, Alivar smirks, holding up a small, weathered bag like a trophy. "Got it."

"Yep. Piece of cake," Fenris grunts.

Zaria rushes past me, her face pale with worry. "I'll get the healers!" she calls over her shoulder before vanishing out the door.

Lutin shuts the door behind them with a sharp click, and I find myself moving toward Alivar, my steps unsteady. I wrap my arms around him, ignoring the grime and blood.

"Thank you," I whisper, my voice thick with emotion.

He chuckles, though it's a weak sound. "My pleasure." I can feel his exhaustion in the way he leans into the embrace.

I pull back, my gaze scanning his battered frame, noting every tear and every bruise. "Are you okay?" I ask, my voice trembling.

Alivar winks, as if to reassure me. "Perfect."

The door bursts open again not a minute later, and Zaria reappears, flanked by two fae women. They're identical, from the pale blue gowns they wear to the golden blonde hair cascading down their backs. Their features are delicate, their blue eyes piercing, but it's the translucent, shimmering fairy wings that steal my breath.

The healers stop short when their gazes land on Alivar and Fenris. Their eyes widen in shock, taking in the extent of their injuries.

Alivar tosses the brown satchel at the closer healer, his tone filled with authority. "The fairy first."

The two healers exchange a glance, then nod in unison, their movements efficient as they hurry toward the bed.

"Let's hope it works," Fenris mutters, his voice low.

I turn, stepping up to Fenris, my concern outweighing the chaos still lingering in the room. His injuries are impossible to ignore. I reach up and gently cup his face, tilting it side to side to examine him more closely. His skin is warm beneath my touch, blood staining the tattoos on the side of his head.

Fenris's hand comes up, resting softly on mine. His fingers lightly curl around my wrist.

"I'm fine." His voice remains low and steady.

A weak smile tugs at my lips. "That's my line," I counter.

He doesn't look fine. Not even close.

There's a gash running along the side of his head, blood dripping sluggishly down to his neck and matting the dark ink of his tattoos. His bottom lip is split, swollen, and angry-looking. A particularly nasty wound slashes across his bicep, and the subtle limp in his step confirms the toll his body has taken.

"I'm a hybrid shifter," he reassures me. "We heal fast. I promise."

I nod reluctantly, not trusting myself to argue. The logical part of me knows he's right, knows he'll recover in time, but that doesn't stop the ache of worry. Tentatively, I rest my head against his chest, closing my eyes for just a moment. His heartbeat is strong and steady beneath my ear, and I let it calm me.

His arms come around me, pulling me into a warm, solid embrace. For a fleeting moment, I feel safe, my mind being transported back to when we were kids, and he'd hold me like this when I was upset.

Fenris steps back, his expression soft. "We got this, My Queen."

"I sure hope so."

When I turn around, my eyes catch on Lutin and Senka, their expressions grim, their frowns deepening with every passing second. It's not just their worry that catches my attention, though. The healers are giving me strange looks, a mix of curiosity and unease flickering across their identical faces.

Chapter Fifty-One

Maxon

"What the fuck do you want?" I sneer, my throat dry as sandpaper. Each word grates out of me like broken glass.

The shadows have been gathering for hours—maybe longer. It's hard to tell anymore. At first, their swirling, restless movement was easy enough to dismiss, blending into the edges of the dim cavern. But now? Now they're everywhere. Pressing, breathing, suffocating. I can feel them in my head, clawing at the fragile threads of my patience. My fingers twitch with a restless urge. I'm tired. Agitated. Ready to crawl out of these goddamned bones just so I can incinerate every last one of these things.

Then, the shadows move. No—they peel. They unfurl and step forward, becoming her. Yumekui. Her body seems woven from the tendrils of darkness that still ripple and stretch across the cavern, tethered to her. Her lithe form almost glows against the void of her own making.

That damn smirk is on her face, cocky and infuriating as ever. But it doesn't fool me. Not really. I see the flicker in her eyes—the tight line of worry she's trying to hide.

"The Master wants to see you." Her voice coils around me like smoke, insinuating itself where it's not welcome.

And just like that, I hate her all over again. Not just for her smugness, but for the way her words work their way into my head, dragging my will with them. No matter how much I resist, no matter how much I hate it, I feel myself bending—cracking under the weight of her command.

She sees it too; her blood spells are working.

Yumekui leans over me, her every movement deliberate, calculated to mock and remind me of just how much control she has. The chain around my neck loosens as her slender fingers unhook it from the wall. Her hands move with practiced ease as she frees my wrists, the wyvern cuffs leaving behind raw, angry marks on my skin.

"Now," she says, her voice mocking, "be a good pet and behave."

The word pet grates against my nerves like nails on stone. A growl rumbles low in my throat, a primal sound born of anger and frustration. Her smug expression falters for a heartbeat. She pauses, crouching down in front of me with an unsettling elegance, the silk of her white kimono pooling around her like liquid moonlight.

Her hand snaps up, gripping my face with a strength that betrays her delicate frame. Her nails bite into my skin, sharp as daggers, drawing thin lines of blood that drip down my cheeks. I don't flinch, but the sting only fuels the fire burning inside me.

"Behave." Her voice is a command, low and venomous, her crimson eyes boring into mine. They flick back and forth, searching, daring me to defy her. "Now stand."

She lets go with a shove, and I rise, slow and deliberate, towering over her. I could snap her in two if I wanted, and I know she knows it. The smirk that curls her lips is proof enough—she's daring me to try.

Yumekui doesn't flinch. Instead, she reaches up, her slim fingers curling around the back of my neck, her nails grazing the base of my skull. She pulls me down, and I let her, though my fists clench at my sides so tightly that my knuckles ache. Her tongue darts out, quick and serpentine, licking the blood from my cheek in one maddening swipe.

My body stiffens, every muscle coiled with the effort of restraint. It takes all of my willpower not to lash out, to slam her against the cold stone walls and remind her that I'm not some broken thing she can toy with.

Yumekui steps back, that infuriating smirk still playing on her lips, as though she knows exactly how close I am to snapping. Maybe that's what she wants.

With a sharp tug, she pulls me toward the exit by the chain attached to the bones around my neck.

Chapter Fifty-Two

Everly

The healers depart leaving the scent of herbs hanging faintly in the air, mingling with the quiet tension that has taken their place. Now, everyone is seated around my chambers, their faces lit only by the flickering glow of lanterns and the fire crackling away in the hearth. No one speaks. Tension radiates off them—my companions, my confidants—each grappling with what the next few days will bring. There is unity in our silence, even if it trembles under the strain of what is to come. Outside, the night deepens, cloaking the world in darkness, as if the stars themselves are holding their breath. Time is moving, relentless and indifferent. A creeping reminder that we are mere hours away from departure.

With a deep breath, I shift my attention. "Fenris, can you bring my armor with you to Escalle?"

"Of course," he replies without hesitation. "I'll ready the armies to head out in three days." He scratches his head thoughtfully. "Raiden and I talked it over and decided it would be best to send the troops in small groups leading up to the third day. Less chance of raising suspicion that way."

"How long will it take to get there from here?"

Fenris considers it, glancing briefly at Raiden before answering. "Depends. If we take the road through Mistyglade, it's about a twenty- two hour journey. But if we cut through the forest, we can make it in eighteen. The forest is faster, but more dangerous."

"And depending on where we come out in Ethereal Peaks, we could still be days away from Escalle. The terrain between the two is unpredictable." Raiden states.

I sigh, running through the details in my mind. "So, we have roughly four days to locate the Skythari Nomads if we want to meet the armies in Escalle on time?"

"Yes." Fenris nods. "But we won't cross the border into the Outlands until we're all together. We can't risk splitting up once we're that close."

Raiden steps forward, his silver eyes steady. "We do this as one. We have a better chance if we stand united. Who knows how many bodies the Shadoweaver has at her disposal. She has had centuries to amass an army."

I visibly shake, my arms crossing in an attempt to ward off the unease slithering through me. But the fire that burns through my veins is stronger, and I straighten. It's time.

Everyone exchanges glances before quietly leaving the room, the door softly clicking shut behind them. Mia and Scarlett stand, pulling me into a hug. My heartbeat is so loud and fierce at this moment that I think I might pass out. When we finally pull apart, there are tears glistening in each of our eyes, words not quite enough to cover the unspoken fears.

Scarlett reaches up and brushes her fingers gently through my hair, her tone quiet but fierce. “You need to be careful,” she murmurs, her voice breaking slightly. “Don’t make me go ape shit crazy on the faerie world. Cause you know I will.”

I let out a choked laugh, pulling her back in for another hug. “I promise I'll do my best,” I say, trying to reassure her even as my own nerves hum with uncertainty.

When we step back, Mia takes my hand, her face serious. “We’ll hold down the fort. Scarlett and I have decided. We’re going to learn to fight. We want to be able to help.”

I tilt my head, a small smile lifting the corner of my lips. “That’s probably a smart idea. Lutin and Senka will be more than capable teachers.”

“But won’t they need to stay on guard here to keep up the ruse?” Scarlett inquires, concern knitting her brows.

Biting my lip, I give Mia’s hand a squeeze before letting go. “They will need a break, and Raiden has set up a rotating guard roster to make sure there’s always coverage outside the chamber doors. I want you both to stick close to Lutin and Senka. And Fenris will be around for a few days–”

Mia groans dramatically, throwing herself onto the sofa with a roll of her eyes. “Ugh, Fenris? He’s impossible!”

A loud laugh bursts from me at her exasperation. “Yes, he’s infuriating,” I agree, joining her by the sofa, “but he’s also fiercely protective. He’ll keep you safe, even if he drives you insane in the process.”

Scarlett chuckles, giving me a playful wink that Mia doesn't miss. She narrows her eyes, looking between us suspiciously. "What was that look?"

"What look?" Scarlett feigns innocence, though a mischievous grin tugs at her lips.

I laugh, leaving them to their banter as I cross the room to my wardrobe, opening the doors and letting my fingers brush over the fabrics within. They stop on an elegant black warrior-style dress. The upper portion has a fitted bodice with a V-shaped neckline. The sleeves are long and fitted, giving a streamlined look. A wide belt with intricate detailing at the center cinches the waist, adding both structure and a subtle accent to the outfit. The skirt flows down in soft, draped layers, reaching the ground and adding a sense of movement to the ensemble. It seems to convey a sense of power, mystery, and resilience. I pull it out and lay it on the bed, my attention shifting to Nix. Her color slowly but steadily returning.

"I'm just going to have a quick shower because it might be a while before I get another chance," I say.

My heart pounds, a frantic rhythm echoing the nervous flutter in my stomach as I step into the shower. This is it. I'm actually leaving the safety of the castle to find the Skythari Nomads in hopes they can help me get to Maxon. I sigh, the fleeting image of the white beast still vivid in my memory. To earn their trust, a bond must grow . . .

Closing my eyes, I tilt my face into the spray, letting the water wash over me as I silently pray to Morrigan for her guidance.

Chapter Fifty-Three

Maxon

The Shadoweaver's shadows snake out like living tendrils, wrapping around me. They lift me effortlessly, dragging me closer to her in slow, deliberate movements until I'm suspended just inches away. Her black-orbed eyes fix on me, the tiny pinprick of light at their center glowing eerily.

She doesn't speak at first. Her gaze is careful, studying, drinking me in. The inky black dress she wears clings to her body like liquid oil, shifting and undulating with an unnatural pulse. The shadows that dance around her seem darker today, heavier, their movements almost aggressive.

The way her anticipation thickens the air between us is suffocating. She wants to say something. But of course, she doesn't rush. She never does.

"How have you been, Your Majesty?" she purrs, her voice smooth and serpentine.

Her form floats gracefully around me, a predator circling its prey, testing its boundaries. I don't answer. I won't give her the satisfaction. My silence is my only defense.

"I wonder how your mate is faring without you," she continues, her tone dripping with glee, the kind that revels in other people's pain.

The words hit like a slap, but I keep my expression still. She stops in front of me, leaning close, her cold breath brushing my cheek as she whispers into my ear.

"I have something I think you'll want to see."

"Doubt it," I snap, my voice sharp, though I can already feel the chill of dread creeping up my spine.

The Shadoweaver pulls back, and her lips curl into a slow, knowing smile. Her skin is ghostly pale, unnaturally white, almost glowing in the torchlight. The effect is haunting. She looks like death itself, smiling at me as though savoring her victory.

"You know"—she begins, her voice like silk wrapping tightly around my throat—"how I said I can see through the eyes of those I control?"

A cold wave crashes over me. Dread pulses through my stomach, clawing its way into my chest until the tension makes it hard to breathe. Her grin widens, harsh and cruel.

"Let me show you," she whispers.

Before I can respond, her hands latch onto either side of my head. Her nails dig into my skin, sending lightning bolts of pain through my skull, but it's nothing compared to what comes next. My vision blurs and then collapses into darkness, only to return in flickering pulses of light.

When my sight finally steadies, I'm no longer in the cavern. I'm in my chambers in the castle. I see Raiden and Zaria hovering near the bed, their expressions tense. Two royal healers bend over someone lying on the mattress, their faces grim. In the corner, two women I've never seen before standing apart from the group, whispering.

Tristan. Kian.

And then my breath catches in my throat.

Everly.

She's standing in front of a battered Fenris, cupping his face, her delicate fingers brushing his skin with a tenderness that makes my blood boil. Worry creases her brow, as she looks him over.

She looks like a goddess descended—perfect, serene, beautiful. The sight of her, of them, ignites something primal in me. Jealousy twists with rage, burning its way through my veins.

The Shadoweaver's laugh echoes faintly in my ears, even here. But it doesn't matter. All I can see is Everly, her touch, her care.

And I can't decide what hurts more; that she looks so radiant or that her hands aren't on me.

Everly leans against Fenris's chest, his arms wrapping around her in a brief embrace. He then steps back, creating space between them.

I know, deep down, that she would never betray me. Everly is too kind and loving, her gentleness making such a cruel act unthinkable. I know this in my soul. But knowing doesn't stop the ache that builds, sharp and relentless. Seeing her in another man's arms—even if it's innocent—feels like a knife slipping between my ribs. It isn't jealousy, not exactly. It is the unbearable thought that maybe someone else could provide her with something I can't. Something she needs.

Chapter Fifty-Four

Everly

I pull the hood of my cloak up over my head as we step out of the damp, shadowed tunnel, the cool night air brushing against my face like a whisper of freedom. Zaria stays right on my heels, her footsteps quiet but sure against the uneven ground. The earthy scent of moss and damp stone fades, replaced by the crisp, woodsy aroma of the grove. The tunnel led us past the castle walls and into this stand of elm trees, their branches intertwining like skeletal fingers above us, barely allowing glimpses of the starlit sky.

The faint crunch of leaves beneath our boots is the only sound at first, until the beating of wings cuts through the stillness, and through a gap in the branches, I see Raiden.

"They are a hundred yards ahead," Zaria whispers, barely audible. Her breath fogs faintly in the cool air, and I nod, tightening the grip on my cloak.

The soft chirping of crickets rises around us, a gentle backdrop to our hurried steps. I spot Raiden's massive form first, his broad shoulders and immense wings silhouetted against the faint moonlight filtering through the canopy. Even in the shadows, he's impossible to miss, a towering figure of quiet strength. Three other shapes linger with him, but it's the flash of red hair that catches my eye. A smile tugs at my lips when I see the small figures.

Malick and Gideon stand by the horses, who, restless but silent, paw at the earth, their breaths misting in the cool night air. All of them turn toward us as we step into the clearing.

"Ready?" Tristan's voice cuts through the stillness, his expression as stoic as ever. His watchful eyes search mine as we approach.

"Of course," I reply, my voice steady, though apprehension tightens something deep inside me. The fear is there—alive, constant, pressing in—but so is the determination. For Maxon, I would walk through fire. At least now we're moving, doing something to bring him back, and that alone brings a tiny measure of relief.

I turn to Malick and Gideon, offering them a soft smile. "Thank you for getting the horses here undetected."

"Anything for you, Your Majesty." Malick bows deeply, his tone filled with unwavering loyalty.

Before I can respond, there's a sudden blur of motion. Gideon rushes forward, his small frame moving with a speed that takes me by surprise. Kian steps instinctively to block him, but Gideon ducks under his arm with startling agility and slams into me. His tiny arms wrap tightly around my middle, and he buries his face against my chest, his body shaking as a sob escapes him.

"Thank you for saving my brother," he chokes out, his voice muffled and trembling with raw emotion.

Startled, I blink. My arms move instinctively, wrapping around him as I lower my cheek to rest gently on his head. His hair smells faintly of wild grass and hay.

"You don't have to thank me for that, Gideon," I whisper, my voice soft but firm. "I'd do it a thousand times over."

Gideon pulls back, his face flushed, and swipes at his damp cheeks with the sleeve of his worn, dirt-streaked tunic. Malick immediately steps forward, wrapping a protective arm around his younger brother's shoulders and pulling him close.

"He's a little emotional," Malick explains, his voice light but not unkind.

Embarrassed, Gideon ducks his head, his hair falling into his eyes.

"We're all emotional right now," I assure him gently. "Don't worry about it."

Raiden steps up to the boys and ruffles both their hair. "There's no judgment here. If there were ever a time for raw, unchecked emotion, it's now."

Malick straightens, his hand resting firmly on Gideon's shoulder as he raises his other fist to his chest in a gesture of respect. "Good luck," he says solemnly. "May Morrigan guide you and ensure your safe return."

"Thank you," I reply, dipping my head. "And you—stay safe and out of trouble while we're gone."

Malick huffs a soft laugh as I move over to Storm, who stamps his hoof impatiently. His coat gleams in the moonlight, breath visible in soft, rhythmic puffs.

Behind me, Zaria and the others move to their horses. Zaria is riding Nova, her snow-white coat standing out among the other horses.

The air is thick with the kind of anticipation that wraps around your chest and refuses to let go. Tristan helps me onto Storm before mounting his horse.

As I adjust the reins in my hands, Raiden catches my gaze, his intense silver eyes locking onto mine.

"Ready?" he checks, his voice low but steady.

"Ready," the single word is firm, though my pulse quickens.

Storm shuffles beneath me, his muscles coiling like a spring ready to release.

Before anyone can signal to move out, a distant, rhythmic sound catches our attention. A steady drumming of hooves on the earth, faint at first but growing louder with each passing second. Instinctively, my breath catches in my throat, and my eyes dart toward Raiden, questioning what to do. His gaze meets mine, and with deliberate calm, he raises a finger to his lips, a silent command to stay still and quiet.

We all freeze, tension rippling through us like an electric current. Each second feels stretched thin as we sit in silence, hearts pounding in sync with the approaching sound, waiting to see if the rider will pass us by.

Then, through the still night air, the moonlight reveals a dark shape moving across the meadow in our direction. At first, it's only a shadow—a blur against the pale grass—but as it gets closer, the details sharpen. I glance at Zaria, her nervousness mirroring the unease twisting through me. Neither of us speaks, but the question hangs between us: friend or foe?

The horse finally comes into clearer view. Its sleek, midnight-black coat gleams faintly under the silver light, but something is off. It takes a moment to register what it is. The animal isn't carrying a rider.

"Stand down," he orders, making us all trade confused looks.

The black horse slows as it approaches our group, and I'm struck by its luminous golden eyes. A wave of magic moves over my body like a soft breeze, and in seconds, Nero stands in front of us, arms crossed over his bare chest. His long black hair reflects the moonlight as his golden eyes roam over our small group.

"Going somewhere?" he inquires in a lightly joking tone.

"Nero?"

He bows low, the movement graceful and fluid, then starts toward me. His bare feet glide over the crisp autumn leaves, not a single sound betraying his steps.

"Your Majesty, I see you are sneaking off, but I insist I join you."

Raiden sighs next to me, and I peer over at him.

"He would be useful in a fight," he admits.

"You're a horse?" I ask, bringing my attention back to Nero who is now stroking Storm's neck.

Storm nudges him gently, and I'm surprised, because I've never seen him be kind to anyone else besides myself and Maxon.

"I'm a púca, Your Majesty," he replies, the word rolling off his tongue like a melody.

"A púca?" I repeat. I do recall something like that being mentioned before, but I never connected the dots. The name rings faintly familiar, dredged up from half-remembered tales whispered in my childhood, but the details remain elusive.

“Yes,” he confirms, the smile never leaving his lips. “A shapeshifter, a trickster, and your most loyal ally.” His voice holds a strange mix of sincerity and mischief, making it impossible to tell whether he’s teasing or utterly serious.

Storm nudges him again, and he chuckles softly, rubbing the horse’s muzzle with practiced ease. The sight is disarming, a rare moment of calm in a night already filled with too much tension.

I glance at the others who all shrug. With a deep breath, I look down at Nero. “You have given me no reason not to trust you. But if you so much as sneeze in the wrong direction, I will hang you with my vines.”

Nero smiles and bows. “I would expect nothing less.”

Before I can answer, Nero shifts back into his horse. Storm snorts, and then there’s no hesitation. With a powerful surge, he takes off in a sprint, his massive hooves pounding the ground with an almost deafening rhythm. We burst from the trees and into the meadow. Our surroundings blur around us as he moves, swift and untamed, like a force of nature. I lean forward, bending low over his neck, my fingers gripping the reins tightly as the wind lashes at my clothes and hair.

The night swallows us whole, the vast expanse of the meadow stretching out endlessly. Kian and Tristan flank Zaria and me, their presence steady and protective, while Raiden leads the charge, his dark form cutting through the night like an arrow. Valric brings up the rear.

After an hour of relentless riding, my legs scream with every movement, and my fingers are stiff and numb from the cold night air. The river we've been shadowing begins to narrow, its frothing waters cascading with unrelenting speed. The sound of the rushing current grows louder, echoing off the surrounding terrain.

Raiden raises his fist, and we slow in unison, our horses transitioning from a steady canter to a careful trot before coming to a halt.

"This looks like the best place to cross," Raiden notes, his eyes fixed on the turbulent river. "The current's strong, but it's narrow enough."

I frown, staring at the churning water. It's vicious, a wild force determined to drag anything into its depths. Beyond the river, the Feyglades loom dark and mysterious, shrouded in mist. And farther still, the jagged outline of the Ethereal Peaks rises against the horizon, faintly illuminated by the sliver of moonlight breaking through the clouds.

Raiden tugs at his horse's reins, guiding it toward the riverbank. I can see the animal's hesitation, its ears flicking back nervously as its hooves paw at the ground.

"Wait!" I call out, and glance over my shoulder at Valric, his sharp gaze meeting mine as he gives me a small, firm nod. He doesn't need to say more; I know exactly what he's thinking.

Damn it. I haven't practiced enough with water magic to feel confident, but what choice do we have?

"I'll see if I can slow the current." My words remain steady despite the swirl of uncertainty.

Slipping off Storm's back, I let my boots crunch against the smooth, damp stones that line the river's edge. Kian is right behind me, dismounting with practiced ease, and following closely. His presence is as solid as ever, and I can feel his protective instincts flaring to life, an invisible shield around me.

With a deep breath, I step closer to the river. The spray from the rushing water dots my face, cold and biting against my skin. Noticing a relatively calm area a short distance away, where the rocks provide some protection from the strong currents, I cautiously make my way across the slippery rocks.

Kneeling, I press my hands into the icy current. It nips at my fingertips, the chill shooting up my arms, but I force myself to hold steady.

I close my eyes, shutting out the world around me, and let the sound of the river fill my mind. I focus on the hum of my magic, the way it stirs in my chest, rising and twisting like a living thing. The chill of the river is almost grounding, anchoring me to the present as I coax my magic forward, urging it to respond. The water laps gently at my hands, a soft, rhythmic sound, and I send my magic out, feeling it swirl with the current like an invisible hand. I imagine the current slowing to a lazy pace, barely rippling as it winds its way through the landscape. Then as almost an afterthought, words fall from my lips in a hush whisper.

"A aibhne fhiáin, cuir do ghearán i gcéin,
Faoin ngealach gheal is spéir airgid réidh.
Le duille is cloch, le toil bhog na cré,
Bí séimh anois — bí ciúin, bí socair.

Lig don shruth scíth a ghlacadh, lig don fhearg dul i suan,
Tabhair pas dúinn don chosán atá á lorg againn."

The soft murmur of voices, like the rustle of leaves, draws my attention, and I open my eyes.

The river is almost motionless, the gentle current barely disturbing the golden flecks and sparks of magic that flare within the water, a physical manifestation of my magic.

"I knew you could do it," Valric remarks, urging his horse forward and stepping into the river.

I stand frozen, a wild rhythm drums in my chest as I watch him cross. Kian bumps my shoulder, a light contact that makes me turn to look at him.

"Good job." He gives me a wink, and gestures with his head to the horses. "Come on, let's get going."

We walk over to the horses, and he holds his hand out, boosting me up onto Storm's back. I gather up the reins, my attention on Nero as he crosses the river next.

I follow closely behind Tristan and Zaria as we cross the river in single file, Kian right behind me. The water swirls around our horses' legs, the current pushing against my magic. My grip on Storm's reins is firm, guiding him forward while his muscles tense beneath me, each step measured and cautious. The current pushes hard, but my magic holds steady, forcing the water to slow and part just enough for us to pass.

Ahead, Raiden, Nero, and Valric are already waiting on the far bank, their silhouettes outlined against the backdrop of the dark Feyglades. Raiden sits tall in his saddle, his wings partially spread as if ready to take flight at any moment. Valric's hand rests on the hilt of his sword, his watchful eyes scanning the surroundings.

Storm snorts, his ears flicking back and forth as the river's chill seeps through his legs, but he presses on, trusting me. The horse climbs the muddy bank, almost desperate to get out of the water. As soon as Kian reaches the bank and his horse scrambles up onto solid ground, I turn back toward the river. My focus sharpens, and I reach for my magic once more. It hums beneath my skin, warm and pulsing, as I pull it back into myself.

The moment my magic dissipates, the river roars to life. The sound is deafening, a violent rush that drowns out everything else for a moment. I linger, watching the current surge and swell, reclaiming its wild dominance.

We ride well into the day and the sun now sits high in the sky. My stomach rumbles, but I don't want to stop. The long grass of the glade sways in the warm breeze, the mountains ahead growing larger by the hour, making my heart thrum in anticipation.

I slump a little in the saddle, my legs attempting to relax, and ease the pain in my back. Storm must sense my fatigue, because he lets out a loud neigh. His pace slows, and the other horses follow his lead. Raiden turns in his saddle to meet my gaze, and I must look pretty bad, because he immediately turns his horse for mine, pulling it alongside Storm.

"Why didn't you say you needed a break?"

I shrug, not wanting to appear weaker than the others. "It didn't seem important."

"Everly, you're the most important person here. If you need rest, say so."

I frown, ready to argue, but he doesn't give me a chance. He is off his horse and handing the reins to Kian as he reaches for me, lifting me from Storm's back.

He carries me over to a log and I poke him in the chest. "You can put me down. I know how to walk."

Raiden smirks, and I can see amusement in his eyes. "Not so sure you can. You aren't used to riding long distances, and we have been riding almost nonstop for eight hours."

I roll my eyes. "Put me down."

"As you wish." Raiden places my feet on the ground, my legs immediately buckling, and he catches me before I crumple to the ground. Embarrassment heats my neck and creeps up to my face as he guides me over to the log.

"Thanks," I mutter, plonking down.

"It's happened to all of us at some point," Tristan assures me, handing me a piece of crusty bread and some cheese.

My mouth waters as I reach for it. Kian hands me a canteen, and I gratefully take that too, guzzling down a mouthful of cool liquid before stuffing a piece of bread in my mouth. I am so hungry.

"We should reach the base of the mountains by nightfall. We will set up camp for the night and continue fresh in the morning."

Chapter Fifty-Five

Everly

The crackling of the fire is soothing, a rhythmic warmth that lulls me into a fragile sense of peace. I close my eyes and reach inward, seeking the thread nestled in my chest. It's always there, faint but persistent, connecting me to him. I let my focus slip away from the world around me, following the golden thread as it winds through the dark recesses of my mind. There's no resistance this time, no barriers to push past. The thread is a glowing beacon, guiding me forward.

"Maxon," I whisper, my voice tentative, barely audible in the stillness.

But something feels wrong. The sensation creeps over me like a shadow, heavy and cold.

The darkness around me shifts, giving way to an open expanse. Abruptly, I'm standing on a windswept cliff, jagged rocks plunging into a roaring ocean below.

The waves crash violently, the sound thunderous, drowning out everything else. Spray from the sea reaches me, cold and sharp against my skin, and I shiver, wrapping my arms around myself as the salty air clings to me. I turn in a slow, hesitant circle, searching.

Then I see him. Maxon stands behind me, his figure still and ghostly in the dim light. His face is pale and drawn, the familiar warmth in his expression dulled. My chest constricts painfully, and before I can stop myself, I rush to him. Eyes roam over his form, noting the hollowness in his cheeks, the way his clothes hang off him like he's been shrinking away from the world. He's losing weight, and it hits me like a blow to the chest. My lip trembles, but I force myself to hold it together.

His hands lift to cup my face, his touch gentle and familiar. His thumb brushes over my cheek, and the simple, tender gesture unravels me.

"Stóirín," he breathes, leaning closer, his face burying into my hair. He inhales deeply, as if the scent of me is enough to anchor him. "I've missed you."

"And I've missed you," I reply, my voice shaky. "But you seem sad. What's wrong?"

I reach up, cupping his face in my hands, tilting it so I can see into his eyes. Those eyes—the deep violet I know so well—flicker with hints of gold and red, like autumn leaves falling through a twilight sky. His magic dances there, wild and restless, yet muted, locked away.

Maxon's hand closes around my wrist, pulling one of my hands from his face. He presses a soft, lingering kiss to the inside of my wrist, his lips warm against my skin.

"You are so beautiful," he murmurs, his voice a low, aching rasp.

"A chroí," I whisper, trying to keep the tremor from my voice. "Talk to me. Please."

He doesn't respond—not with words. Instead, Maxon leans down, his lips brushing mine. The kiss is soft, achingly tender, carrying a weight of emotion that threatens to break me. It's as if he's pouring every unspoken word, every fear, every longing into this single moment. My stomach tightens, a knot of unease pulling tighter and tighter. Something is wrong. I can feel it, like the distant rumble of a storm closing in.

Breaking the kiss, I wrap my arms tightly around him, pressing my head to his chest. His heartbeat, faint and uneven. "Maxon," I say softly, my voice trembling, "we're coming for you. We're on our way–"

"Don't say anything more," he interrupts, his tone sharp and cautious. "I'm not sure if she can hear us."

"Who?" I ask, barely above a whisper. "Yumekui?"

He shakes his head slowly, as if shaking off invisible chains. "The blood magic," he murmurs, his voice heavy with exhaustion. "It's getting harder to fight."

A wave of panic slams into me, stealing my breath.

"What can I do?" I blurt out, desperation lacing my words.

Then a thought flickers in my mind. Mates can heal each other through shared blood. Would that work with a spell?

Can my blood wash away the evil trying to take over his mind?

It's worth a try.

"Feed from me," I plead.

Maxon stiffens, his hands gently gripping my arms as he pulls back to look at me. "I don't want to hurt you." His voice is strained with a mix of longing and restraint.

"You won't."

"I barely stopped last time," he argues, his tone carrying a dark edge of self-recrimination.

"But you did." I reach up, cupping his face and forcing him to meet my gaze. "I trust you, Maxon. Take what you need to survive until I can get to you. Please."

For a moment, he doesn't respond, his jaw tightening as an internal battle rages within him. Then, unexpectedly, his expression darkens. "I saw you and Fenris." He keeps his voice low, a faint growl vibrating beneath his words.

I blink, startled by the abrupt change in subject. "Me and Fenris?"

"In our chambers," he clarifies. "He was wounded. You were comforting him."

"How?" the question slips from my lips, confusion swirling like a rising storm.

Maxon's eyes narrow, his voice heavy with doubt and pain. "Do you love him?"

My head jerks back as I stare at him, stunned. "What? No!"

Grabbing his hand, I press it firmly to my chest, over the frantic beating of my heart. "It's only you, Maxon. You are the other half of my soul."

His fingers graze my cheek, his touch achingly tender. "Losing you . . . isn't something I would survive," he murmurs. "Your smile, your kindness, your heart of gold—those are what keep me going. But if you want to be with someone else . . . I'd let you go. I'd give you that."

Anger flares hot and fast, and before I can think, I punch him in the stomach. "Don't be stupid!" I fume, my voice trembling with frustration. "Fenris is just a friend. You, Maxon, are my life, my mate, my soul. No one could ever replace you. So don't you dare die on me, okay?" My chest heaves with the force of my words, my emotions burning through me like wildfire.

For the first time, a spark of life returns to Maxon's eyes, and a smirk plays at the corners of his lips. "Fiery as ever," he growls, dragging me closer until our bodies are pressed together. His mouth crashes down on mine, the kiss fierce and full of unspoken promises.

Then, without hesitation, his fangs pierce my neck. The initial sting fades quickly, replaced by a warm, dizzying pull as he drinks. He's tentative at first, but as the blood flows, his grip on me tightens, his arms crushing me to his chest. My hands bury themselves in his hair, holding him just as fiercely.

After a few moments, Maxon pulls back, his lips stained with crimson. His eyes are brighter now, glowing faintly with renewed energy. "Someone's coming," he warns, his voice urgent. "I have to go."

Before I can protest, he kisses me again, softer this time, lingering as if trying to memorize the feel of me. "Be careful," he whispers against my lips. "I love you."

A sob escapes me as he steps away, his form fading into the darkness like a shadow consumed by the night.

"I love you, too," I whisper into the emptiness, my hands clutching the spot where he just stood as I'm left alone once more.

Chapter Fifty-Six

The Skythari Nomads

We stand on the ridge, the peak of the snow-dusted mountains stretching beneath our feet, and watch from our hidden vantage point. The sun dips low in the sky, casting a golden glow across the snowy valley, illuminating the group below. Among them, the woman with sun-kissed hair goes still, her entire body stiffening as she realizes they are being followed. A ripple of awareness passes through her companions, but she senses it first—an instinctual reaction, sharp and immediate.

We haven't interfered yet, merely observing. It intrigues us that a frostflare has been guiding her for days, leading her across treacherous terrain, closer to us. But something else is out there now, something stalking her and her companions, its presence thickening the air with danger.

It isn't us—not this time.

Our orders are clear: don't interfere unless trouble finds its way to our doorstep.

"We can't continue," the one with the sun-kissed hair speaks, her voice carrying on the wind as she turns to face her companions.

The tension in her shoulders betrays her calm tone. "If we try to outrun whatever is out there, there's a good chance it will follow us to the Skythari Nomads. I won't win their trust if I bring danger to their home. We need to deal with it now."

Shock rolls through our group like a wave. A few of us exchange quick glances, disbelief flickering across our faces. My sister, standing beside me, whispers, "Since when do the high fae care about anyone but themselves?" Her voice is so soft, but I hear the clear disbelief in her tone.

Below, we feel the disturbance before the attackers crest the snowy hill. A group of ogres, hulking beasts with thick, meaty limbs, move swiftly toward the fae. Their speed defies their size, their heavy bodies charging through the snow, barreling toward their prey. The ground rumbles beneath them, snow kicking up in plumes. The air around them grows sharp with the scent of impending violence.

The fae react as one, their instincts honed and deadly. The draconian male is the first to act, his massive wings spreading wide as he leaps from his horse, launching himself into the air with a powerful beat of his wings. His sword gleams, catching the light reflecting off the snow.

Another fae shifts seamlessly into her leopard form, her body sleek and agile, fur rippling as she drops low to the ground, eyes locked on the approaching ogres. She is a predator, pure and focused, muscles coiled and ready to strike.

The silver-haired fae with his bow and arrow drawn charges forward, his horse moving as one with him, hooves pounding the ground as he releases arrows in rapid succession. Each shot is accurate, the arrows cutting through the air aimed at the oncoming beasts. The black horse with the golden magic races toward the ogres with incredible speed.

Meanwhile, the remaining two fae soldiers stay back, forming a protective wall between the ogres and the woman with sun-kissed hair. Their stance is clear; they will defend her at all costs, even if it means their lives. There is no hesitation, no faltering. The bond between them is stronger than fear.

"Who is she?" I wonder out loud.

We watch, tension thrumming through our veins, unsure of how this will play out. Our gazes flick between the battle unfolding below and the woman at the center of it all. She isn't retreating, isn't running. Instead, she stands her ground, her hand resting lightly on the hilt of a blade at her side, watching her companions fight.

"She's not like the others," my sister whispers, her eyes narrowing as she studies the woman.

The ogres bear down on the fae, but they are met with a swift, brutal counterattack. The draconian swoops down from above, wings tucked close in a lethal dive. His sword flashing silver in the sunlight, cleaving through the first ogre with terrifying grace. Blood sprays in an arc, painting the white snow red as the beast crumples without a sound. He moved like a phantom, too fast to follow, a living storm of steel. The leopard shifter leaps into the fray, claws flashing, teeth bared as she tears into their thick hides. Arrows whizz past, finding their marks in exposed flesh, bringing the ogres to their knees.

Still, the battle is far from over.

We remain on the peak, watching, waiting. This is no longer just an observation—it is a test. The woman with the sun-kissed hair has drawn trouble to the edge of our lands, but how she handles it, how she navigates this danger, will determine whether she is truly worthy of our attention—or our intervention.

Chapter Fifty-Seven

Everly

I sit frozen for a heartbeat, my pulse hammering in my chest as the ogres crest the hill behind us. Storm shifts restlessly beneath me, his hooves stamping the snow, sending flurries into the air.

My eyes flick to Raiden, who meets my gaze. We don't need to speak—his look says everything.

Stay put, we will handle this.

I want to snort at the warning glare he sends me, but I just hold his stare with my own.

His attention goes to Kian and Tristan, and without another second's hesitation, he takes flight, his wings spreading wide, dark and powerful, as he launches himself from his horse. His two swords are already drawn. Zaria follows immediately, her movements smooth and effortless as her form shifts, magic swirling around her in a soft breeze.

I feel the whisper of her transformation brush against my face, a reminder of the primal power at her command. She drops to the snow, her leopard form sleek and deadly, muscles coiled and ready to pounce. She is beautiful and powerful.

My own magic stirs beneath my skin, a thrumming pulse of energy that quickens in response to the chaos unfolding around us. I can feel it licking at my senses, eager to be unleashed, but I force myself to stay grounded. Valric, riding hard behind Raiden and Zaria, lets loose a barrage of arrows, each one finding its mark with unerring precision. One of the ogres staggers, an arrow embedded deep in its neck. It stumbles but doesn't fall, not until Raiden descends from above, sword flashing as he drives the blade through the back of the ogre's neck, severing its spinal cord in a brutal final blow. The beast crumples to the ground, lifeless, as the others continue their charge.

Nero is a blur of movement over the white snow, his powerful form eating up the distance in no time.

Tristan and Kian flank me, their swords drawn as our horses dance back and forth in agitation.

Two ogres break free from the fight, their heavy footfalls shaking the earth as they lumber toward us.

Tristan and Kian move forward in unison, creating a barrier between me and the approaching threat.

Kian glances back over his shoulder, his expression lit with a dangerous sort of amusement.

"Ready?" The word is filled with an almost boyish enthusiasm that belies the danger before us.

"Sure." I grip the reins tightly with trembling hands.

The ogres don't slow. Their beady eyes gleam with malice as they close the distance, their guttural snarls growing louder. The air feels charged, heavy with the promise of violence.

Kian shifts his weight slightly, settling into a fighting stance. "Good."

Something nags at the edge of my awareness as I watch the ogres get closer. Nymeria and Anika went ahead earlier, scouting the area, and we haven't heard from them since. My heart skips a beat as I stretch out my senses, searching for them amidst the chaos. I close my eyes, allowing the snowy landscape to fill my mind, sweeping my magic across the terrain. The cold bites at my skin, but I try to focus on finding my wolves.

There.

Several miles ahead, I find them perched on a rocky outcrop. My connection with them flickers, and I press harder, my magic circling them like an insistent hand, tugging them back toward me.

Return. I demand silently, sending the pulse of my will through the bond we share.

The faint hum of their acknowledgment fills the bond, a subtle shift in their focus as they begin to make their way back, their howls floating on the breeze.

The sound of a low growl snaps my attention back to the battle. Zaria's leopard form springs forward, claws slashing through the air as she tears into an ogre's side, her movements fluid and lethal. Valric's arrows rain down with deadly accuracy, and Tristan and Kian stand like stone, swords ready to cut down anything that gets too close.

My magic crackles beneath my skin, begging to be used, but I hold back, waiting for the right moment. My fingers curl around the hilt of my sword, and I unclip the cloak from my neck, letting it fall from my shoulders.

I slip from Storm's back, my boots landing in the snow.

Tristan's attention darts over his shoulder at me and his eyes widen. "Everly, get back on the horse!"

Ignoring him, I focus on the task at hand and draw my sword from its sheath in a single smooth motion. The wind picks up around me, tearing at my clothes and whipping strands of my hair across my face. The icy sting is a distant ache, drowned out by the adrenaline coursing through my veins.

I bring my gloved hand to my mouth, biting down on the fingertip with more force than necessary, and yank the glove free. The cold bites at my exposed skin, like little needles, but I welcome it.

Crouching low in the snow, I dig my bare fingers into the frozen ground, feeling the earth tremble beneath my touch.

Valric told me I don't need physical contact to summon my magic, that I am strong enough to call it forth without it. But it's easier this way, the connection more immediate, more visceral. And right now, I need that. I need the surge of control, the pulse of power at my fingertips.

My fingers curl into the snow as I glare at the approaching ogres, my breath fogging the air in quick, determined puffs. The rage I've been holding back since the attack on Skora ignites within me, and my magic rises from deep in my core, bursting outward.

It's raw, unrestrained, a fierce energy that flows from me and sinks into the ground beneath.

The earth responds.

The ground quakes in rhythm with my heartbeat, a deep rumble that spreads in every direction. I sense my magic threading through the soil, a pulse of life and power that thrums beneath my fingertips. The horses nearby shift nervously, hooves stamping as they feel the tremors. They sense the power, too, their bodies tense and uneasy as they dance back and forth, uncertain.

The ogres are close now, their guttural growls filling the air, their massive fists clenching as they prepare to attack. But I'm ready. The earth beneath them shifts, and for the first time, I see hesitation in their eyes, a flicker of doubt as they sense the power rising from the ground.

I smirk, letting them feel that fear, letting them know that they've walked into something far greater than they anticipated. The cold snow melts beneath my hand, a thin layer of frost giving way as my magic takes root. It spreads through the earth like wildfire, unseen but felt, growing stronger with every second.

And then, with a long calm exhale, I let it go.

The ground erupts.

Jagged spears of earth shoot up from the snow, aimed directly at the ogres' path. The force is immediate, and the ogres scramble to dodge the deadly spikes. But they're too slow. One of them is impaled, the earth piercing through its thick, meaty body with a sickening crunch. The other roars in fury, losing its momentum, faltering under the sudden assault.

I rise from my crouch, magic still humming in my veins. The other ogres have ceased their battle, their eyes fixated on me—a blend of fear and morbid curiosity etched upon their brutish faces. Then, with a deafening roar that shakes the very mountains, the ogres abandon their fight with my friends. As they charge toward me, the ground trembles beneath their massive feet.

Lifting my palm up in a sweeping motion, I send a fierce gust of wind barreling into the remaining ogres. They stop their charge, lifting their arms to try to block the onslaught of snow and wind.

I walk forward, anger singing in my veins, ready to take on the remaining four ogres. Raiden and Zaria are already engaging one, Valric another, as the two stragglers come for us. Adrenaline sings through me, and I tighten my grip on my sword, my teeth clenched.

Suddenly, my mating bond flares to life, a foreign magic stirring in my blood. My steps falter in the snow as I draw it to the surface, curious. A fiery path of magic trails down my arm, engulfing my sword in flames. I lift it, turning it in my hand.

Did I somehow summon Maxon's fire, did he open the bond for me, sharing his dragon's fire?

I don't have time to think about it as two ogres are on Tristan and Kian, swinging their fists with the fury of a demon. Kian is knocked from his horse and Tristan jumps, launching himself, sword raised at the ogre.

A rush of adrenaline has me running, the ground lifting to meet me, pushing me forward. While the beast is focused on Tristan, I lift my sword, slicing at the backs of his knees. The sword surprisingly cuts clean through the flesh, the ogre instantly falling to the ground. My sword sings, demanding more, the flames burning brighter than before. With a snarl, the ogre rolls over, ready to launch itself at me when Tristan's sword pierces through its chest.

I spin around frantically, searching for Kian. My stomach lurches when I see him pinned beneath the last ogre, its massive body crushing him into the snow. His sword is knocked from his hand, his form struggling against the weight. I falter as I watch him lose the battle. Panic pounds through me and my vision tunnels, adrenaline surging like wildfire in my veins. Before I even register the movement, I'm closing the distance in a blur. My sword is already raised, and with a scream of raw fury, I drive it into the ogre's back, straight through its heart.

The beast lets out a guttural roar, its body jerking violently as flames erupt from the wound, consuming it in seconds. I scream again, my anger ripping through the cold, as the ogre's body rolls off Kian and crumbles, disintegrating into ash and embers.

Panting, I sink to my knees in the snow. My body trembling from the exertion, my sword falls from my grip, the flames extinguished as quickly as they appeared.

The cold snow seeps into my clothes, but I barely notice it. My lungs heave as I try to catch my breath. My pulse is still pounding, the adrenaline refusing to ebb, and I can feel the aftershocks of my magic pulsing beneath my skin.

For a moment, I just kneel here, staring at the ash and the snow, my mind struggling to process what just happened.

The sound of wings flapping overhead pulls me back, and I glance up just in time to see Raiden landing beside me. His wings fold against his back, and the warmth of his presence is a stark contrast to the cold biting at my exposed skin. He kneels next to me, his hand landing gently on my back, a reassuring weight that grounds me.

"Are you okay?" Raiden's voice is low, concerned, but steady.

I nod, unable to speak just yet. My throat is raw from screaming, my pulse still thundering in my ears. I can feel his eyes on me, the heat of his hand spreading through my body, chasing away the lingering cold.

"Kian?" The sound of Zaria's worried voice has my head snapping up. She's kneeling in the snow next to Kian, tapping his face lightly, but he remains motionless.

I scramble to my feet, sinking in the snow as I stagger over to him and fall to my knees by his side. His face is paler than normal, and his breathing shallow. I lean over him, cupping his face.

"Kian?"

"Those ogres were ready for war," Tristan murmurs. "I've never seen any behave so bloodthirsty."

Valric steps up behind me, his shadow falling over me with Nero by his side in human form.

Tears prick my eyes, and I grit my teeth, tasting the salt of frustration on my tongue. My magic is growing again, a heat that feels both familiar and foreign simmering beneath the surface. I command it to spread, to reach out and search for injuries, for anything to mend. I try to summon that same unthinking focus I had with Nova. Back then, I didn't even notice I was using magic. It was effortless, instinctual—a simple thought transformed into action without hesitation or control.

But this time, it's different. My mind is too aware, too burdened by doubt and desperation. The warmth in my body pulses, but it doesn't reach where I need it. The magic feels trapped, stubbornly refusing to move beyond my skin.

"It's not working," I mutter, frustration tainting my voice.

"What's not working?" Zaria lays a hand on my arm.

"I healed Nova after the attack on the way to the Evergreens. Maxon told me to keep it a secret. I just . . . I don't know how I did it."

Zaria's warm brown eyes widen, and she blinks. "You can heal?"

I shrug, looking back down to Kian. "Maybe the first time was a fluke."

Valric grunts next to me. "Was no fluke, My Queen."

I look over my shoulder at him in confusion. "What?"

"Your mother was a healer. She would often wander the forest in search of injured animals or sick trees and give them the boost they needed. But it comes at a price."

"Why didn't you tell me this during training?" I demand.

"Why didn't you tell me you've healed before?" he volleys back immediately.

My mouth opens, but nothing comes out. "Touche," I finally concede. "Well then, how do I heal him?"

"He will heal on his own in a few hours," Valric utters simply, turning and making his way over to the horses.

I sit here stunned for a second before jumping to my feet and charging after him.

"Valric!"

"Yes, Your Majesty?" He spins around so fast I almost crash into him.

"How do I heal him?"

"You don't."

"But–"

"He will live. You shouldn't waste your energy on healing him. There will be more battles to come."

Chapter Fifty-Eight

Everly

Back in Storm's saddle, I hold the reins tightly as we make our way through the deepening snow. The silence between us is thick; even Storm's hooves fall muffled against the fresh powder. Valric has taken the lead, riding ahead, giving me ample time to glare at his back. Why wouldn't he tell me how to heal Kian? Yes, he is fine now and riding between Raiden and Zaria, but still, this is a part of me that I wish to know.

"Your Majesty," Tristan's voice breaks into my dark thoughts. I turn, drawn from my brooding, and meet his steady gaze.

A sigh escapes me, and I force a small, weary smile. "Call me Everly, please. It's just us here."

Tristan's nose wrinkles, as if I've just suggested something scandalous.

"But you are the queen," he objects, his voice quiet but insistent.

"Yes, but right now, I'd prefer to be Everly," I reply, a faint teasing lilt slipping into my tone.

"Very well. You dropped these." He holds out my gloves. I completely forgot about them. I've barely noticed the cold since the fight.

"Thanks, Tristan." I reach out and take the gloves, slipping them into my satchel.

"It's going to be nightfall soon. We need to find shelter," Raiden announces.

Nymeria nudges my leg, drawing my attention down to her. *'There is a rocky outcrop about a mile up the mountain that will offer the shelter you need.'*

With a grin, I lean down and run my hand over Nymeria's head, her fur warm and soft beneath my fingers. She tilts her head up to meet my gaze, her amber eyes wide and alert.

"Thanks, sweet girl," I murmur, my voice low and grateful. She gives a soft huff, and I like to think it's her way of saying, *Of course.*

"Nymeria says there's a rocky outcrop a mile up the mountain," I impart, looking at Raiden. "It'll give us shelter from this wind."

Valric turns his horse to face us, casting a glance at me before his gaze shifts down to the wolves padding alongside our horses. His stern expression eases as he watches them, his usual formality softening into something almost warm. The snow falls more heavily now, and I notice the wolves shaking it from their coats every few steps. They look like shadowy ghosts.

A grin tugs at Valric's lips as he addresses the wolves directly. "Nymeria, Anika," his voice carries over the whistling wind, "you two want to show us the way?"

Nymeria's ears prick up, and she looks to her sister as if exchanging a wordless agreement. Then, with a sharp bark, she bounds forward, her paws silent against the snow as she takes the lead.

'We are being watched.' Anika's ears perk up as she scans the darkness beyond our shelter.

I stare into the flames but show no outward emotion to her words.

'You sure?'

'Yes.'

My eyes flicker to the darkness beyond the flames and I let my magic rise the way I did that time when I wanted to find Zaria.

'They aren't a threat.' Nymeria yawns, laying her head down on her paws.

'How do you know?'

Anika tilts her head, looking at me curiously. *'They have been watching us since we entered the valley leading up to the mountains.'*

My breath catches. '*Why didn't you say something sooner?'*

'We were scouting.'

I huff out a breath and shake my head at her simple explanation. *'Isn't that the point?'*

"Is everything alright over there?" Raiden's voice rumbles softly, his gaze flicking toward me with a hint of concern from where he's seated, leaning back against the stone wall.

"Everything is fine," I reply, offering a small, reassuring smile. He gives me a skeptical look. His shoulders relax slightly, but he's watching me closely, reading my expressions.

Everyone needs rest, especially Kian and Raiden. If I mention that we are being watched, no one will get any sleep. Zaria is already curled up by the fire next to Raiden, her small frame snug against his side, her breaths soft and steady. Across from them, Tristan lies on his back, staring up at the ceiling as if he were counting every mark in the stone. Then there's Kian, lying off to the side, face half-buried in his cloak, though I know he isn't sleeping either.

Kian's injuries have been healing so slowly, and it worries me. Even after all this time, he is still struggling, occasionally wincing. Tristan healed remarkably quickly after the ambush on the road to the Evergreens, but Kian is different. I remember Zaria telling me that the high fae possess magic, and the strength of that magic reflects in the shade of purple in their eyes. Tristan has the deeper purple, whereas Kian's are the softest lavender. But the fact he's still hurting. It tugs at me in ways I can't ignore.

I bite my lip, worry creeping in.

Just then, Valric comes in, stamping his feet to shake off the fresh layer of snow dusting his cloak. He gives each of us a long look, his gaze lingering on Kian, then on me.

"We should all get some rest," he suggests quietly, brushing the snow from his shoulders. "I'll take the first watch, followed by Nero."

I nod, though the urge to volunteer burns on my tongue. I know none of them will agree to have me on watch. I peer over at Nero. His golden eyes, reflecting the firelight, look distant, as though his mind is somewhere far away. I can't help but wonder if he regrets tagging along with us.

Sensing my gaze, Nero raises his eyes from the fire and stares directly at me. His eyes are curious, as if he's trying to read me. The intensity of his stare makes me feel oddly exposed, though neither of us says a word.

After a moment, Nero gives a slight nod, the barest dip of his head, before leaning back on the hard ground. To my surprise, he doesn't bother with a blanket, shirt, or bedroll. He simply lies there, bare-chested, the cold seemingly no match for him. The firelight dances over the black tattoos that cover his entire body, and I can just make out faint scars that crisscross over his skin, hinting at battles fought long before our paths crossed.

I watch him for a moment longer, wondering what thoughts lie hidden behind those golden eyes.

Chapter Fifty-Nine

Maxon

I'm being led by a fucking leash through the tunnels once again. I can sense Yumekui's delight at having me at her mercy, at treating me like her fucking pet. Everly told me she has a plan to get me out of here. The spark in her green eyes was enough to make me believe in it. But she didn't tell me what that plan was, and for good reason. If they were somehow able to infiltrate my mind—to pull secrets from me—I don't want her to know Everly's plan. Not even a hint.

It occurs to me that when I emerged from my vision with Everly, her blood served as an antidote. It acted as a cleansing force, dispelling the sinister, almost sentient blood magic. Although I was completely clear-headed when Yumekui arrived, I pretended to be dazed and obedient, wearing a temporary mask.

My boot catches on a jagged rock, and I stumble forward, the leash jerking me so hard that the wyvern bones digging into my wrists and neck pull tight, sending a sharp jolt of pain through my nerves.

My hands clench, itching to reach up and tear this leash off, but I know better than to resist. Not now. Not here.

The thick, black cloth bag over my head smothers my senses, blocking out everything but the faint, suffocating scent of stale air and stone dust. I can't see a damn thing, can't even catch a whiff of the damp tunnels around me. But sound? Sound is something I can't shut out. The echo of footsteps bounces off the walls, coming from all directions—muffled conversations, the clanking of chains, groups of people moving about.

I don't bother asking where we're going. I already know Yumekui won't tell me. She lives for this, for the suspense of drawing out the unknown, letting it seep into my bones like venom. Like any filthy demon, she feeds on pain and misery, thriving on the power it gives her, savoring each twist of agony and confusion as if it's some twisted delicacy.

I'm pushed in the back and then two hands clamp down on my shoulders, forcing me down until I fall into a chair. Then the sack is ripped off my head, and I blink, my eyes adjusting to the light. I see Yumekui's back as she retreats to the far wall and kneels down, head bowed.

"I see you've healed again, but not without scarring." The Shadoweaver's piercing gaze goes to Yumekui.

"What do you want?" I growl.

She smiles. "I want to share a meal with you."

I frown in confusion, my eyes narrowing as I tip my face forward.

"And after, you can call that mate of yours."

"You're fucking dreaming." I smirk.

In an instant, the Shadoweaver is up and rounding the table, her movements smooth and predatory. Her hand lashes out, grasping my face in an iron grip. Nails—long and razor-sharp—dig into the skin of my cheek, forcing my head up so that I'm looking directly into those dark, soulless eyes. Her face is mere inches from mine, breath icy against my skin.

"Call your mate," she hisses, her voice now edged with impatience. "I know you can. I know you and she meet between planes, that you feed from each other. How else could you heal so well." The Shadoweaver's eyes narrow, as if daring me to deny it. "Now. Call her."

My jaw clenches, and a fire burns under my skin, a fire I wish I could unleash.

"Stubborn, are we?" she sneers, her fingers tightening, nails pressing harder until I feel the sting of blood beneath them. "Well, I know a few things, and your mate's little trick to deceive me failed."

My heart lurches and I do my best to maintain an air of indifference. The Shadoweaver lets go of my face, pushing me backward, and making the chair rock.

"Did she think that sneaking out in the middle of the night would work?" The sinister laugh that follows sends a shiver down my spine. "I thrive in darkness, as do my pets."

"Go fuck yourself!" I snarl. The fire burning deep in my chest moves outward like lava flowing through my veins.

The Shadoweaver tips her head back and laughs, the sound grating.

"I am surprised though. She is stronger than I was led to believe. The human world didn't leave her as weak and broken as one would have thought." She leans her hip on the table, her long nails tapping on the hard surface.

I can't stop my smirk from forming. Everly is stronger than we ever gave her credit for. Just because she looks soft, with her delicate features and kind demeanor, doesn't mean she can't be fierce. It doesn't mean she can't hold her ground when the world tries to push her down.

"Where is she going?" the Shadoweaver demands, cutting through my thoughts.

"I have no idea, and even if I did, I wouldn't tell you."

"I can have Yumekui get into your mind. It's much easier if you just tell me."

I laugh and shake my head. "Go ahead," I taunt, my tone almost dismissive. "Everly has told me nothing of her plans."

The flicker in her eyes is unmistakable, like starlight piercing through the darkness—bright and piercing. "She is in the Ethereal Mountains. Why?"

I shrug, deliberately casual, and tilt my head slightly as I meet her gaze.

Her lips curve into a tight smile, but it doesn't reach her eyes. "Prince Alivar has aligned himself with your mate," she says, her voice suddenly sharper, cutting the conversation in a different direction. "So, I think it's only fitting to send him a warning."

The words hit me like a blow, and my mind flashes back to the marching—a memory so vivid it makes my pulse thunder. My chair scrapes against the floor as I surge forward, my hands slamming onto the table.

"Don't you fucking dare," I snarl, my voice low and dangerous. Fury ripples through me, tightening my muscles and darkening my vision.

The Shadoweaver doesn't flinch. Instead, a slow, almost taunting smirk spreads across her face, and she straightens, exuding confidence and command.

"Oh, My King," she purrs, her voice dripping with mockery, "but it's done. My creatures will descend on the City of Starlight tonight."

I lunge, but before I can move an inch closer, Yumekui appears in a swirl of shadows, her grip iron-tight as she tugs on the chain around my neck. The force yanks me back, my body straining against her pull.

"No!" I roar, my fury burning hotter with each passing second. My glare locks on the Shadoweaver.

She watches me, calm and unbothered, as though my rage is nothing more than an inconvenience.

"If you tell me what she is up to, I can call off my army."

I grit my teeth, my jaw popping under the pressure. She sighs and waves me off.

"Very well."

With that, I'm dragged from the cavern.

Chapter Sixty

Everly

The early morning sunlight bouncing off the fresh snow is almost blinding, filling the air with a crisp, shimmering brightness. The cold bites, but the beauty of it all is distracting. I squint, adjusting the hood on my cloak as I trudge through the powder toward the horses. Their breaths form little clouds, hanging briefly before vanishing into the morning chill.

The sound of the snow crunching under my boots is oddly calming as I reach for the bag of oats, approaching Storm. His ears flick forward, alert, and he watches me intently. I hold out a handful of oats and he steps forward, his breath warm against my palm as he carefully nibbles the food. His dark eyes, framed by his thick, glossy lashes, are as expressive as ever, and I smile, lost in the silent connection that exists between us.

Once he finishes, I drop the bag back down and step closer, running my hands gently over his cheeks, feeling the softness of his coat beneath my fingers.

"You're such a beautiful horse," I whisper, feeling an unexpected swell of emotion.

Storm presses his nose into my shoulder, and a soft laugh escapes me. I'm not sure if he's looking for more food or just offering his version of comfort, but either way, his presence steadies me.

"We're going to get him back, Storm," I promise quietly, more to myself than to him.

A flicker of movement in the snow catches my eye, and I turn to see a frostflare perched gracefully atop a rock jutting out from the snowdrift, watching me with an almost unnerving stillness. Its silver eyes catch the light, gleaming like polished diamonds, and as it shifts, its fur seems to ripple like water caught in sunlight, almost as if it were made of frost and moonlight woven together.

It watches me, head tilted slightly. A slight smile pulls at the corners of my lips as I watch the frostflare in return. Then, with a graceful sweep of its tail, it turns and vanishes into the snow-dappled shadows. I watch the place where it disappeared for a moment and see figures approaching. I blink, my mind not quite catching onto what I'm seeing. Am I hallucinating?

I take several steps forward, waiting for the apparition to disappear. But it doesn't. The figures are still approaching. The sound of Raiden's wings reaches me before I see him, a deep, rhythmic beat that vibrates the air. And then, in an instant, his massive, hulking frame appears before me, blocking everything else from view.

I hear a soft rustle, and Valric steps up beside him, silent and steady. His hand rests on the hilt of his sword.

I glance over to where the others stand at the edge of the rocky outcrop, swords drawn and at the ready. But it's Anika and Nymeria who truly catch my attention. They're lounging off to the side, each with their head on their paws, tails flicking lazily. They don't look worried at all. I know that if anything truly threatened me, they would be the first to leap to my defense. Plus, the frostflare didn't seem worried either. It was more like he was trying to draw my attention to the group.

Pulling my shoulders back, I gather my courage, ducking under Raiden's wing, and stand in front of him to face the group of six fae that have stopped a few yards away.

My mouth falls open in awe, my arms falling slack at my sides as I stare. These fae are unlike any beings I've ever seen, stunning in a way that seems to defy both nature and magic. Their skin is a pale, icy blue, covered in intricate white markings that swirl and dance over their arms and faces. Every exposed inch of their skin is covered in these symbols, as if they were etched by winter itself.

Despite the biting cold, they seem utterly unaffected, dressed in flowing garments that ripple in the wind. Thin leather belts hug their waists, with arm guards to match. Leather necklaces hang around their necks in layers, each one with a different stone. Every one of them carries a bow slung across their backs, quivers filled with arrows.

Their hair, as white as freshly fallen snow, whips around their faces in the wind, framing high cheekbones and sharp, ethereal features. But it's their eyes that truly capture me. They're the most striking shade of blue I've ever seen, shimmering like gems, clear and intense, as if each holds a piece of the northern skies.

One of the women steps forward, her intense blue eyes locked on me as if I'm the only person here. "We have been watching you." Her voice is soft and haunting, carrying on the wind like a whisper.

"That's not creepy at all," I hear Kian mutter from behind.

"My wolves made me aware of your presence last night," I reply, keeping my voice steady. I sense Raiden and Valric tense beside me, their postures tightening.

The woman tilts her head, a look of curiosity crossing her delicate features. "Yet you didn't sound the alarm or send your warriors to find us?"

I shrug, giving her a small smile. "It was cold," I explain lightly. "They needed rest, and honestly, I doubt they would have found you."

"Hey," Raiden objects, his wings shifting slightly in irritation. I glance up at him, meeting his gaze with a raised brow.

"Well, the Skythari Nomads have managed to stay hidden this entire time, haven't they?" I pause, giving Raiden a pointed look. "I didn't mention it because you wouldn't have rested. You need to rest, Batman—you're running on fumes."

Raiden grunts in response. I glance back at the fae woman who watches our exchange, a faint, unreadable smile tugging at the corner of her lips as if she finds our banter amusing—or maybe just curious. It's hard to tell with her, with all of them, really.

The other fae remain silent, but their eyes glimmer with that same intensity, as if we're all pieces of some puzzle they're trying to decipher.

"You are different from other high fae. Who are you?"

"My name is Everly. I'm the last true blood druid heir. I've come seeking your help."

The fae woman raises an eyebrow in surprise. "The princess died along with her family many years ago."

A cold sweeps through me at her words, and images of my mother's last moments flash through my mind.

"Mother, please!" I cry, clawing at her arms. "Don't leave me."

She shakes me firmly to get my attention. "Everly, listen. You have to go."

I stop crying and feel the warmth of my mother's gaze as I look into her moss green eyes. So many emotions flicker through them as she stares at me.

"I'm so sorry, Everly."

The sounds of howls fill the night air, and the horses draw nearer. Mother spins around, drawing her sword. She slowly looks around, her eyes carefully scanning the area. Spinning back to me swiftly, she places a tender kiss on my forehead before whispering words in an old, forgotten language. Pulling back, her eyes fill with tears, and I feel the pressure of her hands on my chest as she pushes me away. I stumble backward, my hand instinctively reaching for her as I fall. I watch in horror as an arrow pierces her chest and blood instantly spreads across the front of her dress.

Then I'm falling.

The world around me slips away, and I fall through the ground. I fall for only a few seconds before I am suddenly lying in a grassy meadow, the sun's heat warming my skin.

I shake my head, trying to dispel the images. "My mother sent me through the Faerie gate into the human world, sealing it closed behind me." I drop my gaze. "I came back through the gate two months ago, and have slowly been gaining my memories back."

The woman is silent for a long moment. "I'm not sure I believe you."

"I'm telling the truth. I was sent to find you; I need your help."

"Who sent you?"

I hesitate.

The fae woman crosses her arms and waits.

"Ancient spirits and the guardians of the land guide her," Nero's voice sounds from behind me.

A gasp rings out among the group and the woman steps closer, her arms dropping. "You spoke to the Guardians?"

Their reactions prevent me from turning and questioning Nero.

"Yes." I can sense the others coming to stand closer, and the group in front of me shifts uneasily.

"We have only come looking for aid. The Shadoweaver has taken the king of the unseelie fae hostage. We need your help to rescue him. Can you take me to your chief?"

The group exchanges uncertain glances, their eyes flicking toward one another. A quiet tension hums in the air. Finally, the one in charge turns her attention back to me, her gaze unreadable.

"Please," I say, my voice catching slightly before I steel it. "Just let him hear me out. I wouldn't be here if it weren't important."

The woman's face softens for only a second but I see it. "I will take you to our chief and he will discuss this with you. From what we've witnessed, you seem like good people." Her eyes harden slightly. "Don't make me regret this."

I hold my hands up. "You won't."

The fae woman turns, her movements smooth and graceful. "My name is Iridessa." Her voice is like the crackle of ice in the wind. She stops and turns slightly, gesturing to the fae standing beside her, nearly a mirror image save for her hair, which is intricately braided into dozens of tiny plaits. "And this is my sister, Onora. If you have any questions, you will direct them to us."

"Okay." I nod, my gaze drifting over the group. The other fae stand tall and still, their posture reminding me of my own companions, poised and alert, yet as rooted as trees in a winter forest.

"Are you the chief's daughters?" I inquire, curiosity getting the better of me.

Iridessa and Onora both blink in surprise, their perfect composure slipping for just a moment. At once, the other fae move, stepping protectively in front of the sisters, hands poised on their bows, and spears raised slightly. I hold up my hands in apology.

"Oh, sorry! I was just asking. It seems like you're in charge."

Raiden's arm sweeps out in front of me in a protective arc, his powerful form pulling me back. He casts me a look, one that's part warning, part exasperation.

"The queen would not harm you," he urges, looking back at the group of Skythari Nomads. "She is not like that. She is kind, and she values the strength of allies."

"I wouldn't let any harm come to you," I agree, my eyes meeting Iridessa's and Onora's in turn. Raiden and Valric inch closer to me, the heat of their bodies pressing in around me.

Onora's icy-blue eyes soften, and she gives a slight nod. "We know this. We heard what you said before the ogres attacked." Her gaze flickers toward the fae guards in front of her, and she offers a small, wry smile. "They are just like your companions. Overprotective."

A smile tugs at my lips, and she mirrors my expression. There's a warmth in her smile that feels like the first touch of sunlight after a cold winter, subtle yet sincere. In this moment, the air between us shifts, a quiet understanding passing that feels like the beginnings of friendship.

Chapter Sixty-One

Everly

We follow the nomads on foot, leading our horses by the reins. Riding feels rude and out of place when they are walking. The silence between us is thick, filled with a cautious tension that hangs in the cold air. Everyone remains on high alert, their gazes flicking back and forth, every muscle taut and ready.

Only a few of us seem at ease—Iridessa, Onora, the wolves, and, surprisingly, me. Iridessa and Onora walk with quiet confidence. They all do, their movements light and effortless through the snow. Even their feet do not sink into the snow like ours. Anika and Nymeria pad along at my side, tails low but relaxed, their heads turning occasionally to meet my gaze, as if reassuring me they're watching over us all.

I cast a sideways glance at Iridessa, and she catches my eye, giving a small, reassuring smile.

"Your wolves are beautiful," she observes softly.

"They are. I rescued them when they were pups, and they never left my side. It pains me to think they were alone for so long when I was sent to the human realm."

Both wolves press in on each side, and warmth floods our unique bond.

"I could only imagine what it was like being sent away. One day, I would love to hear your story, but for now, we are here."

I frown, confused. There is nothing in front of us but the snowy valley. I can't even see any trees.

Iridessa waves her arm in the air in a fluid motion, and suddenly, the white markings that lace her skin blaze to life with a powerful, ethereal glow. The light sweeps outward, washing over the landscape with a pale brilliance that seems to seep into every corner of the world around us. I stop in my tracks so abruptly that Zaria bumps into me. She stumbles back, catching herself, and we both gasp as the snowy, barren landscape that stretched endlessly before us just moments ago begins to shift and ripple.

In an instant, the wilderness transforms, as though a veil has been lifted. Huts materialize, nestled beneath icy boughs, their chimneys whispering smoke into the cold, crisp air. A market comes into view with vibrant stalls overflowing with strange goods, their canopies fluttering softly in the winter winds. The fabrics, woven in colors that seem almost too vivid for this snowy mountain range, sway like soft mirages, inviting us into this hidden realm.

"Oh, wow," I murmur, barely able to believe my eyes.

"Yeah . . . " Zaria breathes, her voice barely above a whisper. I glance at her and catch the same mixture of awe and disbelief mirrored in her eyes.

Before we can take it all in, Iridessa's voice slices through the wonder with a tone as cold and unyielding as the snow beneath our feet. "You may keep your weapons," she instructs, her gaze sweeping over us with a quiet but unmistakable intensity. "But if you raise them against us, you will be killed on the spot."

I see Raiden stiffen out of the corner of my eye, but I step forward and smile, giving a slight bow of my head. "You won't have any trouble from us."

Iridessa dips her head and her shoulders relax. "Come. My father isn't a patient man."

The fae villagers stop what they're doing, their movements freezing mid-action as they turn to stare at us. Their expressions range from open-mouthed shock to narrow-eyed distrust, the tension thickening as more and more eyes fall upon us.

Each fae here shares the same striking coloring: icy-blue skin that seems to shimmer faintly in the cold light, hair so white it almost blends with the snow, and piercing blue eyes that glimmer like shards of glass. They are beautiful in an otherworldly way, like living statues carved from ice, each one uniquely crafted but unmistakably bound by a common essence.

Beside me, Zaria shifts closer, her arm hooking in mine.

Finally, we come to a stop in front of a large structure that stands apart from the others, rising imposingly against the snowy backdrop. It's a curious blend of styles: part ancient hut, part conical tent, with a peaked roof that stretches upward in an elegant taper.

Two fae women step out, coming to an abrupt halt, their vivid blue eyes widening on our group. Iridessa and Onora ignore them and open the heavy wooden doors, motioning for us to follow.

The warmth inside is heavenly, and I sigh audibly, feeling my muscles relax. I didn't realize I've been holding myself so rigid. Spinning slowly, I let my eyes trail upward, tipping my head back to take in the vast rafters overhead. Wooden beams crisscross high above, their edges softened by time and wear. The faint scent of pine and something older—earthy and ancient—fills the air. My steps falter as an unexpected wave of familiarity washes over me. This place . . . it feels like something I've known before, though I can't place why.

Valric steps up beside me, his presence solid and steady. He tilts his head slightly, watching me as though he knows exactly what I'm feeling. "You recognize it, don't you?" he inquires softly, his voice careful, almost reverent.

I tear my gaze from the ceiling and turn to face him, furrowing my brow. "What?"

Before he can answer, a sudden wave of magic sweeps through the room. It's strong and commanding, yet wild, like a storm breaking free. My own magic stirs instinctively in response, curling and coiling beneath my skin as if answering a call.

"Princess," a deep voice booms, echoing off the stone walls, "or should I say, Queen."

I whip around, the words striking like a thunderclap. Two males have entered the room, their imposing figures framed by the doorway. My first thought is that they're warriors—everything about their stance radiates power and discipline.

They're both tall and broad-shouldered, sturdier than the high fae I'm used to seeing, though not quite as massive as Raiden. There's something primal about them, something ancient and unyielding. They remind me of the Vikings I've read about in stories, their presence larger than life.

The first male wears a heavy pelt draped over his shoulders, the dark fur contrasting sharply with the worn leather straps and belts crisscrossing his chest. His white hair is braided tightly, falling over one shoulder like a cord of silver, and the scar running down his jaw gives him a harder edge. The second male mirrors him in many ways, though his hair is tied back loosely, and he carries several daggers at his waist.

Their eyes are striking—a pale blue so piercing they seem to look straight through me. But there's something else there, too, something familiar.

I can't stop staring. These men don't just look like warriors—they look like the kind of beings who belong to stories, myths, legends. Their presence makes the room feel smaller.

The one with the scar steps forward with a grin stretching across his face.

"Valric, you're looking good for your age, old man," he greets him like an old friend, his voice warm and teasing, before slapping Valric on the shoulder with enough force to make the older fae shift slightly.

I stand there, mouth agape, trying to process what I'm seeing.

What is happening right now?

Days we have been planning, endless hours of discussing strategies and contingencies, Valric never once mentioned knowing the Skythari Nomads—or, apparently, their leader. This wasn't just an oversight; it was an outright omission.

My gaze flicks to Raiden, and the storm brewing in his eyes tells me he's thinking the same thing. His lips press into a tight line, and the tension rolling off him is palpable.

"Sorry," I interject, my voice harsher than I intend as I interrupt their reunion. "How do you two know each other?"

Valric and the man both turn to face me, their expressions so similar in their mix of surprise and calm composure that I almost roll my eyes.

"Vera–" the nomad begins, but I cut him off, holding up a hand.

"It's Everly," I correct him. Vera was only used by those closest to my family. Was this man in my parents' inner circle?

The scarred man's grin softens into something more respectful as he dips his head. "My apologies, Your Majesty," he replies smoothly.

Before I can respond, Raiden steps up beside me, his arms crossing over his broad chest. The imposing stance only adds to the simmering irritation radiating from him. "It would have been nice to know you knew the Skythari Nomads, Valric," he chides, his voice a low rumble.

Valric's eyes shift briefly to Raiden, his expression unreadable. "Forgive me," he replies, though his tone suggests he doesn't feel particularly apologetic. "But this was Everly's journey. She was leading the way with the frostflare. It was not my place to intervene."

Raiden lets out a low grunt, clearly unimpressed with the answer, while I shake my head. Being left out of the loop doesn't sit well with me, and I doubt the others will appreciate it either.

The scarred man steps forward again, his posture commanding yet open, and when he speaks, his voice carries the weight of authority. "My name is Barak, Chief of this tribe in the Ethereal Peaks."

Then, with a slight turn, he gestures toward the second man who entered with him. "Do you remember my son, Kaden?" Barak's voice is softer now, though it still carries the weight of the room. "You and Fenris used to play with him whenever you visited. My daughters weren't born until after . . . well, after the tragedy that led to your parents' deaths."

The air seems to still as his words settle over us. My stomach tightens, and I struggle to keep my face neutral. The memories he speaks of linger at the edge of my mind, hazy and fractured, like the remnants of a dream. Kaden.

The name stirs something faint, but the images are elusive.

Before I can chase the threads of recollection further, my focus shifts to the fae standing beside Barak. He's tall and lean, with the unmistakable bearing of a seasoned warrior. His sleeveless tunic reveals arms corded with muscle, and a well-worn leather belt cinches his waist, supporting a deadly-looking axe that rests at his hip. His silver hair is tied back loosely, a few strands falling free around his angular features, and there's an ease to his stance that speaks of confidence and readiness.

When his gaze meets mine, a faint smirk tugs at the edges of his mouth. His eyes, the same piercing blue as the other Skythari Nomads, seem to take me in all at once, as if he's weighing and assessing me. But there's no challenge in them, only respect.

With a smooth motion, he bows slightly, pressing his fist to his chest. "Vera," he addresses me, his voice low and warm, the smirk softening into something closer to familiarity. "It's been a while."

I swallow hard, resisting the surge of frustration that rises in me. The spell locking my memories feels crueler in moments like this, when the pieces are so close yet just out of reach. I wish, more than anything, for it to break completely and release the flood of names, faces, and moments I've been denied.

But wishing doesn't make it so, and I refuse to let my disappointment show. Instead, I square my shoulders, forcing those feelings down. "I wish I could say I remembered," I admit.

Kaden's smirk fades, replaced by a flicker of understanding. "You will," he says simply, as if it's a certainty.

Barak's gaze flickers between us, his expression unreadable. "You've come this far, Everly. The rest will come when you're ready."

A half-huff, half-growl falls from my mouth. "We are in need of your assistance."

Barak winks. "Straight to business then."

"The Shadoweaver has the king, and I was told you have something that could help rescue him."

Barak rubs his jaw and motions us with his head to the seats around the fire. We follow, and I'm surprised by the sheer size of this place; from the outside it didn't look that big.

"We will get some food and drinks sorted." Onora links her arm with Iridessa, who looks ready to argue.

"Thank you, daughters." Barak offers a grateful smile.

Kaden stands near the fire, his tall frame silhouetted by the dancing flames. He's positioned just to the side of his father's chair, his stance similar to the way Tristan and Kian stand near mine.

Raiden, Zaria, and Valric take their seats without hesitation, their postures varying from relaxed to wary. I slowly take a seat, nerves buzzing like a swarm of bees running riot through my body.

Barak's intense gaze flicks to me, assessing. "So, Your Majesty. What is it you think we have that can aid your rescue mission?"

I hesitate, my eyes flicking to Valric, who nods. "I was told," I begin carefully, "that you possess beasts capable of avoiding detection by the Shadoweaver's magic—creatures strong enough to break the chains holding the king captive."

The words leave my mouth with more confidence than I feel, but inside, I'm guessing. The riddle the Witte Wieven gave me is maddeningly unclear, and this theory has been the only conclusion I've been able to draw.

Barak's expression changes subtly, his eyes widening for a brief moment before a small smile curves his lips. He leans back in his chair, the firelight casting shadows across his weathered features.

"I have no such thing in my possession, young one," he says calmly, and disappointment coils tight inside me.

Before I can respond, he leans forward, his hands resting on his knees, his voice lowering. "These creatures you speak of cannot be tamed. They are not ours to command. No one owns them."

The flicker of disappointment sharpens into curiosity, my hands clenching in my lap. "So, you know what I speak of?" I ask, trying to keep my voice steady.

"Aye," he replies, his tone weighty. "But if you want their help, you must prove yourself worthy."

"And how do I do that?"

Barak and Kaden exchange a look, something unspoken passing between them. The moment feels heavy with significance, but before Barak answers, Onora and Iridessa return, each balancing trays laden with food and drink.

"Thank you," I murmur as Iridessa passes me a steaming mug.

She dips her head slightly, stepping back to take her place at her father's side.

Barak turns back to me. "You'll need to complete the Gauntlet," he says simply.

I stiffen, the unfamiliar term sparking both intrigue and apprehension. "The Gauntlet?" I echo, my voice wary.

"If they find you worthy," Barak continues, "they will approach you. They choose their allies, not the other way around."

Raiden bristles at my side, the tension radiating from him almost tangible. "What is the Gauntlet?" he demands, his deep voice cutting through the moment.

Barak shifts his attention to Raiden, his expression blank. "A trial," he explains. "A test of strength, will, and spirit. Only those who pass are deemed worthy."

"And those who fail?" Raiden presses, his jaw tightening.

Barak's smile returns, though it holds no humor. "They don't return, and if they do, they bear the brunt of the trials," he answers bluntly, his words settling over the room like a heavy blanket.

The air is thick with unspoken questions, but I refuse to let the gravity of his statement dissuade me. "Then I'll do it," I say firmly, my voice cutting through the silence.

Raiden tenses beside me, clearly wanting to argue, but he doesn't speak. Barak's eyes meet mine, and something in his expression shifts—approval, perhaps, or respect.

"So be it," Barak accepts, his tone final. "The Gauntlet awaits."

Chapter Sixty-Two

Maxon

"Your mate has disappeared from our detection," Yumekui's voice cuts through the air as she storms into the cavern, her usual infuriatingly calm demeanor nowhere to be found. She kicks a rock across the floor, the sharp sound echoing against the walls.

I tip my head back against the wall, a hollow laugh escaping my throat as I close my eyes, the edges of my smile teasing. Of course, Everly has figured out a way to hide herself. She is not as naïve as everyone thinks.

The quiet lasts barely a moment before I feel her presence—close, too close. I open my eyes as Yumekui straddles me, her kanzashi pressed hard against my throat, the tip biting into my skin just enough to draw a trickle of blood. Her ruby eyes burn with unrestrained fury, her lips curling into a feral snarl.

I glare up at her, refusing to flinch. The fire under my skin flares in response, the dragon's magic surging with raw, unrelenting power. It roars to be unleashed, clawing at my restraints, and I wince at the brutality of it. My body trembles as it sweeps through me, but Yumekui must mistake my shaking for fear. Her wicked grin widens, her expression dripping with sadistic delight.

"How is she doing it?" she hisses, leaning closer, the words slicing through the air like a whip.

"How would I know?" I snap back, my voice strained but defiant.

Her grin vanishes in an instant, replaced by a cold, calculating look. And then, without warning—without her usual taunts or drawn-out threats—she leans forward, pressing her lithe frame against mine. I barely have time to register the movement before her fangs sink into my neck.

The pain is immediate and excruciating, a white-hot burst that radiates from the point of contact. I clench my teeth so hard I hear a faint crack under the strain, my fists curling tightly at my sides. My fire surges wildly in response.

Yumekui's grip tightens on my head, her fingers tangling in my hair as she draws deep, greedy mouthfuls of my blood. I feel the pull of it, the draining sensation that leaves me dizzy and disoriented, but I refuse to give her the satisfaction of a sound.

She finally pulls back, her lips stained crimson, her eyes half-lidded with something too close to pleasure for my liking. "You're hiding something," she purrs, her tone smooth and dangerous. "But don't worry. I'll find out."

My voice cuts through the charged silence, low and seething. "Fuck you."

Yumekui tilts her head, a slow, deliberate movement as her lips curl into a predatory smile. She rocks her hips against my thighs, a taunting motion that sends a spark of rage surging through me. "I could . . . " she purrs, her tone laced with mockery, her eyes glittering with wicked amusement.

My magic snarls beneath my skin, coiling like a spring ready to snap. "I'll kill you," I hiss, the words trembling with barely restrained fury.

She laughs, light and musical, as if I've told a delightful joke. In a blur of motion, she leaps off my lap, her bare feet whispering against the cold stone floor. Blood still stains her lips, and she takes her time licking it away, her tongue slow and deliberate, as though savoring every drop.

"You'll never leave here." Her voice, smooth as silk, carries the weight of a threat. "Not until you're mine."

"Again, fuck you," I spit, venom dripping from every word.

Her smile widens, growing sharper, more dangerous, as she tilts her head once more. "Soon, I'll have enough blood to control you. Blood magic can be tricky, but with a few more feedings," her eyes narrow, her words wrapping around me like a noose, "and with runes etched in our combined blood, you'll worship the ground I walk on."

The world shifts beneath me as her words sink in. My breath hitches, and dread courses through my body like ice, freezing me in place. That's what she's been doing?

She sees the realization flash across my face, and her satisfaction is palpable. The corners of her smile twitch higher as she takes in my speechlessness. "Oh, don't look so shocked," she chides, her voice dripping with false sweetness. "You're stronger than most, but even you can't fight this forever."

Satisfied with her handiwork, she turns and glides toward the door, the hem of her white silk kimono trailing behind her.

Chapter Sixty-Three

Everly

I grip my sword tightly and draw in a deep, steadying breath. Letting it out slowly, I focus on calming the wild rhythm of my heart. All I have to do is make it to the other side. Easy-peasy, right?

With a quick glance at Valric, I meet his unwavering gaze. His eyes are steady and filled with quiet assurance. A subtle nod follows, his expression exuding a confidence I'm not sure I fully share. His lips move soundlessly, forming words meant only for me; *You got this.*

The silent encouragement settles in my chest, a warm, steadying force against the turbulent storm swirling inside me. His belief in me is comforting, even if I'm not sure I share his confidence. I shift my focus to the snow-covered slope ahead. It's steep, dotted with sparse trees and jagged rocks that jut out like teeth.

Beyond it lies a stone wall and an unforgiving expanse of ice. My task is clear: navigate the obstacles and reach the other side of the valley before sunset. The problem is, the path ahead doesn't look forgiving.

Before I can dwell on it too much, Kaden steps up behind me, holding out a strip of red cloth. His expression is a mix of sympathy and mischief, his lopsided shrug adding a touch of apology.

"Sorry," he says. "But you've got to be blindfolded."

"What?" The word bursts out of me in disbelief, my grip on the sword tightening.

"It's the rules," he explains simply, as though this ridiculous twist is perfectly reasonable.

Before I can argue further, he steps closer, placing the red cloth over my eyes and ties it securely at the back of my head. Darkness envelops me, and I resist the urge to rip it off. His hands land on my shoulders, squeezing gently.

"Just open up your other senses, and you'll be fine," Kaden says, his voice low and reassuring. "The Vera I knew before loved this game."

I snort softly, shaking my head. "The girl you knew had a lot more faith in herself."

"I believe in you," Kaden replies, and there's no teasing in his tone now—just certainty.

I hear his steps retreat, leaving me standing at the top of the slope, blindfolded and clutching my sword. I take another deep breath, trying to focus on the sounds around me—the crunch of snow underfoot, the faint whistle of the wind as it brushes against the trees.

This is going to be anything but easy.

The darkness brings my fears bubbling to the surface. Panic, familiar and unwelcome, creeps in like a long-lost friend. The Witte Wieven cautioned me that I would have to confront my fears.

"When the horn sounds, you may begin," Chief Barak's deep, authoritative voice rumbles from somewhere behind me. "The rules are simple: keep the blindfold on and make it to the other side."

My stomach knots, a cold wave of unease washing over me. The horn blasts a moment later, its echo bouncing off the mountains like a warning. My heart leaps into my throat as I force myself to step forward.

I know I'll need my magic if I have any hope of succeeding. Almost as if in response to my thought, it unfurls within me, a wave of energy wrapping around me like a protective shield. The sound of my blood pounding in my ears nearly drowns out everything else.

My breaths come heavy and fast, panic clawing at my chest.

"Calm down, Everly," I mutter, trying to ground myself. "It's just a test."

A test that can severely hurt you if you make one wrong move, I chide myself.

I take another step forward, snagging a boot on a rock hidden beneath the snow. My stomach lurches as I stumble, arms flailing for balance. I catch myself just in time, planting my sword in the snow for support, and cringe, knowing George won't be happy with me for using the weapon in that way.

Drawing on the elements, I focus on letting them guide me. The wind brushes my face, tugging at my clothes with subtle persistence. Trusting the sensation, I turn and follow the direction it seems to urge me toward. From my left, a branch creaks, the sound sharp and clear against the soft hush of the snow. I tilt my head, listening.

The whistle of an arrow pierces the air, slicing through the silence. Instinct takes over, and I lift my sword just in time, deflecting it with a metallic clang. The force reverberates up my arm, but I don't falter. I keep as still as possible, listening for another.

Behind me, I hear Raiden's voice rise in fury. "You said nothing about her being under attack!" he roars, his anger palpable even from a distance.

Valric's response is carried away by the wind, lost as I refocus on the challenge before me. My pulse is still racing, but I force myself to slow my breathing, steadying the rhythm. Each inhale sharpens my focus; each exhale releases the tension in my limbs.

Two more whistles sound in the air, and I tilt my head, concentrating on the direction. Letting my muscles relax, I lift my sword, arcing it through the air to hit both arrows in succession. I stand there for a few seconds, waiting. When no other arrows sound, I start moving again.

The snow crunches underfoot as I cautiously make my way down the slope into the valley below. The soft brush of fur against my legs, startles me. My magic reaches out instinctively, connecting with the presence—it's the frostflare, its energy bright and wild.

The creature nudges my leg, almost impatiently, urging me to move left. Trusting its guidance, I adjust my path. I try to send magic out to map the area for me, like it did when I found Zaria. But with panic so close to the surface, I can only manage a few yards ahead.

A low rumble reaches my ears, faint at first but growing louder with each passing second. My stomach drops to my toes, and the ground beneath my feet shudders, sending a jolt of fear through me.

I spin around, trying to pinpoint the source of the noise, but all I achieve is disorientation. Which way am I heading?

Panic pulls taut, but it enhances my senses too. I feel it—a faint pull, like a thread tugging at the edge of my awareness. My magic comes alive, stretching outward, guiding me to the source of the disturbance.

Avalanche.

The realization slams into me like a blow to the chest. My head snaps to the side as golden waves of magic ripple out from me, blanketing the landscape. The world shifts, and I can see the landscape around me through the magic as it paints the terrain in glowing golden detail. There—a rocky outcrop to my left. It might not be much, but it's my best chance.

The snow is coming fast. I don't waste another second.

Boots pound the snow packed ground, as magic surges beneath me, hardening the earth and giving me traction. The rumble becomes a roar, thunderous and all-consuming. I grit my teeth, lungs burning as I push myself harder, the rocky outcrop growing closer with each step.

I reach it just as the avalanche crashes into the valley. With a desperate dive, I slide beneath the outcrop, curling into myself as snow and debris surge overhead. The roar is deafening, the force of it pressing down like a physical weight. For one breathless moment, I am completely surrounded—by sound, by movement, by the raw power of nature.

Then, silence.

I lie there, trembling, the adrenaline coursing through me like fire. The moment is fleeting, but it feels like an eternity, etched into my memory as vividly as the golden magic still shimmering faintly around me. Slowly, cautiously, I exhale and let my head fall back against the rock with a thud.

"That was too close."

Gradually, I shift from my cramped hiding place, muscles stiff and trembling with adrenaline. The air is eerily still, thick with a muffled quiet that presses against my ears. Somewhere above, snow still settles, but all I hear is the echo—dull, haunting—bouncing through the hollow space around me. It fills me with instant dread.

With a shaking hand, I reach forward and my fingers swipe through the empty air. Encouraged, I inch forward on my knees, snow grinding beneath them, sharp and wet as it seeps into my breeches. I flinch at the chill, but push on.

Then . . . my palm hits a wall of snow.

My heart gives a single, hard thud. I press against it, move sideways, feeling along its surface. All around me, the world has become a coffin of ice and snow.

I'm trapped.

You're okay. It's okay.

The words sound hollow, but I repeat them anyway, trying to keep the panic at bay. My breathing quickens, rising with panic despite efforts to stay calm. The confined space feels smaller by the second.

I just need to dig. That's all. I just have to dig.

I let go of my sword—the hilt has been welded to my palm with tension, and my fingers ache from the release. I flex them, trying to restore feeling. They're stiff, almost numb.

Sliding my hands along the cold walls, I inhale slowly through my nose, then exhale through pursed lips, trying to stay in control. Magic stirs faintly in my chest, a flicker of warmth. I reach for Maxon's fire, willing it to come to my hands, to spark, to burn a way out—but there's nothing. Not even a wisp of heat.

Fine. No fire. Just me.

I press my hands against the softest patch I can find and begin to dig.

It takes me longer than I want to claw my way out of the snow. My arms ache with exertion as I drag myself from the cold, wet tunnel and into the fresh, open air. The faint sound of cheers rises up behind me, and a smile creeps across my face. I take a deep breath, feeling the relief wash over me. Yes, I am still alive.

Climbing to my feet, blindfold still in place, I look around, my magic sweeping over the landscape once again. Less than a hundred yards ahead is the wall I have to get over. I head in that direction, easily navigating the terrain now. I pick up the pace, not too sure how much time passed while I was digging my way out of my icy tomb.

Unease slithers through me and my fingers flex around the hilt of my sword. Sensing something is off, but I can't pinpoint exactly what it is. It's more like a gut feeling, my intuition screaming at me to slow down and listen. A prickling sensation moves between my shoulder blades, but I push on, not wanting to waste any more time.

I slow as I near the towering wall. An eerie hollowness twists in my stomach, and the tingling sensation crawling over my skin grows clearer, setting every nerve on edge. The hair on the back of my neck rises, and I feel the unmistakable pulse of my magic, a warning I should have heeded sooner.

Before I can react, a gust of wind slams into me with enough force to knock me off my feet. I cry out as I'm sent backward; the world tilting. I hit the snow, the impact jarring, the sword slipping from my grasp. Panic flares, and I scramble upright, my hands blindly searching the freezing ground until my fingers graze the familiar hilt. Relief floods me as I drag the weapon back to my side, clutching it tightly.

With the blindfold still in place and the sword gripped in my hand, I push myself up to stand on shaky legs, gasping in shallow breaths. That's when I feel it—my magic vibrating through me with a sense of urgency, a ripple of insight. I glance up and freeze. I didn't notice before, but now I see it clearly; a deadly pit of spikes lying hidden at the base of the wall.

Are they trying to kill me?

I should've listened more closely to what my magic was trying to warn me about. Swallowing hard, I force myself to focus.

Standing at the edge of the pit, I scan the expanse before me for any sign of a path across. It yawns wide and deep, easily fifty feet from me to the wall on the other side. Jagged rocks litter the bottom like the teeth of some ancient beast. There's no going around it—the wall goes on for miles, the pit stretching endlessly in both directions, disappearing into the hazy distance. How I didn't notice it before is beyond me.

My attention is drawn below and I look down to see golden tendrils of magic weaving their way around several of the larger stones. They shimmer faintly, forming delicate arcs of light that loop through the air and anchor themselves into the stone. A bridge?

The hum of warmth in my chest grows stronger as I reach for the earth beneath me. My magic responds eagerly, and tendrils of vines snake down my arms, slithering across the ground like living extensions of myself. Rocks begin to rise in the air from the bottom of the pit, forming a path across. The vines weave around the rocks, anchoring each stone in place.

I shuffle forward slowly, fear lodging in my throat as I place my foot on the first rock, testing its stability. It holds. Arms out wide for balance, I carefully make my way across, one step at a time. Adrenaline courses through me, my senses heightened. One mistake and those spikes will be greeting me.

I reach the final stone and leap, landing at the base of the wall with a soft thud. Relief floods me, but it's short-lived. Where I stand is barely a foot wide, and as I glance up at the towering cliff face, I realize there's no way I can climb it while holding my sword, and leaving it behind isn't an option.

With a resigned sigh, I slide the blade into the belt around my waist, silently praying it won't cut me as I climb. The cold metal presses against my hip as I glide my hands over the wall, searching for a handhold. I imagine a pattern of protruding rocks forming an even path to the top. My magic flares in response, the stone rumbling beneath my palms as rocks jut out from the surface in a staggered formation.

A grin tugs at my lips despite the stress as I reach for the nearest handhold and begin to haul myself upward. Every movement is deliberate, my muscles straining with the effort, fingertips digging into the rough surface of the stone.

Sweat beads along my spine, a sharp contrast to the biting chill that cuts through the air. I focus on my breathing—slow and steady—as I climb, the wind growing fiercer with every foot I gain.

Somewhere along the way, my braid has unraveled, and now my hair whips wildly around my face, caught in the relentless gusts.

Reaching the top, I haul myself over, every muscle trembling from exertion and adrenaline. My breath comes in ragged gasps as I cling to the edge, glancing out over the unforgiving landscape ahead. Below me, a sheer drop stretches into a rocky abyss. Two ropes are anchored to the top of the wall, swaying faintly in the wind. Beyond them lies the frozen expanse of the ice lake, shimmering ominously under the faint light, and beyond that, the dark silhouette of the valley's edge marked by the distant tree line. Safety.

Kaden downplayed the challenge, calling it a *simple obstacle course.* As I stare at the daunting obstacles ahead, his words feel like a cruel joke.

"Okay," I mutter under my breath, rolling my shoulders to loosen the knots of tension. "You've got this."

I inch along the top of the wall, each step intentional as loose stones shift beneath my boots. My vision wavers, exhaustion dulling my focus, and the golden glow of the landscape map in my mind begins to flicker, as if vibrating in warning. A faint sound catches on the wind—a low, ominous whistle that raises the hairs on the back of my neck. I turn sharply, and my foot slips on the unstable rock.

I scream, my arms pinwheeling as I desperately try to catch my balance. For a heart-stopping moment, I'm sure I'll fall. My lungs heave as I steady myself, but the relief is short-lived. A dozen flaming arrows arc through the sky, their fiery tips painting trails across the dim magic horizon. They're heading straight for me.

Instinct takes over before I have time to think. My arm snaps up, crossing in front of me, a surge of power coursing through me. Vines burst from my skin, twisting and interweaving until they form a living shield. The first arrow strikes with a hard thud, sending a jolt through my body. Another follows, then another, each impact vibrating through the vines. I stumble under the strain, a gasp escaping my lips as I brace myself against the force, my boots shifting on the loose stones.

The onslaught ends as abruptly as it began. When no more arrows fall, I lower the shield, the vines retreating back into me, and the arrows fall to the ground below. I don't waste time catching my breath. Scrambling for the rope, I grab hold and begin my descent.

The rough fibers bite into my palms as I slide down, my boots skidding against the icy stone wall. My hands burn, but I don't stop. The moment my feet hit the snow-covered ground, I'm off.

I sprint toward the edge of the lake, the cold air slicing through my lungs. My sword bangs awkwardly against my thigh with every step, but I push forward, the adrenaline driving me faster. The ice lake looms ahead, a frozen expanse that would be treacherous even without the arrows. After days of riding and dealing with the elements, my body is already fatigued, but the fire burning in my soul for Maxon drives me harder than before. He needs me, and I will do anything to have him back in my arms.

Chapter Sixty-Four

Everly

I skid to a halt at the edge of the lake, my boots kicking up a spray of loose snow. The cold wind rushes over the frozen expanse, cutting through my clothes and whipping my hair away from my face. Surprisingly, the blindfold remains tightly fastened, not slipping an inch despite the chaos so far. I resist the overwhelming urge to rip it off. Doing so would mean forfeiting the trial—and losing any chance of gaining the nomads' help.

Taking a steadying breath, I draw my sword from my belt. The last thing I want to do is slip on the ice and cut myself. With cautious steps, I ease onto its slick surface which is treacherously smooth beneath my boots. My foot slides, and I immediately shift my weight, arms spread wide to maintain balance. Each step is a calculated gamble, and it takes several agonizing moments to adjust to the slippery terrain.

I grit my teeth, wishing I could take this blindfold off. It's fairly easy to navigate the golden magical landscape, but seeing it with color and detail would be significantly better. The temptation to pull it off gnaws at me, but I shove it down. Barak claimed this trial would test my resolve, my focus.

Halfway across the lake, the air seems to shift. A deep vibration ripples underfoot, subtle at first, then stronger. I freeze, holding my breath as the ice quakes faintly beneath me, the sound of cracking spreading like a spiderweb in my ears.

I crouch slightly, pressing one hand to the ice and sending a pulse of magic into it. The icy surface hums in response, and I feel it—the water beneath, churning and moving with unnatural speed. Something is down there, circling me.

The realization sends my pulse skyrocketing. I focus harder, pushing more magic into the ice, trying to sense exactly what lies beneath. I follow the currents, gold ribbons of magic brushing against something large and alive.

My stomach knots as I abruptly pull back and stand, wiping my palm on my breeches. Whatever is under the ice, it's circling closer.

I attempt to move quicker, but I just end up slipping on the slick ice. Adrenaline pumps through my body, setting my pulse racing as I fight to stay calm. Then, it hits me; an unsettling stillness, as if the world is holding its breath.

A deafening crack splits the air, the sound echoing through the frozen landscape as something heavy crashes into the ice from underneath. The force of the impact sends a tremor through the surface of the frozen lake, making me stumble sideways.

The creature hits the ice again. This time, shards of ice fly through the air, several hitting me. I reach up, my fingers touching something hot and sticky on my cheek. Blood.

Whatever hit the ice explodes from the water, its massive form landing on the surface of the lake, making me slip and wobble. Panic has all thoughts fleeing my mind as I stand in front of this giant . . . My head tilts, and I try to concentrate on what is in front of me.

Confusion has me wanting to tear off the blindfold. But instead, I slowly crouch down, the cold seeping through my clothes as I set my sword down carefully on the ice. I press my hands against my knees, drawing in a long, trembling breath, and then rise to my full height, lifting my hand out in front of me.

I'm panting with a mix of adrenaline and wonder. I lower my head, blocking out the world, and let the minutes stretch as I stand perfectly still.

And then I feel it—a warm, wet nudge against my outstretched palm. My breath catches.

The creature presses closer, its muzzle firm but cautious as it sniffs me. I stay frozen, barely daring to breathe. Then, to my astonishment, it leans in further, its head slipping over my shoulder to tuck me securely under its neck.

A voice fills my mind, soft yet resounding, like a wave crashing against the shore.

'I missed you, young one.'

I startle, my knees nearly buckling from the shock.

'You were gone so long I assumed you were dead, but it is you.'

Holy shit.

Thoughts whirl as realization sinks in. The kelpie—this majestic, otherworldly creature—is speaking directly into my mind.

Only Nymeria and Anika have ever done this, thanks to the bond we share. But this? This is something entirely different.

"How?" I whisper aloud, my voice shaky.

The kelpie doesn't answer, just nuzzles me again with a tenderness that feels impossibly familiar. My arms move on instinct, wrapping around its thick, muscular neck. Its hide is damp and cold to the touch, but there's an undercurrent of warmth, a thrumming energy that pulses like a heartbeat. I squeeze tighter, wishing I could see her properly—not just the faint, golden outline my magic reveals through the blindfold.

The kelpie lifts her head, her powerful neck shifting beneath my hands. With a gentle nudge, she presses her nose under me, lifting me effortlessly until I'm seated on her back.

My hands clutch at her mane as she rears slightly, then takes off across the ice with a smooth, gliding gallop. A startled laugh bubbles up from my chest, escaping into the cold air. It's pure, unrestrained joy, a moment so surreal and exhilarating that all my fear melts away.

But the joy is short-lived.

Without warning, a memory slams into me like a tidal wave—raw, vivid, and so overwhelming it nearly knocks me from her back. Except it isn't my memory.

I watch as a figure cloaked in black approaches the lake's edge, cradling a baby in their arms. My breath catches as realization dawns—it's me. A tiny, helpless version of myself, barely able to crawl, placed delicately on the frozen shore.

The memory shifts to that moment in time, and I feel the icy plunge, the bone-deep cold as I fall into the water. Panic floods my body, and I thrash about, withering in the icy water, sending out a desperate pulse of magic—a scream for help.

And then she is there, beneath the surface, to pull me from the depths. The kelpie saved me.

The memory fades, leaving me gasping for breath, my grip tightening on her mane as we streak across the frozen lake. My mind reels trying to process it all.

'Someone had stolen you from your crib and left you at the lake's edge, sending you to your death, but something about you called to me, and I couldn't let you die.'

I have no words.

'Thank you for saving me,' I whisper.

'After that day, anytime your mother visited, she would bring you here to see me.'

A tear slips down my cheek, and a dull ache spreads through me. *'I wish I could see her again.'*

'She is with you.'

Within seconds, we reach the edge of the lake, and the kelpie slows, coming to a stop. Gently, I slide from her back, my boots crunching in the snow as I land. I pause for a moment, one hand resting on her flank, listening to the soft puff of her breath.

"Couldn't have made it without you," I murmur, my hand trailing along her side. I sense her bowing her head, then with a shimmer and a splash, she transforms into her water form, racing back to the heart of the lake. Watching her leave, I wish, yet again, that I could have gotten a proper glimpse of her.

Out of nowhere, a blast of hot air swirls around me, the sudden warmth a stark contrast to the icy cold I've been enduring. The force of it raises goosebumps on my arms, and the hair on the back of my neck stands on end. I freeze, every instinct on high alert. A deep, resonant growl rumbles from behind me, so low it vibrates through the air and in my bones.

Swallowing hard, I turn ever so slowly.

My breath catches in my throat as I see the creature looming behind me. Massive and regal, it radiates raw power and an otherworldly presence. Before I can take in the full scope of what I'm seeing, my blindfold loosens. I reach up to grab it, desperate to keep it in place, but it slips through my fingers, floating gently to the ground.

Light floods my vision, and I instinctively squeeze my eyes shut, overwhelmed by the sudden brightness. For a moment, I simply stand there, blinking rapidly, trying to adjust. When I finally open them fully, the sight before me steals the air from my lungs.

Towering above me is a white lion, its size dwarfing even my wolves, who are already massive in their own right. Its fur gleams like freshly fallen snow, and from its back spreads a set of enormous, feathered wings so white they seem to glow. The feathers ripple as the lion shifts, catching the faint light in a way that makes it seem ethereal, almost unreal. It huffs, a sound both commanding and strangely gentle, a cloud of warm air billowing from its nostrils.

This is no ordinary creature. This is a luxaryn—a being of legend. And it's breathtaking.

I stand perfectly still, hardly daring to breathe as it begins to circle me, each step silent despite its immense size. I can feel its magic brushing against mine, soft yet potent, like the whisper of a storm on the horizon. Its presence is overwhelming, its energy probing, testing, as if it's trying to decide whether I'm worthy of its attention.

The air thrums with tension as it moves behind me, out of my line of sight. My muscles lock in place, not from fear, but from a profound sense of reverence. Suddenly, I feel its tail curl around my waist. The gesture is surprisingly intimate, almost possessive, and I fight the urge to reach out and touch it.

I remain still, letting it finish its assessment, until a familiar voice cuts through the moment.

“You left this on the ice.”

I blink and turn to see Kaden approaching, a wide grin plastered across his face. In his hand, he’s holding my sword, the blade catching the light as it sways slightly in his grip. His eyes flick to the luxaryn, then back to me, as though this entire encounter is perfectly normal.

His grin widens. “Guessing you’ve made a new friend?”

The luxaryn huffs again, this time almost in amusement, as if answering for me.

Chapter Sixty-Five

Everly

The Skythari Nomads have outdone themselves, hosting a feast so grand it seems to light up the entire encampment. Fires burn bright, casting a warm glow over the gathered tribe as laughter and music fill the air. The rich aromas of spiced meats and freshly baked bread mingle with the sharp tang of the mountain air.

The mood is infectious. Even Raiden, usually so serious, seems to have relaxed, his deep chuckle carrying across the gathering as Kaden tries to teach him one of their traditional drinking songs. Zaria and Iridessa are caught up in a lively dance, spinning and twirling with a grace I can only envy.

But as much as I want to join in, I'm finding it hard to fully embrace the celebration.

My thoughts keep straying back to Maxon, bound and suffering under the Shadoweaver's cruel magic.

The weight of his captivity bears down on me, a relentless reminder that while this is a victory, the true battle still lies ahead.

I sit at the edge of the firelight, a warm mug cradled in my hands, its heat doing little to thaw the icy knot of worry that seems to be a constant now. I've wanted to leave already, to put this win to use and set out to free Maxon. But I know better than to let impatience drive me forward unprepared. The Gauntlet pushed me to my limits, and though the few cuts and bruises I got have already healed—thanks to my magic—I can feel the deep ache of exhaustion settling into my muscles. A night's rest isn't a luxury at this point, it is a necessity.

Magic tingles at my fingers as I drop one hand and swirl it around above the snow beside me. Slowly, a sprout forms, pushing through the snow. It's a vibrant green against the white, though the flower that blooms has icy-blue petals.

Barak approaches, a tankard in one hand and an unreadable expression on his face. He lowers himself onto the log beside me, the firelight dancing in his piercing blue eyes.

"Ice lily." He gives a pointed look down at the flower.

"I've never seen a lily like this," I whisper, watching the petals shimmer a soft crystalized blue.

"You did well today," he says simply, his voice low but firm. "The luxaryn don't always choose to pair with someone, even if you finish the Gauntlet. You have a pure heart, Everly. Just like your mother."

"Thank you," I reply.

The words feel hollow, almost disconnected from me. I made it across—that much is true—but everything that led to this point presses down on me. I should feel triumphant, maybe even proud. Instead, all I feel is tired. Barak studies me with a kind of measured patience. The flames flicker across his weathered face, throwing shadows that make his expression hard to read.

"You've earned the respect of the tribe tonight," Barak continues, taking a long drink before setting the tankard down. "But respect is only the beginning. You need to prove you will be a strong leader."

"I understand." I meet his gaze.

"Do you?" he questions, his brow raising slightly. "The Gauntlet was a test, yes. But it was only a taste of what's to come. The kelpie interfered and helped you across the lake, where most don't make it to the other side."

His words settle heavily on me, but I nod, determination hardening in my gut. "By the sun, the moon, and the stars, I will do whatever it takes," I declare firmly.

Barak studies me for a moment longer, then inclines his head. "Rest well tonight. Tomorrow, your true journey begins."

As he walks away, I lean back against the log I'm sitting on, my eyes drifting up to the stars glittering against the inky-black sky. He's right, I need rest.

Nymeria and Anika move silently by my side, their presence a comforting shadow as we make our way to the small hut Zaria and I have been assigned to share. The cool night air carries with it the faint scent of pine and the distant hum of laughter and music from the still-active feast. My wolves remain vigilant, their watchful eyes scanning the shadows, though I doubt there's any real danger here among the Skythari Nomads.

At the edge of the village, three luxaryn rest like silent sentinels. Their feathered wings catch the moonlight, giving them an otherworldly glow. They are as still as statues, but I know better than to be fooled by their calm appearance. The one that has chosen me—the one whose piercing gaze I've felt all evening—watches me still. Its eyes are like twin beacons, tracking my every move with a quiet intensity that sends a shiver down my spine.

Kaden's words echo in my mind: *They're perceptive creatures. They read more than your actions; they read your heart, your intentions.*

I didn't fully understand his meaning until now. It isn't just about trust; it is about baring my soul, letting the luxaryn see every shadow, every secret. The thought is unsettling, but there's no avoiding it. Whatever bond I am forming with this creature, it goes far deeper than I expected.

Inside the hut, the soft glow of a single lantern casts flickering shadows across the wooden walls. Zaria has already slipped inside, her gear carefully stowed, and is sound asleep when I enter. Nymeria and Anika settle near the door, their watchful eyes never leaving me.

I drop onto the small cot with a sigh, rolling my head to ease the lingering tension from the day. Peering over my shoulder, I glance out the small window, my gaze drifting back to the luxaryn at the village's edge. It hasn't moved, but I can still feel its presence.

Lying back on the cot, I let out a slow, measured breath in an attempt to calm the storm churning just beneath the surface. But the moment my eyes close, my thoughts rush straight to the bond—and to Maxon. It quivers faintly, like a thread pulled too tight, vibrating with unease. I can feel it fraying at the edges, weakening with every second, and the realization claws at me.

Panic flickers—sharp and breathless. If the bond breaks . . .

I press a hand to my ribs, as if I could hold it together by sheer will. The silence around me only makes the absence louder.

I need to see him. Now.

Chapter Sixty-Six

Maxon

My mind drifts, heavy and sluggish, as I sit here, head lolling forward every few seconds. Sleep claws at me, demanding surrender, at the same time that my body screams for sustenance. I need sleep, I need food, and blood, but most of all, I need Everly. My throat is parched, every swallow a razor's edge. My gums ache insistently, a reminder of the hunger that gnaws at me. It's been a few days since I fed from Everly, and the punishment my body has endured since then has been pure torture.

I barely register the touch at first, too lost in the haze of exhaustion. Then gentle hands cup my face, firm yet impossibly tender, lifting it upward. My eyes flutter open, and instinct stirs—a snarl building in my throat, ready to lash out at whoever dares to touch me. But the sound dies before it can form.

Jeweled green eyes stare back at me, shimmering with tears. Her tears. My breath catches, the sight cutting through the fog like a blade.

"Stóirín," I whisper, the word escaping me on a breath.

Her lip quivers, and she leans closer, her voice trembling but strong enough to wrap around me like a lifeline. "A chroí." My heart.

Everly's face is radiant despite the shadows, her beauty undiminished by the worry etched into her features. She leans forward, her soft lips brushing against mine in the gentlest of kisses, a touch so fleeting and delicate it feels like a dream. The sweetest scent of roses and jasmine fills my lungs, chasing away the damp stench of the cavern.

"You smell amazing," I groan, my cracked lips parting on an inhale. "Like home."

"I am your home," she breathes. "I'm coming for you, Maxon. I promise. I won't leave you here."

I close the gap and press my lips to hers. "I know, but you shouldn't be here. If they find out, they can trap you. Please, you need to leave."

"You need to feed first." She maneuvers herself on my lap, and lifts my bound wrists over her head. I slip them around her and down her body to rest against her lower back. Her skin is warm and soft beneath my fingers. Without hesitation, I pull her in tighter, needing the contact. My cock stiffens against her, aching from the nearness of her, from the sweet, maddening heat radiating between us.

"You smell amazing." I murmur.

Without taking her eyes from mine, she drags her hair over one shoulder and brings her neck closer. "Feed. Keep up your strength. I know you're trying to keep your pain from me, but I can feel the bond weakening, Maxon. Drink. Please." There is a slight wobble in her voice that gives me pause.

I lean forward as much as the bones around my neck will let me and run my tongue over her skin. Everly shivers in response, pressing closer. My fangs descend, sharp and eager, piercing her flesh with a primal urgency. The moment her blood fills my mouth, it's as if the world snaps into focus. Her warmth, her taste—so familiar, so intoxicating—surges through me like a bolt of lightning, setting every nerve alight. My senses sharpen; the pain of my captivity dulls beneath the heady rush of her essence.

Driven by instinct, I rock my hips upward, desperate for the friction my body craves. Everly's breathy moans echo around the cavern, a melody that fuels the fire raging inside me. Her hands fumble at my waistband, trembling with haste as she works my pants down just enough to free me. The cool air hits my cock briefly before her warm fingers wrap around it, her grip firm yet tender, her touch electric.

She guides me to her entrance, positioning herself above me. When she sinks down, her heat envelops me completely, and I'm lost—dizzy, overwhelmed by the sheer intensity of her. My teeth sink deeper, drawing in more of her blood as she grinds down on me, rocking her hips with a rhythm that leaves me undone. The cavern around us fades into insignificance; all that exists is her—her taste, her scent, her body moving with mine.

My orgasm builds swiftly, a storm raging through my core. I force myself to withdraw my fangs, reluctant but knowing I can't take too much. I lap at the wound on her neck, savoring every drop, my bound hands pressing her harder against me. The wyvern bones tighten, digging into my wrists, but I don't care. I just want more of her, all of her.

Everly's lips find mine, hot and desperate, her kiss a blend of sweetness and fire. Our bodies melt together, her inner walls clamping down around me as I thrust upward, meeting her every movement. My control shatters as she takes me deeper, her slick heat driving me to the edge.

"Fuck," I snarl, the word ripped from me as my climax hovers just out of reach, the tension unbearable.

Everly tips her head back, a sweet cry tearing from her lips as she trembles around me. Her walls spasm, gripping me like a vice, and I explode inside her, my release rushing through me in waves so powerful I see stars. My cock pulses as my body shudders. Her name falls from my lips in a broken whisper. A faint golden light washes over us and my mind clears completely. Has her blood been healing more than my physical wounds?

Then I feel it—the way her form begins to flicker, to fade. Panic lances through me. I don't want her to leave. Not yet. Not like this.

I need to tell her about the attack, but how many days have passed? Does she already know?

Her fingers trail softly across my cheek, her touch featherlight as her edges blur further.

"Maxon," she breathes, her voice a faint whisper, a ghost of a sound.

And then she's gone, leaving only the lingering scent of roses and the ache of her absence.

Chapter Sixty-Seven

Everly

I stand in the snow at the edge of the village, my eyes glued to the horizon. The sun is just beginning to crest over the jagged peaks in the east, casting a golden glow that sets the sky ablaze with hues of orange and pink. Despite the breathtaking beauty, my heart feels unbearably heavy. My thoughts linger on Maxon, his weakened form from last night etched permanently into my mind. Whatever they're doing to him, it's taking a toll.

Yet, amidst the heartache, there's a faint solace—a constant hum in my chest. After my visit, our bond feels stronger, more present again. I draw a slow breath, letting the cold air fill my lungs.

A flash of movement catches my eye, and I spot Nymeria and Anika bounding up the slope toward me. The wolves slipped away early this morning, likely hunting in preparation for our departure. Their silvery white coats are dusted with snow, their tongues lolling in apparent satisfaction as they frolic in the powder, carefree and wild.

I sense someone approaching from behind, and peer over my shoulder. Kaden. He's bundled against the cold, his sharp features softened by a smile as he lifts a hand in greeting. I force myself to return the gesture with a small smile of my own, though I know it doesn't reach my eyes.

He stops beside me, watching the sunrise. The silence between us feels mutual, comfortable.

"I'm coming with you," Kaden says, speaking first.

I frown and look up at him. "Why?"

"I can help. I want to help."

I pull my cloak around me tighter as I turn to face him. "We don't know what we're up against."

"All the more reason to have me come along. I know the luxaryn, I have bonded with my own. We will accompany you."

I bite my lip and glance out over the snow-capped mountains, an icy cold wind whipping my hair across my face.

"I'd love all the help I can get," I whisper.

"Good. Now, do you wish to fly to Escalle?"

I snap my head back to him, my eyes going wide. "Fly?"

"Yes. You and I can fly on the luxaryn. The others will have a guide to the base of the mountain, and it's a straight two-day ride from there. But we can be in Escalle by nightfall."

The weight of indecision presses down on me. "I . . . I can't leave my friends."

Nymeria and Anika bound over, rubbing against my body, jolting me slightly. *'We can get them to Escalle safely,'* Nymeria offers.

'I know you can, but I'm not going to simply take the easier path because I'm able to.'

Kaden's kind eyes watch me, as I struggle with the decision.

"Queen Vera, you need to bond with your luxaryn. This journey into the Outlands rides on you being able to communicate with Aetheris, the same way you do with your wolves."

I frown, pursing my lips. He's right, I know he is. But guilt at leaving the others eats at me.

"Your friends will be fine, and I'm sure they know what's at stake," Kaden adds.

"Fine," I relent. "I will fly so I can bond with the luxaryn, but we watch over the group as we do."

Kaden grins, inclining his head. "As you wish, Your Majesty."

A shadow falls over us, long and shifting against the snow. I squint up, lifting a hand to shield my eyes from the glare of the sun. My breath catches as I spot them—two massive luxaryn circling gracefully above. Their snow-white fur shimmers like frost under the golden rays. The creatures descend, their enormous wings spreading wide as they glide down effortlessly. The ground trembles faintly as they land a few yards away, their powerful claws sinking into the snow. They fold their wings against their broad backs, the motion smooth and practiced, before puffing out their chests as they stride toward us.

I can't take my eyes off them. These beasts, reminiscent of lions but so much more, radiate an aura of majesty and command that takes my breath away. Their long tails swish behind them, and their piercing silver eyes seem to hold so many secrets.

The luxaryn halt a short distance from us, lowering themselves to sit on their powerful haunches. Even in this position, they tower over us, their massive forms casting an imposing presence.

Kaden, however, is utterly unfazed. With the ease of someone accustomed to their magnificence, he steps forward and places a hand on the neck of the nearest luxaryn. Its fur ripples under his touch, catching the light like spun silver. The beast lets out a low rumble, almost a purr, and leans slightly into his hand. Even standing tall, Kaden barely reaches its shoulder, the beast towering over him by at least a foot.

I remain rooted in place, mesmerized by the scene. The bond between them is undeniable, a connection forged through trust and respect. As Kaden turns to glance back at me, a faint smile tugs at the corner of his lips as though inviting me to step closer.

"This is Starfire." Kaden rests his palm on the luxaryn. "And that is Aetheris." He motions toward the luxaryn who chose me yesterday.

I swallow down my nerves and step closer, my hand trembling as I reach up to touch Aetheris.

My fingers sink in, shifting through the strands, her fur is so soft and warm. I smile and look up, anticipation pounding in my chest.

"They are magnificent," I breathe.

"Want to go for a ride?"

I give Kaden a look out of the corner of my eye, making him laugh.

"Come on, a practice run." With fluent ease, he walks around the side of his luxaryn, and the creature stands, his hand gripping the mane as he launches himself onto its back, settling in.

"Ahh . . . " Is all I can manage.

Aetheris shifts and nudges me with her nose.

'Come little one,' she beckons, startling me.

With shaking hands, I reach up and grip her mane. Suddenly, Aetheris's tail wraps around my middle, hoisting me up and onto her back. My hands grip the mane tightly as I clamp my legs down hard. Nerves and adrenaline flood my body.

"I'm not so sure about this," I mutter.

'I won't let you fall.'

Without warning, Aetheris launches into the sky, her powerful hind legs propelling us upward in a single, fluid leap. Starfire follows closely behind. The force of their take-off sends a blast of snow swirling around me, the cold biting at my cheeks. A scream escapes my throat, carried away on the wind before I can even process it.

The ground beneath us disappears rapidly as we soar higher and higher. Cold wind tears at my hair and stings my face, my breath catching as I cling tightly to the luxaryn's mane with a death grip. The vast expanse of the land stretches out in all directions, breathtaking and endless. The village shrinks to a speck below, the forests sprawling like a sea of green, while the mountains in the distance rise like jagged teeth against the horizon.

The icy wind whips past me, harsh and relentless, but I hardly notice. My eyes sting and water, though I can't tell if it's from the cold or the overwhelming rush of emotions surging through me. A strange bubbling sensation builds—somewhere between laughter and tears—as my heart pounds wildly.

I grip Aetheris tighter, my fingers digging into her silky mane for stability. It's impossible to ignore the sheer power of her wings as they beat rhythmically, each stroke propelling us further into the vast, endless sky.

I close my eyes for a moment, letting the chaos within me meld into a single, indescribable feeling.

Chief Barak adjusts the strap of his fur-lined cloak as he addresses us. "We have topped up your supplies. It shouldn't take more than two days to reach Escalle. My guides will lead you down the mountain through the rougher terrain."

Valric claps the older man on the shoulder. "Thank you for your hospitality, old man."

The camaraderie between them brings a flicker of warmth to my chest. Despite their contrasting temperaments, the bond they share is clear.

Before I can voice my gratitude, Iridessa and Onora step forward, their spears glinting faintly in the sunlight. They carry themselves with the grace and strength their lineage is known for, though their expressions betray a quiet reluctance.

"We are assisting your friends down the mountain," Onora says softly, her warm smile a gentle reassurance that eases some of my tension.

"Thank you."

Onora hesitates for a moment, exchanging a glance with her sister before continuing. "We wish to accompany you to the Outlands to save your mate, but our father forbids it."

Her words stir a pang of guilt, though I know Chief Barak's reasoning is sound. I reach out, clasping her hand in mine. "Your father only wishes to keep his daughters safe, and I don't blame him."

Iridessa's lips press into a thin line as her attention lands on her brother with a spark of indignation.

"Kaden gets to go," she huffs.

"He is helping me bond with my luxaryn," I explain gently, hoping to ease her frustration.

The sisters exchange a look, their disappointment evident despite their understanding.

"I will visit again, once this is all over. I'd love to bring Maxon here."

That seems to break through their melancholy, their faces lighting up with identical smiles.

"Promise?" they ask in unison.

"Promise."

Nero strolls over with a relaxed confidence that seems to command attention without effort. My gaze catches on the black tattoos winding over his skin, their shapes eerily reminiscent of the white markings of the Skythari Nomads.

"I will ride Storm down the mountain, if that is okay with you, My Queen." Nero's deep voice is smooth as he stops beside us.

I glance at Onora, and it's impossible to miss the way she drops her gaze, her cheeks blooming a soft, rosy pink. She fidgets slightly, her composure slipping for just a moment.

"That would be great, Nero. Thanks," I reply.

Nero dips his head in acknowledgment, a faint smirk tugging at his lips. Then, with a deliberate grace, he turns to the sisters. Reaching out, he takes each of their hands in his, his movements fluid and practiced.

"I appreciate the beautiful company and your hospitality," the words come out rich and laced with charm as he presses a light kiss to the back of each hand.

Both sisters stand frozen, their mouths falling open in surprise. The faintest hint of color rises in their cheeks, and I have to fight the urge to laugh at the scene.

Nero releases their hands with a casual flourish and throws me a playful wink before sauntering off toward the horses, his every step exuding a kind of effortless magnetism.

Chapter Sixty-Eight

Everly

I rub my hands over my face before letting out a long breath, then send a prayer to whoever is listening for the strength to do what needs to be done today. We reached Escalle by nightfall yesterday evening, the dense woods around the village shrouded in an eerie silence that made every sound feel amplified. The small cluster of houses were illuminated only by the faint glow of lanterns, their flickering light casting long, dancing shadows across the cobblestone streets. The armies were camped outside the village walls, Fenris and Alivar having arrived only that morning with the last of the soldiers.

I was devastated to hear that the City of Starlight was attacked two nights ago while the city was sleeping. Ogres, giants, and deadlings swarmed the walls. Yet Alivar still showed up for me, for Maxon.

With the first rays of sunlight piercing through the mist, we gather in the village hall. Maps were spread out on the central table, weighed down by mugs of steaming tea and small rocks to keep them from curling.

After a lot of back and forth, we decide that the primary group will attack from the valley, aiming to draw the Shadoweaver's army out of hiding. It's a bold strategy, as the valley itself is a natural choke point, wide enough for an army to advance, but narrow enough to create vulnerabilities if an ambush were sprung. It is there that the clash will begin, with the main force acting as both bait and hammer.

Meanwhile, I, along with Kaden and the luxaryn, will infiltrate the cave system. I shiver remembering how the air crackled with tension as the plan was explained; nervous glances were exchanged, yet I stood firm in my decision.

Locating Maxon will be the most challenging aspect of our plan, but the luxaryn cloaking my presence will buy me the necessary time. Not to mention the verse says only they can break his chains.

Now, I'm pacing my private tent as the countdown begins. We ride out in less than an hour to cross the veil into the Outlands, heading straight for the Deadlands where the cave systems are.

When Fenris took me out to see the veil this morning, I was in complete awe. At first, I couldn't see the veil at all. It wasn't until he pointed it out that it came into focus. It's just a shimmer in the air, like the wavering heat off sunbaked stone, barely noticeable against the eerie stillness before me. But as my eyes adjust, the magic reveals itself. A shimmering, white barrier stretches endlessly before me, pulsing faintly, its woven threads of power both beautiful and menacing. It isn't just a wall—it is a prison. And beyond it, trapped within this forsaken land, are those who have been banished, sealed away from the world they once knew.

To the west the Mistyglades stretch into the distance, its rolling fog dancing over the long golden grass, before giving way to the skeletal remains of a forest. The trees in the Outlands have been stripped of vibrance, their colors muted to lifeless grays and browns, their gnarled branches twisting like grasping fingers toward a sky choked with heavy clouds.

The Outlands look exactly as I expected—dead.

At the sound of approaching footsteps, I look up just as Zaria enters the tent, the flap swinging behind her.

"Kian told me you were in here. Are you ready?"

I stand and approach the large, heavy wooden chest Fenris had delivered, its dark wood gleaming under the dim light. My fingers tremble as I unlatch and open the lid. Inside is the armor George made me.

"Will you help me put it on?" I request over my shoulder.

"Of course."

Together, we carefully fit the armor over my fighting gear. The metal plates gleam faintly in the flickering torchlight. Zaria's hands move deftly, strapping everything in place. She tugs at the final buckle, ensuring it's secure, and steps back to inspect her work.

"All that's left is your sword," she notes, her voice softer than usual.

My hand closes around the weapon, its energy vibrating under my palm.

"Raiden isn't happy you're going in alone."

I sigh, meeting her worried gaze. "I won't be alone. Kaden will be with me."

Her brow furrows, the crease between her eyebrows deepening. "Exactly. Raiden doesn't know him, and you are our queen."

"Taking more people could draw attention. This mission requires stealth."

Zaria steps closer, her hands landing gently on my shoulders. She gives me a small, bittersweet smile, the kind that speaks of reluctant acceptance.

"We know," she whispers softly. "We just don't like it."

I place my hand over hers, squeezing lightly. "I'll be careful."

Her smile doesn't falter, but I see the worry lingering in her eyes.

The tent flap opens and Alivar steps inside. His eyes roam the armor, and he lets out a low whistle. "You look amazing."

"She looks like a warrior," Zaria agrees.

"A queen ready for war," he adds with a wink.

"That's exactly what I am, Alivar." I heave a sigh.

He steps aside, pulling the tent flap open for me. "My army is ready and waiting."

A storm of emotions swirls inside me—relief, fear, something close to disbelief—but above it all, gratitude rises like a tide. Alivar owes me nothing, yet he's given more than I ever dared ask for. That kind of kindness and loyalty doesn't just sit quietly in your chest. It stays, settles deep, and humbles you.

I let out a deep breath and nod. "Okay, then. Let's go."

It's time to rescue my mate.

Zaria leads the way, stepping outside first. I move to follow, but Alivar's hand lands on my arm, stalling me. When I glance up into those sharp amethyst eyes, my heart stalls. Flickers of blue flash in their depths, the silver ring around them sparking with life as he steps closer.

"I want you to be safe. If shit goes down, you need to retreat. We can try again."

I frown, opening my mouth to argue, but Alivar doesn't give me that chance. He steps outside and disappears into the crowd.

From my vantage point atop Aetheris, I survey the assembled armies, eager to fight for the king's return. In a central position, Storm stands tall alongside Raiden, Tristan, and Kian, his onyx coat shimmering. There is no way he was going to sit this one out. With a snort and a pawing hoof, the loyal warhorse stands ready, eager to aid his king in whatever way he can. I've given Nymeria and Anika strict instructions: stay close to him, watch each other's backs, and be ready for anything. Nero catches my eye and gives me a slight nod, the magic around his body making the air tremble.

As I let my gaze roam over the armies, doubt claws at the edge of my mind. What if they die? What if I'm sending them to their deaths?

'Then it happens,' Aetheris answers in my mind.

I jerk at the matter-of-fact response, my fingers tightening in her mane.

'I don't want people to die,' I reply.

I've noticed since the flight here that our bond has strengthened and now rests calmly next to the wolves'.

'It is inevitable. Everyone here knows the risks.'

'Doesn't make me feel better.'

I look down at my engagement ring, the gold band and crystals catching the sunlight. I promised Maxon's court I would return with him, and I plan to do just that. This is for him.

Soon he will be by my side again.

Nothing will stop me.

My attention lifts again to the bleak expanse of the Outlands—silent, scarred, and watchful. No beasts, no scouts, no sign of movement. It is too quiet and I don't like it.

Ahead, the mountains rise like the ribs of a long-dead titan, jagged and shrouded with shadows.

The army begins to advance, boots crunching dry earth as they head toward the valley. With the attack on the City of Starlight only a few days ago, we are assuming the Shadoweavers numbers to be low, and hoping to meet with little resistance.

'When we enter the mountain,' Aetheris continues, striding forward with Starfire, *'we'll need to release the cloak surrounding the army. The distraction will draw her forces out. But we will remain hidden from the Shadoweaver as we descend into the caves to find your king.'*

I turn to Kaden. Our eyes meet. His expression is all grim resolve and unspoken trust. He nods once, firm and final.

'Starfire found a side passage,' he tells me. *'A hidden entrance near the main opening. While the army engages hers head-on, we'll slip inside—quiet, fast, unseen.'*

I nod, gripping the hilt of my sword in one hand and the white mane of Aetheris in the other. Into the belly of the beast we go.

Chapter Sixty-Nine

Maxon

I turn my head to the side and spit the blood from my mouth, the metallic tang lingering on my tongue. My jaw aches, but I force a grin, the defiance burning brighter than the pain.

"Is that all you got?" I rasp, glaring up at the ogre looming over me. My voice is hoarse, cracked from hours of this twisted game, but the edge in my words slices through the air like a blade.

The ogre sneers, his cracked lips curling into a grin that reeks of cruelty. Without a word, he draws his massive arm back, muscles bulging like coiled ropes beneath his mottled green skin. The moment hangs suspended in time, and then the blow lands, knuckles like boulders crashing against my face.

The force jerks my head to the side, stars exploding behind my eyes.

My vision swims, but I refuse to let the darkness win. Not yet. Not while there's fight left in me.

I'm hanging from that fucking hook in the ceiling again. My arms are stretched above my head, wrists raw and bleeding where the wyvern bones cut into my skin.

The hook creaks faintly with every movement, a mocking reminder of how trapped I am. My toes barely scrape the cold, damp floor, offering no reprieve from the agony tearing through my shoulders.

But I won't break. Not for him. Not for anyone.

I force myself to look up, blinking away the blood trickling into my eyes. "You hit like a goddamn pixie," I spit, a smirk tugging at my swollen lips. It hurts to smile, but the pain is worth it to see his face twist with rage.

As I draw in a shallow, rattling breath, I feel the faintest breeze whisper across my battered skin. It's so subtle, like a dream slipping through the cracks of my reality, and on that breeze is the unmistakable sweet scent of roses. My mind clings to it, desperate for a lifeline in this hell. Everly.

A smile stretches across my face as I close my eyes, the pain receding for just a moment. Her golden, silk-spun hair fills my vision, shimmering like sunlight caught in a web. Those sparkling green eyes, so full of innocence and sweetness, seem to pierce through the darkness, grounding me even though she's not here—can't be here.

The breeze shifts, carrying with it a ripple of change, and my instincts flare. A sense of movement draws my attention to the cavern entrance.

My eyes snap open.

She is here.

A bright, white light breaks through the darkness outside the cavern, and the massive form of a luxaryn steps into the light. Its entire form shimmers in the dark, lighting its way. The otherworldly creature spreads its white-feathered wings as it lowers its enormous head. With a guttural roar, the beast shakes the air itself, the deafening sound reverberating through the chamber. The walls tremble, and rocks and debris cascade from above in response to its fury.

And then she appears.

Everly.

She slips off the luxaryn's back with the grace of a whisper, landing softly beside the towering beast. Her presence is ethereal, her every movement deliberate and unshaken. The fire and determination in her eyes radiates like a beacon, and for a moment, I forget the pain, forget the hook, forget the blood dripping from my face.

All I see is her.

My mate.

My soul.

My queen.

The ogres reel from the luxaryn's roar, stumbling back in stunned confusion. Their eyes dart between the beast and the golden-haired woman who now stands before them. When they finally regain their composure, one of them steps forward with a growl, his voice dripping with suspicion and malice. "Who the fuck are you?"

I can't help but grin through the pain, wiping the blood from my chin with a flick of my shoulder.

"That"—my voice is hoarse, but filled with pride—"would be my mate."

The ogre sneers, his brows furrowing. "The one the Master is after?"

"The one and only."

My smile widens, and I spit another mouthful of blood onto the cavern floor.

Chapter Seventy

Everly

The steady drumbeat of adrenaline and anger pounds through my body. Every part of me is trembling, but I slip smoothly from Aetheris's back, my boots landing on the ground, and face the two ogres, their ugly sneers sending my hackles up.

Aetheris let out a deafening roar, the sound splitting the air like a crack of thunder. The force of it sends the ogres stumbling into each other. I rest my hand on her side, my eyes going to Maxon, who is chained to the ceiling. A cold wind hits the length of my spine, but it's nothing compared to the anger I'm feeling.

How dare they hurt my mate!

My magic pulses in response to my emotions. The air around me crackles, thick with energy and raw emotion. Golden light flickers at my fingertips, barely contained, and the ground trembles beneath my feet as if the very world can feel my wrath building. My vision narrows, not from fear but from purpose.

"Who the fuck are you?" one ogre sneers, and I'm actually surprised, because this is the first time I've heard one speak.

Maxon answers before I can. His voice is rough, but the smirk on his face has my heart leaping in my chest.

"That"—pride lights his eyes—"would be my mate."

The ogre doesn't look convinced, his brows furrowing. "The one the Master is after?"

"The one and only," Maxon confirms, his smile widening.

'Get him out of those bones, or chains, whatever they are, and I'll handle these two,' I say to Aetheris.

I cast a quick glance down the dark tunnel behind me. Kaden took the left path, and I went right. A knot of worry twists in my chest as I think of him. I hope he's okay. Though this place has been eerily empty so far.

My grip tightens around the hilt of my sword as I step into the cavern. The air is damp and heavy, carrying the faint, acrid scent of ogres, damp earth, and blood.

"Well, well," one of them rasps, his voice like gravel sliding down a mountain. "Imagine the reward we'll get for capturing her."

I raise my sword, meeting their gazes with defiance. They don't know. They can't know. I am not the same weak, pathetic human they might have expected a month ago.

'*You were never weak or pathetic,*' Maxon's voice surges through the bond, strong and steady.

I glance toward him, suspended there, and the way he believes in me stirs something deep—steadying, strong. Aetheris moves around me, heading in Maxon's direction, unfazed by the ogres.

"Well?" I begin, drawing their attention to me. "You going to come get me?"

The two ogres don't wait. They trudge forward, their massive fists flexing, each step shaking the ground beneath my feet. I steady my breathing, planting my feet firmly. If they want to fight, they are about to learn just how much I've changed.

With a burst of speed, the first ogre lunges, swinging a meaty fist. I sidestep easily, his fist crashing into the stone wall where I've been standing. The second ogre comes from the side, his arm swinging in a wide arc. I duck, feeling the rush of air as his strike narrowly misses me.

"You'll regret that," he growls, his grin turning feral.

I smirk. "Will I?"

The bond pulses again, a ripple of encouragement from Maxon.

Magic surges through me, flowing like liquid stardust from my fingertips into the trembling earth. The ground beneath us groans, a deep rumble reverberating through the cavern as I channel my power. With a forceful gesture, a sharp pillar of jagged earth and stone erupts from the ground, its edges gleaming like a predator's fang. It strikes true, impaling the nearest ogre with brutal precision. His massive body is lifted off the ground and pinned against the cavern ceiling, the pillar piercing clean through him.

A wet, guttural gurgling escapes his throat, his blood cascading down the pillar in dark, viscous streams that pool on the ground below.

I let a smirk tug at the corner of my lips, the thrill of control and power momentarily intoxicating. Turning, I fix my gaze on the remaining ogre. He hesitates, fear flickering in his beady eyes as he glances between me and the macabre scene behind him.

"Your turn," I challenge, my voice low.

With a fierce roar, the ogre charges, and in this moment, Aetheris's claws strike through the chains holding Maxon to the ceiling. My heart skips as he falls to the hard, unforgiving stone floor. The distraction leaves me open, and the ogre's fist connects with my shoulder, sending me sprawling across the ground. A sharp pain pulses through me as I try to draw in a deep breath.

Oh my god.

That hurt.

A rattling wheeze escapes my lips as I fight to roll onto my hands and knees, my body aching with the effort. Though the armor softened the blow, the impact still hurt like a bitch.

I hear Maxon snarl, the sound echoing around us, and I lift my head. Less than a foot away, the ogre freezes, turning slightly. I grit my teeth and attempt to blow my hair away from my face. Aetheris's jaws carefully clamp over the bones around Maxon's neck, the last of his restraints. Hope surges as the bones clatter to the ground.

Maxon stands, blood covering his entire body, his fists clenched at his sides as his chest heaves. A raw and primal fury that radiates from him like a storm about to break.

"Get away from my mate," he snarls.

I watch in awe as his eyes ignite like kindling.

Then, the fire erupts.

Flames ignite across his skin, racing along his arms and shoulders, wreathing him in a fiery aura. The heat is immediate and intense, forcing me to shield my face with my arms. His flames are wild, untamed, yet they don't harm him. Instead, they seem to feed off his rage, growing larger with every second.

The ogre takes a step back before it turns to run, but it's too slow. Maxon raises his hand, and with a guttural roar, he unleashes a torrent of fire straight at the creature.

The ogre's scream is a sound I'll never forget—a mix of terror and agony as the fire engulfs it. The acrid stench of burning flesh fills the air, and I gag, covering my mouth. I can barely breathe, but I can't tear my gaze away from the scene before me.

Maxon doesn't stop. His flames' roar with a life of their own, feeding on the ogre until there's nothing left but ash. The fire dims, leaving the scorched ground and a few smoldering embers where the ogre once stood. Only then does Maxon's fury begin to wane. The flames recede, flickering out as quickly as they came, leaving his skin unmarred but still glistening with sweat and blood.

He turns to me, his glowing eyes dimming, replaced by the familiar warmth I've always known. For a moment, he looks like he's about to collapse, but he steadies himself, his gaze locking onto mine. There's a softness there now, a vulnerability.

"Are you hurt?" His voice is hoarse and full of concern.

I shake my head, unable to find the words to respond. Instead, I stand and take a tentative step toward him, my heart still racing. He doesn't move, letting me close the distance between us. When I'm finally within reach, I place a trembling hand on his chest, feeling the rapid beat of his heart beneath my palm.

We don't speak for a long moment, just take each other in, the air thick with unspoken words and emotions. Maxon's hand reaches up, brushing a strand of hair from my face, his touch gentle, yet filled with intensity.

"You are so beautiful, My Queen," he murmurs, his voice low and reverent.

A tear slips down my cheek, and I reach up with both hands, cupping his face to draw him closer. Our lips meet, and the world seems to pause, leaving only the softness of his kiss and the warmth of his embrace. My stomach flutters as his tongue sweeps in, claiming me in a way only he can.

Then I feel the sharp punch of his panic down the bond. Maxon pulls away, his fingers gliding over my hair, and smoothing down my braid. My body alights at the sensation.

"You shouldn't have come for me. She has been waiting," Maxon sighs.

Anger rises swiftly, burning the back of my throat. "I know."

A soft nudge at my back from Aetheris causes me to break away from Maxon, though his arms immediately encircle my waist, pulling me closer, refusing to let me go. His mouth seeks mine, the kiss neither innocent nor sweet, but one of strength. Of love.

Maxon lifts his head. "We need to go," he stresses, reluctantly releasing my waist and taking my hand.

'I will lead the way.' Aetheris turns for the exit.

"No," I refuse, my voice soft but unwavering. "I want you to take me to her."

Maxon lifts an eyebrow in surprise, his gaze narrowing as I look up at him. "Why?"

"I want to see the Shadoweaver for myself," I answer, my voice gaining strength. "Prove that they won't win. Ever."

Maxon's gaze shifts to the tunnel, his indecision evident. I can see the conflict in his eyes, the desire to protect me warring against the knowledge that this is something I must do. Then, without another word, his features harden.

"Okay," he mutters, his jaw tightening. "I wouldn't mind seeing her face when she realizes she can't stop this."

I turn to Aetheris and scoop up my sword. "Go find Kaden. Get him out of here. We won't be far behind."

Aetheris dips her head in acknowledgment. '*Don't do anything foolish*,' she warns before disappearing into the tunnel.

Chapter Seventy-One

Everly

I stare into the cavern's shadows, pulse hammering violently in my ears, the surge of blood rushing through my veins like a warning—sharp, urgent, impossible to ignore. The air feels dense and oppressive, shadows clinging stubbornly to every surface. The torches along the walls flicker wildly as if a storm is brewing inside. The magic imprisoning the Shadoweaver is clear before me—a shimmering veil of ancient power, vibrating just four feet away. It pulses with energy, and like opposing magnets pushing against each other, the force repels me, keeping me from drawing closer.

"Where?" I ask, peering up at Maxon.

I can feel his magic, its wildness flowing from him in waves. He wants to storm in there and fight, but he's holding back.

"She's in there. What worries me is we haven't seen the demon," he murmurs in a low growl.

A sudden noise pulls my attention back to the cavern. I frown, my gaze shifting to another entrance on the far side. My breath hitches, confusion washing over me as I spot Mia being shoved roughly through the doorway. She stumbles, her feet catching on the uneven ground, and she lands hard on her hands and knees. A sharp gasp escapes her lips, but she quickly flips her hair back and twists to glare into the shadows behind her, a snarl curling her lips.

My mind is struggling with what I'm seeing. Senka strolls into the cavern with a smug smirk painted across her face. My heart plummets, a hollow ache blooming in my chest.

It can't be.

"Senka?" my voice trembles, echoing off the cavern walls.

Senka doesn't respond. She stands motionless beside Mia, her lilac eyes giving nothing away. The silence between us is deafening.

Maxon's warmth radiates against my back as he steps closer. His presence is steady, grounding. The shadows in the corners of the cavern shift unnaturally, writhing and twisting like living things. Laughter—soft, mocking, and inescapable—starts to rise, filling the cavern with its eerie resonance.

"Senka, let Mia go," I command, my voice firm despite the quiver that runs through me.

Nothing. Not even a flicker of acknowledgment. The distance between us feels like a football field when in reality it's no more than a hundred feet. Panic rises swiftly, making my palms sweaty.

"Senka," Maxon growls, his tone a low, dangerous rumble.

That gets her attention. Her eyes flicker, and for a brief moment, I see something—remorse? Regret? But it's gone just as quickly, replaced by a hardened expression, her features set in stone.

“Where is Lutin?” I demand.

I’m almost afraid to hear the truth. The possibility claws at my mind; were they in on this together? A sick alliance to betray us all? Is Scarlett okay? My thoughts race faster than my words.

Senka’s eyes find mine. Then, the single word falls from her lips like a stone into a still pond.

“Dead.”

The world tilts for a moment. My heart skips. I don’t know whether to believe her or not, and yet the finality in her tone doesn’t allow much room for doubt.

“How?” I manage, my voice thin.

Her lips curl. “Me, of course. He never saw it coming. His neck broke like a twig.”

My breathing picks up, shallow and rapid. The room feels colder, heavier. The sharp, bitter taste of rage rises in my throat. My magic stirs unbidden, coiling tight like a serpent ready to strike.

In the distance, the deep, guttural roars of the luxaryn reverberate through the cave system, shaking the stone walls around us.

“Mia,” I whisper, my voice threatening to break.

Mia’s soft, brown eyes meet mine. They’re brimming with tears, but she straightens her shoulders, her voice emerging stronger than I expected.

“You got this, E. With or without me, you got this.”

Her words hit me like a punch to the gut, and I shake my head, refusing to accept the possibility of losing her. I take a step forward. The shadows around us whisper, a cacophony of taunts and jeers. The laughter crescendos, a cruel and haunting sound that seems to come from everywhere and nowhere all at once.

"Senka, let her go," Maxon orders, his voice tight with restrained fury. I can feel the heat radiating from him, his body trembling against the strain of holding back. His magic—the dragon's fire—is building beneath his skin, an inferno begging for release.

Suddenly shadows converge behind the two of them, and I watch as two hands form from those shadows and grip Senka's head, giving it a sharp twist. Senka's eyes widen for only a second before her lifeless body falls to the ground. Then, without a second to comprehend what's happening, the shadows surge forward, entwining like living tendrils of darkness. They move with terrifying speed, latching onto Mia. Their inky forms coil around her head, and she gasps, her wide, tear-filled eyes locking onto mine.

"I love you, Everly," she whispers.

Her eyes flutter closed, and for a brief moment, time seems to freeze. Then her head jerks, twisting at an unnatural angle. The sickening crack reverberates through the cavern like a thunderclap, and the world crashes down around me.

"No!" my scream rips through the air, raw and broken, echoing off the cavern walls. The sound carries my anguish, ricocheting wildly until it feels like the entire world is screaming with me. Rocks and debris rain down from above as the ground beneath us trembles violently, the quake a physical manifestation of my grief and fury.

The shadows loosen their hold, and Mia's lifeless body crumples to the ground like a puppet with its strings cut. My world narrows to her still form, everything else blurring into a haze of red. Fury and grief swell inside me, an unstoppable tide crashing against the fragile walls of my control. My magic ignites, bursting free in a fiery wave that rolls across the ground, shaking the very air around us.

"Everly, stop!" Maxon's voice is distant, drowned out by the roar of my emotions and the pounding of my heart. His hands grip my arms, trying to hold me back, but I twist away with a savage strength I didn't know I possessed.

I tear free from him, my vision tunneling as my focus locks on the barrier ahead. My hands are already moving, my dagger drawn in a single, fluid motion. The blade's edge bites into my palm as I slash it open, the sting barely registering through the storm raging within me. Blood wells up, warm and bright against my skin, and I run toward the barrier without hesitation, my hand raised and dripping crimson.

I faintly hear Maxon's voice yelling my name, but it's not enough to stop me. I need to save her. If there's a chance, I'm taking it.

My palm meets the barrier, and the second the blood connects with the magic holding the Shadoweaver, it dissolves, falling like a shimmering waterfall to the ground. I hear Maxon curse behind me, but I run forward, dropping to my knees beside Mia. I gather her in my arms, holding her tightly against me. The ground shakes and tears stream down my face.

"Please, no," I beg Morrigan and the gods to release her back to me.

The cavern ignites in a fiery blaze as Maxon's magic swirls around us, forming a forcefield of protection. The shadows hiss and retreat.

"Mia? Mia, please, please come back to me," I cry, rocking her back and forth in my arms.

My hand rests on Mia's cheek, and I close my eyes, pushing my magic into her. Warmth encases me in a golden glow, and I feel Maxon's magic right there beside mine, the two entwining and pulsing with love and life.

Mia stirs, and I think my mind has finally fractured.

Maxon's magic and mine combined pulse into Mia as I chant over and over to release her back to me. Mia twitches in my arms, a soft breath falls from her lips, and I sag in relief. She is alive.

Maxon crouches down and grips my chin, lifting my face to his. Pain and fury line his features.

"Let me carry her." He wipes away my tears.

The walls begin to crumble around us. Maxon's fire won't protect us from a cave in. He scoops Mia into his arms as I stumble to my feet, swiping up my dagger and turning to follow Maxon. The second he draws his fire back, Raiden appears in the entrance. His silver eyes are glowing as he takes us in.

"Come on, this way!" he yells over the rumbling on the earth.

Maxon inclines his head, waiting for me. I take off after Raiden, my magic swelling again as I do my best to keep the roof from falling on us as we run through the tunnels. My adrenaline overrides my panic at the thought of being trapped, but I can feel it at the edge of my mind, ready to take over if I let it.

I hear the echo of a sinister laugh, a sound that seems to bounce off the walls of my mind, reverberating until it fills every corner of my thoughts. And then realization hits at what I've done. The reality strikes me like a sudden plunge into an icy lake, freezing my breath and constricting my ribs. I've set the Shadoweaver free.

Chapter Seventy-Two

Everly

I burst out into the open-air gasping, my hands landing on my knees, as I try drawing in a lungful of clean air. Each breath burns, and my body trembles from the exertion. I peer over my shoulder, my lungs still heaving, and spot Maxon standing tall behind me, Mia firmly in his arms. He's covered in dust and debris, blood smeared all over his bare chest and face. I know he is still in pain, but he holds my friend with such care.

A piercing howl cuts through the momentary calm, freezing me in place. The sound is raw and furious. My head snaps toward the source just in time to see Fenris in wolf form barreling toward us, his massive frame scattering soldiers who leap out of his path. He skids to a halt mere steps away, his chest heaving as his wild eyes sweep over me. Before I can react, he shifts, and his arms wrap around me tightly, crushing me against him.

"Thank fuck," he growls, his voice rough with emotion. "When the caves started collapsing, I–"

His words cut off abruptly. His body goes stiff, his arms dropping away as though he's been struck in the back. Confused, I follow his gaze and see where his attention has landed—Maxon, or more precisely, Mia.

Fenris's expression darkens, his features twisting into a mask of rage. "What the fuck?" he snarls, his voice low and dangerous. "How did she get here?"

Maxon's jaw tightens, but he doesn't respond.

I step forward, my voice coming out quieter than I intend. "Senka. She betrayed us."

Fenris's eyes snap to mine, the fury in them tempered only by a flicker of disbelief.

I choke down the lump rising in my throat as Fenris steps closer, his movements deliberate yet trembling. His hand reaches out, brushing a stray strand of hair from Mia's pale forehead. His chest heaves with unspoken emotion, his breaths uneven and raw.

He glances up at Maxon, and their eyes meet—a silent exchange, heavy with gratitude and shared pain. Slowly, almost reverently, Maxon passes Mia's frail body into Fenris's waiting arms.

Fenris pulls her close, his grip tightening as though to shield her. His head bows, his lips grazing her hair in a fleeting, tender touch before he presses his cheek against her head.

"She is alive, but barely," I whisper, coming to stand beside them. "The Shadoweaver broke her neck. I don't know how, but we managed to heal her." Words get stuck in my throat as I look at her. "I don't know what damage has been done. Can you take her to the healers?"

Fenris dips his head. “Thank you for bringing her back. I . . . She . . . I will take care of her,” he finally says.

I watch as he turns, carrying my best friend toward the horses.

Maxon pulls me into his arms, his familiar scent surrounding me, and I break. Floods of tears swell and cling to him.

‘Everything will be okay, Stóirín.’ Maxon’s arms tighten around me, his arms holding me up.

‘I wasn’t thinking straight. When I saw her, I just . . . ’

‘Shhh . . . I know. It’s okay, we will figure it out.’

Our camp, a fragile sanctuary carved from the desolation of the Deadlands, sprawls at the mountain’s base. Make shift tents dot the rugged ground, fabric rustling in the cold breeze that sweeps down from the jagged peaks. Fires burn low, casting flickering shadows on the weary faces of those gathered. The air smells of smoke, blood, and earth—a stark reminder of the battle we just survived.

We aren’t planning to stay long. This is a pause, a temporary reprieve to give the injured time to recover, to allow their wounds to close enough that the journey ahead won’t tear them open again.

Around several large piers set up in the center of the camp, seelie and unseelie alike move with grim purpose. Old animosities are forgotten as they work side by side, dressing wounds, sharing supplies, and passing out bowls of food and water.

My eyes follow Maxon as he makes his way around the camp. He should be resting. His own body bears the marks of the battle—deep cuts, bruises, and the exhaustion that I can feel through our bond. But rest isn't in his nature, not when others still suffer. He moves through the camp, his steps slow but steady, checking on every soldier who fought to rescue him. Even in his weariness, there is strength in the way he carries himself, a quiet determination that seems to lift the spirits of those around him. The soldiers who meet his gaze straighten, even if they are barely able to stand.

"Hey, how are you holding up?" Zaria's soft voice rings out next to me.

Turning, I wrap my arms around her. "I'm okay. How are you?"

Her arms tighten around me. "I'm okay."

Pulling back, I see Raiden standing behind her. "I'm sorry, Batman. I didn't–"

Raiden shakes his head. "Everly, you did what you had to. I understand, and if it was Zaria in there with her, I'd do the same, and you know it."

I nod, tears lining my eyes again. "But I . . . " my voice trails off. My emotions are too volatile. There is no excuse. I chose my friend over the safety of the realm. What kind of queen am I?

Nolan's words echo in my head. *You're weak. We need someone who is cold and calculated and not emotional.*

Zaria wraps her arm around me, and I rest my head on her shoulder.

'You are everything I could want and more, Stóirín. Don't you ever forget that. Your kind heart is what had me entranced from the start,' Maxon says in my mind, his love and unwavering support soothing my frayed edges.

"Everly, we are in this together. The Shadoweaver won't stand a chance," Zaria assures, with more conviction in her voice than I feel.

"So, the Shadoweaver *is* free from the prison?" one of Raiden's soldiers demands, his eyes landing on me.

I flinch, feeling the weight of his accusing gaze, and quickly step away from Zaria, nervously biting my thumbnail. I know the accusation is coming, but my stomach still plummets, a cold dread washing over me. Nymeria and Anika step between me and the gathering crowd. A silent reminder to them not to try anything. My eyes move over the soldiers, and I spot Kaden and the two luxaryn coming our way.

"She didn't have a choice," Fenris growls, appearing in front of me.

"Like hell she didn't!" one soldier shouts.

The tension crackles, a tangible force threatening to snap. Raiden steps forward, his hand shooting up, his presence commanding immediate attention. "She is your queen, and she will be respected!" he bellows, his deep voice carrying over the unrest. The commanding edge in his tone silences the soldier's protest, though resentment still flickers in their expressions.

I feel it before I see him—Maxon's fury, a fiery torrent burning through the bond we share. He approaches with deliberate strides, his anger an almost physical force that presses against me. As he reaches my side, his voice cuts through the taut air.

"What's done is done," he declares firmly, his words clipped but resolute. "We will deal with the threat. Everly did what she had to do to save a friend. You can't say you wouldn't do the same if it was your sister, brother, or best friend in there."

I swallow hard, my gaze sweeping over the soldiers who have gathered, their faces etched with fatigue, anger, and fear.

"I'm sorry," I mutter, my voice carrying the weight of my guilt.

Maxon's hand finds mine, his grip firm, grounding me in the moment. His eyes scan the crowd, daring anyone to challenge him. "None of you were there." His voice is low but commanding. "You have no idea what happened, so none of you can pass judgment."

A flicker of movement catches my attention. Kian, Tristan, Fenris, Kaden, and Zaria—each of them battered and worn, their faces pale and drawn—step forward, forming a line of solidarity at our side. Their presence speaks volumes, a silent declaration that whatever happened, they stand with us. The soldiers shuffle uneasily, their anger faltering as their gazes dart between us. The unity in our stance seems to dim the embers of rebellion, though their unease still lingers in the charged air. I glance around the camp, my eyes scanning the crowd, but there's no sign of Nero or Alivar. I haven't seen them since we first set up camp. They didn't look injured—tired, maybe, but not hurt.

Maxon's voice rises, cutting through the quiet. "The Shadoweaver was never going to give up. Her power reached beyond her prison. She would have poisoned our minds in an effort to get free. She did it before, wiping out the druids. If we stand strong, stand together, the Shadoweaver won't break us."

Chapter Seventy-Three

Maxon

Slowly, I push into her, my movements deliberate and unhurried. This isn't something to rush—I finally have her back in my arms, and I intend to savor every moment. Each thrust is measured and deeper than the last, a steady rhythm that binds us closer with every motion. My hands tighten, fingers tangling in the cascade of her silky golden hair, pulling gently to tilt her head back, exposing her neck.

I grit my teeth as she tightens around my cock, the feeling like the most intoxicating elixir, sending waves of pleasure coursing through me.

I trail my lips along the exposed curve of her neck, letting my teeth scrape lightly down the column of her throat. Her soft moan spills into the air, igniting a fire in my chest as she arches into me, her pelvis grinding against mine to meet my thrusts.

The connection between us feels electric, each touch, every sound weaving a tapestry of longing and fulfillment that I never want to end.

My voice is a low growl, the words “mine, you're all mine” coming out rough and hoarse in my native tongue as I build us up.

“I missed you,” she whispers, fingers gliding over my face. My eyes meet hers, and my stomach tightens with lust, hunger, and adoration.

Scooping her up, my hands slide under her back, and I lift her into my arms as I continue to move inside her, both of us lost in each other. Her legs wrap tightly around my waist as I kneel on the bed of furs and blankets. Everly's soft hands land on my shoulders as she starts moving over me, her breathy moans making my head spin.

Reaching up, I brush the hair from her face, rubbing my nose along hers. “I fucking missed you, too.”

My hands glide up her back, fingers tangling once more in that hair I adore. It feels like silk against my skin, and I can’t resist threading my fingers through it, pulling her just a little closer. It took every ounce of willpower to focus on the mundane tasks of bathing, eating, pretending I wasn’t aching for this moment. Now, with her in my arms again, nothing else matters.

Everly’s bare breasts press against my chest, her hardened nipples brushing my skin and making my cock throb inside her. The friction is maddening—sharp, electric—every slight movement sparking deeper hunger. Her breath ghosts over my lips, warm and shallow, and when she whispers my name, it’s pure sin—soft, breathy, and dripping with want. I grip her hips, holding her against me, the heat between us building, unbearable and addictive.

"You need to feed. Raiden told me if–"

My low growl fills the air, silencing her next words as anger burns through my veins. Everly pulls back to meet my eyes, her fingers continuing to move through my hair, creating a soothing sensation on my scalp that eases my anger.

"Don't say another man's name while I'm moving inside of you."

Understanding and love flood her eyes, and she rocks her hips, grinding down hard, my cock hitting so deep inside her we both moan.

"A chroí, feed."

My gums tingle, and I know my canines have lengthened. Everly drags her hair over her shoulder, giving me access to her neck. I trace my tongue slowly up the curve of her throat, savoring the softness of her skin beneath my lips. She shivers in response, and I can't help but smile against her neck, feeling the warmth of her breath on my shoulder, and the tremor of anticipation that ripples through her. I lower her onto the furs, the firelight licking across her skin in waves of gold and shadow. I stretch over her, possessive and hungry, my mouth finding the tender beat of her pulse. I kiss her there—slow, deliberate, worshipful—before thrusting into her, hard and deep, claiming her in one unrelenting motion. At the same instant, my fangs pulse with need and sink into her flesh. She cries out, her body arching to meet mine, to take more. Her blood floods my mouth—sweet, warm, and utterly her. It fills me, overwhelms me as my mind and body are swept away by the rush of pleasure and power that comes with each swallow.

'Tá sí foirfe,' a low, rumbling growl echoes in my mind.

'Yes, she is perfect,' I reply.

A roar from outside shakes the tent, a deep, guttural sound that rattles the earth beneath us, but I don't stop. I don't even flinch. I keep drinking, keep thrusting into Everly's sweet, molten heat, my focus solely on her. The world outside is nothing compared to this moment—nothing compared to the feeling of her body against mine, her warmth, her energy, her essence.

Her nails dig into my shoulders, the pressure grounding as her body trembles beneath me. I feel the tightening of her muscles, the way she moves against me, her orgasm building to its peak. Then, with a cry that tears through the air, she screams my name, the sound both raw and beautiful, filling me with a sense of possessiveness.

I can feel it; my dragon, he is near. The connection between us is undeniable. His presence swells, a low, approving hum reverberating through my chest. He recognizes her, my mate. She is ours. The approval pulses through me, setting fire to my veins.

"Mo dragan. Ceadaíonn sé mo chomrádaí," I breathe, letting go of her neck.

"What was that?" she pants, her voice breathless, still trembling from the force of her release.

Without answering, I flip her onto her back, my body shifting over hers as I slide back inside her, the heat of her tightening around me, pulling me deeper. I lean over her, my breath ragged, and whisper, "My dragon . . . He's here."

Everly's green eyes widen, a flicker of something between awe and uncertainty flashing across her face. Before she can speak, I drop my head, my lips finding her nipple, my teeth grazing it lightly before I clamp down, sucking hard. She gasps, fingers threading through my hair, tugging me closer, urging me to stay there, to give her more.

The sensation of her fingers in my hair only heightens the connection. She pulls me up, the sting in my scalp sending a pulse of lust straight to my cock. Then, I feel it—a sharp sting as her fangs sink into my neck. The moment she drinks, a wave of pleasure crashes through me, sending sparks of electricity all over my body, making my balls tingle with the force of it.

"Fuck," I grunt, the sound raw and primal as I drive deeper into her, my thrusts becoming harder, faster. Every part of me burns with need—my body, my mind, my dragon—all of it consumed by her.

Chapter Seventy-Four

Everly

I slip out into the cool predawn air, leaving Maxon asleep in the tent. I need space—time to gather my thoughts, to reconcile the weight of what I have done. The camp is still, save for the faint rustle of tents shifting in the breeze and the occasional murmurs of the sentries on patrol.

Nymeria and Anika spot me as I leave and follow, their footfalls silent as always. I quietly make my way through the camp, ducking out of view of the soldiers patrolling the area. Reaching the edge of the camp, I find a rocky outcrop, its rough texture cool beneath my hands as I climb, wanting solitude to watch the sunrise.

Reaching the top, I take a seat and let my legs hang over the edge. Both wolves lie down beside me, their eyes moving around our surroundings. Unconsciously, I stroke my fingers through their fur as the sun bursts across the sky.

Thoughts of the previous day invade my mind.

I rescued Maxon, brought Mia back to life—but at what cost?

My heart sinks as I think of all the soldiers—their trust, their loyalty—and the growing disappointment that must be festering among them. I did the one thing I had sworn I wouldn't. The weight of my failure settles over me, heavy and unrelenting.

A flicker of movement catches my eye. A shadow glides across the ground, swift and silent. I frown, tilting my head to the side. What was that? I scan the horizon, but the shadow is gone as quickly as it appeared. Perhaps it was just a trick of the early morning light, or maybe fatigue playing games with my mind. Shaking my head, I exhale and pull my cloak tighter around me.

The silence stretches, broken only by the distant rustling of leaves and the soft murmur of the wind. The sun creeps slowly into the sky, spilling hues of gold and crimson across the landscape, but its warmth does little to ease the chill settling in my bones.

Then, without warning, a fierce gust of wind slams into me. I throw up an arm instinctively as dust and leaves whip through the air. The ground trembles beneath me. A deafening rush of air fills my ears, followed by the unmistakable thud of something massive landing nearby.

When I lower my arm, my breath catches in my throat. A colossal dragon stands before me, its black and red scales gleaming in the morning light, shifting and rippling like liquid fire. Its piercing eyes lock onto mine, intelligent and unreadable. The sheer power radiating from the beast is enough to make my pulse quicken.

I jump to my feet but remain frozen to the spot, heart pounding, unsure whether to run or kneel.

Nymeria and Anika lift their heads, their ears twitching, but stay nestled at my feet, unbothered.

Even though the dragon is on the ground and I am on this rocky outcrop, it stands a few feet above me. Sharp, jagged horns protrude from its head, and his reptilian eyes burn like embers as he stares down at me. I know now that this is Maxon's dragon, and he is massive.

Before I can speak, the dragon's magic washes over me, calming almost.

'You have set events into motion that cannot be undone,' he says, his tone neither angry nor forgiving, but simply factual. *'Now, you must face the consequences of your actions.'*

The harsh sting of tears burns my eyes. I fought so hard to save the people I love, to rewrite fate itself, but in doing so, I have unleashed something far worse than I could have imagined.

The dragon stares at me, his massive head tilting to the side. Those big, fiery golden, reptilian eyes focused solely on me.

"What am I going to do?" I whisper.

'Fight,' the dragon's low, rumbling voice answers in my mind.

"I didn't mean for this to happen. I can fix this." The words feel hollow even as I speak them. Can I?

The Shadoweaver was bound by powers far greater than mine. Who am I to think I can undo this catastrophe?

The dragon's eyes narrow slightly, and he lowers his head until his flaming golden gaze is level with mine. *'Fix it? Oh, child, you cannot even fathom the depth of the chaos you have unleashed. But fear not—your part in this tale is far from over.'*

Something moves above us, its shadow sweeping across the ground. Several shouts ring out among the soldiers as a roar splits the air.

The dragons have returned.

To be continued . . .

Acknowledgements

I want to thank everyone who has taken a chance on my books. I truly appreciate your support. It means the world to me. I want to thank my mum for always allowing my imagination room to grow. I had quite the vivid imagination as a child. The idea of exploring hidden paths fills me with a thrill I can't quite put into words. There's something about the unknown—the possibility of stumbling upon a secret passage, an untouched grove, or a forgotten relic—that sparks a deep sense of wonder in me.

I think this fascination started after watching *The Goonies*, I was completely hooked on the idea of adventure. Hidden tunnels, cryptic puzzles, secret maps—I wanted to be part of it all. I'd daydream about finding an old, dust-covered journal filled with clues leading to something incredible.

I even took my curiosity into the real world. I remember walking home from school, tapping the pavers with my foot, listening closely for a hollow sound. Maybe—just maybe—one would be loose, revealing a secret tunnel beneath. I imagined it leading somewhere magical, a place no one else had discovered. Of course, I never found a hidden entrance, but the *idea* of it was enough to keep my imagination running wild.

That sense of adventure, of chasing the unknown, still lives in me today. It's why I love storytelling—because even if I never find a real hidden path, I can always create them.

I want to thank my inner circle. You know who you are! The ones I message at all hours of the day, either excited or stressed, ready to throw in the towel or share my tears. Love you lots. I wouldn't have gotten this far without you.

www.ingramcontent.com/pod-product-compliance
Lightning Source LLC
Chambersburg PA
CBHW070540310726
48982CB00010B/1422/J

* 9 7 8 1 7 6 3 6 4 9 5 4 5 *